DRUGS TO
FORGET

DRUGS TO FORGET

RACE AGAINST BIOTERROR

MARTIN GRANGER

RedDoor

Published by RedDoor
www.reddoorpublishing.com

© 2018 Martin Granger

ISBN 978-1-910453-51-3

A CIP catalogue record for this book is available from the
British Library

Cover design: Megan Sheer

Typesetting: Tutis Innovative E-Solutions Pte. Ltd

Print and production managed by Jellyfish Solutions Ltd

To Jacqueline

One

The explosion could be heard five blocks away. In the cafés of downtown Harare people steadied their spilling coffee. They were not the first to feel the blast. The German Ambassador was given a brief warning by a flash of light, then a muffled sound, and then silence. A few minutes later he slowly opened his eyes to see a cloud of dust swirling through a large hole in the once-tiled roof. He was on his back, legs pinned to the floor by some sort of concrete object with iron bars sticking out of it. A man in a flak jacket wearing a black beret shone a torch into his eyes and mouthed something. It took a while for him to realise the man was shouting, but he couldn't hear a thing.

The embassy was a small unassuming building with ornamental porticos and art deco styled bay windows. It had a yellow German plaque on the wall bearing the familiar black eagle. That was now all in the past tense. The plaque had disappeared along with half of the front wall. Special Forces climbed over the rubble to pick through the debris. Three members of the clerical staff, two of them African, were dead, buried under bricks and mortar. Those in the back offices had survived; some just covered in dust, others like the ambassador with broken bones. They carried him out on a stretcher.

Within hours a forensic team were picking over the details. A crude bomb, an effective one but crude nevertheless. Probably did more damage than intended. It had been placed under a structural pillar, one under investigation by the embassy's surveyor. A crack had been reported several weeks ago. But even if the bombers had not meant to bring down half the building, it was no consolation to the dead.

Lloyd Bamba showed his ID to a uniformed officer. *Journalist, Zimbabwe Times.* He was waved away with a threatening gesture of an M4 machine gun. After taking some surreptitious pictures with his phone he retreated and went back to his office. The files on bombings in Harare were sketchy. The mid-eighties, a huge explosion blamed on South African covert forces rumoured to be targeting the liberation movement in exile. The late nineties, a blast in the Sheraton, the venue for a Commonwealth summit. Closer to home, two attacks on his rival newspaper *The Daily News* in 2000 and 2001. Allegedly instigated by Zimbabwean security forces for its anti-presidential propaganda. Seemingly no connective thread with any of them. Lloyd turned to his editor.

'Can't seem to find a common lead, I'll have to go back when the dust has settled.' He suddenly realised the pun. 'I mean that metaphorically; when those twitchy guys with guns have relaxed a bit. Any ideas?'

The editor turned his screen towards Lloyd. 'Only this on WikiLeaks; from their Global Intelligence Files. Some sort of chatter about that bomb blast in Harare Central Police Station around election time. Police blamed the opposition party, others citing ZANU-PF. One common theme though.'

Lloyd peered at the text on the screen. 'Which is?'

'All of the authors, including the US Defence Intelligence Agency, agree that there are no active militant groups in Zimbabwe.'

Lloyd went back to his desk and started downloading the photographs from his phone. One caught his eye. He enlarged it and examined the image on his laptop.

'By the look of this, I think that might have just changed.'

※

Lloyd waited until dusk to make his way back to the embassy. This time he went via the grounds of the polytechnic. He entered the main building and climbed the staircase to the top floor. From here he had a view across Prince Edward Street and towards the roof of the damaged embassy. The area had been cordoned off and an armoured car sat at the entrance. He could see that if he approached the site from the girl's high school there was a small gap in the perimeter where he might gain access. He descended the stairs, strode across the street and through the high school as if he belonged. To a passer-by he would be taken as a teacher. Parts of the embassy were draped in orange striped tape, a few disinterested soldiers hovered around. Lloyd crossed one of the lawns confidently as if taking a short-cut home. No one seemed to notice. As he had anticipated the vigilance level had dropped and it was getting dark so he cast few shadows. He took out his phone, studied the picture and made his way to the spot. There it was. Under a piece of rubble a charred piece of paper. He was bending down to pick it up when he was startled by a shout.

'Halt, don't move. Put your hands on your head.'

Lloyd was wondering how he was going to put his hands on his head without moving when a steel barrel was thrust into his back.

'On your head, I said,' snapped the voice.

Lloyd slowly crumpled the paper into a ball and put his hands into the air.

'Turnaround!' The order was shouted.

Without lowering his arms Lloyd gradually rotated his body to face an intimidating soldier who was aiming his gun at him.

'Oh it's you,' barked the soldier. 'The journalist. I thought I told you to disappear.'

'Only doing my job,' said Lloyd quietly.

'And my job is to shoot intruders,' retorted the soldier.

'I'm sorry, I thought that...'

'I'm not interested in what you think. Get out, and if I see you here again I'll shoot first and ask questions afterwards.'

Lloyd deliberately lowered his arms, keeping his fist tightly closed. 'I'll go, but if there's anyone that can give me an interview...'

'You're pushing it son. Get out of my sight or the only interview you'll get is in a prison cell.' The soldier gestured to the exit with his weapon. 'Now!'

Lloyd picked his way across the masonry, the concrete and dust crunching underneath his feet. He didn't look back. He had what he had come for in his right hand. A leaflet left by the bombers. One of probably many that they had placed to promote their cause. The only problem for them was that the explosion had been so immense that the pamphlets had been scattered to the winds. A bombsite wasn't the place to read it so Lloyd made his way to the Book Café on the corner of Sixth Street. The café was a place for actors, musicians and writers. A space where artists liked to exchange ideas. It had been shut down for a while but now had relocated to a building near the Holiday Inn. It was the one place where Lloyd felt comfortable. There was a show on that night and people had started to gather in the bar. He ordered a beer and sat at a small table in the corner. The ball of paper in his hand was badly damaged. He slowly unwrapped it and smoothed it out on the table top. It was charred and torn but he could still make out the cheap printing. The grammar was poor but the message was clear. The West should stop exploiting African resources or they would get more of this. Lloyd assumed 'this' referred to the destruction by the bomb. The top portion of the pamphlet was missing but he could just about make out a logo. A capital E was followed by a large X, the strokes of which extended above the letters either side of it. Lloyd put two and two together and guessed at the acronym. WEXA; the Western Exploitation of Africa. The name was not unfamiliar to him. Despite the claims of WikiLeaks' Global Intelligence Files Lloyd had heard rumours about this group in this very café. The gossip was that this was neither a pro or anti-government lobby, but an extremist group with a grudge against Western involvement in African affairs. No clear-cut agenda apparently, just a small group of very angry young men. They were thought to be harmless malcontents. Well they weren't harmless now. Lloyd folded up the paper and made his way back to the office to write up his piece.

Three thousand kilometres away in Brazzaville a Zimbabwean nurse sat in her hotel room. To all intents and purposes she was a volunteer there to help the overloaded Congolese health service. She had travelled incognito and wished for no publicity. The Ebola outbreak was not meant to be talked about. But her experiences in Sierra Leone had made her the perfect candidate. She knew how to diagnose the disease and cope with the grieving relatives of the dead. Burying the contaminated bodies without contracting the virus was one of the keys to preventing it from spreading further. She had arrived a week ago and been through the local induction course. Now she was preparing for her first site visit away from the banks of the Congo. She was on the top floor and could see Kinshasa in the distance over the vast brown river. Many people confused the two regions: the Republic of the Congo on one side and the Democratic Republic on the other. Salina was not one of them. Her brief had been very clear. She turned away from the window and reached into her canvas medical bag. A smooth black object, something like a glasses' case, nestled in one of the pockets. The metal hinge creaked slightly as she opened it. Inside a glass vial and a plastic syringe. She screwed the long needle onto the syringe and inserted it into the rubber membrane of the vial. Slowly she pulled back the plunger and held it up to watch the liquid draw through. The needle was extricated, and with a flick of her finger the bubble dispersed. She rolled up her sleeve and gently pushed the needle into her arm. Insurance, that's all it was, but what she was about to do was far more dangerous than her normal practice. She replaced the equipment into the case and snapped it shut. Now for a shower and bed; it would be a long day tomorrow.

The health district vehicle turned up at 7.00 am. It had seen better days. Bald tyres, rusted wheel arches and a smashed-in headlight. Salina threw her bag in the back and sat beside the driver. The air-conditioning wasn't working so she wound down the window. It was as hot outside as it was in but, as the car moved into the traffic, there was at least some breeze caused by the movement. The driver didn't have much to say for himself so she sat there in silence watching the crowded city. They passed the airport and drove away from the river along the N1 to Geula. It was humid as one would expect on the fringes of an equatorial river basin but at least it wasn't raining. It was the beginning of the wet season and Salina had already experienced one of the apocalyptic thunderstorms that threw water from the sky. The road had become impassable and her earlier visit had to be aborted. Now the road was clear, fringed by walls of red mud and the thick dark green vegetation beyond. The journey was only forty kilometres but the vehicle was so slow that it took nearly two hours to cover the distance. Salina reached for the water bottle in her bag; it was warm but she drank some anyway.

The driver pointed out of the window. 'There, just beyond those trees.'

She turned around to see a small clearing and a wooden house with two pitched roofs at right angles. It was constructed like a log cabin, only the logs were ten centimetres wide; despite this it was neat enough. The driver pulled off the road and stopped about a hundred metres from the house.

'That's as far as I go, I'll stay in the car.'

Salina threw him a disapproving glance before opening the door. He shrugged his shoulders as he passed her the bag. She slung it over her shoulder and marched towards the house. A young boy in ragged clothes ran out to meet her. She would have loved to have hugged him but she held up her hands for him to stop, took a mask and gloves from her bag and gestured for him to show the way. The interior was lit with kerosene lamps. A woman with tear-streaked cheeks greeted her and became effusive with thanks. Salina nodded politely and without taking the woman's hand moved towards the bed in the corner of the room. It was the last stages; she could tell that at a glance. She had already been told about the fever, diarrhoea and vomiting. Now she could see a rash and severe bruising around the man's face. He was moaning, doubled up with stomach pain. This was the nineteenth reported case, but the authorities wanted them to be kept quiet, or denied. Her job was to keep the patients comfortable and ensure as little contact as possible on burial. She despaired at the former; she had few drugs in her bag. As for the contact, the wife and little boy would take some persuading.

Salina placed her gloved hand on the man's forehead. It was dripping with sweat. A small stainless steel container with its vacuumed glass lining was in her pocket. It unscrewed easily. She placed a cotton bud into the patient's mouth, moved it around gently and then placed the tip into the container. A few turns and the rubber seal was tightened. Her work was done but the little boy looked up at her with pleading eyes and so she took off her gloves, reached into her bag and pressed some painkillers into his palms.

'Give these to him with plenty of water. Plenty of water, you hear me?'

He nodded. By his look he knew, as she did, that these ineffective tablets would be vomited out within minutes.

The return journey was as silent as the one on the way out. Salina was glad of it. She and the driver knew that the man would be dead within days. But it would be another nurse accompanying him for the burial. She would be flying back to Zimbabwe, a precious cargo in her hands.

Two

Seek assistance, seek assistance. The orange light flashed on the panel.

It was nine-thirty in the morning and Tottenham Court Road Tube station was heaving. A queue started to build up and some of the commuters were becoming frustrated. Long sighs, mutterings and impatient body language filled the hall.

The woman looked dazed as she turned around to stare at the crowd. A man, wearing an expensive looking raincoat, pushed his way through and glanced at the card in her hand. A slightly grubby, cream coloured business card of some sort.

'I'm afraid you're trying to put the wrong thing into the ticket barrier.' He gently took the underground ticket from her other hand. 'Here this should do it.'

The ticket shot through the slot and the gates swung open.

'About bloody time,' came a shout from behind them.

The woman walked through the barrier and stared first at the business card and then at the various exits around her. The man in the raincoat had followed and, seeing that she had some difficulty in making a decision, asked her if he could help.

'I need to get to this address,' she said staring into the distance.

'Do you know this area of London?'

She turned to look at him, this time straight into his eyes. 'I don't know. Who are you?'

He saw that she was frightened, and possibly disturbed, but he had come this far. 'That's not important. Let me look at that card, I'll see if I can give you directions.'

The address showed a number in Soho Square, just around the corner. He placed his hand on the woman's elbow and steered her towards the Oxford Street exit. 'Look, I'm going that way so why don't you come with me.'

She did so without a word, from time to time moving her head to peer at the traffic or the passers-by. They turned left into Soho Street and then into the square.

'Here, that's your number. I have to get to work now. Are you sure you'll be alright?'

She turned to him with a strange smile and then compared the number on her card with the one on the imposing door in front of them. 'Yes thank you, you have been very kind.'

It was the last he would see of her as she purposely strode up the steps to the offices of Bagatelle Films.

✻

Nathalie Thompson was trying to get her head around the science. It wasn't easy.

'So, if a bioterrorist could find a way of storing an inactive Ebola virus, they could carry it anywhere without being detected?'

Doctor Styne stepped away from the whiteboard. He wasn't used to such direct questioning. He had been asked to meet with this young film director to give advice on his speciality of virology. He had thought it would be for some sort of educational or pharmaceutical video. Now he was beginning to realise that this company was involved in something far more sinister and he wasn't sure that he should be here.

'Well yes, but I thought you were interested in how viruses worked.'

'Just wondering. Sorry, carry on, you were describing the lipid cycle.'

'The *lytic* cycle.' Styne picked up a felt tip marker, and returned to the whiteboard. 'As I said viruses don't eat, grow or reproduce on their own. They need a host, like you or me. They've a protein coat which recognises and attaches the virus to a suitable cell.' He drew a crude diagram on the board. 'Then they insert their DNA into that cell so they can use the host to enable them to reproduce.'

9

'What, bore a hole and shove it in?' asked Nathalie scribbling notes on to her pad.

He looked at her over his glasses. 'Not quite, but you said you didn't want an academic account, so close enough.'

They were interrupted by a knock. Stefanie, the producer's PA, put her head around the door. 'Sorry to butt in but there's a woman who says she must see you.'

Doctor Styne looked puzzled. 'Me?'

'No, not you Doctor Styne, Nathalie. The woman has a business card with Nathalie's name on it. She's in quite a state. I don't think she really knows why she is here and I don't quite know what to do with her. Perhaps you could just give her a few minutes and she might go away.'

Nathalie looked at Doctor Styne.

'Go ahead, I'm fine as long as I get back for half twelve.'

The woman was sitting in Stefanie's office turning the card around and around in her hands. She looked to be in her late forties, brown tangled hair and no makeup. Nathalie had never seen her before.

'I understand you wanted to see me.'

The woman looked up in surprise. 'I'm not sure.' She thrust the card into Nathalie's hands. 'Is this you?'

Nathalie studied the card. It had seen better days but it was hers all right. *Nathalie Thompson. Documentary Film Director. Bagatelle Films.* The Soho Square address was where she was standing right now.

'It's my card. Where did you get it?'

The woman looked at her with watery eyes. 'I don't know, I was hoping you would tell me that.'

'I'm really sorry I can't remember meeting. What's your name?'

'Esther, Esther…'

'Esther what?'

'Esther.' The woman looked confused and anxiously took back the card as if it was some sort of comforter.

'Esther, I'm afraid I should be in a meeting right now so how can I help you?'

Esther stared at the card and then at Nathalie. 'Is this you?'

Nathalie glanced at Stefanie and sat in a chair beside the woman.

'Okay, let's start again, I'm Nathalie Thompson, where do you come from Esther?'

The woman looked around the office and then at her own hands as if searching for the answer. 'Nathalie Thompson.'

'Yes that's right, where do you live Esther?'

Esther raised her head and looked straight into Nathalie's eyes. 'I don't know, I really don't know.'

Nathalie glanced at Stefanie again. 'Esther, can I leave you with Stefanie for a moment whilst I fetch someone who I'd like you to meet?'

Stefanie nodded back knowingly as Nathalie returned to the meeting room. She explained the situation to Doctor Styne. He seemed intrigued.

'I'm no neurologist but I'll have a chat with her if you like.'

'Just don't want to throw her out on the street as some kind of nutter in case she is really not well,' explained Nathalie. 'Follow me, she's just in the next office.'

Doctor Styne followed and was introduced to Esther.

'Hello Esther, I understand you've come here to meet Nathalie.'

Esther looked troubled. 'Nathalie?'

'Yes, Nathalie, the young lady standing beside me. You've come to meet Nathalie.'

'Have I?'

'Esther, how old are you?'

'I think I had a birthday recently.'

'Are you married?'

Esther gazed around the room again, squinting her eyes struggling for the answer. 'I don't think so.'

'Esther, where do you live?'

She slowly shook her head. 'I don't know, I can't remember.'

Doctor Styne pointed to the card in Esther's hand. 'That's Nathalie's card, who gave it to you?'

The woman looked at the card closely. 'Nathalie, yes I need to see Nathalie.'

'Can I take your pulse Esther, I'm a doctor.' Esther shrugged her shoulders and held out her wrist.

Styne looked at Nathalie and Stefanie, 'Well she knows what a pulse is; do you have a thermometer in the office?'

✳

Geoff Sykes was in his office juggling with the paperwork of eight television programmes. Stefanie told him about the woman and he unsympathetically wrote it off as a scam.

'It's obvious, the woman has found a card on the pavement and wants to nosey around in our office. See what the film industry looks like from the inside.' He threw a wad of files at her. 'If the woman had my scheduling problems then she's welcome to it. Has that researcher come up with anything more on that Zimbabwean terrorist group yet?'

Stefanie was used to Geoff's rants. She was also used to managing more than one task at a time. She glanced at the row of international clocks on the wall.

'We are expecting a call any time now. Lloyd's got to be careful, he said he would telephone as soon as he could get a private moment. And, as for the woman, I believe she's genuinely lost her memory. The doctor's in my office with her now; I think he would like us to call for an ambulance.'

'Doctor?'

'The virologist that Nathalie's meeting.'

'What's he got to do with it?'

'Nathalie asked him to check her out, after all he *is* a clinician.'

'We're not running a bloody hospital. She is meant to be mugging up on Ebola viruses, not playing nurse to every vagrant that walks in.' He glanced up at the knock and saw Nathalie's head appear around the door. 'Talk of the devil.'

Nathalie laughed, 'My ears were burning so I've come to set the record straight. That vagrant, as you so call her, is quite distressed. The doctor thinks she's got TGA and should be seen by a neurologist.

He knows a colleague at his hospital who he is referring her to. We've sent for an ambulance, so we should be getting back to work very soon, mugging up on Ebola viruses, I seem to remember.'

'Enough of your cheek. Of course if the woman is distressed we should do everything we can.' Geoff was about to turn back to his paperwork when he looked up again. 'What's TGA?'

'Transient global amnesia. Not uncommon apparently. It's really weird, she can do stuff pretty normally but she hasn't got a clue who she is. Keeps on asking the same questions. Am I Nathalie Thompson? The doctor says it could be due to cerebral ischaemia.'

'What's that?'

'Could be a lack of blood supply to her temporal lobe. A sort of mini stroke.'

'Sounds dangerous.'

'Could be, that's why we stopped work and are sending her to hospital.'

'Okay, okay fair enough. But why did she have your card?'

'No idea, could have just picked it up somewhere and the address was all she had to cling on to. I've never met her before.'

The phone rang. Geoff looked at the incoming number and shooed Nathalie and Stefanie from his office. 'I've got to take this, make sure the woman's okay and finish off with your doctor. Lloyd's going to be phoning any moment and I want Nathalie to personally take the call.'

It was approaching mid-morning and Bagatelle's offices were becoming busier. A film crew had just come in from the Far East and were stacking dusty equipment boxes in the hallway. Helmeted motorbike couriers stood at reception waiting to take the rushes to the edit suites and a graphic designer struggled to manoeuvre their portfolio through the main doors. The paramedics didn't seem out of place as they pushed their way through the melée into the lobby. Doctor Styne chaperoned the woman out of the lift and handed her over with a note that he gave to the driver of the ambulance.

'Just keep her calm and introduce her to this guy. I telephoned and he knows she's coming.'

The driver nodded and, with his colleague, helped the woman into the waiting vehicle. The blue light flashed as they drove off without the siren into the London traffic. The doctor returned to the meeting room and spoke with Nathalie.

'I'm sorry, but I have to go soon. I'm afraid that little episode has interrupted our meeting.' He handed her a pamphlet. 'This is something I give to my patients, you may find it useful.'

'Probably not the sort of thing I'm looking for,' thought Nathalie, but she took it all the same.

Doctor Styne began to pack his briefcase. 'Have you tried to contact the pharma companies? I'm sure they could give you info on how they're trying to stop viral epidemics.'

Nathalie could see that the doctor was subtly telling her that this was all she was going to get out of him. 'As it happens I have but, as soon as I mention the word bioterrorism, they shut up like clams,' she said. 'Just like you,' she would have liked to have added.

Styne noticed the awkwardness and started to make his way to the door. He stopped as Nathalie tapped him on the arm. 'I'm sorry Miss Thompson but...'

'No, that's fine. I'm really grateful for what you've taught me. I was just going to ask you to get in touch if you hear anything about that woman with memory loss. I'd really like to know.'

Doctor Styne lowered his shoulders and shook her hand. 'Of course, Miss Thompson; if I see my colleague I'll ask him, and if there's any non-confidential information I'll give you a call. Best of luck with your programme. I'll see my own way out.'

She was about to say she would escort him to the door but the meeting-room phone rang so she merely waved and picked up the receiver. It was Stefanie.

'Lloyd's on the phone. Geoff said that he particularly wanted you to speak to him directly.'

Nathalie had been waiting for this call for several days. She sat down and grabbed a writing pad from the meeting desk. 'Put him on.'

Lloyd worked for the *Zimbabwe Times*. A couple of months ago he had written an article on an unusual Ebola outbreak in Harare. Ebola had been hardly heard of in Zimbabwe and no one could trace the source. The government had put the virus down to a random infected passenger travelling from Sierra Leone. But Lloyd had chased the story up and could find no such carrier. During the same period, the German embassy had been blown up; three people had died. Rumours were rife concerning a terrorist cell called WEXA and their possible involvement in the bombing. Lloyd believed that the Western Exploitation of Africa group may have something to do with the Ebola outbreak. His newspaper article had coincided with Bagatelle Films' intention to produce a programme on bioterrorism. Lloyd had agreed to moonlight from the paper and to feed the London production company with information.

Lloyd's husky voice came down the line. 'I think I've found them.'

Nathalie twirled the pencil in her hand. 'You sure you can talk?'

'Yes, it's fine. They think I've gone outside for a smoke.'

'So where are they?'

'About two fifty kilometres south of here, place called Shurugwi.'

'Are you sure?'

'Can't say for sure. Went to a late bar in Harare. Known for dissidents. Put it about that I was a sympathiser. Wished I could do something. A guy tapped me up. Said if I wanted to help he knew a few people.'

'Can you depend on him?'

'Not completely, but my other sources seem to think it's the real deal.'

'What's the next move?'

'I think you need to come out here. Play the Western activist. A campaigner for the rights of Africans. As a team I think we could get in there.'

Nathalie chewed on the pencil. 'The Ebola? Can you tie them to it?'

'That's a dead end at the moment. Government heavies are watching me on that one. I think you'd have a better chance of getting into the hospitals. Another reason you should come out.'

There was a long pause broken by a sharp noise as the pencil broke in two.

'Okay, I've spent enough time on my rear doing biology lessons. I'll ask if they can raise expenses for a short field trip. When's the best time for you?'

'I'm meant to be having my annual holiday next week. The paper still doesn't know I'm doing this so that would be a good time.'

'If I can get a visa in time you're on.'

'Don't apply for the journalist accreditation, it'll hold you up and blow your cover. If you're caught reporting or even blogging you'll be in the shit, so make a cover story as an African aid worker or something. Someone is coming, I better go. Stefanie has got my uncle's e-mail, don't use mine. Let me know if you can make it.' The line went dead.

Three

The fly landed on the brown folder which was resting on her lap. She stared at it willing it to go away but it did not stir. Just like her in this queue. Nathalie had never been to Central Africa before and now she was realising why. The cream-walled admissions office was lined with tubular metal chairs filled with passengers in transit, all with glazed eyes. She had been sitting here for more than an hour and hardly anybody had moved. Two rows in front of her was a long windowed desk, like an old-fashioned post office. Behind this desk sat two khaki-uniformed men alongside two piles of khaki folders. The fortunate passengers who were at the head of the queue were having their papers stamped, again and again. The sound echoed through the still fetid air.

Nathalie had been overjoyed when she heard that Geoff had a contact at an African aid organisation. He had filmed for them before and must have done them some favours for they were very generous with their cooperation. Within a week she had a back story, an NGO visa, and an invitation to visit two hospitals in Harare. The watchword was 'immunisation'. A complete blackout on AIDS and Ebola. She could handle that, a general chitchat about the children's immunisation programme and an on the side conversation with a caring nurse. That's if she got that far. The NGO visa didn't seem to be pulling any weight in this queue or, if it was, God help the others.

'Miss Nathalie Thompson, Imunaid?' An assistant was calling from the front desk.

Nathalie jumped up. 'Here,' she called expectantly.

'You are number fourteen. Please take a seat.'

She sat down again. It was pointless protesting, this was Zimbabwe's bureaucracy; probably a vestige of old colonial days. If she wanted to get in the country she would have to play along. She used the time by rehearsing the plan in her head. Visit the hospitals, chat up the immunisation nurses to get an outreach visit to the bush, check out any possible Ebola cases at the same time. Lloyd said he would set up a meeting in the countryside, south of Harare. It would be safer that way. It sounded simple but this was the easy part. Coming back with a film crew would be another matter altogether.

It was late by the time she had been 'duly processed' and Nathalie was unaware of her first African blood orange sky as she closed her eyes in the taxi on the way back to her hotel. Stefanie had booked her in at the Holiday Inn. It was characterless but complied with the Trip Advisor commendation of clean and convivial. Nathalie had learned that boring franchise hotels with working WiFi were a lot better than chic boutique hotels when you were on a job, so she hadn't complained when she had seen her accommodation on the recce sheet. Besides, the staff were great, no problem with the check-in, Bagatelle had prepaid – and, with the swift help of a porter, the luggage was in her room. Couldn't have been more different than the experience at the airport arrivals hall. She flopped on the bed and scanned some of the hotel's literature. Room service, WiFi and unmissable sights. Here she had to smile. Top recommendation, the nearby Epworth balancing rocks attraction. These rocks were world-famous. Granite rocking boulders, naturally perched on one another. If she had the time they would be worth a visit, but what made her smile was the reference to their image on the Zimbabwean banknote. The Zimbabwean banknote had been obsolete for years as a result of hyperinflation. It became so bad that some of the notes had to have trillion dollar denominations. Nathalie had been briefed on the problem and had been given a wad of US dollars, probably the best currency from one of the eight used in Zimbabwe. These were safely tucked into a money belt alongside her smart phone which she now pulled out to check her e-mail. There was one from the Central Hospital in Harare inviting her to a meeting the next morning and a more cryptic message from Lloyd attaching a bunch of numbers. It was too late to ring the hospital so she merely typed a confirmation hoping they would get it before she arrived. She worked out that the numbers Lloyd had given her were for a pay-as-you-go phone. She stored them and tapped the speed dial. A telephone was answered but no voice came.

'Hello, anyone there?'

Still no response.

'Hi, Lloyd is that you? It's Nathalie.'

The familiar rasping voice came from the other end. 'Yes, it's me. Just wanted to check that it was you that was calling. How was your trip?'

'Trip was fine, admission into the country a bloody nightmare. Are you on for tomorrow afternoon?'

'Yes, it's better than I thought. Mentioned your name and showed them the fake blogs we'd mocked up expounding on your militant views. Think they really fell for it. Got very excited, want to expand their network. I think that they're a crazy dangerous group but amateurs for all that.'

'Don't know which is more dangerous, professional terrorists or amateur ones. You're sure this will be safe?'

'Can't guarantee that but I've arranged to meet in a public place. A small bar in Ruwa.'

'Ruwa?'

'It's a village on the Harare-Marondera Road about twenty kilometres south-east of your hotel. If you're not changing your mind I'll pick you up at a service station on the outskirts of the city; I'll text you the address.'

'I've not come all this way to back out now. We need real contacts if we are going to make this programme. The TV channels hate reconstructions and hearsay from journalists. I've got a meeting at the hospital in the morning. Would three o'clock in the afternoon be okay?'

'Perfect, I told them we'd be there early evening. Should give us plenty of time to talk and plan our story.'

'See you at three then.'

Lloyd disconnected the phone without saying goodbye and moments later a ping indicated that he had messaged the rendezvous address. Nathalie checked the location on her maps. A short taxi ride from the hotel. If her meeting at the hospital tomorrow morning went well she would have time to come back and change. She didn't want to turn up in a terrorist camp wearing her Imunaid gear. It was going to be a busy day.

✳

The hospital was a red brick, square horseshoe sort of building. Its 1930s' metal windows reminded Nathalie of her old secondary school. A woman brushed past carrying a baby as she opened the door for an old man whose leg was cased in a plaster cast. The reception held the typical hospital antiseptic smell. She held her large Imunaid lapel badge towards the man at the desk and informed him of her appointment. Without replying he thumbed through the scruffy book in front of him in slow motion. Nathalie closed her eyes and took a deep breath. She hated this sort of suspense. Was there an appointment or wasn't there? She opened her eyes to see the man listlessly turning a page first one way and then another. She leaned over the desk to look at the scrawled ink handwriting on the faintly lined paper.

'There,' she said, jabbing a finger at the page. 'There, Nathalie Thompson, Imunaid, to see Sue Jones, from the immunisation programme.'

He looked up at her with his bloodshot eyes, scrawled something into the book and handed it to her. 'Sign here please ma'am.'

Nathalie did so and asked for directions. The man merely nodded to a row of torn canvas and metal chairs against the far wall.

She sat there, uncomfortably in her smart suit, feeling out of place amongst the ragged clientele. Half an hour later she was about to explode with frustration when a spick and span nurse came into the lobby and surveyed the scene. She spotted Nathalie almost immediately.

'Nathalie Thompson? I'm so sorry, a bit of an emergency I'm afraid.' She raised her eyebrows. 'Understaffed, like most hospitals. Please, follow me.'

Nathalie was doing so at a brisk walk down the corridor when they were interrupted by a commotion. A young African man was being manhandled by two burly security guards. He was struggling and shouting loudly, his heavily accented voice echoing around the passageway. Nathalie and Nurse Jones had to flatten themselves against a wall to let them pass.

'What was all that about?' asked Nathalie. 'What was he shouting about his sister?'

Sue Jones straightened her uniform. 'Not the first time. He's a young lecturer from the university. The poor man's sister has an infection and has been in the isolation ward for months. Sadly but not surprisingly they won't let him in to see her. He won't accept it. Thinks the hospital's hiding something from him. Anyway...'

'Is that the lady with Ebola?'

Sue Jones reddened. 'Where did you hear that? No of course not, Zimbabwe doesn't have Ebola. It's a hospital infection that's all, very contagious but just an infection.'

Nathalie was experienced enough to know when and when not to press things further. She made a mental note of the young man's face and profession and changed the subject.

'Of course, now you have your immunisation outreach programme, you must be very proud of it.'

Sue Jones visibly relaxed. 'Absolutely we are. Do you know that through this programme we have immunised more children for the triple vaccine than the UK? A lot of people may look at Zimbabwe as a backward country. Not so. Even with vast distances through difficult terrain we get vaccines to these kids.'

Nathalie smiled at her. 'I know. That's the reason I'm here. Can't wait to see how you do it.'

The morning meeting went better than expected. Nathalie took copious notes as Sue Jones explained their outreach programme.

Each local district had a depot which held the frozen vaccines. Every week a team drove a Land Rover that towed a refrigerated truck to prearranged outposts and kraals. Here the parents would line up their kids to be vaccinated. These vaccinations were recorded on yellow record cards. Thousands had been printed and distributed throughout the whole country. This was interesting stuff but it was more than that for Nathalie, it was a means of access to the places she wished to film in.

'Sounds amazing. Would it be possible for me to go out on one of the rounds? It would be really good to see it in practice.'

Nurse Jones looked down at her fingernails. 'I'm not sure about that, there is only limited space in the Land Rover. There's the driver and the two immunisation nurses, and of course I'd have to get authorisation from my superiors.'

'As you can see I'm quite small, I'm sure they could squeeze me in. As for your superiors, you could tell them that Imunaid have some contacts in the charity business who may be able to get a film crew to video the project. There's a huge programme on British television called 'Child Aid'. It raises millions of pounds for good causes. One short video could fund your programme for a year.'

'Of course, if you put it like that, I'll certainly ask them.' Nurse Jones looked at her watch. 'You said you wanted to see how and where we centrally stored the vaccines. If you come with me I'll show you, we just have enough time before my next meeting.'

Once more Nathalie followed Nurse Jones down the winding hospital corridors. The noises and aromas were familiar. Squeaky trolleys, humming machinery and that all-pervading antiseptic smell. What was less familiar were the images through the small windows in the ward doorways. Rows of sick patients under mosquito nets. HIV was prevalent in Zimbabwe, yet few admitted to it. These patients were simply labelled with diseases such as influenza, pneumonia or organ failure. At one crossroad in the corridor Nathalie noticed the sign for the isolation unit. She deliberately dropped her notepad and a few minutes later took the opportunity of the nurse bumping into a colleague to say she would go back for it. There was a security guard at the entrance to the unit. Parked outside was a drugs trolley. Nathalie bent down to tie her shoelace and took note of the packaging labels. *XEBO vaccine Biomedivac* was printed on a number of the boxes. No Ebola in Zimbabwe then.

She heard her name being called and hurriedly made her way to the corridor junction. It would really blow her cover if she was caught nosing around the isolation unit. All her good work on visiting the outreach programme would be undone. The voice was getting nearer and she could see the nurse's hat among a crowd of straggling patients. It was too late; she frantically struggled to think of a good excuse. Suddenly a porter swung into view, pushing a gurney around the corner. Nathalie took the opportunity to slip into the opposite corridor before retracing her steps to look as if she had come from a different direction. She was just in time. A flustered Nurse Jones was standing at the junction looking for her.

'Oh there you are, I thought you had got lost. Sorry, I got caught up in a conversation. I must get to my meeting now. Would it be possible for you to come back and view our vaccine store at another time?'

'Of course,' said Nathalie. 'I'm here for the week, and I'd like to meet again soon to see what your people say about my going on your next outreach programme. Just tell me the way out.'

'I'll have to escort you I'm afraid. If you give me your telephone number I'll let you know their decision by tomorrow.'

Nathalie didn't push her luck and meekly followed the nurse to the exit. She'd got more than she expected. Confirmation of an Ebola patient, the drugs that were given, the patient's relative as a possible future contact, and a possible means of getting a film unit into the country. If the afternoon's meeting went as well then Geoff Sykes would be an extremely happy man.

✳

It was only a twenty-minute taxi ride back to her hotel. Nathalie stared out of the window at the grey domino-like skyscrapers of the city. She had only been in the country a few days but it seemed that Harare was one of the most unattractive capital cities that she'd ever visited. Her mood was lifted by Emmanuel, or Manny as he liked to be called, the Holiday Inn doorman and all-round fixer.

'Welcome back Miss Thompson, I hope you had a good morning. Can I persuade you to take a little lunch in our restaurant?'

She'd only met this guy once and he was already treating her as a regular.

'Thank you Manny, I've a few things that I have to do. Would it be possible for me to have a club sandwich and some fizzy water in my room?'

'Of course Miss Thompson. I'll send it up right away.'

Nathalie went to her room and started to prepare for the afternoon's rendezvous. She exchanged her business suit for a pair of torn jeans and a sloganed T-shirt. She put her passport, phone and Imunaid documentation into the hotel safe and keyed in a passcode. If she was searched there would be no way of these guys tracing her identity. Lloyd had arranged with Bagatelle to send some background on Nathalie's 'pro-African rights' campaign. The ideology was militant and indirectly incited terrorism and so they had changed her name to Nathalie King. They had also not given her any hard copies in case these were intercepted by government officials. Lloyd said he would prepare something for their meeting. Recalling all this deception made Nathalie nervous and she jumped as there was a sharp knock on her door.

'Best club sandwich in Harare Miss,' came the cheerful voice from the corridor.

Nathalie unlocked the door and Manny wheeled in a trolley bearing a pretentious silver dome and an ice bucket containing a bottle of sparkling water.

An hour later and Nathalie was speeding along the Mutare Road towards Ruwa. The skyscrapers gave way to low-rises and then to scrub. She noticed the sign to Epworth on her right-hand side. Perhaps if she had a day to spare she would visit its famous rocking boulders. She secretly thought that she'd rather be doing that this afternoon. The closer she was getting to this rendezvous the more nervous she felt. It had all sounded rather exciting in the London production office but now, sitting in the back of this taxi under dark cloudy skies, any glamour seemed far away.

The service station was a modern concrete slab mounted on four pillars alongside a car accessories shop and a pay booth. She recognised Lloyd from the photo he had e-mailed to London. 'Easy to notice me, I'm half and half,' he had written. He was standing by an old Ford Mondeo dressed in jeans and a tan leather jacket holding a small canvas holdall. She paid the taxi with US dollar bills. They didn't seem to use coins here so she added a generous tip. Lloyd strolled up to her.

'I wouldn't flash that money around,' he said. 'Best not to get noticed.'

Nathalie thought that a strange introduction. She followed him to his car and once inside made a deliberate move to shake his hand.

'Good to meet you at last Lloyd. Thanks for setting all of this up.'

Lloyd took her hand. 'Yeah, sorry. Good to meet you too. I'm just trying to get focused, you know.'

Nathalie looked at her watch. 'We've not got much time so why don't you give me an outline of the plan.'

Lloyd unzipped the holdall and showed her a bunch of papers. 'As I said, the meeting is at three. These guys are convinced that you are some sort of activist and they need a contact in Europe. They are not a big group but they have big ambitions. They're pissed off with the West exploiting Africa, and not too keen on what they see as their corrupt government, so they'll do anything to expand their cause. I've used some of the technology at my newspaper to mock up some stuff to show you're a sympathiser. They've seen blogs on the internet, I thought this might give them a bit more confidence. We don't want to be late so I'll tell you more on the way.'

Lloyd stuffed the papers back into the bag and put the car into gear. Soon they were making their way south, at speed, along the dual carriage highway. Nathalie was about to ask how they could find out more about the possible connections between the group and the Ebola case when she noticed a massive cavalcade approaching them in the other lane. Motorcycle outriders, flashing lights and huge black sedans with darkened windows. Lloyd hesitated, and then put his foot down. It all happened in the blink of an eye. The blur of the cavalcade rushing past. Two motorcyclists peeling off from the rear. Bright flashes from the objects they were carrying. The ripping of tyres and the squeal against the tarmac. Lloyd wrestling with the wheel and the world outside turning. The ground, then the sky, and now the earth, this time spilling and churning through the windows. Nathalie felt a sharp pain in her ribs and moisture on her forehead before everything faded to black.

Four

The concrete was hard, wet and cold. The pale green brick walls rose from the floor to a small square of light standing about three metres above. To one side was a single metal bed covered in a sheet and a grey blanket, to the other a row of white bars. Nathalie felt sick. She put her hand to her head and pulled it away to see a patch of sticky dark red blood on her hand.

'Shit, what a mess, where in the hell am I?'

She didn't know if she had spoken or just thought the words. She turned sideways and tried to rise onto her hands and knees. The room seemed to spin, she closed her eyes. She was sure she was going to be sick, but no vomit came. Using the bed as a support she stood and opened her eyes once more to look at – look at what? A room, a cell? Yes it was a cell. Just like she'd seen in American movies. Bare walls, a single sink, a bed and a row of metal bars. Painfully she lowered herself onto the bed and lay back. Her body ached all over. What was all this about? Then slowly, like pieces of floating jigsaw, her memory formed a picture. She was with Lloyd, that's right Lloyd, in his car. Going somewhere. Two guys on motorcycles. Wheeling around and pointing something at them. No not something, guns. They had been fired at! Must have hit the car's tyres. Oh Christ that was it. The car had rolled over and over. What in the hell was she doing in here? The room went dark again.

She was woken by the noise of the metal door being unlocked. A tall African guy in a khaki uniform with a large stick at his waist entered the room.

'Ah, awake, good. Come with me.'

'Excuse me, who are you and where in the hell am I?' slurred Nathalie, trying to come to her senses.

'*We* shall be asking the questions. Get up and follow me.' This was said more roughly and he began to grab at Nathalie's arm.

'Okay, okay, I'm coming. Let go I'm bruised all over, that really hurts.'

The man ignored this, pulled her to her feet and pushed her through the open door.

She was half dragged, half pushed, along the echoing corridor. It really was like an American movie. A row of white barred cells, some empty, others containing sleeping inmates. It was hot and the place stank of stale urine. A thick metal door stood in their way. The guy with the big stick took it out of its holster and rapped on the door loudly. Moments later, a rattle of keys and it swung open. The noise boomed through Nathalie's head. She swayed a little and was pressed through into the light. Another uniformed man met them at the bottom of a narrow staircase. She couldn't manage the stairs so her two guards took her by the elbows and literally dragged her to the top and deposited her on the floor of the landing.

'Wait here.'

She had little option. Her legs were so weak that she could hardly stand let alone wait somewhere else. With difficulty she manoeuvred herself into the foetal position and tried to get the bearings of her surroundings. She was in a wooden floored anteroom. Behind was the metal door to the staircase, now closed. To the sides, other doors, more domestic looking. Like the floor also wooden, painted dark green with small wire-glassed windows. Two incongruous orange plastic-backed chairs rested against one wall. She crawled up to them and managed to use one to assist her onto the other. She had been told to wait, so she sat here waiting.

It was Tom Finch's first day. It was early summer in London, the T-shirts and floral cotton dresses were out and people were making the best of it. Tom had never felt better. A year ago he had been sweating over biochemistry exams and now he was about to join the film industry. He couldn't believe his luck; there must have been dozens of candidates, all with media degrees and work experience. He'd gone in with a science degree and a few months as a hospital porter. No chance. But the letter in his hand said otherwise. Two o'clock, Bagatelle Films, Soho Square. Why two o'clock, and not first thing, he had no idea, yet here he was. The intercom crackled and a voice asked him to come up.

He hadn't seen Geoff Sykes' office, he had been interviewed in the boardroom, but it was exactly as he had anticipated. Television screens, international wall clocks and framed film awards.

'Tom, sit down, has Stefanie offered you a coffee?'

Tom nodded.

'Right, I'll get down to it. Sorry couldn't meet earlier, I was out of the office. Wanted to brief you personally. I first want to reiterate that this job could be dangerous. This isn't a schools' programme on bacteria. Bioterrorism isn't to be taken lightly and you could be meeting some very unpleasant people.'

'I was told that at the interview, I said I'm okay with it.'

'Yeah, but saying you're okay with it and actually doing it is another matter. We really won't take offence if you change your mind.'

'No, I've thought carefully, I really am good about it.'

'Okay I'll take your word for it.' Geoff took a thin file from his desk and handed it to Tom.

'The reason we've hired you is your knowledge of biochemistry and you've had some experience of hospitals. In your hands is the proposal we sent to the BBC and A&E Networks in the States. As you'll see it promises quite a lot. They've accepted the proposal but shooting it is going to be a lot more difficult than writing it. That's where you come in. We've got a few leads in Afghanistan, Indonesia and Zimbabwe, leads but no real hard facts. We'd like you to use your science background to firm some of them up.'

Tom's pulse started racing. 'You would like me to travel to some of these places?'

'Possibly, the brief is pretty open, it's up to you. We need you to research real stories and get credible contacts. We haven't got an unlimited budget but it's good enough and, if you've got enough evidence to go somewhere, we'll pay your expenses.'

'That's great. I mean, if it's really worth going then I'll...'

Geoff leaned back and gently waved his outstretched hands. 'You're a bright guy, I'm sure you won't be using our budget for a travel holiday. Now your film director is a lady called Nathalie Thompson. She's experienced, used to travelling and shooting abroad and, although she may not look it, quite tough. I think you'll like working with her.'

'Will I meet her today?'

'No. She's in Zimbabwe following one of our stories.' Geoff pointed at the file. 'To save time I'd like you to investigate the stuff on Indonesia. From your CV it's right up your street. There's been a leak of a weird strain of bacteria from some sort of Mickey Mouse laboratory in East Java. Apparently it's not natural but manufactured. We know this because a swab of a patient in the Royal Free was sent to the London School of Hygiene and Tropical Medicine. I would suggest that's where you start. Would be a good idea to get a dossier on it and some sort of story before Nathalie returns at the end of the week. I'm sure she will be grateful for any help she can get.'

❋

Geoff Sykes could not have spoken truer words. For at that moment Nathalie was sitting in front of a plain Formica table, behind which was a very large, very imposing African policeman.

'Before you ask for your lawyer, I've lost the number, okay?'

Nathalie stared at him in disbelief. 'I wasn't going to ask for my lawyer, I was going to ask for the British Ambassador. What in the hell am I doing in here?'

'Ah, not a local then. I'm afraid I've lost that number too.' The policeman leant forward menacingly. 'Name?'

Nathalie's head was spinning. She was just about to let out her name when she went cold. Name? In the car, where she presumed they'd found her, she was going under the name of Nathalie King. 'Shit,' she thought. 'If they've found those documents they must think I'm a militant activist.'

She tried stalling for time. 'Sorry I feel a bit sick, my head really hurts, can I have a glass of water?'

The policeman sat upright and spoke into the corner; presumably they were being watched and recorded somewhere. 'A glass of water, now.'

Nathalie used the time to think. It made sense that they had found the papers, why else would they have locked her up? On the other hand, who had shot at them to cause the car crash in the first place? Perhaps she was just a victim of attempted armed robbery. But if she was a victim why was she being treated like this? The glass of water was brought in. She had run out of time so she thought the best thing to do was to tell the truth.

'Nathalie Thompson, my name is Nathalie Thompson. I'm a British citizen and I would like to see the British Ambassador.'

'Oh so you have a name. Nathalie Thompson,' drawled the officer, writing it down on his notepad. 'And so Nathalie Thompson where is your ID?'

Nathalie could sense a glimmer of hope. He hadn't challenged her on her name, perhaps they hadn't found the papers.

'In the hotel, I left them in the hotel. Silly of me I know, I put all my stuff in the safe. I was told that…' She paused, she was going to say she was told that Zimbabwe could be a pretty lawless place, but this seemed a bit tactless with the stern face of the law in front of her. 'Just forgot to take it with me,' she finished lamely.

'Take it where?'

Oh Christ, Lloyd. What had happened to him? Had they got him too? And if so what story was he telling. She had seen all this on TV. Split the people up, get them to tell their stories, check out the differences.

'My friend, is he okay?'

31

'Your friend?'

'Yes my friend, he was driving the car, the one that crashed. Did you get the guys that did it?'

To her shock the policeman laughed.

'The guys that did it. That's a good one.' The policeman put his pencil to his lips and seemed to make a decision.

'Right, before we go any further I'm going to check out your story. What hotel are you staying at?'

Nathalie felt that the conversation had turned the corner. She was still worried about Lloyd but she had to look after her own skin first. 'The Holiday Inn, Harare, on Fifth Street. Ask for Manny, he'll vouch for me and get you my passport.'

The policeman left the room and Nathalie spent the next half-hour praying that the police were too busy to send someone to search her hotel room. She might prove that she was Nathalie Thompson, the problem was that her phone would show her as Nathalie Thompson the television journalist and not Nathalie Thompson the Imunaid worker. Still it would be better to be deported for journalism than life imprisonment for assisting terrorists. Her luck was in. A smiling Manny entered the room with her interrogator and her passport. Just her passport she noted.

'Can you identify this woman as Nathalie Thompson staying at your hotel?'

'Yes Sir, that's her. The British Imunaid worker. I personally hailed a cab to get her to the central hospital this morning.'

'Bless you Manny,' thought Nathalie.

'The hospital, can they vouch for her?'

'I don't know Sir, you will have to ask them Sir.'

The policeman looked first at Nathalie and then back to Manny. He handed Manny his notebook, asked him to write down the name of the hospital and then told him to go.

Nathalie held out her hand for her passport. 'Can I go now then?'

The policeman put her passport in his pocket and gestured for her to sit down.

'Not yet Miss Thompson, there are a few things we need to clear up.'

Nathalie inwardly groaned.

'The guys that did it, as you so colourfully put it, were the personal bodyguards of the president of Zimbabwe.' He paused awhile waiting for this to sink in.

'There is a law here, Miss Thompson, that when the presidential cavalcade passes, no matter what side of the road you're driving on, you are expected to stop. This is by presidential decree and is for security reasons. Anyone failing to do so can be stopped by any means. Any means. You get my drift?'

Nathalie nodded slowly. This sounded a crazy rule but she had heard that crazy rules were the norm here.

'We have interrogated the driver of the vehicle who claims that he was showing an aid worker the countryside and was heavily engaged in conversation when the cavalcade passed. He also claims by the time he noticed it his foot slipped from the break to the accelerator. All very convenient don't you think.'

Nathalie tried not to show her relief. Lloyd was alive and, by the sound of it, metaphorically kicking.

'We are not very convinced by this argument and as a passenger you may also be implicated in the charge.'

Nathalie closed her eyes again. This was not good.

'However, I have decided to wait for a report from the hospital, just to see how important your work is here. We don't want to cause yet more friction between our countries do we?'

So her freedom all depended on Nurse Jones. Nathalie hoped that she had made a good impression, and that her promise of financial aid had got through to the right people.

The answer came sooner than she expected. Later she was to hear that the senior health officer was obviously very influential, with friends or perhaps even relatives in high places. The hospital was desperate for the money and had told the police that Imunaid were indispensable. She was a critical part of the outreach team and was scheduled to leave with them in the next few days. Prison and the scandal associated with it was out of the question. Nathalie was asked to fill in a form, verifying her good and fair treatment and told that she could leave. She had been shot at, bullied and practically assaulted but she would forego all of that to just get out of this place. She signed the form subserviently and was shown to the outer office. There, sitting in a corner, was Lloyd. His face was black and blue and a small streak of blood was running from his ear. Yet he greeted her with a smile.

'Nathalie, good to see you're all right.'

'I'm not sure about all right, but it's good to see you too. Shall we ask to go out of the back door?'

Lloyd leaned over to whisper in her ear. 'No. We'll go out the front door together. Make a big show of it.'

She looked at him quizzically.

'Tell you later.' He held her hand and together they walked into the sunlight.

Lloyd strolled slowly outside the entrance to the police station as if looking for a taxi. He asked Nathalie to do the same, making sure that passers-by could see her.

'News travels fast in Harare, and you're looking good especially with those bruises.'

'I don't get it,' said Nathalie.

'Neither will these rubber necks,' replied Lloyd. 'It will start a lot of rumours.'

'Why would you want to do that?'

'Two people, one a white girl, coming out of a police station covered in cuts and bruises. Our little terror group will love it. If they weren't convinced that you're a militant activist before they definitely will after this, especially if I can put the word around.'

'Clever, but what will your paper think.'

'They'll just think I'm an arsehole for not stopping for the President's motorcade. Look here's a taxi, you take it, go back to your hotel and clean up. I'll contact you when I've remade the meeting. You still want to go through with it don't you?'

'Yes of course,' said Nathalie automatically, getting into the cab. She was so dazed that she didn't know what she wanted to go through with, it seemed like the right answer at the time.

Manny greeted her at the hotel like a long lost friend. 'Miss Thompson, what an experience. Let me help you to your room. They told me you were in a car crash and they didn't know who you were. I'm glad it's all sorted out now. Is there anything I can get you? Would you like me to call you a doctor?'

'No, I'm fine Manny, thanks for bringing my passport. Did you notice my phone in the room?'

'All safe and sound Miss.' He winked at her. 'I didn't think you would have liked the police rummaging through your personal messages. They can get so misinterpreted sometimes.'

'You're an angel Manny. Just send a mug of hot chocolate up to my room. What I need now is a long warm bath.'

He called the elevator for her and rushed off to the kitchen. Nathalie entered her room and started to run a bath. She checked the safe for her phone and found it just as Manny had said but with a couple of new messages on it. One was from the hospital saying that they would have great pleasure in taking her on the next outreach visit in two days' time. The other was from Geoff asking her to call. She dialled his number.

'Hi Nathalie. How's things.'

Nathalie decided not to tell him about the afternoon's events. That could wait for later. 'Fine Geoff, just got a note saying they're up for me going on the immunisation outreach programme. I mooted the fact that we might be able to video it and they seem keen on the idea. Sneaky way of getting our film crew into the country.'

'Great news. I was just going to update you on this end. Your new researcher, Tom, started today. Seems very keen. I've put him onto the Java story. He's got an appointment with the School of Tropical Medicine tomorrow. Hopefully we'll have something for you when you get back. How's Lloyd's contacts working out?'

'Looking promising. I've met Lloyd, he seems to know what he's doing. Should be able to get a meeting with these guys soon.'

'Okay, be careful, it can be rough out there.'

'Tell me about it,' thought Nathalie, rubbing her bruised thigh.

'Anything else Geoff? My bath is about to run over.'

'No I don't think so…oh yes, one thing. That woman with memory loss who came into our office.'

'What about her?'

'Your doctor friend has just rung to say that she regained a little of her memory. Seems that she was on some sort of drug trial.'

'What drug trial?'

'No one knows. Apparently she just walked out of the unit this morning.'

Five

The Portland stone art deco building known as the London School of Tropical Medicine and Hygiene stood a few blocks away from the British Museum. Tom had passed it many times on his way to Goodge Street Tube station. This time he paused and stood at the main entrance looking up at the ornate carving above the doorway.

'Apollo and Artemis riding a chariot,' came a voice beside him.

Startled, Tom looked around to find a bearded man carrying a slim tan briefcase. 'Excuse me?'

'Apollo and Artemis. You know, two of Zeus's kids.'

'I beg your pardon?'

'Sorry, I'm Doctor Goodfellow.' The man looked at his watch. 'I recognised you from your Facebook page. You have a meeting with me in five minutes.'

'Oh,' said Tom relieved and putting out his hand. 'Pleased to meet you Sir.'

His hand was taken warmly. 'Philip will do. Come in. It's a nice day, we can sit in the courtyard.' He tapped his briefcase. 'I read your e-mail and have pulled out a few papers for you. The doctor gestured for him to enter. 'After you. It's the school's logo by the way.'

The courtyard was a contrast to the stripped classical facade. It was hemmed by a seven-floor glass building set within a vast atrium. Philip Goodfellow noticed Tom staring up in wonder. 'A good use of the space and very practical don't you think?' He gestured for Tom to sit down at a small table at the foot of the structure. 'You know this place is Shakespeare's loss and world medicine's gain don't you?'

Tom was becoming used to this man's eccentric manner and decided to play along. 'It's built on an old site of the Globe or something?'

'Good guess but not quite. In 1913 the National Theatre Committee purchased the land to build a Shakespearean theatre on it. Fortunately for us, about ten years later the Rockefeller Foundation put up two million quid to build the school. Best money they ever spent.' He waved his hand towards the glass building. 'We've been making improvements ever since.'

Tom shuffled in his chair wondering how to get around to the topic of bioterrorism. He was used to talking to professors, but this had normally been in tutorials as an undergraduate; now he had to appear as a hard-bitten journalist. He needn't have worried, Doctor Goodfellow noticing his unease opened the subject for him.

'Your office tell me that you are looking for background information for a documentary film you're making. Sounds fascinating. Well I think you might have come to the right place. We've been making more tests on that bacterial sample I told your Mr Sykes about. Extraordinary results. What do you know about gyrase inhibitors?' Once more Doctor Goodfellow had thrown Tom another question from left-field.

'Gyrase inhibitors? I've heard about them, sadly didn't revise that part of the syllabus.'

'Syllabus?'

'I did microbiology at Imperial, but don't remember that part of the module.'

'Shame, an important destructive mechanism in the reproductive process of bacteria you know.'

Tom felt the interview was getting away from him; he hadn't come here to retake his exams. 'Doctor Goodfellow, I don't want to appear rude but...'

'But you haven't come here for a lecture on bacteriology.'

'I didn't mean...'

'No, I know you didn't, but if you're going to make a film on bioterrorism and use our laboratory work as a story then I'm afraid you might have to listen to one.'

'Okay,' replied Tom, lengthening the 'kay' part of his answer.

Doctor Goodfellow clapped his hands. 'Right, here goes. The bacteria that we found in the sample is unique. Never come across it before. It reproduces using an enzyme called DNA gyrase.' He paused. 'You know what an enzyme is don't you?' Seeing Tom's expression he continued. 'Of course you do. This enzyme helps a bacteria reproduce. It relieves the strain while double strand DNA is being unwound.'

Tom nodded recalling an image from the back of his mind. 'Yes that's right. Something called helicase does the unwinding doesn't it? The two strands have got to be separated so the bacteria can reproduce. Then they are coiled up again. I seem to remember we twisted the coils of our phone chargers to bunch them up to demonstrate how they can get inside their tiny casings.'

'Exactly, I use the same analogy with my students. To get to the point, that's not an abnormal process, what's strange here is the speed with which our sample replicates. The helicases look like they're on speed. Incredible rate of bacterial duplication. We've broken the enzyme down and there's nothing like it in nature. Could be synthetic. And if it is, someone's made it. This bacteria is pretty unpleasant and so if there is some laboratory out there producing it then they're up to no good.'

'An agent for bioterrorism?'

'Possibly. We've traced the patient's background. Of course I can't divulge any of this to you.' Philip Goodfellow placed an open folder onto the table between them. 'And I'm afraid the police aren't interested, however it would be good if someone followed it up wouldn't it? Fancy a cup of coffee? The machine is just around the corner; terrible stuff but hot and wet, you know.' Goodfellow got up and strolled out of the courtyard.

Tom stared at the folder in front of him. By twisting his neck around he could see a name and laboratory address typed on one of the sheets. An Indonesian name and an address in eastern Java. He wasn't sure if this was legal but he took his phone out of his jeans' pocket and took a quick photograph.

The sun blazed through the blinds creating stripes across the room. One of them danced across Nathalie's face. She woke, turned over in the bed and then groaned. She had spent all of yesterday in the same bed but her bruises still hurt like hell. Still, she could thank her lucky stars that she wasn't resting in that cell. If it wasn't for Manny. She propped herself up on the pillows and reached for the hotel telephone.

'Room service? Orange juice, buttered toast and a very large cup of coffee please. That's right, room 361.'

The day in bed hadn't been wasted. She had contacted the Central Hospital and they had been more than helpful with the arrangements. The promise of charitable funding had obviously worked. A minibus with some of the nurses would pick her up from her hotel and take her to the nearest local immunisation depot. There, after a brief overnight stay they would relocate into the outreach Land Rover with its refrigerated trailer. Then bingo! One of the outreach locations was in a kraal village near Shurugwi. Nathalie could hardly believe her ears. As soon as they put the phone down she had rung Lloyd. Could their meeting with WEXA be arranged to coincide? He said he would do his best. That was twenty-four hours ago. Not a peep out of him since. She took her breakfast tray from Manny and removed the pretentious little cardboard covering from the orange juice. Her mobile beside her began to flash. The number looked familiar.

'Lloyd?'

'You've a charmed life. They're up for it. Really keen. I think they caught some of the rumours of us coming out of the police station. Are you sure you can get away from the outreach programme long enough to make it worthwhile?'

'That's fantastic Lloyd. I've been thinking about that. I'll tell them that I have to do a technical recce. Meet with a sparks or some other sort of film crew. You could be my sound man. I'm sure we could join up and creep away for half an hour.'

'You think they'd buy it?'

'Why not? The film business can be a bit mystical. I'm sure we could pull the wool over their eyes.'

'Wool?'

'Never mind. They don't know anything about filmmaking, I can make it sound very techie, essential that we sort out the audio and lighting before we shoot it.'

'If you say so. I'll arrange the meeting in a hut in a nearby kraal; you could say that you'd like to film in one and need to discuss the setup.'

'Sounds good, I'll have to think of a way of keeping them out of it.'

'Yeah, I'm sure our bunch of terrorists won't want an immunisation team to listen in. That reminds me, don't mention anything about the embassy bombing, they don't know I know anything about that. We're just there to support them with their publicity campaign. If they start talking about more devious things we'll only listen, yeah?'

'Don't worry, I'll take your lead, just see if you can nudge them around to talking about Ebola.'

'I'll do my best. By the way, I should've asked, how are you? Recovered yet?'

'On the mend. And you?'

'Still walking, I'm sorry about the crash. Didn't want to stop in case they searched our papers.'

'Yeah, what happened to them? I was so confused yesterday, forgot to ask.'

'I was still conscious after the car rolled so I threw the bag into the bushes. It's probably still there. Haven't dared go back in case someone follows me.'

Nathalie closed her eyes and tried to remember the location. Of course, nothing. She had been completely knocked out. She couldn't even remember the terrain leading up to the accident.

'You don't think anyone would find it?'

'Well, the Bush was pretty thick and I threw it as far as I could. With a bit of luck if we get a storm the papers will get soaked anyway. I wouldn't worry about it. The police have checked who you are with the hospital and are satisfied.'

Nathalie was about to pursue the matter when their call was interrupted by a knock at her door.

'Okay, here's someone to clean my room. I'll text you when we are on the road, and you can let me know where we can meet.'

'Will do.' Lloyd closed the call without saying goodbye.

The minibus was early. Nathalie felt like royalty as she surveyed the entourage that waited for her in the hotel lobby. They stood as she entered and Sue Jones introduced her to them one by one; the district medical officer, the senior nurse responsible for the outreach programme, and two immaculately dressed immunisation nurses in their white uniforms.

'I wasn't expecting...' Nathalie tailed off as Nurse Jones glanced at her furtively.

'We are honoured to have the district medical officer with us today. He will explain the programme on our way to Gweru. It's a four-hour drive and I hope you don't mind, we've booked you in at the Midlands Hotel.'

'Midlands Hotel?'

'Yes, the best hotel in Gweru. You see, the team need to pick up the vaccines from the refrigerated store first thing tomorrow morning.'

Nathalie was becoming concerned. 'But I thought you said we were going to Shurugwi.'

Nurse Jones smiled. 'Sorry, I assumed you knew. Gweru is not far from Shurugwi district. It's just that there's no, how shall I say, suitable accommodation there.'

Nathalie shrugged her shoulders. 'Oh that's fine then, I'm not too fussy where I...I mean I'm sure your arrangements will be...'

Noticing the impatience on the medical officer's face Sue Jones interrupted her and suggested that they make a move.

The minibus had seen better days and the further they drove from Harare the rougher the road became. For the first part of the journey the district medical officer droned on and on about health statistics and the importance of information systems. Nathalie tried to concentrate but every time the vehicle hit a pothole she nearly screamed out with pain from one of her multiple bruises. Thankfully after an hour the medical officer seemed to run out of things to say so Nathalie had time to relax. She pressed her face against the window. The sprawling low rise buildings of the Harare suburbs had now turned to scrub, with the occasional tree forming a silhouette against the threatening skies. A crack of thunder was followed by a lightning flash and then a torrent of water hit the windscreen. The driver reached for the dashboard and the windscreen wipers scraped across the screen only to come to a halt in the middle. The scene outside became a streaked blur. The minibus slowed and veered from side to side as the driver unwound his window. Holding grimly on to the steering wheel with one hand he reached around to try to wipe the windscreen with the other. It was hopeless, and dangerous. With each attempt the bus slew into the side of the road. The two nurses looked really scared so Nathalie, realising that she was the VIP passenger, tapped the driver on the shoulder.

'Wouldn't it be better if we stopped for a while, just until the storm cloud passes over?'

The driver turned around and looked for some assistance from the chief medical officer. As he did so the bus struck another pothole and they all nearly hit the roof.

'I think Miss Thompson's right. Pull over for a few minutes and, while we are waiting, you could take a look at that windscreen wiper.'

The nurses' expressions turned to relief as they rearranged their crisp uniforms and repositioned themselves in their seats. The driver disappeared into the deluge and made some futile attempt to repair the wipers. The rain came down harder driving into the thin metal shell of the bus like nails. Nathalie tried to clear the steamed-up window with her elbow but the condensation kept reappearing. Although it was nearly midday the sky above was black. The road was becoming hardly visible, covered in a stream of red mud.

Nathalie began to wonder whether stopping was a good idea. But the rain eased off as quickly as it had arrived and the sun began to filter through the cloud cover and splinter through the raindrops on the windows. The chief medical officer looked at his watch and leaned out of the window to shout at the driver.

'Hurry up man, I have to get to Bulawayo before nightfall. This is disgraceful; when did you last service this vehicle?'

The wiper began to slowly squeak across the screen as if in protest.

'Bulawayo?' queried Nathalie. 'I thought we were going to Gweru.'

The driver climbed back into his seat, dripping water onto the medical officer beside him.

'Nurse Jones and I are going on to Bulawayo after we've dropped you off at your hotel,' said the medical officer irritably. 'That's if we ever get to Gweru,' he added brushing the drops from his jacket.

The rest of the journey was driven in silence. The morose driver with saturated clothing shuffled around in his seat trying to keep the minibus away from the ruts of red mud in the deteriorating roads.

Nathalie looked around at her fellow passengers. So, Sue Jones and the medical officer were not going on the outreach programme. That left the senior nurse and his two assistants. A lot easier to cope with if she was going to slip away to meet up with Lloyd and the WEXA group. She studied the face of the senior nurse. He hadn't spoken a word to her after their initial introduction. He seemed shy but she could sense something deeper under his gentle demeanour. The badge on his khaki epauletted shirt read *Joseph Karasa*.

'Well Joseph,' she thought, 'I wonder whether we could get to know you a little bit better?'

The Midlands Hotel in the centre of Gweru looked more like a mosque than a hotel. It was constructed of tiers of white arches and accompanied by a minaret-looking clock tower. The minibus pulled up at the entrance in the town square and the driver jumped out to take their luggage from the back. The chief medical officer stayed seated and he turned around to shake Nathalie's hand.

'This is where we part Miss Thompson. I'm afraid, because of the conditions, we are running late and Nurse Jones and I have an important meeting in Bulawayo. I do hope you'll excuse us for departing so suddenly.'

'Of course,' replied Nathalie, stepping out of the bus. 'A pleasure to meet you. I look forward to seeing you again when we return with the film crew.'

'Absolutely, if I'm around. It would be good to see the project through, my diary permitting, you understand?'

A hotel porter was disappearing through the sliding glass doors with her luggage, and Nathalie suddenly realised that her transport was about to vanish.

'Oh by the way, how do I get back to Harare?'

'Not a problem, Joseph will look after you. We're dropping him and the nurses off at the transport depot. The Land Rover is in for repair so they will pick you up tomorrow morning in the Toyota. After you have finished the rounds they'll drive you back to Harare before nightfall. Now if you'll excuse us we must go.'

'Charming, I'm sure,' thought Nathalie, as the minibus pulled away. 'Great hospitality.'

She turned and walked into the hotel lobby. It had that 1950s colonial feel. She handed her passport to the reception desk and filled in the obligatory forms. She was given her key and, to her surprise, a note from the slot under her room number. The porter led her to her room, put the luggage on a small standing rack and waited for his tip. He seemed satisfied with the US one dollar bill and shuffled off down the corridor. Nathalie glanced into the shower room and placed her hands flat on to the bed. The mattress felt sturdy enough and the room, although not to the standard of the Holiday Inn, was adequate. She sat on the bed and opened the note in her hand. On it were simply the words *room 206*. She looked at her key. The number on the fob was 229; 206 would be on the same floor.

'In for a dollar,' she thought, and leaving her luggage untouched made her way to the corridor. The simple plaques on the wall pointed the way. She turned the corner and gently tapped on the door of room 206. It was opened almost immediately.

'Ah Nathalie,' exclaimed Lloyd. 'I was expecting you earlier.'

Six

They had the Midlands Hotel coffee shop to themselves. Nathalie played with the spoon in her saucer whilst Lloyd gave his explanation.

'It wasn't difficult. I'm a journalist; a couple of calls to the hospital and find you're the star of the show. Coining money from a big Western charity, that's the way they see it.' He looked around at the drab surroundings and snorted. 'Being accompanied by the big cheese and put up in a glamorous hotel in Gweru. To soften you up I think.'

A door creaked in the far corner, they both turned to look but it was only the wind.

'Well the big cheese has left me on my own. In other circumstances I would be a bit pissed off but I couldn't have arranged it better.'

'Yes I heard he had an urgent meeting in Bulawayo. That's what gave me the idea to meet you here. The WEXA group are getting nervous. I mentioned that you were undercover with the immunisation team. They didn't seem to like that. Too many people.'

'Shit.' Nathalie threw the spoon onto the table. 'You mean to say I've come all this way and they have chickened out.'

Lloyd picked up the spoon and carefully replaced it into the saucer. 'Not exactly.'

'Not exactly, what does that mean?'

'That's the reason I've spent hours travelling through rivers of mud to get here.' Lloyd put his elbow on the table and rested his chin in his hand. His deep brown eyes stared into Nathalie's.

'Okay, sorry I'm tired, bloody awful journey like you. Will they meet us?'

'I think so. As long as it's later this evening. They've given me a rendezvous location, but there's no guarantee. As I told you they're a bit of an amateur outfit, a fickle bunch.'

'Yeah, an amateur outfit that bombs the German embassy and murders three of its occupants. They weren't fickle that day were they?'

'That's the problem. And it makes it more dangerous. They are unpredictable.' Lloyd started to get up from his chair. 'It's quite a drive, if we are going to get there by dusk we ought to get going.'

Nathalie hesitated.

Lloyd sat down again. 'Changing your mind? I wouldn't blame you, we could call it a day now if you want; I'll just invoice my expenses.'

'No it's not that, I'm up for it. It's just that I haven't got a car; my friendly medical officer left me stranded.'

'Well I didn't come by bus. The garage lent me a jeep whilst they are beating my car wreck into shape. You needn't look so worried; I don't think the president's cavalcade will be driving where we are going.'

The road was even rougher than the one from Harare. The afternoon's rain had turned the dusty thoroughfare into a river of slime. Nathalie noticed that Lloyd had tied bundles of sacking and plywood boards onto the back of the jeep. He was obviously used to these conditions. Their progress was slow. Every two or three miles the vehicle slithered sideways and became bogged down in the mud. Eventually there was an impasse. No matter how hard he tried Lloyd couldn't make the thing move another inch. He was gentle on the accelerator yet still the wheels spun and dug the jeep deeper into the mire. Nathalie got out to push but was blinded by the rust-coloured spray that covered her from head to foot. Lloyd switched off the engine and climbed down from the cab. For the first time since she had met him Nathalie saw Lloyd break out into a broad white smile.

'If you could see yourself.'

Nathalie wiped the mud from her eyelids. 'I can imagine.'

Lloyd reached into the back of the jeep and pulled out the sacking and boards. 'Here, you push those under that wheel, and I'll do the other.'

Fifteen minutes later and they were on their way again, Nathalie caked in red mud and Lloyd with the same white smile.

The thunderous clouds had given way to sunlight and a purple-tinged sky. The sun itself appeared huge against the flattening horizon. Dusk in Central Africa, especially after a rainstorm, was really something. In the distance they could see a group of small round huts with conical thatched roofs. Their shadows were already lengthening against the bare earth clearing.

Lloyd squinted against the light.

'I think this is it. The settlement was abandoned some months ago. They said if we got here before nightfall they would be waiting for us.'

'Can't see a car. Maybe they got stuck like we did.'

'No, I think I can see fresh tyre tracks. Someone could have dropped them off. We'll soon know anyway. I'll park here, the scrub's a bit thick to drive right up.'

Lloyd pulled off the track onto the verge and put the handbrake on. They sat in silence for a few seconds listening in the still air. Not a sound.

Lloyd opened the driver's door with a creak. 'We'll try the hut on the right first, I suggest we go together.'

Nathalie nodded and followed him. This wasn't the first time she had met 'undesirables' but it didn't make it any less scary. The first hut was about four metres in diameter and was made of daubed dry mud. The exterior was probably painted in a cream wash but under the current sky it appeared a burnt orange. Lloyd peered into the small opening. Nathalie stood to one side and waited. A few moments later Lloyd stood up, shook his head and pointed to the next hut twenty metres away.

'Your turn,' he said quietly.

Nathalie trod over the scoured earth, avoiding the strange constructions made out of twisted dried branches which were thrust into the ground. They looked like some sort of giant basket weaving but were probably the foundations of an unbuilt dwelling. The second hut was slightly larger, still circular, with an exposed brick base beneath the mud superstructure and thatched conical roof. The doorway was higher and she had no need to stoop as she entered the interior. It was dark, very dark. After a few seconds the light from the vent in the roof outlined three seated figures in the smoky atmosphere. They resembled some sort of African mujahideen. Cross-legged, wearing headscarves that partially obscured their faces. They would have looked threatening apart from the fact that the scarves were made from the colourful floral fabric worn by Zimbabwean women. Nathalie beckoned Lloyd into the hut as the man in the middle began to stand.

'Welcome,' he said in a rather shaky voice.

'As frightened as me then,' thought Nathalie.

Lloyd nodded, thanked them for the invitation and introduced Nathalie.

They were asked to sit and were offered a mug of dark hot tea which one of the men poured from a blackened kettle resting on embers in the middle of the floor. The hole in the roof was not an efficient way of removing the smoke from this open fire and the soot in the air began to claw at Nathalie's eyes.

'Zimbabwean,' said one of the men proudly.

'Taganda tea, grown to the east of here,' explained Lloyd. 'Big export.'

Nathalie normally didn't drink tea, but she wasn't going to say so here. She nodded politely and took the steaming enamel mug in both hands. She could sense the nervousness amongst the group so decided to head straight in.

'I understand that you would like some publicity in Europe for pro-African rights on the global stage,' she said as calmly as she could.

The three men stared at her blankly. Perhaps this was going a little bit above their heads.

'You think that Africa is being treated unfairly by the West,' she added. 'I agree. Your resources have been completely exploited.'

This seemed to hit a better note. The man in the middle spat on the ground. 'Exploitation, that's right. And it's no better with so-called independence. Before, they stole our goods, now it's embargoes and sanctions.'

The smaller man to the right nodded in agreement. 'That's why we're doing something about it.'

The first speaker, possibly the leader, gave him a hard stare. 'But that's our business. Muzi here says that you have sympathisers in the West, contacts that can help us. Yes?'

Nathalie was about to ask who Muzi was when she realised that it must be a name that Lloyd had given them. This was getting complicated. Lloyd was a Zimbabwean journalist pretending to be a sympathiser, and she was a television director pretending to be an aid worker pretending to be a rights' activist. She had to be careful with her words; the machetes on these guys' laps didn't look too friendly.

'Yes,' she said simply.

Lloyd, or Muzi as he was now referred to, obviously had had a few encounters with these guys. He spoke to ease the tension. 'Nathalie is obviously guarded with what she is prepared to say. What I do know is that she can offer you two things. First, she has access to the media in the West; not a random internet sort of thing but broadcast television with huge captive audiences. Second,' he turned to Nathalie and put one finger to his lips. 'Second, and I know that she can't tell you more until we get to know you better, she has contacts. Contacts in the West who are very sympathetic to your cause and will go to extreme lengths to make it known.' Lloyd accentuated the word *extreme* and, when he had finished, took a slow long draught of tea to let his sentence sink in.

The small guy used this pause to jump in excitedly. 'What extreme lengths? Will they...' His utterance was cut short by the thwack of the flat blade of a machete across his chest.

'My friend is jumping the gun. We too must be guarded, as you put it, until we get to know each other better. This television thing? It's almost impossible for foreign journalists to bring cameras into the country. How do you propose we can get our message across Miss Nathalie?'

'Will they what?' Nathalie was thinking, but she put that thought out of her head and played along with the game.

'Well, as Muzi…' She still had a job working around that name. 'As Muzi has probably told you I have been given access to study the immunisation programme here. My associates at home are interested in obtaining some inside information on our fellow sympathisers. This was one way of getting into the country. We initially just wanted to touch base, but we've had a stroke of luck.'

Nathalie paused and held out her mug for a top-up of her drink. It had the dramatic effect that she intended. The guy in the middle reached for the kettle and poured the tea slowly.

'And this stroke of luck is?'

Nathalie took her time and sipped from the mug. She had them now, she could feel the suspicion melting away. 'That the ministry here seems to think it will be a good idea if we televised it. A great boost for the country's prestige, besides the great boost for their coffers.'

'So how does that help us?'

Nathalie put down the drink and spread her hands. 'If we can get you in the can at the same time putting your message across, pointing out what you *would* do if nobody listens, then I have plenty of broadcasters who would transmit it.'

The one who had been silent throughout leant over and whispered into his colleague's ear. The guy, who now Nathalie was mentally referring to as 'the middleman', nodded slowly and took a cigarette packet from his jacket. He opened it slowly as if trying to make a decision. He offered a cigarette first to Nathalie and then to Lloyd who both declined. Without using his fingers he took a cigarette into his lips and then bent forward to the smouldering embers to light it. The smoke added to the acridity of the air.

'You say, you would point out what we "*would* do". What do you mean by that?'

'My associates assume that you are not just a pacifist group who want to whinge on television.' Nathalie made as if to rise. 'If that's who you are, then best of luck to you but we're not interested.'

The middleman put out his hand and waved it for her to keep seated. 'And if I said we are more active than passive?'

Nathalie resumed her cross-legged position. 'Then I would say the more active you are the more interested we would be.'

'And besides televising our views, you and your associates could assist us with some of these activities?'

She shrugged. 'Why else do you think we are sitting here?'

The shaft of light coming through the doorway was turning to a darker shade of red. But by now their eyes had become accustomed to the murky interior. To one flank of the three men was an oil drum on its side and a pile of brushwood. On the other, an old twelve-volt battery. What this was for Nathalie could only guess at. To recharge their mobile phones perhaps? Besides the open fire and kettle the rest of the hut was bare. No kitchen equipment, no beds. They obviously weren't going to stay the night. So who brought them here and who was going to collect them?

Lloyd broke the silence. 'I believe what Miss Nathalie is trying to get at is, how far do you propose to go? She's not just interested in a protest group marching with banners and all that, she wants action.'

Nathalie had the impression that the group were beginning to listen. It was now or never. 'Ll…Muzi's right,' she said interrupting herself just in time. 'You may have seen from our press that we've been campaigning peacefully for some time; lobbying ministers, sending petitions to CEOs of mining companies. Their response, zilch, nothing. Zimbabwe is an independent state for Zimbabweans. Is it hell. Africa is exploited for its minerals by huge international conglomerates and sold cheap drugs that the West don't want. Look at the state of your country. Crap infrastructure, ghettos of poverty, racked with malnutrition and disease. It's time to act. And none of you lot seem to have the guts to do anything about it.'

Her rant had the desired effect. Middleman stood up and beat his own chest. 'Do nothing. That's how little you know. We have already caused damage to a Western embassy, and we have a cell plotting to do further damage on their own doorstep.'

Nathalie's eyes widened and she tilted her head to one side. 'On their own doorstep? You have explosive experts in the West?'

The small guy also got to his feet. 'There are more weapons than bombs. We have experts who can do even wider damage.'

Nathalie felt she had them on a run. 'You mean chemicals?'

'Or even worse; disease. We could give them a dose of an African disease. Poetic justice, don't you think?'

She could sense that the quiet guy was becoming agitated. His overeager colleagues were saying too much too soon. Staying seated he spoke for the first time. 'My friends are eager to prove themselves. But I would like you to prove yourself. Yes we have a plan, but we need a little assistance from indigenous people within Europe.'

'Indigenous,' thought Nathalie. 'Unusual word; educated guy, perhaps not as naive as Lloyd thinks.' She leaned forward as if asking him to continue.

'From our background checks, we think you can provide that assistance, but we will need more reassurance that you are genuine. So first let us see how our little television programme goes. And just to show you how active we are...' He nodded to the two standing men. 'Just a little demonstration to show what we do to people who double-cross us.'

Nathalie almost fell back into the dying embers of the fire as Middleman roughly grabbed Lloyd and pulled him to his feet. The smaller man seized his wrists and stretched Lloyd's arms over the rusty oil drum. Nathalie watched with horror as the 'not so naïve' silent guy slowly got up and used two hands to lift his machete over his shoulder.

She would never forget Lloyd's scream.

Seven

It had been nearly a week since Tom Finch had visited the School of Tropical Medicine. He was feeling rather satisfied with himself. Geoff had been pleased with the information he had obtained and had encouraged him to follow through with the investigation. Several days on the internet and, with a few visits to some pharmacology departments, he had come up with a very plausible story. Someone in Indonesia was researching and producing drug resistant bacteria that could replicate at speed in almost any condition. In the wrong hands this bacteria would cause havoc. A perfect weapon for a bioterrorist. On the other hand of course, it could be pure research to produce experimental bacteria for new drugs. There was only one way to find out: visit the laboratory. He had been weighing up the ways he could ask to do this when Geoff had suggested that he learn a little bit more about the industry, a trip to see some editing perhaps. Tom would have preferred to be on a plane to East Java but he could be patient and, after all, a month ago he would have given his eye teeth for such a visit. Stefanie met him at the top of Wardour Street.

'Great, you're on time. I've been asked to show you around a typical edit suite and a graphics studio.'

He followed her brisk walk down the street as she continued. 'We used to hire cutting rooms; you know, places where they physically cut film to make programmes. Now it's all digital. Geoff hates it but I think you'll find it interesting.'

It was another warm day and the streets were teeming with people in shirtsleeves and flimsy frocks. Stefanie marched him past numerous eateries and windows displaying sex toys and lurid underwear. There was a buzz about the place. Casually dressed media types appeared to be talking into the air until one spotted the small smartphone wire hanging around their necks. Surabaya could wait, today Tom would enjoy the Soho life.

The square mile around Soho in London, sometimes called the Golden Square Mile, is the home of the British film industry. Hundreds of media production offices, sound studios and editing facilities line its streets. Some in glamorous three-storey buildings, others in small cramped basements. Behind their walls lie miles of cables and thousands of screens. The productions here vary from corporate videos to stunning animated advertising and broadcast television programmes. Tom had some inkling of the technology but this was the first time he would be introduced to professionals in action.

Stefanie stepped into a side street and pressed one of the bells alongside an unpretentious looking door. 'Here we are, *Reels*; it's just one of the suites that Bagatelle is hiring at the moment.'

Tom looked up at the rather unimposing brick facade of the building. 'Hiring?'

'Yes, Geoff doesn't own any editing equipment, says that technology moves too quickly. Also some weeks we are editing five films at once, and others none at all, so it's impossible to know in advance what equipment...' She was interrupted by a distorted voice coming from a small grilled speaker. Neither of them could make it out but a loud buzz indicated that someone had remotely unlocked the door. Stefanie pushed it open and they walked inside. A narrow stone staircase faced them.

'Not very salubrious I know but Geoff hates spending money on flash reception rooms and cocktail cabinets.' Stefanie threw up her eyes. 'As long as the equipment is up to date and the editor knows what he's doing.'

Tom followed Stefanie up the stairs and into a corridor that led off the first mezzanine. She knocked on a rather grubby white painted door.

'Come in.'

Stefanie opened the door to reveal a small room crammed with technology. A mini NASA, as Tom would later describe it. A man with his back to them was staring at three television screens. Two contained moving pictures and the other a series of numbers and icons.

'Take a seat, won't be a moment, just want to render this bit.'

Tom looked around the room, which didn't take long. Behind the edit desk and to one side of the door was a small worn two-seater sofa and a cluttered side table. Tom and Stefanie perched on the sofa and waited. The editor was typing something at speed on a strange looking keyboard. It was like the one that Tom used with his PC but it had multi-coloured keys. As the editor typed, the images on the screens changed. On one appeared a sheet of flame, on the other a close-up of a fire hose. The images then froze and the man in the chair swivelled to face them.

'Sorry about that. Done. Just got to wait for the machine to catch up now. Doesn't matter what software you put into these things, still have to sit watching this annoying bar crawl across the screen.'

'Bob, this is Tom. Tom this is Bob, one of our regular and most skilful editors.'

'Tell that to Geoff next time he gets my invoice will you?'

Stefanie ignored this remark and asked Bob if he would give Tom an overview.

'Geoff says that if you're learning to make films it's best to start at the end,' she concluded.

Bob gestured for Tom to sit in the swivel chair alongside of him.

'There won't be an end if I spend too much time teaching all his new recruits.' He turned back to face the screens. 'But I'll quickly talk you through it. Here we're making a documentary film on arson for Channel 5. A week ago the director gave me the rushes and I loaded them into bins.'

Tom peered at the row of numbers. 'Bins?'

'Yeah, a hangover from celluloid days. We used to have a big canvas bin to hang all the strips of film in. Now I load different categories of film into different digital bins. For instance, here I've put all the fire shots, here all the interviews, and here the scenes at the fire station.'

'So you can find them quickly?'

'Exactly, then I take the director's storyline and try to make sense of it. Sometimes we have a voice-over first and sometimes it's written afterwards, to fit the pictures.'

'Doesn't the director tell you what order to put the pictures in?'

'Occasionally, but mostly it's a team effort. One day you should come in with your director and watch us in action. Who are you working with?'

'Someone called Nathalie. I've not met her yet, she's meant to be flying back from Zimbabwe this morning.'

'Well you're in good hands there. Send her my regards.'

'Will do. We are meant to be meeting this afternoon but she's not contacted the office recently; busy or poor communications from Africa I suppose.'

There was a cough behind them and Tom turned round to see Stefanie tapping the watch on her wrist. 'Sorry to interrupt you two boys but if we don't get a move on we won't get to that meeting. I still have to show Tom an animation studio.'

The studio was in the Haymarket so they made their way back towards Wardour Street to hail a black cab. Stefanie filled in the background.

'*Magic Touch* is owned by Oskar, a guy Geoff used to use as a freelancer in the days he directed films.' Tom gave her a glance. 'Yes I know, hard to believe but he hasn't always been sitting behind a desk grunting out orders. Anyway, Oskar has made it really big in the CGI business. You'll see a big difference to the edit suite we've just visited. He has at least twenty of the world's top animators working for him. You've probably seen their work on major feature films. Oskar does documentary work for Geoff for old times' sake.'

The cab pulled up outside an imposing architectural facade. Stefanie paid the cab driver and they walked into the glass-fronted lobby.

'All our opening credits and anything that needs 3-D graphics are done here,' explained Stefanie pushing the elevator call button.

'I hear that you might need animation to explain how viruses and bacteria work, is that right?'

If he was honest, Tom hadn't really thought about that. Sounded like a dream come true. The ability to describe all the things he normally did as rough sketches on paper by spectacular 3-D animation. He tried to hide his excitement from Stefanie and just nodded nonchalantly.

The lift doors opened and they made their way into the glass-surrounded reception area. A huge screen in one corner was showing a loop of the studio's show reel and scattered around on shelves were dozens of small statues which Tom assumed to be film awards. A girl with pink hair bounced up to Stefanie.

'Amazing to see you, it's been ages.'

They kissed on both cheeks. Stefanie gestured to Tom. 'This is Tom. I've been let out to show him some of the facilities we use. He might be helping Nathalie with the animation for the bioterrorism doc we're doing. Is Oskar around?'

'Yes he's about to go out for lunch but I'm sure he'll give you a few minutes.'

Oskar was all that Tom expected from an art director. Tall, blonde ponytail and a logo-plastered T-shirt. He spoke with a soft, slightly Polish accent.

'Hi, let me show you around. Medical stuff eh? We used to do quite a lot of that. May have some basic models stored to keep your costs down.'

Tom thought that this was slightly jumping the gun; he didn't have an idea of what was needed yet, but he didn't say anything. The studio was as amazing as the show reel. Rows of computers and screens attended by young hipster artists, most of whom were around Tom's age. The room was surrounded by vast posters containing colourful images. In one corner a man was sitting surrounded by the scattered innards of a computer. In another, two young women were bouncing a coloured ball on to a mat of artificial grass.

Oskar saw Tom staring at them. 'Don't ask. Working out some sort of advertising storyboard probably.'

59

Tom was shown various projects on the screens but they didn't make much sense to him. Artists were plotting a series of mathematical algorithms, others constructing wire-framed objects.

'You don't have to understand how they do it, just give them a really good brief on what you want,' said Oskar. 'Too many of our clients think they're bloody artists. What we need is what they want the audience to feel, think, or understand, and we'll do the rest.'

'That's telling you,' interjected Stefanie. 'He's just letting off steam, wouldn't dare say that to his big advertising clients.'

'You've known me too long Stefanie,' said Oskar with a grin. 'Don't worry, we'll look after your new prodigy. Just let me have your budget and schedule when you get one. Now if you'll excuse me I have a lunch date to catch up with.'

※

The production meeting had been set for two-thirty. Stefanie and Tom had grabbed sandwiches on the way back to the office and were now eating them in the boardroom. Between mouthfuls Tom kept nervously flicking through his notes.

Stefanie tapped him on the arm. 'He won't bite you know. He may not show it but I gather he thinks you're rather good.'

'Who's rather good?' asked Geoff bursting into the room.

'None of your business,' replied Stefanie. 'I thought you said two-thirty prompt. Tom and I have been waiting here for at least a quarter of an hour.'

'See Tom, what I have to put up with, insubordination and mutiny. As it happens Miss Moneypenny, I've been waiting for Nathalie; not like her to be late. I suppose we'll just have to start without her.

Stefanie was used to Geoff Sykes' faux misogyny and played along with the game. 'Well Mr Bond, we've had another letter from Arts and Entertainment – in the States,' she added for Tom's benefit. 'They are happy to join in with co-funding but want to have a bit more flesh around the proposal. You must admit it's a bit sketchy at the moment. Locations in Indonesia, Zimbabwe and Afghanistan with evidence of bioterrorism. All we have at the moment is Tom's report on a possible laboratory in Surabaya and whatever Nathalie has come up with on her Harare trip. Nothing at all on Afghanistan. Only some vague report from Reuters quoted by that guy you hired to do the first proposal.'

Geoff sat on the edge of the table and flipped open his file. After a few moments studying the papers he came to a decision.

'To be honest, I never really expected us to film in Afghanistan, too bloody dangerous. We left it in because it sounded topical at the time. It's only a forty-five minute programme. I'm sure we can fill it with Indonesia and Zimbabwe, after all they are two huge countries. Even the Americans know that much geography.'

Stefanie slowly shook her head. 'I must apologise for the lack of political correctness from my employer Tom. He likes to exaggerate from time to time.'

Geoff repositioned himself into a chair and leaned back. 'Okay, fair enough, but I'm sure we can satisfy our benefactors with a bit of creative writing. Tom, you sound like you're on to a good story. Where have we got with that?'

Tom noticed that the notes in his hands were shaking so he put them down. 'As I mentioned in my report…'

'Yes yes, I've read it, move on.'

'I think the professor's hunch is right. I've gone through their results with other labs, they all think the bacteria has been synthetically manufactured. In the wrong hands it could be a lethal weapon. What I can't prove at the moment is if the bacteria was manufactured for selling to terrorists or for testing out new drugs.'

'So how do we prove which it is?'

'I've checked the address of the laboratory in Indonesia where the infected guy came from. On Google Earth it looks like a warehouse in a small village just outside Surabaya. Doesn't look like a top state-of-the-art research lab that a pharma company would use.'

'And?'

'I suggest we go out there and take a look.'

'Could be an expensive trip if you're wrong.'

'Yeah, but if it's legit, we could still tell the story of how dangerous making artificial bacteria is.'

Geoff looked at Stefanie. 'The boy learns fast. Can you check out hotels, flights and costs et cetera. We can give it to Nathalie when she arrives, see if she wants to go.'

Tom disguised his disappointment by changing the subject. 'I hope you don't mind but there's been something that's worrying me.'

Geoff opened his hand, 'Go ahead.'

'If we find that this laboratory is really making biological weapons for terrorists shouldn't we tell the police rather than just film them?'

'Good point young man. It's a dilemma that many an investigative documentary maker has. But to appease your conscience, I'll tell you the answer. We film them first and then we tell the police.'

'But...'

Geoff held up his hand and closed it into a fist. 'Think about it. Tell the police first.' He uncoiled his thumb. 'First of all, which police? The ones in the UK, the ones in Indonesia?' He opened up his index finger. 'Second, what evidence do we have? Film them, put them on TV – guilty as hell.' He waved his third finger in the air triumphantly. 'Finally, if nobody appears to be doing anything about it, we can show it to the world.'

Tom sat there, a little bemused. 'I suppose if you put it like that.'

'I do. Now the Ebola thing. Last thing we heard from Nathalie is that she was going on an immunisation recce. Sounded like she could get a film crew into the country. Good news, always difficult doing concealed camera stuff. Crap quality and you don't always get what you want.'

Stefanie rose from her chair. 'She's over an hour late, her flight was meant to come in early this morning. If you don't mind I'll check with the airline, see if there's been a delay.'

She was saved the trouble by Nathalie appearing at the door. 'Delay I should say so, two hours trying to clear customs.'

'Ah, the prodigal returns,' said Geoff. 'Here take a seat, coffee?'

Nathalie pushed her trolley bag into one corner and took the chair next to Geoff's. 'No thanks, people keep telling me I drink too much coffee. Sorry I'm late, where are we up to?'

'No problem, you're just on cue. Ebola. Any progress?'

Nathalie reached into her shoulder bag and pulled out a bunch of papers and her mobile phone. The phone looked like it had been hit with a sledgehammer.

'Oh that,' said Nathalie seeing the expression on their faces. 'Dropped it from the hotel balcony. That's why I haven't been in touch. Didn't think Zimbabwe landlines would be very secure and it seemed a bit crazy to waste time looking for the Gatwick payphone when I was due here. Anyway, I made these notes on the plane.' She passed them to Stefanie. 'Excuse the handwriting.'

Stefanie took them resignedly. 'I'll tidy them up and let you see them before we send them in to the commissioners. They want an interim report,' she added.

'Bugger the report,' exclaimed Geoff. 'Have we got a film or haven't we?'

'Good chance,' said Nathalie. 'Visited the hospital in Harare, a definite Ebola case. Met with a so-called terrorist group. They're definitely up to something. I'm pretty sure that there's a connection there.'

'Such as?'

'They're keen to have a sympathiser in the West who can cross borders without being noticed. Putting two and two together I think they'd like to plant some sort of biological weapon to scare people. I don't think it's big scale, just enough to draw attention to their cause.'

'And Lloyd, is he still on board?'

'Ah Lloyd,' said Nathalie. 'That's another story.'

Eight

Nathalie cast her mind back to the terrifying scenes in the Shurugwi hut. The smoke-laden interior; Lloyd's arms being stretched across the curved sides of an oil drum; the lifting of a machete; and the screaming tear of metal as it tore into the container creating an eerie gash in its edge. Lloyd had nearly fainted. His shout was replaced by the laughter of the three men.

'That's what we do to people who double-cross us,' the quiet one had said. 'I trust that if we share our plans, you will keep them to yourselves.'

Nathalie had decided to spare Bagatelle the precise details. 'Lloyd is a bit nervous at the moment, he was threatened at our meeting. You know the sort of thing – split on us and we'll come looking for you. But I think he'll come round.'

Geoff took Nathalie's notes from Stefanie and studied them.

'You think we can depend on his continued support? What sort of guy is he?'

'Difficult to read him. Plays his cards close to his chest. Must be living in that sort of environment. Thought-Police everywhere.' She remembered his broad smile when she was covered in mud. 'But underneath I think he's okay. In it for ethical reasons, not just for the prestige of getting his stuff on TV.'

Tom had kept quiet since Nathalie's arrival. Nobody had introduced him and he hadn't wanted to interrupt, but he thought that if he was meant to be a researcher on this project he ought to say something.

'Um, hello I'm Tom. Started doing some research on the project whilst you were away. If they threatened you, do you think they're suspicious in any way?'

Nathalie turned to him and put her hands in front of her eyes. 'Oh God, how rude of me. Sorry Tom. I heard that you had been hired.' She stood up and walked around the table to shake his hand. 'I was so shattered after the flight and airport fracas that I didn't think to introduce myself. As you have probably gathered I'm Nathalie, the person who is meant to be directing this programme.'

Tom reddened as he took Nathalie's hand. 'No problem. I can see your head's in other things, don't worry about me.'

'That's no excuse, I'm really sorry.' Nathalie perched on the table beside him. 'You were saying, about them being suspicious. I think that people in that position are suspicious of anyone, we're no different. But if they really thought we were up to something I don't think they would be prepared to be filmed.' She turned to Geoff. 'If it's okay by you I've made an arrangement to shoot the immunisation project and use it as a cover to meet them again.'

Geoff looked up from the notes, 'Sounds good to me, but it looks as if you've got a lot on your plate. Tom here has located a suspicious laboratory in eastern Java for you to look at. Possible production of biochemical weapons. I suppose you could move on to Indonesia with the film crew after your shoot in Zimbabwe, but you wouldn't have the chance of a recce.'

'Too risky,' replied Nathalie. 'I don't know enough about it yet. Also, I need to check out my own laboratory. The guys who are making this anti-Ebola vaccine I came across in the Harare hospital, I think they're based in Slough.' She looked at Tom. 'Tell you what, why doesn't Tom fly to Java on his own and see if his story holds water. If it does, and the timescale fits, I could follow along with the film crew later.'

Geoff tidied his papers on the table top with a sharp tap and got up to return to his office. 'Fine, that's settled then. Nathalie checks out Slough and Tom flies to Java. Time's short so tomorrow would be good. Stefanie could you make all the arrangements?' He didn't wait for the reply.

Tom sat there mouth open. Nathalie saw his face and laughed. 'Don't worry, he's always like that. I think it's time for you and me to catch up.' She looked at her watch. 'I give in, I've only been on the wagon for two hours but it's no use, I really do need a coffee. Why don't we pop around the corner to *Nude Espresso,* and we can have a good chat without being disturbed.'

✳

Biomedivac House was a slick futuristic building jammed against an industrial Victorian skyline. The curved central facade was partially filled by an immaculate circular lawn and fountain. Either side, white granite paths led up to the glass rotating doors. It had not been difficult for Nathalie to get an interview. The promise of publicity on broadcast television was too much for Professor Townes and he had agreed to meet at short notice. To prepare, she had looked him up on the internet. Whiz kid professor of pharmacology at a prestigious Oxford college. Ground-breaking papers on plasmid DNA, cholinesterase inhibitors and C-type lectins. Nathalie couldn't pretend to understand all of the science but it was obvious that this guy was very bright and a key opinion leader in his field. On more digging she discovered that a few years ago he had put all of his, and possibly a lot of the bank's, money into Biomedivac, a company in which he was a majority shareholder. To all accounts and purposes the company was doing very well: a new anti-Ebola vaccine with glowing trial data and a drug in development for Alzheimer's disease. Where he fitted into the Zimbabwe puzzle she had no idea, but she was here to find out.

As she reached the entrance bearing the corporation's logo, Nathalie realised that she had visited the company before; not at this building but at an office in Berkeley Square. That was several months ago at the beginning of the project when she was scratching around for ideas on transmittable diseases. They were most unhelpful she recalled. One mention of a film about bioterrorism and they had shut up shop. This time she had better take a different tack.

The receptionist was polite and efficient. 'Please fill in this form and take a seat,' he said without a smile.

Nathalie looked at the form. A standard but rather thorough questionnaire. Name, occupation and address, followed by a series of multiple-choice questions. Had she been in contact with any diseases recently? Had she had any operations? Did she suffer from any chronic illness? It was more like an insurance form than a visitor's information list. She filled it in giving Bagatelle's address and, ensuring that the answers were benign, gave it back to the receptionist.

The young man placed the form under a scanner and entered some information on his computer. 'Thank you Miss Thompson. Professor Townes will be with you shortly. Please make yourself comfortable.'

'More like MI5 than a pharmaceutical company,' thought Nathalie as she sat in one of the easy chairs and picked up one of today's papers.

She had just finished the leader column when a balding middle-aged man entered the lobby from one of the rear doors. He passed through the security gate and proffered his hand.

'Good morning, Professor Townes, sorry about all the admin.' He turned to the reception desk. 'Philip, please give Miss Thompson her badge and let her through will you?'

Philip reached under his desk and gave Nathalie a large plastic badge with her image printed on it. Seeing the surprise on her face Professor Townes pointed to a small camera in the corner of the lobby.

'We have to keep security tight here. I assume you'd like to look at our laboratories and we have stringent conditions,' he said as an explanation. 'But first, come to my office and we can discuss what sort of article you're working on.'

Nathalie gave him the full spiel. Bagatelle was working on a proposal for BBC's *Horizon* – a programme about frontier science. They had heard that Biomedivac were pioneers in biotechnology and had recent successes with antivirals. Fortunately, Townes hadn't heard of her visit to their Berkeley Square office and immediately warmed to the idea.

'Sounds good,' he said. 'I've always loved *Horizon*, a great science series, very balanced, not like some of the tabloid television you get nowadays. As long as we steer away from the confidential proprietary stuff, I'm sure we could help you. Would you like to take a look at the laboratories? I've a spare half-hour, could show you around now if you like.'

Nathalie said that would be ideal and soon found herself wrapped from head to foot in white overalls and an astronaut-looking headset. The laboratory looked like something out of a sci-fi movie. Stainless steel tanks, brightly painted aluminium walkways and glass cabinets containing vials of coloured liquids. Identical white-suited operators moved gingerly between the apparatus.

'These are the fermentation tanks,' explained Professor Townes, his voice muffled through the helmet. 'We use biochemical engineering techniques to produce antiviral vaccines and are now working on an exciting new drug for Alzheimer's disease.'

Nathalie was desperate to interrogate him on the Ebola vaccine but decided to keep her powder dry and to appear interested in the Alzheimer's project.

'Alzheimer's, a terrible disease. You think you have a cure?'

'An absolute cure, too soon to say, but the early trials are promising. How much do you know about biochemistry?'

'Wouldn't say a lot but I have a science degree, so try me.'

'You may have heard of amyloid plaques. They are lumps of protein that can gather in the brain. To cut a long story short these plaques can produce synaptic failure and memory loss. Without giving too much away I can tell you that we are working on the production of enzyme inhibitors, a pair of chiral molecules which can interfere with the substances that can short-circuit the synapses.'

'And does that work? Stop the Alzheimer's that is?'

'So far so good. As I said, at the moment we are in early stage trials and only producing a small amount of the product. But if the results continue as they are we should be scaling up in our Morocco plant soon.'

'Morocco?'

'Yes, that's where most of our drugs are manufactured once they have been approved.' Professor Townes rubbed his gloved finger and thumb together. 'Cheaper out there.'

Even though he was clad in a suit and mask Nathalie could see that the professor was relaxing in her company. She decided to tackle the Ebola issue.

'Is that where you make your vaccines?'

'Yes we have a couple of products, the latest being an anti-Ebola virus vaccine. Perhaps a thing you could cover in the programme. People are always moaning that pharmaceutical companies just produce drugs for the West. Here we have a brand-new vaccine that not only protects people from the disease but assists the recovery of those already with it.'

'Has it been used a lot?'

'It's been approved by the FDA and is on the market. We are collating the data now. Let's say I'm very optimistic.'

Nathalie saw her cue. 'The vaccine, before you gave it to people, did you have to try it on the virus in the laboratory first?'

'Yes of course, first computer models and then the real virus in laboratory conditions. That's why we have to be so careful with visitors. There's some dangerous stuff in here.'

'So where do you get the actual virus from?'

'Africa mainly. There have been a number of outbreaks in recent years, patients have been sampled and the virus kept under strict confined conditions. A lot of bureaucracy to go through. Can't afford for it to escape.'

'So you can keep the virus alive in test tubes and bring it back here?'

'Not quite as simple as that but, yes, our bespoke incubation containers can hold the active virus. We have special couriers and customs arrangements; very expensive.'

'And you test your drug on the virus in this very laboratory?'

'Viruses; there's more than one strain and we need to know it can be effective against all of them.' He noticed Nathalie looking at the glass cabinets. 'Oh you needn't worry, no Ebola virus here at the moment; all under lock and key in a very safe place. Our suits are to protect the laboratory from us rather than the other way around at the moment.' The professor looked up at the wall clock and gestured towards the door. 'Now, I have a meeting to go to so if you don't mind I'll hand you over to one of my assistants. We have a very good canteen if you want to stay for lunch.'

The so-called canteen looked like a five-star restaurant. White tablecloths, sparkling glassware and heavy cutlery. Nathalie was shown to a table by a smartly dressed waitress and informed that Professor Townes' assistant would be with her shortly. Within minutes a young man with long blonde hair pulled out a chair from the other side of the table. To her dismay she recognised him. It was the same man that she had met in Berkeley Square a few months ago.

'Pleased to meet you.' No mention of the previous visit. 'James has asked me to treat you to lunch.' He handed her a piece of vellum paper. 'The sole is very good'.

Nathalie took the menu and studied the young man. It wasn't apparent whether he recognised her or not.

'Thank you, if you recommend it I'll have the sole.'

'Wine?'

'No thank you, just fizzy water if that's okay.'

'Two soles and fizzy water it is then,' he said gesturing to the waitress. 'Rob Barnes by the way, so-called assistant to the director.'

From the way he said 'so-called' Nathalie could tell he was unhappy with the title. 'Well Rob I understand Professor Townes has filled you in on the reason for my visit. I wondered if you could tell me anything more about the science.'

'The science, yes.' Rob picked up his knife and spun it between his fingers. 'He told you that did he? Said I could tell you about the science?'

Nathalie looked at the knife, you could cut the atmosphere with it. 'He did mention that you had worked on the Alzheimer's project.'

Rob gave out a spluttered laugh. 'Worked on it? You could say that. In fact my PhD thesis started the whole thing off. Not that I got the credit for it. Oh yes, one small footnote somewhere I think.'

The bottled water arrived and Rob poured out two glasses. Nathalie was taken aback with his frankness. The last time she had met him he was this reticent young man who gave her short shrift. Now he seemed to be ready to wash his dirty linen in public. She took advantage of the opportunity.

'So your thesis was on Alzheimer's?'

'Indirectly. I discovered the two chiral molecules that inhibited enzymes from stopping APP making B amyloid. It transpires that one of them reduces plaques in Alzheimer's patients. Without my work there would be no drug.'

Nathalie didn't have a clue what APP was but this guy was really bitter. Good material for information. 'Did you work on the Ebola vaccine as well?'

'No, before my time, but *my* drug, at least I call it my drug, and the vaccine are making Biomedivac very attractive for a takeover. Not that my few shares will make much of a difference.'

Nathalie didn't know where this was going but she stoked the fire a little more.

'Who's the interested party?'

Rob looked around the canteen, they were virtually the only customers but he leaned forward and lowered his voice. 'A huge US drugs' conglomerate, Zormax Pharmaceuticals – I expect you have heard of them – put in an offer. I'm not even consulted.'

'The takeover. A good thing or a bad thing?'

They were interrupted by the arrival of two plates of steaming Dover sole. Rob thanked the waitress, picked up his fork and waited for Nathalie to start. Noting the etiquette she began to fillet her fish.

'A good thing or bad thing?' she repeated. But the interruption had spoiled the disclosure.

'Hard to say,' he said, putting a mouthful of sole flakes into his mouth. 'Really good fish,' he added changing the subject.

The telephone vibrated in her pocket. She didn't want to take the call in front of Barnes so she put her laptop bag on the table and asked him to mind it while she excused herself.

'The ladies are over there, first on the left in the corridor,' said Rob, pointing to the door behind her.

'Thanks,' muttered Nathalie, not wanting to disillusion him.

She found the toilets, entered a cubicle and locked the door. Her phone had stopped vibrating. She checked the screen. Not a number she recognised, possibly a nuisance call. She turned off the silent key, slipped the phone back into her pocket, left the cubicle and washed her hands out of habit.

On her return she found Rob Barnes waiting for her. She sat down and replaced the napkin on her lap.

'Oh you shouldn't have stopped eating, it'll get cold.'

'Manners,' replied Rob distantly. 'Anyway, here's your stuff safe and sound,' he added pushing her bag towards her.

The rest of the meal was small talk. Nathalie probed further but he kept side-stepping the issues. Rob Barnes had obviously been provoked into this mood by a recent encounter and had finished letting off steam. The waitress cleared their plates and Nathalie turned down the offer of a dessert. She said her goodbyes and returned to the reception where she handed in her badge.

'Don't worry, we destroy them,' said the young man. 'Data protection you know.'

Nathalie didn't know and would not have been surprised if her data had been kept on the system for all time. This was a very strange place and Rob Barnes was a very strange man. Throughout lunch she became sure that he had known that they had met before. He must have had his reasons for not bringing it up and she had no desire to remind him that she was working on a bioterrorism project so she hadn't addressed the issue. She had just circumnavigated Biomedivac's fountain on her way out when her new phone rang. A different ring tone than she was used to so it took some time for her to realise that it was hers.

'Hello?'

The familiar gruff voice came from the other end. 'About time, I thought you were coming back here for lunch.'

'Oh Geoff.'

'Who in the hell did you think it was?'

'New phone, haven't stored my numbers yet. Lunch? Yes I was invited to stay here. Very interesting visit too.'

'Any further leads?'

'Possibly, but more questions than answers. What I do know is that active Ebola can be transported in the right conditions, and that these guys can do that. The weird thing is I've just met a malcontent employee who pretends not to recognise me from an earlier encounter. He must have his reasons but right now I'm not sure what they are. I'd like Tom to do some research on a pharma company called Zormax. Maybe some answers there.'

'No can do at the moment I'm afraid; our sorceress Stefanie applied for his Zimbabwe, Afghan and Indonesian visas the day we employed him. He is on his way to Java now.'

Nine

A loud ticking sound could be heard above the drone of the aircraft. It took Tom a while through his disturbed sleep to work out what it was. He was lying on his wrist watch of course. It was the first time that he had made a long-haul flight. Barcelona with his parents, and Berlin and Paris whilst at university were his most distant locations to date. Two or three hours at the most. The flight to Jakarta was more than sixteen with a stopover at Kuala Lumpur; most exotic. It had all been a bit of a whirl. Stefanie had bundled him to the airport with travel documents and a visa. There was no direct flight to Surabaya so he would have to spend the night in Jakarta and take an internal flight the next day. The next day. It was very confusing, the time difference. Yet this is what he had signed up for; film production and foreign travel. He would make the most of it. The noise of the engines changed as the aircraft made its descent. He was told that they would have a short stopover and it would be possible to get off the plane whilst it refuelled. They wouldn't be allowed out of the airport but at least he could say he had been to Kuala Lumpur.

The landing wasn't smooth and a few things fell from the lockers as the plane taxied towards the in-transit hall. *Bing Bong* and a singsong thin announcement came from the tannoy.

'Welcome to Kuala Lumpur. In-transit time will be one hour. The penalty for smuggling drugs is death. Thank you.'

Tom had never heard a threat in such a pleasant tone before. The lilting accent sounded as if it was the overture to some sort of Asian musical. Tom emptied his pockets of his paracetamol and stuffed them into the webbed basket on the seat in front of him. He was leaving nothing to chance.

The in-transit lounge was more interesting than he had anticipated. Fascinating shops selling alien wares and a huge glass cabinet full of enormous beetles. Whether these were for sale or just for display he couldn't make out. He purchased a digital camera with a zoom lens – it was very cheap – and after a few circuits of the hall made his way back to the plane.

Stefanie had booked him in at the POP! airport hotel in Jakarta. The plane had landed at around seven o'clock local time. Tom couldn't get his head around this. The aircraft had taken off from Heathrow at about the same time, whether it was today, yesterday or tomorrow he couldn't quite make out. Fortunately the hotel was just outside the airport perimeter, and it wasn't long before he was slinging his holdall onto the lobby desk. He now understood what the exclamation mark stood for. The reception was stark white with blocks of bright lurid colours, like the set of a children's television programme. He signed himself in on the yellow plastic counter and was shown to his room. Equally stark and lurid. Lime green bed head, bright orange door and a stainless steel semi-circular shower in the corner. He was shattered and abandoned his original plan to seek out the nightlife of Jakarta. Instead he made his way to the restaurant and picked out a harmless vegetable stew steeped in coconut. At least, unlike in a lot of Europe, vegetarian food in Asia was not hard to come by. He rolled the receipt into a straw shape, flattened it and tied it into a knot. Habit. He then realised that he should keep it for claiming expenses and slid it into his wallet. Recalling the efficient Stefanie and the bustling offices of Bagatelle he suddenly felt very lonely on this side of the world.

※

Nathalie had been busy. She didn't like loose ends and, annoyed with Geoff bundling Tom off so soon without telling her, had spent much of the time on researching Zormax Pharma. Of course she had heard of them, had even worked for them on a corporate film some time ago, but she had no knowledge of the company's recent activities or portfolio. It wasn't difficult to find out, they were one of the world's largest drug companies and their publicity was everywhere. Like many of the larger Pharma outfits, they were increasing their size by picking off the smaller fry; their latest acquisitions included a number of minor biotech companies researching anti-cancer drugs. Now it seemed they were on the lookout for treatments targeting the next big disease area, Alzheimer's. If Biomedivac's trial data were as Professor Townes claimed then they would be good for the taking. She had no idea if Zormax had anything to do with her bioterrorism trail but there was something about Rob Barnes that unsettled her. Her return trip to Zimbabwe was in a week and Tom was checking out the Indonesian lead. It was worth a punt, so she called her friend at Medical Films and set up a meeting.

✳

'Nathalie, lovely to see you.' The tall girl in horn-rimmed glasses gave her an air kiss on both cheeks.

'Great to see you too Veronica,' said Nathalie. 'Long-time.'

'Absolutely. Know you're here on business so won't waste time with chitchat. I've dug out some stuff on Zormax for you, think you'll be interested, come on through.'

Veronica led her along a brightly-lit corridor to a viewing room with a large screen at one end and an overhead projector in the ceiling.

'Thought you might like to see this. Coincidentally, we're making a couple of videos for Zormax right now. This one – a boring talk by the CEO – speech for the troops sort of thing, and another educational film on Alzheimer's disease. They must be launching a drug for that soon or why would they be bothered? Of course this is all highly confidential and, if any of it gets on TV, nothing to do with us.'

Nathalie had known for some time that Veronica wanted to work for Bagatelle, why else would she be so helpful. 'Naturally, wouldn't want you to lose such a big client. Don't know if this leads anywhere but if it does we'll be very discreet, and I'm sure Geoff will be very grateful,' she added.

As Veronica had indicated the interview with the CEO was very boring. A man in a pinstriped suit giving a stilted presentation, sometimes to the camera, sometimes glancing at the unseen interviewer. Perhaps the director was too deferential to the guy to take proper retakes. However, twenty minutes in, the talk became more interesting, to Nathalie anyway. It would be Zormax policy to aggressively take over smaller biotech companies that had promise in the Alzheimer's and antiviral areas. To do this they would need to pay the lowest share price possible. Any mechanisms in achieving this from their worldwide senior management teams would be well rewarded. The video came to an end and Veronica returned holding a large file.

'The educational video we're working on is still being scripted. You must remember the sort of thing from your freelance job with us.' Veronica threw up her eyes. 'Twenty-seventh draft!'

Nathalie did remember. Corporate films tended to go that way. The marketing managers were Steven Spielberg wannabes; if they could make a change they would.

Still that wasn't why she was here. 'Your client – is based in the States?'

'The ultimate boss yes, but our immediate client is in the UK. The film will be used for both audiences.' Veronica slapped the overfull file onto the table. 'That's the problem, neither party can agree on anything.'

'You've had meetings here?'

'Yes, here and the United States, every bloody week.'

Nathalie took out her phone and showed Veronica a couple of surreptitious photos she had obtained at Biomedivac. Well, they had taken her picture; why shouldn't she take theirs.

'Recognise either of them?'

Veronica flicked the images back and forward. She pointed to the image of Professor Townes. 'This one no.' She scrolled to the photo of Rob Barnes. 'This one, yes. Saw him at Zormax's UK head office this week, in deep conversation with some of the senior staff. Very shifty character.'

'Very shifty indeed,' thought Nathalie.

✳

Surabaya, the capital of East Java was very hot in July. The sweat ran down the back of Tom's shirt. Despite the comfortable bed, he had slept little the night before and was having strange problems with his balance due to the jetlag. He hailed a cab at the airport taxi rank and showed the driver the piece of paper that Stefanie had given him. The Sun Hotel, Sidoarjo. He was told that the journey would take about thirty minutes. It wasn't exactly where the supposed laboratory was located but Stefanie had told him that this was the nearest decent accommodation. She had asked the hotel to provide him with a driver and a vehicle for his three-day stay. He should ask for them on his arrival. The road conditions were better than he expected and the taxi was soon speeding away from the urban sprawl into the countryside. The scenery was alien to Tom. Palm trees luxuriated between the rice fields and the twin peaks of two blue-tinged mountains loomed in the distance. He looked at his map, these were the twin volcanoes of Arjuno and Arjuna. Volcanoes? They looked pretty peaceful today. He took out his new camera and wound down the window. The driver turned around in annoyance as a rush of hot thick air swept into the cab.

'Sorry, just taking a few photos.' He waved his camera in case the man didn't understand.

The driver grunted, shrugged his shoulders and turned his eyes back on to the road. Some minutes later Tom sensed the approach of another town. The shanty shacks turned to more substantial buildings and the skyline ahead indicated that they were nearing Sidoarjo. The Sun Hotel was an L-shaped five-storey building. A rising driveway ended in a concrete canopy guarding the front entrance. Tom paid the driver, who took the money with a scowl, and walked up to the lobby to check-in. There was nobody around so he rang the bell on the desk. A young man, wearing a batik shirt over a chequered sarong, appeared from a side door and held up his right hand.

'Apa kabar,' he said with a smile.

Tom had been reading his guidebook in the taxi. 'Baik, baik, saga,' he said awkwardly. 'And before we go any further that's all I know I'm afraid.'

'No problem, we hope you have a good stay,' replied the man in stuttering English. He passed Tom a piece of paper. 'You sign this, I take your bag.'

The guy looked so frail and slender Tom wondered whether he should carry the bag himself but this seemed impolite so, after the formalities, he followed Rafi – as he called himself – into the lift and to his room on the first floor.

'Anything you wish dial zero; we here to help.'

Tom took his bag and pressed a 50 000 rupiah note into his hand. 'Oh there is one thing, my company should have arranged a car and driver for me. I'd like to use it after lunch.'

The young man looked puzzled. 'After lunch?'

'Yes,' said Tom mimicking the action of turning a steering wheel. 'Car, driver, after I eat.'

Rafi giggled, copying Tom's mock driving. 'Car, after you eat.'

Tom took that as a yes, nodded politely and closed his door. After taking a shower he unpacked his few clothes onto the fitted wardrobe shelves and, grabbing the hotel folder and his phone, flopped back onto the bed. He sent a short text to Bagatelle confirming his arrival and then looked for the room service menu. There was a page of long Indonesian names with crude translations underneath. They obviously didn't have many English tourists here. The *pork fat knokles* sounded disgusting but further down he saw something he recognised, '*gado gado*', he probably couldn't go wrong with that. He looked at the time on his phone, a bit early to eat and he was still suffering from jetlag; maybe a short nap before lunch. As he put the folder back on the side table a piece of paper fell out. He noticed that some of it was written in English. '*Massage in your room*'. He was aching all over, these oriental massages were meant to be very good; you could pay a fortune for them in London. He dialled the internal line, zero.

The gentle lilting voice came from the earpiece. 'Mr Tom? Car arriving at two o'clock.'

'Yeah, great. Thanks. I was wondering Rafi, it says here that the hotel can provide a masseur. Is that possible now?'

'Sorry, no understand.'

'Massage, it says here that you can provide massage.'

'Ah yes, massage. Man or woman?'

Tom didn't really know why that mattered. His shoulders were aching like hell. Perhaps a guy would have a firmer touch. 'Man. Can he come now?'

'Of course Mr Tom. Come to your room.'

Tom put down the phone, wrapped a towel around his waist and lay face down on the bed. When at last there was a soft knock at the door he was nearly asleep.

'Come in,' said Tom soporifically. 'I've had a shower so you can start when you want.'

He felt the smooth soft hands on his back. Small for a man but powerful. Thumbs pressed into the muscles behind his shoulder blades. Tingling. A trickle of oil meandered down the gullies on either side of the spine. The hands became firmer, caressing the lower back and loosening the tension.

'Turn over please.'

Tom was startled, it was Rafi's voice, but he was too relaxed to make any comment. He did as he was told.

'Oh, hairs on chest, very sexy.'

Tom noted that Rafi had removed his shirt and was standing there like a classical statue, a torso like porcelain wrapped in the blue sarong.

'You very tense Mr Tom.' He placed his hands around Tom's neck and rhythmically stroked the tendons. Tom closed his eyes. Another drizzle of oil. Fingers moved across his nipples and down towards his stomach. He felt a frisson of arousal.

Rafi had also noticed this and started to unwrap the towel from around Tom's waist. Tom opened his eyes to find that Rafi had stepped out of his sarong.

'Whoa Rafi, I said massage not…'

Rafi looked crestfallen, in more ways than one. 'But Mr Tom, I thought…'

Tom pulled the towel around his thighs and sat up in the bed. He breathed heavily, he was still dizzy; stimulated.

'Sorry Rafi, a mistake. Another time, another place perhaps, but I'm working, have to keep my mind on the job.'

It wasn't evident that Rafi understood all of what Tom said but he seemed to get the gist. He lowered his eyes. 'You working. Me sorry too Mr Tom.' Picking up his sarong and wrapping it around his waist he quietly left the room.

✻

It was four o'clock in the afternoon when the driver and car arrived. Two hours late, not bad by Indonesian standards. Tom had spent the time in the hotel's restaurant. After his enormous plate of gado gado he had sketched out his plans for the afternoon. The laboratory address was difficult to find on a map, and he thought he would have difficulty in instructing the driver, so he had with him a Google Earth printout of the area. The village or town looked like a rural industrial park from the air. Low-lying warehouses flirted with anonymous flat-roofed blocks in a clearing between the palm trees. An internet search revealed that a well-known yoghurt corporation occupied some of the plots, but there was no mention of the company that he had photographed from the open folder at the School of Tropical Medicine. Judging from the time it took to get to the hotel from the airport the plant was probably about an hour away. The sun set early and fast in this part of the world. He would have to go now if he wanted to see it in daylight. The driver spoke no English. Tom showed him his Google Earth printout with the route marked in red biro. The driver turned it around and around in his hands until he found what he thought was the right way up. He pointed at the sun and gestured towards the car. They would have to hurry. The road wasn't as good as the one to the airport and the old Hyundai made heavy weather of it. The driver kept looking out of the side window, shaking his head and waving at the sinking sun. Tom rolled his fingers around each other to indicate that he wanted to go on. They were now surrounded by paddy fields, the horizon filling with the silhouettes of the twin volcanoes. The light was amazing, casting long distorted shadows of the car across the potholed road. The sun sank lower and lower, not a building in sight for miles. Tom was just about to tell the driver to turn around when his chauffeur motioned towards something in the road ahead of them. There was just enough light to make out the sign of the approaching town.

'Stop, wait here,' said Tom slowly, putting his hand up like a policeman and then signalling vigorously to the ground.

The driver braked and sat folding his arms. Tom got out of the car and pointed to his watch. 'I'll return in one hour,' he said, moving his finger around the face.

The driver looked nonplussed, pulled out a packet of cigarettes from his top pocket, tapped it on his wrist and put one of the protruding sticks into his mouth.

'I'll go now, please wait here,' said Tom, as deliberately as he could.

The guy stared at him blankly, struck a match and lit the cigarette. A slow stream of smoke coiled from his nostrils.

Tom gave him a wave, put up his thumbs, pointed to the ground once more, turned and walked towards the buildings in the near distance.

The business park was haphazard. Concrete structures seemed to have been laid down at random. No planning or organisation apart from one area where a smart group of whitewashed buildings sat behind a low wall bearing the name of the well-known yoghurt company. The lights coming from the industrial windows were becoming brighter. Tom looked at the sky; blackness was sweeping in, the buildings were swiftly moving into shadow. He rummaged around in his shoulder bag, found his powerful LED torch and used it to light the way along the gravel side roads. Glass crunched underfoot. The beam picked out a low corrugated-roofed structure, windows all blown out. Not a soul in sight. A few hundred yards further down the road Tom noticed more lights leaking through some black foliage. Stepping off the path he made his way through the trees and was abruptly halted by a chain-link fence. He shone the torch along the metal wire and settled on a large white sign with red lettering. *SUPAYA METU.* It meant nothing to him but it didn't look friendly. He followed the fence for another fifty metres and could now see the outline of a two-storey industrial unit within the perimeter. Using the zoom lens on his camera he peered into the winking lights. Someone in a white coat moved through the frame. Focusing more deeply he could make out benches and glassware. A laboratory, very much like the ones he had worked in at university. Further along the fence he found a depression where a tree root had lifted the wire. The earth was soft and it didn't take long to scrape a hole large enough to crawl through. It was only twenty or thirty metres to the corner of the building. A few steps across the grass scrub and he would be able to get a clear shot with his camera through the nearest window.

He didn't know what direction it came from but it was on him in a second. A loud rustle and a blur of hair. The creature lunged at him and sank its fangs into his leg. He opened his mouth to scream but a large hand came from behind and clamped it shut. Tom began to struggle when an arm wrapped itself around his waist in a vice-like grip. He was helpless, frozen to the spot in pain. Waves of panic overwhelmed him. He was unable to move an inch.

Ten

A large boot swept from behind and dug into the ribs of the dog. It let go of Tom's leg, squealed and ran into the undergrowth. A gruff voice whispered into his ear.

'Don't move, don't speak and keep your eyes open.'

There was an accent, but it wasn't Indonesian. Indian, or even Scots? Tom's leg hurt like hell, blood was seeping through his light cotton trousers. He felt sick but had no opportunity to disobey his captor as there was still a large hand clamped around his mouth. The voice spoke again.

'We ought to get out of here, if they see that dog with blood in its mouth they'll come looking. Now keep very quiet and turn around very slowly.'

The hand slipped from his mouth and moved on to his shoulder. Tom was gently spun around to confront a large white man wearing a black ski hat.

'Pleased to meet you, I'm Nick Coburn, friend of Geoff Sykes. Now follow me back under that wire and I'll see what I can do with that leg of yours.'

Tom was dizzy and confused, he was sure he had heard the name Geoff Sykes. Who was this guy? He meekly followed the man and was helped under the fence. Nick Coburn propped him against the base of a palm tree, pulled out a knife and cut off Tom's trouser leg below the knee.

'Not too deep, you'll be all right.' Nick took a flask from his back pocket. 'Now this will sting, but don't shout out, we're still within earshot.'

The warning came just in time, a searing pain knifed into his leg as the liquid was poured onto the wound. It was all that Tom could do to stifle a scream.

'Good lad,' said Nick ripping a strip of Tom's trouser leg and using it as a bandage. 'Hurt me more than it did you; that was a fine malt.'

Tom had started to compose himself. It was obvious that this guy wasn't from the laboratory. He had a rugged yet friendly face and had mentioned the name of Geoff Sykes, but what on earth was he doing here at nightfall in the middle of an Indonesian jungle?

'Geoff Sykes? You said the name Geoff Sykes. Who are you?'

'Thought I said that? Coburn, Nick Coburn, mate of Geoff's. Well maybe he wouldn't put it that way, let's say an employee. Now let's get you back to my jeep and I'll fill you in.'

'Your jeep? I've come in a car.'

'Oh, that buggered off the minute you were out of sight. Lucky for you I hired a 4x4; didn't take much time to catch up.'

Still in a daze Tom was helped back to the main road. Nick was right, his driver was nowhere to be seen and, instead, a pristine Cherokee jeep was parked on the verge. They got in, Nick spun it around and they were on their way back to Sidoarjo.

'Sitting comfortably?' Nick glanced down at Tom's leg. 'Okay perhaps not, but here's the story. There I was lounging in the Hong Kong Mandarin at a client's expense when I get a call from Mr Sykes – has a young researcher next door. Next door! Typical of Geoff. Think he had a prick of conscience, sending a young kid into the lion's den. Anyway thought you might need a bit of help. Knew I had a few contacts with some gentlemen in the Surabaya police force and paid me his usual miserly rate to come over. So here I am.'

Tom stared at the burly Scot, the accent was obvious now. 'You work for Bagatelle?'

'Not exactly, odd job man. Met Geoff some years ago; from time to time he finds me useful. If I can help out…'

'As a film director?'

'No way, no head for cameras. Military background; a few contacts, you know the sort of thing.'

Tom didn't but could make a shrewd guess by looking at the man's frame and scarred face. He'd been pretty useful with that dog.

'I haven't thanked you for what you did back there.'

'No problem, as I said odd job man.'

'How did you find me?''

'Not difficult, was told where you were staying and your boyfriend told me where you were going.'

'Boyfriend?'

'Well he seemed pretty keen on you; guy at reception, was worried about your driver. He was right there. Would have been a long walk back.'

'I told him to wait.'

'Hundred thousand rupiah would have been better.'

Tom sat back and pondered his position. The jeep's headlights ran against the grasses at the side of the road. The rest was pitch black. Not a dwelling, not a light. He had found the laboratory, he was sure of that, and they didn't want intruders, but wasn't that the case for all industrial plants? And this guy, he sounded kosher but could he be sure? A few probing questions might help.

'What's Geoff told you about the project?'

'Not much, never was good on detail. Understand you're following up on a possible terrorist lead. Think that building back there is manufacturing some sort of biological weapons. If it is, a stupid way of finding out. Stumbling around there in the dark.'

'Natasha the director asked me to take a look.'

'You mean Nathalie. Nice one Tom, always good to check out who you're talking to. Great girl, I'm not supposed to say that; why, I'm not sure? Great woman sounds crap. Nathalie wouldn't give a toss what I called her. Good at her job that one. Anything else you'd like to ask me?'

Tom felt that listening to Nick's soft Scottish tones was like hearing a British Airways pilot's announcement during turbulence, comforting in an alien environment.

'Just being careful, I'm still in a bit of shock if I'm honest, don't want to make any more cock-ups.'

'No worries laddie, you sit back and take a rest.' He turned a wrist to look at his enormous watch. 'Wouldn't ring Geoff now, it's about lunchtime there; he's grumpy at the best of times. We'll go back to the hotel for a meal, check in with your office and have an early night. First thing in the morning, we'll sit down to make a plan over breakfast. How does that sound?'

✳

Tom's breakfast was a slice of papaya and a glass of mango juice. Nick had already eaten and was making a few phone calls.

'Any more news from your governor?' he asked, throwing his cell phone onto the table.

'Internet down but we exchanged a few short texts last evening. He said that you knew what you were doing.'

'Praise indeed,' said Nick pushing a fork into one of Tom's slices of papaya. 'I wouldn't go that far but I think we've hit lucky.'

Tom raised an eyebrow.

Nick looked around, the coffee shop was empty. 'Yesterday evening I called an old friend at the Surabaya police station. We met on an op a few years back. Asked him about the lab. He said he'd make some enquiries, just been on the phone to him this morning. You going to eat that papaya?'

Tom pulled the plate of papaya away from Nick. 'What did he say?'

'No wonder you're so skinny if that's all you eat. Shall I ask Rafi to rustle up some more of that chicken porridge? I could do with another bowlful.'

Tom winced. 'Chicken porridge? No thank you. The papaya is fine as long as you don't keep eating it all. Your guy, what did he say?'

Nick sat down at the table opposite, pulled out his phone and scrolled through the texts. 'Gita Suparmanputri,' he pronounced slowly.

'Gita who?' said Tom.

'I'm not saying it again; one of my mate's cousins. And before you say it, not that coincidental, I think the whole population of Java is one of his cousins.'

Tom shook his head. 'You're losing me.'

'This Gita thingamajig happens to work as an assistant at our hideaway laboratory. Just out of university, got a job there about a month ago, had to sign some sort of secret agreement. Not that secret as she seems to have blabbed it halfway round Sidoarjo district.'

Tom's jaw dropped. 'What is she doing there, you think she knows something? Can we talk to her?'

'Whoa there Tom, softly softly. We don't want to go jumping in with our two left feet again do we? Let's find out where she lives, what she does in the evenings and perhaps we could casually bump into her.' Nick started to key in a number on his phone. 'And when I say we, I mean you. I'm sure she will feel more comfortable being chatted up by a young tourist than a six foot three war veteran don't you?'

It was one in the morning in London and Nathalie couldn't sleep. She got out of bed and powered up her computer. The Rob Barnes' thing was still worrying her. She pulled back the blind from her Fulham flat window. It had been raining and the streets were streaked with the reflections from the sodium lights. A car passed, the spray falling from its tyres; she was not the only one up tonight. The computer bleeped at her, ready for business. She sat down at the keyboard and typed in the words Alzheimer's, Biomedivac and Zormax. Nothing more other than the familiar corporate spiel. She switched the engine to Google Scholar, an in-depth academic site. The information and papers here were quite abstruse but she had enough scientific background to get the gist of them. Robert Barnes' name came up more than once. First as a co-author under Professor Townes, and then in a couple of more obscure articles for a trade pharma magazine. Reading between the lines she detected a cynicism of recent Alzheimer's research trial results. No company was mentioned but it wouldn't take an expert too long to tie these in with Biomedivac.

The projection of lights from another passing car fanned across the ceiling. Nathalie got up to close the blinds and returned to try an alternative search word – Ebola. Another connection with Rob Barnes. This time a more subjective article in an epidemiological journal. The premise that the recent Ebola outbreaks may have come from African bats and how the fight against it should be renewed with progressive antiviral medications. No mention of the success of Biomedivac's latest drug. Professor Townes would not be at all pleased. But perhaps this fascination with Biomedivac and their drugs was taking her away from her real purpose: exposing WEXA's threat of giving the West a dose of an 'African disease'. She still had not heard from Lloyd and her immunisation shoot in Zimbabwe was scheduled for seven days' time. He had been left alone long enough, she would call him first thing in the morning.

✳

The Foreplay Club was in the middle of Surabaya not far from the city zoo. Nick had thought that most appropriate when he had heard the club's name. He and Tom had spent the day in the Sun Hotel phoning around and checking out the area. Fortunately it was a Saturday and Nick's policeman friend had discovered that Gita visited her parents in Surabaya every weekend and was not unknown to party in the city. A few more calls involving the resources of the Surabaya police force and they found out that Gita and a friend were planning to go to the Foreplay that evening. At midnight Nick and Tom took the Cherokee jeep and made good time on the sparsely trafficked roads towards East Java's capital. On the outskirts Tom struggled with the map.

'It says here it's on Aditawarman Street, but if you just follow the signs to the zoo I'm sure we'll find it.'

Nick slowed as he hit the city traffic. 'Bloody marvellous, as long as you know the Indonesian for zoo we are well in.'

'It's a tourist place, there's sure to be a sign in English, or perhaps a symbol like an elephant.'

'Would have been easy if Ebenezer Sykes had booked a jeep with a satnav; have you tried maps on your phone?'

'No signal.' Tom glanced up. 'Look there, told you, elephant.'

'In the bloody city?'

'No, not a real one, on the sign. Left here now.'

The wheels of the jeep screeched as Nick slew it round the corner at the last minute. 'A bit more warning next time young Tom but, you're right, here's the zoo, we must be close. There's a hotel coming up, I'll park in there. Two white guys, they'll think we're residents.'

The Foreplay Club was housed in a mall. Shops by day, bars by night. Young girls dressed in too-tight skirts hovered around the entrance waiting for a promising partner to pay their entrance fee. The fee was a hundred thousand local, about eight US dollars, and Tom and Nick were offered a packet of complimentary cigarettes and a free beer as they made their way to the neon lit bar. Nick downed his in one and raised his eyes in surprise when the barman asked for two hundred thousand for his second.

'That's nearly twenty dollars, more than New York.'

The barman didn't reply, just waited for his money. Nick handed it over.

'Good job I'm not thirsty, be bankrupt by the end of the evening.'

They took their drinks to a table in the corner where they could get a good view of the clientele. A DJ, set up on one side of the bar, was playing extremely loud music. The dance floor in the middle was slightly raised and the house photographer was persuading young girls to dance for him whilst he took some shots. Most of the other clubbers stood around the periphery satisfied with taking selfies rather than taking to the floor.

'Rubbish music,' shouted Tom. 'Old-school house and rave, no taste.'

'Thought it might be your thing,' Nick shouted back. 'Loud enough to burst your eardrums anyway. You're going to find it difficult to chat up this young lady in here, that's if we can find her.'

Nick took out his phone and put up the picture he'd been sent.

'Nice-looking girl, a beer for the one who spots her first.'

Tom looked at the photo and ignored the remark. A waiter asked if they would like more drinks and Tom ordered a whiskey and another beer.

'That's for my leg,' he said, passing the tumbler to Nick, taking the receipt and rolling it like a cigarette. 'Sorry it's not a malt.'

Nick nodded appreciatively and knocked it back in one.

'Over there by the door.'

Tom looked around to see two young women entering the club. They were a cut above the others present. Smartly dressed, intelligent faces. One of them sat at a table whilst the other sauntered up to the bar.

Nick leaned over and cupped his hand around Tom's ear. 'Now's your chance, whilst she's on her own. I'll distract the one at the table.' He picked up Tom's untouched bottle of beer and made his way across the dance floor.

Tom had no option other than to approach Gita at the bar. He wasn't used to this but, as Nick said, it was the best way of getting the information. He took a deep breath and sidled up to her.

'Let me get that, and a beer for me,' he said waving a note at the barman. Gita turned to face him and her expression of initial surprise turned into a smile.

'Aren't you a forward one,' she replied. 'And what makes you think I'll take a drink from a stranger?'

'Sorry, didn't mean to be rude but seeing that you were on your own.'

Gita glanced at her companion now sitting at the table engrossed in conversation with Nick. 'Well I wasn't but looks like that's changed. You on holiday or business?'

'Pardon?' shouted Tom.

'Working or tourist,' shouted back Gita.

'Tourist, just finished my degree, on holiday.'

'Me too.'

'On holiday?'

'No just finished my degree, now working.'

'What degree?'

'Microbiology.'

'How funny, so was mine.'

The music was getting louder and the conversation turning into a shouting match. He would have to try to get her somewhere quieter. He remembered the packet of free cigarettes he was given earlier. Tom loathed everything about smoking, but this was the first time he'd ever tried picking up a girl, it might as well be his first cigarette.

He took the pack from his pocket and offered one to Gita. 'It's hot in here, fancy going outside for a smoke?'

'Why not, Dina seems happy enough, there's a courtyard at the back.'

Nick watched the two of them leave the bar and make their way to an alcove in the far corner. He hoped they wouldn't be long, his companion was hard work and racking up the bar bill. Nick had run out of small talk and was pleased when the girl said she was going to the restroom. He took the opportunity to check up on Tom. Avoiding the house photographer he moved around the edge of the room towards the rear exit, a small door half hidden behind a velvet curtain. He stared down the bouncer who stepped aside to let Nick pass. The door opened on to a small tiled courtyard surrounded by a high brick wall. Tom and the girl were nowhere to be seen. A noise came from behind. Just steam from a kitchen flue. The smell of greasy noodles hung in the tropical air. In the wall opposite a metal gate led to a narrow side alley. Nick looked up and down but it was empty apart from the odd fast-food carton. He dialled Tom's number but all he got was the answerphone. He didn't leave a message.

'Fuck you, Tom,' he said out loud. 'How can I be your minder if you just piss off?'

Turning around to return to the club he noticed something wedged in the grille next to the kitchen vent. A rolled piece of paper tied in a small knot. He had commented on Tom playing with it at the table. It was the bar bill. Nick pulled it from the wall and carefully unfolded the chit. One beer, one whiskey and an exorbitant total. But on the chit there was something else scribbled in black, probably from a spent match. The word *SITER*.

'*Siter*, what in the fuck is that meant to mean?'

It was nearly three in the morning. Geoff was going to kill him; losing the little bastard in the middle of Surabaya. 'Look after him he's only a kid,' were Geoff's last words. Still there wasn't much he could do about it now. He would check into that hotel where the jeep was parked and visit the police station at daybreak.

Eleven

The Tube was crowded. The moisture seeping from the wet raincoats clung to the air. Passengers tried to avoid squeezing into each other but it was hopeless. They were packed in like sardines. Some only in T-shirts, others more cannily dressed for the mid-July rain storm. Nathalie was one of the former. She tried to avoid the large man's dripping umbrella. He apologised but there was nowhere else to put it. She suffered in silence and breathed a sigh of relief when the doors slid open at Tottenham Court Road. Half the carriage spilled onto the platform. Nathalie was taken with the flow up the escalator and towards the exit. To her disappointment she found it was still raining. Putting her laptop case on top of her head she half walked, half ran, towards Soho Square.

Geoff was in a bad mood.

'Why don't you dry yourself off in the loo before dumping half of London's downpour onto my carpet,' he growled pointing at Nathalie's sodden case. 'I'll see you in five minutes after I've dealt with this bloody copyright issue.'

Nathalie grinned at him and turned towards the door. She met Stefanie in the corridor.

'Hi Stefanie, Geoff got out the wrong side of bed today?'

'I think he's getting worse. Music company want a two-year licence, and Geoff's client wants it on DVD. Heard him ranting this morning about how in the hell was he to get a DVD that self-destructed after a couple of years.'

'Oh is that all; I thought Zimbabwe had declared war on us or something.'

'Zimbabwe, that reminds me.' Stefanie pulled a notebook from her pocket and flicked through the pages. 'Lloyd rang. Couldn't take your phone call earlier this morning, in some sort of sensitive work meeting. Can talk to you during his coffee break. They're two hours ahead so that means around twelve noon our time.'

'Thanks,' said Nathalie disappearing into the loo.

Exactly five minutes later Nathalie tapped gently on Geoff's office door.

'Don't need to knock, this is a film company not the politburo.'

Nathalie walked in and spun around. 'There, dry as a bone, will you talk to me now?'

Geoff ignored her pirouette and started shuffling through some papers. 'Take a seat. What's all this about that medical video girl, what's her name, something beginning with V?'

'Veronica?'

'Yes, Veronica.'

'What about her?'

'Rang this morning, insisted that she speak personally to me. Wanted to know if I was happy with the information she'd given on some pharma company.'

'Oh?'

'Then she started to pitch for a job. Did I need an experienced producer for my medical films, did I know how many years she had been working in the industry, and on and on.'

Nathalie tried to disguise her amusement. 'What did you say?'

'What do you think I said, not what I was thinking that's for sure. I politely thanked her for her assistance and said that if we ever wanted a medical producer she would be the first person on our list.'

'That was nice of you.'

'Too bloody right it was. What I want to know is what you're doing faffing around with this medical video outfit instead of rooting out some of these terrorists.'

Nathalie moved her computer from her lap and onto Geoff's desk, opened the lid and searched for some files.

'Originally, I was interested in Biomedivac to help me find some background on Ebola.' She spun the computer around so that Geoff

95

could see the image of Rob Barnes. 'Saw this guy back in May. Mention of bioterrorism and I was dropped like hot coals, so recently I tried another tack. Visited their HQ, said we were interested in making an episode of *Horizon* about vaccine research.'

Geoff raised his eyebrows but didn't interrupt.

'Got a completely different response from the big boss, Professor Townes. Really liked the idea, will help out all they can. Trouble was he introduced me to his assistant.'

'The guy on your screen?'

'That's right, Rob Barnes. I thought shit! He'll know it's all a ruse. But no, played along as if we'd never met before. I'm sure he recognised me.'

'So where are you going with this?'

'Well that's it, I'm not sure, but there's something funny going on. Rob Barnes seems to have it in for Townes; mentioned a possible takeover by Zormax.'

'The pharma giant.'

'Yes. So I looked up Veronica. Knew she would like to please you and, I was right, she was very helpful.'

'Lucky I didn't tell her what I really thought.'

'Yes, I should have warned you. Anyway she's making some videos for Zormax. Seems they're really interested in taking over Biomedivac. And from what she says,' Nathalie tapped on the screen, 'this young man is up to his blue eyes in it.'

'So how is this connected to your film on bioterrorism?'

'I really don't know yet. Call it sixth sense. What I do know though is we could do a piece on antidotes. I mean if these guys are threatening the West with an outbreak of Ebola we should also talk about a defence; antivirals, how they work, who would get them in an emergency. All good stuff.'

Geoff nodded. 'See your point. Good shots too, high-tech laboratories, scientists in protective gear. Would give contrast with the Zimbabwean bush and Javanese jungle.'

'That's what I thought. Talking of Java, how is Tom getting on?'

Geoff picked up his phone and scrolled through the texts. 'Okay I suppose, got a typical enigmatic text from Nick Coburn.'

'Nick!'

'Oh yeah, forgot to tell you. Asked Nick to do a bit of babysitting. Tom is very keen but also very wet behind the ears so, as I heard Nick was in the area, I asked him to help out. You know, in case things got interesting.'

'At least he's in good hands. Nick's good at interesting.' Nathalie peered over at Geoff's phone. 'What did he say?'

'You know Nick, need a cryptographer to decipher his texts.' He handed the phone to Nathalie who peered at the illuminated screen.

Met Tom, on to it, few things to sort out but should be okay.

'What's that meant to mean?'

'Your guess is as good as mine; the "okay" bit is reassuring.'

'Yes but I don't like the "should be", Nick's not known for his pessimism.'

'Well the text got through so they've got a signal. I'm sure they would have called if there was a problem. That's why I sent Nick, if he's with him he'll be okay.'

'Suppose so. Anyway back to the antidote idea. You're okay with that?'

Geoff got up and walked towards the window. He prised open the slats of the Venetian blind to stare down at the street below. It was still raining. People were streaming out of their offices making their way to the various boutiques and restaurants in the heart of Soho. He looked at his watch.

'Nearly lunchtime.' He turned towards Nathalie. 'Yes it's a good idea as long as we can get into their labs. I haven't taken you to lunch for ages. How about Sheekeys now Zilli's is closed?'

Zilli's was a name that resonated with Nathalie. It was one of the first restaurants that Geoff had taken her to when she was a raw researcher. If he had meant to impress he had succeeded. A high-class fish restaurant frequented by the aficionados of the media world. Nathalie had been nervous and awestruck. Not so today, she had a phone call to make.

'Would love to Geoff but I've got to call Lloyd. He only has a small window when he can talk so...'

'So you can be taken out to lunch after you have finished the call. I'll ask Stefanie to book a table.'

✳

Lloyd's phone rang and rang. Nathalie was just about to give up when an out of breath Lloyd answered.

'Hi, give me a minute, just let me get out of the building.'

Nathalie continued doodling on her pad. 'Fine, take your time.' She held the handset in the other hand to her ear. Muffled running footsteps and then a door slam.

'Okay, I can talk now. Sorry it took so long to get to the phone, the boss was in my office. Luckily it was on vibrate so didn't have to make any excuses.'

'You okay now?'

'Yeah, sitting under a tree at the back of the building. No one around.'

Nathalie could imagine the scene. Mid-morning heat in Harare, the scrubland at the back of Lloyd's newspaper office, the drone of insects in the background.

'How are you? Still with us?'

'Of course, why shouldn't I be?'

'Those guys in the hut, pretty hairy there for a moment.'

'Take more than that.'

Lloyds's words were more confident than his tone of voice. Nathalie remembered the scream. That wasn't put on. But he obviously didn't want to talk about it so she decided to change the subject.

'I should be there by Tuesday afternoon, same hotel. Bagatelle have managed to hire a full unit. Personally I don't like travelling without a cameraman but Geoff said it would be difficult to get carnets. Usually he says these things for budgetary reasons but this time I think he's right. The less of us in the loop the better. I've spoken to the hire company and they seem to know what they're doing.'

The rattle of blinds drew her attention. Geoff had lent her his office and had left the window open. The summer rain was hitting the window hard and spilling onto the sill. Keeping the handset to her ear she walked over to the casement and pulled the lever shut.

'Sorry, it's raining here and the carpet's getting wet.'

'Carpet, outside?'

'No, it's coming through the window.'

'Oh, yes we get those summer storms too.'

'Not like this you don't; cold, windy and grey here. Not your four-minute high temperature downpour.' Smalltalk, but useful she thought. Lloyd seemed to be relaxing. 'Any progress your end? Those guys still up for the interview?'

'Yes, no change there. But I do have some other news.'

Nathalie breathed a sigh of relief, she had been dreading Lloyd telling her that the WEXA group had backed out.

'News?'

'Yeah, doing some filing for the paper when I came across an old story in the education section. Remembered you talking about a pharma company called Biomedivac and some background research you were doing. There they were in black and white.'

Nathalie had regained her seat at Geoff's desk and nearly dropped the phone.

'Biomedivac mentioned in your newspaper?'

'Yeah, I kept the cutting, give me a second I've got it here in my pocket, I'll read it to you.'

In the far corner of the office a door opened and Stefanie appeared. She pointed to her watch and then made an exaggerated mime of eating with an imaginary knife and fork. Nathalie mimed back, pointing to her phone, shaking her head and holding up her five fingers twice. Stefanie gave her the thumbs up and left the office quietly.

Her phone burst into life, 'You there Nathalie? Here it is. "Star pharmacologist Temba Murauzi wins award for African research exchange."'

'Yeah, but what's that got to do with Biomedivac?'

'That's the company doing the exchange with the university. They've got some laboratories in North Africa.'

Nathalie remembered her conversation with James Townes. 'Morocco?'

'Yes that's right. How did you... Of course, you've already done some research on them. Anyway, this guy is quite a whiz-kid apparently and will be working with their research department. And guess what one of their projects is?'

'Ebola.'

'Got it in one. Thought we could use him to entrap WEXA. You know, tell them that we could get some antidote for their Ebola carriers.'

Nathalie's mind was racing. It was a great idea. Someone who could be filmed in the Biomedivac Moroccan plant talking about antidotes and a means of getting WEXA stitched up on camera at the same time.

Lloyd's voice came down the phone. 'Nathalie, you still there? I've not got long.'

'Sorry Lloyd, just thinking. I've been wondering how we could get real evidence against WEXA. This might just do it. But do you think this guy will play ball? It's quite a dangerous thing we are asking him to do.'

'I'm not sure. Figures that if this guy is into ethical drugs and saving lives then he could be open to helping out.'

'Maybe, but I think we should take it one step at a time. Why don't you contact him and say we're doing a piece on antidotes. Mention we know the big cheese at Biomedivac and it could give him team points. Don't reveal anything about WEXA at this stage. If he seems comfortable with the filming idea then we might be able to bring that up later.'

'Sounds a plan. Must go, got a meeting. I'll try to get in touch with him this evening. Will let you know how it goes.'

Lloyd's phone went dead with the characteristic lack of a goodbye. On cue Stefanie knocked on the door again.

'He's pacing up and down in the lobby, if you want that lunch you better go down and stop him wearing out the carpet.'

'On my way,' said Nathalie folding up her laptop and zipping it into the case. 'Is it still raining?'

'It's eased off. I was going to get you a cab but Geoff says it's only a ten-minute walk. Thinks the traffic fumes will do him good.'

'That and the saving of a taxi fare,' laughed Nathalie.

'He's not scrimping on lunch. You must be in his good books, it's not often he takes his directors out in the middle of the day.'

'Very true,' mused Nathalie. 'The last time was somewhere in the middle of the Cretaceous period if I remember. I wonder what he wants.'

'Only one way to find out,' said Stefanie ushering her out of the office.

Geoff marched her down Greek Street and across Shaftesbury Avenue. Stefanie was right, the rain had eased off leaving pools of water in the curbs and a steam of vapour as the July sun burned the moisture from the roads.

'Have you been to the oyster bar before?'

'Outside my pay grade Geoff,' replied Nathalie, almost skipping to catch up with him.

'Oh it's not too bad, not like the restaurant. You don't have to have oysters; the shrimp and scallop burgers are really good.'

'Your "not too bad" and my "not too bad" probably differ. I bet the burger costs a bit more than a McDonald's.'

'Perhaps, but I'm paying so...'

'So what extra work do I have to do?'

Geoff looked at her askance. 'Nathalie, as if.'

'Only joking Geoff.'

Geoff nodded appreciatively. 'No, it's just that Stefanie has told me that I've been a bit abrasive recently. Should take more care of my staff. Thought you deserved a treat.' He gestured around the corner. 'Down there on the right, the second red door.'

The door was opened for them by a small man in a tailcoat and top hat. Inside was a horseshoe-shaped bar. 'Le zinc', the French would have called it. This 'zinc' was edged in zinc but the bar itself was made of a crazed cream ceramic. Inside the horseshoe, waiters in long aprons scurried like the crabs they were serving between customers who were sitting on tall bar stools. Nathalie noticed a few famous faces amongst the clientele. Geoff helped her onto a towering barstool and eased himself onto the one alongside.

'Glass of wine?' he asked passing her the menu.

'Please', she answered scanning the list. 'The first sauvignon on the list looks good.'

Geoff called the waiter and pointed at the menu. 'Two Loire sauvignons and…?' He looked at Nathalie.

'Fish pie please', she said without hesitation.

'Fish pie and burger and chips', said Geoff interpreting the scallop burger and pommes allumettes from the menu as he handed it back.

'Geoff', said Nathalie scornfully.

'What?' cried Geoff feigning innocence.

The food was delicious. Geoff's designer burger came with all the trimmings and Nathalie's pie was crammed with fish and prawns in a creamy sauce.

'Okay, where are we up to with Lloyd?' asked Geoff gulping down the last mouthful of his wine.

'Interesting phone call.' Nathalie told Geoff about the African pharmacologist and Biomedivac. 'It's an amazing coincidence, Lloyd is trying to meet with him this afternoon.'

'So that fits in with your *Horizon* proposal idea. Shoot a scene with him in Morocco talking about bioterror antidotes?'

'Yes, but it could be more than that. If we can gain his trust we may be able to get him to meet WEXA, pretend to be a sympathiser and offer them some protection from their own weapon.'

'That would be a real coup. I was wondering how you were going to get some hardcore proof on camera. Do you think he'll be up for it?'

Geoff had to wait whilst Nathalie finished the last mouthful of her pie. She rinsed it down with a swig of sauvignon and shook her head.

'We don't know. Neither of us have met him but, as I told Lloyd, if we take it softly softly – do the general antidote scene first – and then see where it takes us...'

'Ah yes the antidote scene. I thought we better get a move on with that so I've written your *Horizon* proposal for you. E-mailed it across to the BBC this morning. Just in case our Professor Townes starts fishing around.'

'That's brilliant Geoff. I was wondering when I was going to get the time to do that.'

'Thank Stefanie, she said you had your hands full. Anyway, I thought I would have a better chance of getting it approved.'

Nathalie pushed him on the shoulder.

'Oi, these barstools are high, you could do some serious damage to an old man.'

Nathalie pushed him again.

Twelve

Nick Coburn had spent a whole day at the police station and had eaten enough rice cakes to last him a lifetime. His police officer friend, Michael, had been apologetic but there was an emergency on; a big jewel heist in downtown Surabaya. The duty officer had been instructed to keep him comfortable and fed. Comfortable was an upright plastic chair on metal legs. The food was okay but boring. Once you'd had one bakcang rice cake you had had them all. Nick had tried to get some information out of the desk team but they had little English and he had no Javanese so little progress there. Past experience had taught him that it would be useless traipsing around a city he didn't know, looking for Tom. Sure he could ask passers-by had they seen a white guy with a local girl, but there were thousands of young white male tourists in Surabaya, most of them accompanied by local females. So he had waited. Michael would be his best bet to find the little bastard.

His patience had paid off. Towards the end of the afternoon the tranquillity of the police station anti-room was broken by an eruption of police officers and alleged burglars. The crooks were protesting their innocence and the officers were challenging this by thrashing around with their truncheons. 'Rough justice,' thought Nick. His friend Michael had pulled out a diamond necklace from one of the captives' pockets. More protests of innocence, more thrashing of truncheons. After ten minutes or so the scuffles died down and the thieves were locked in the cells on a lower floor. All that remained was the distant shouting coming from the stairwell.

'Okay, where were we?' asked Michael, attempting to mend the rip in his uniform with a staple gun.

Nick held out his hand. 'Rice cake?'

'No thanks,' said Michael, turning up his nose at the suggestion. 'I'll send out for some fried chicken later. Catching thieves is hungry work.'

The noise from the cells was getting louder. Michael gestured towards the elevator. 'Let's go upstairs to the analyst room, quieter up there.'

Nick pitched the rice cake into a wastepaper basket like a basketball player. 'Lead the way Columbo.'

The elevator ran to a third floor corridor. At the end a metal door led into a large room filled with humming computer terminals. The room was windowless and lit by cold neon light strips. A dark-haired woman in her mid-twenties, wearing a short-sleeved grey uniform top, was bent over a keyboard in the far corner. Michael walked up to her and tapped gently on her epauletted shoulder.

'Officer Sukarno.' Despite the soft touch she jumped.

'Officer Sukarno, this is Captain Coburn, from England.'

'Promoted to captain and demoted to English in one sentence,' thought Nick, but he held his counsel.

'We are cooperating with Captain Coburn's department concerning an important and confidential international incident,' continued Michael. 'We have a cryptic message here from one of his operatives,' he said holding out his hand for Nick's bar receipt.

Nick prised it out of his top pocket with two fingers and handed the slip to Michael. The police officer in turn gave it to the young woman.

'As you see it has the cryptic message SITER written in what we think is charcoal. We would like you to pass this through your computers and see if it corresponds to some sort of location.'

Officer Sukarno took the piece of paper and smoothed it out next to her mouse mat. She took a dome-like glass paperweight from her desk and placed it onto the receipt. Nick and Michael leaned in unison as she peered through the glass. After a few seconds she sat up almost crashing into the faces of the two men.

'I do not think our digital intelligence system will decipher this code,' she said pan-faced.

Michael was about to protest when she lifted the slip from under the paperweight and handed it back to him. 'You see, you have missread the word. One of the letters did not come out in the charcoal but the object making it, presumably a match, did create some sort of indentation. It's not SITER but SISTER. Does that make your search a little easier?'

Nick grabbed the bar bill from Michael and held it up to the light. 'Shit. Well it was dark.'

'You've had it in your pocket all day,' said Michael. 'I could have asked the duty officer to look it up in the phone book. You needn't have waited to get access to all of this,' he added waving his hands at the roomful of hardware.

'It's too fucking late now,' snapped Nick, feeling angry with himself. 'But as we're here why don't we stick Gita's sister's name into that thing and see what it comes up with.'

It couldn't have been easier. Gita's sister's name and address was on the National Register. After that the most complicated software that they used was Google Maps. The haloed blue dot flashed over a small street adjacent to a canal not far from the harbour.

'Can we look at the street view?' asked Michael.

Officer Sukarno tapped the keyboard. She arced the mouse to show the street. A group of pitched-roofed tightly packed houses fronted a narrow hardcore road and a dark green canal. The area was poor but well-maintained. Gita's sister's house was a small semi-detached concrete bungalow with a minuscule terrace bordering a single window and a small front door. The plasterwork was painted a bright cobalt blue. A sheet was draped over a line obscuring the terrace.

'Bet she would have taken that down if she knew they were taking a picture of her street,' commented Nick.

'I doubt if they have the software to see it so I don't expect they really mind,' said Sukarno pointedly.

Michael looked at the clock on the wall. 'Well, sheet or no sheet, it's going to be difficult to see it soon if we don't hurry. It will be dark by the time we get there.' He casually saluted the young officer. 'Thank you for your time. As I said, this is a confidential international operation so I would be grateful if you would not mention it to anyone, not even your immediate colleagues.'

The woman nodded, pan-faced once more.

Michael turned for the door. 'Okay Nick, I'll take you in the police car. We will park up a block away so as not to scare Tom and the neighbours.'

'Let's hope Tom is there to scare,' said Nick, winking at the young female officer on his way out.

The alley marked as 'Jl Balack Banteng' was only twenty minutes from the police station. Michael drove the police car into the parking lot of a nearby warehouse and tipped the security guard.

'Found it on bricks the last time I left it unattended,' he explained.

'Not unlike the Gorbals in the good old days,' replied Nick. 'Kids used to say, "Look after your car for a quid governor". Tell them it didn't need looking after, they'd show you a rusty nail and say, "Oh yes it does governor".'

Michael pulled out his flashlight from the car, 'East meets West.'

The two men walked swiftly around the block until they reached the canal. The sun had dropped over an hour ago and the homes and bamboos that were clinging to its edge looked like cut-out black shapes against the skyline. There were no street lights here so Nick and Michael trod carefully past the cramped shanty houses, the odd glimmer of light filtering through their windows. The flashlight caught a splash of luminous blue rising up from the curb. Michael dimmed his torch and gestured to Nick. The low coloured stuccoed wall bordered a small terrace.

'No sheet,' hissed Nick.

'Yes but it's the right house,' whispered back Michael. 'I'll stand by the door, you have a look through the window; I've no idea what Tom looks like.'

Nick slid through the small entrance onto the terrace and dropped down on to all fours. The window in front of him was made of latticed wood and the glow from it was making patterns on the small bordering perimeter. Michael edged himself alongside the front door and gave a nod. Nick crawled up to the window and peered over the lower edge. The night was warm and he felt a trickle of sweat run down between his shoulder blades. He pressed his eye to one of the diamond openings in the framework. He froze as a loud noise and light came from over his shoulder. He glanced up at Michael who seemed unperturbed. Merely a passing moped by the canal road. The air was still again, only broken by the incessant noise of crickets. He focused his eyes on the interior of the small room. The window mesh blocked his lateral view so he could only see part of it at a time. Against the far, bare but painted, wall there was a small single rattan couch or bed. Empty. He turned his head to the right squinting to see if he could see the other side. Two women were squatting on the ground looking towards the front door to the right of him. They both appeared distressed, one of them had obviously been crying. It could have been Gita, but with her hair all over the place and face streaked with makeup it was hard to tell. It was impossible to view the inside of the front wall to see what they were looking at but he thought if he could move to another slat he would be able to get a view of the partition to the left. Putting his finger to his mouth, for Michael's benefit, he shifted his weight and changed position. Now he could make out the other part of the room. There sitting on a chair with his hands behind his back was Tom. His head was sloped forward and his eyes closed. He appeared to be unconscious or asleep. Nick made a decision. There was no means of knowing who was behind the door or whether they were dangerous or not. But they had the element of surprise. He pointed at Michael's holstered gun and indicated that they should force an entry. Michael responded by planting his shoulder to the door and heaving with all his might. The door gave way and Nick leapt into the room. The women screamed. A man, who had been standing behind the door, was thrown to the ground. Seeing a knife in his hand Nick stamped on it. The man cried out and let it go. Michael jumped onto his back, pulled his arms backwards and expertly bound his wrists with plastic cuffs.

The noise woke Tom. He opened his eyes, shook his head and tried to take in the commotion happening all around.

'You okay?' asked Nick.

Tom nodded, 'How did you…?

'Boy Scout,' replied Nick, having to raise his voice above the still screaming women. 'Michael, can you ask these young ladies to be quiet and then we can find out what's going on here?'

The man on the floor was groaning and in no state to cause a problem so Michael stepped over the bowls of stale noodles that were lying on the floor and went over to calm the women. Nick took a large leatherman from his pocket and used the knife to cut the rope holding Tom to the chair.

'Okay young man, you've got some explaining to do. One, why the cryptic spook message? Two, why didn't you call me? And three,' he said pointing at the writhing man on the floor, 'Who is this guy?'

Tom rubbed his wrists, and looked at the scene in front of him. A uniformed policeman was comforting two crying women and a man was struggling, handcuffed on the floor, next to a shattered doorframe. He thought he had acted maturely and professionally. He hadn't expected this to happen.

'That guy is Gita's brother. I know it doesn't look like it but I don't think he would hurt anybody. He's just trying to protect his sister.'

Nick picked up the knife from the floor. 'If that's the case what's he doing with this, and why were you all tied up, like a scene out of some movie?'

'It was the only way he could keep me from going with Gita to the laboratory. Now you've brought the police here and have probably made it worse. We've been arguing all day. I'm exhausted but I'm sure I could have talked him round in the end, but now…'

'But now you've been rescued you ungrateful sod,' said Nick dragging up Gita's brother from the floor and propping him against the wall. 'And I've even brought someone from the local constabulary to arrest your bloody kidnapper.'

Tom looked first at Michael and then at Gita's brother who was visibly shaking. 'I don't think you should arrest him. I'm sure we can sort this out. He was coming round to our way of thinking, I know it. It's just really difficult negotiating with someone who can't speak English.'

'What the fuck are you talking about? Geoff said you were a bit wet around the ears but he didn't let on that you were crazy.'

'I'm not crazy, and I didn't ask for a babysitter. I'm meant to be researching a documentary film without drawing too much attention to myself. I thought I was doing that until you smashed open a door bringing an armed policeman with you.'

Nick's head was whirling, he'd never come across anything like this before. A guy who he was meant to be minding, belligerently refusing his help. He rubbed his forehead, 'Okay, Tom Mix; another cowboy if you're wondering; before I set you back on that chair and tie you up again why don't you slowly take us through it. And,' he said pointing to Michael, 'if you need anything from your captor, I'm sure Michael will stand in as translator.'

Tom looked at Gita, who had stopped crying but was looking very frightened, squatting in the far corner of the room. 'Gita are you all right?'

Gita nodded, but her eyes kept darting to and from Nick and her brother.

'It's okay, he won't hurt him. Just be patient while I talk to Nick. Nick, can you vouch that your policeman friend won't take what I'm going to say any further.'

'Michael's a good friend, he'll keep this between ourselves for the time being but I can't promise in the long term.'

Michael nodded, 'Nick has filled me in on some of the background. I'll help out where possible but if it means letting criminals get away with it…'

Tom hesitated. He had little option but to tell his story. Then he remembered what Geoff had told him about the dilemma of filming terrorists. 'Right, it's just that we need a bit of time. I've been paid to get some information for the film. If we do it right then we'll have more than enough evidence for the police. In fact without our investigation they may not have any evidence at all.'

Nick crouched down cross-legged next to his captive, who was now silent and wide-eyed, obviously finding the exchange of English completely incomprehensible. 'Well young Tom, our companions seemed to have settled down so why don't you tell us your story from the beginning. What happened when you and Gita left the nightclub for the courtyard?'

Tom took a deep breath and looked at Gita. 'I'm sorry Gita, I should have told you about Nick. Nick this is Gita, Gita this is Nick. Nick works for the same company that I do. We were both at the nightclub last night and Nick distracted your friend whilst I took you outside for a smoke. It was a setup, I don't even smoke.' Gita just stared at him so Tom turned back to Nick. 'Anyway, in the courtyard we got chatting. I told Gita that I had studied microbiology. That bit's true Gita. So it was natural for Gita to tell me about what she did. Which is why I brought up the microbiology in the first place. The chat was pretty casual until I sensed something was worrying her. I asked her what it was. And she burst into tears.'

For the first time Gita spoke. 'You knew. You did it on purpose.'

'Like I said, sorry Gita.'

Nick got to his feet. 'Enough of all this apologising. If this woman is helping terrorists…'

'I don't think it's like that Nick,' protested Tom. 'She works there but she's not colluding with them. It's only recently that she's got wind of something not being right. That's why she wanted to talk to me.'

Nick walked over to the couch and sat down. 'Okay I won't interrupt again. You're in the courtyard and she started blubbing.'

'She said she had a lot of concerns about her job. But she didn't want to talk about it in the club. Wanted to go somewhere private. Her sister's. I thought it would put her off if I made a phone call so I scribbled a note on the bar bill with a burned match. Didn't have time to write much more, just wanted you to know that I was okay.'

'A bit bloody cryptic,' interrupted Nick; he put up his hand in apology. 'I know, carry on.'

'By the time we got back to her sister's,' continued Tom, 'the sun had started coming up. Riana, that's her sister over there, made us some breakfast and we sat down to talk. Gita is really scared. She knows there's something going on at the laboratory but doesn't know what to do about it. Speaking to me was a relief. The bugs they are making there are really dangerous. Her line manager says that they're for testing new antibacterials, but she can't see any evidence of that. Also, recently she's noticed some irregular exportation paperwork. Some of the stuff is scheduled to be shipped to somewhere in the Yemen and she's pretty sure that the protocols aren't legal. I told her that I could help; know some people who could expose them, if what she said turned out to be true. It was now about lunchtime, neither of us had slept. Gita had just decided to show me to a part of the laboratory where the paperwork was kept when in walks her brother.'

Michael, who had been listening attentively all of this time said something in Javanese to his prisoner. The man jabbered back. A heated argument followed ending with a sullen silence from the brother.

'Sorry to interrupt,' said Michael. 'Just wanted to know the other side of the story. Interested to know why Tom was tied up and what Gita's brother was doing with a large knife.'

'And?' asked Nick.

'Doesn't sound very plausible. Wanted to protect his sister so gently restrained Tom to stop him taking her to the laboratory. Says that she shouldn't go near the place again.'

'That's not far off the mark,' said Tom. 'I wouldn't have exactly said gently but waving the knife about was pretty persuasive so I let him tie me up. Knew it was a bit symbolic, I just wanted to show him I wasn't going anywhere until he really understood what was going on. Problem was the language. We've been arguing all afternoon but I've had to use Gita as a translator. Think I nearly got my point across when I fell asleep out of exhaustion.' Tom paused as he pointed to the splintered wood debris on the floor. 'Then you guys came in, smashing the door down in the process. Next time it might be better if you knocked. This lot are now going to take some convincing to get us access to that lab.'

Thirteen

Tom was wrong. Gita's brother had taken little persuading to change his mind when Michael pointed out that he could be arrested for the kidnapping of an alien citizen and that his sister was at risk of prosecution for collaborating with terrorists. Michael agreed to give them forty-eight hours to come up with a plan and report back to him. Until then he would pretend the whole thing hadn't happened. He returned to the police station leaving them to sort things out between themselves.

Gita's sister was still confused. Her English was not much better than her brother's and she had only grasped bits of the conversation. Gita calmed her and asked her to telephone the lab to report that Gita was sick and would not be in for a few days. The brother was still angry but agreed to keep quiet and leave his sister with Tom and Nick. He left with a wad of Nick's US dollars in his pocket.

After putting what was left of the door back on its hinges, Tom, Nick and Gita made their way to the main thoroughfare and hailed a cab. They returned to the hotel near the zoo where Nick had spent the night. Nick's jeep was still in the car park and they thought the hotel restaurant would be a good place to eat and decide what to do next. The restaurant was empty yet the bored waiter seemed reluctant to serve them. Gita snapped at him in Javanese and he sullenly sloped off to the kitchen.

'I think he thinks you're taking advantage of me,' she explained. 'I've put him right, we should have some hot food soon.'

'We've all got off on the wrong foot,' said Nick. 'Why don't we start again. First of all, what do you two really think is going on in that lab?'

'Go ahead Gita,' encouraged Tom.

Gita took a sip of water from the glass on the table. 'How much do you know about microbiology?'

'Zilch,' said Nick. 'School wasn't my strong point.'

'I'll try to make it simple,' said Gita. 'When I joined the laboratory, they said we were developing new antibiotics. After a while I was told to work on a project synthesising microbes. They were asking us to produce bacteria that had resistance to all known antibiotics. I said that why couldn't we use something like MRSA?'

'MRSA?' interrupted Nick.

'Multiresistant staphylococcus aureus,' explained Tom. 'It's a nasty bug that is really hard to kill with antibiotics.'

'But they said this wasn't good enough for them,' continued Gita. 'They wanted a bacteria that was easy to transmit and had no known antidote. They also gave another specification. It had to be easily transported in simple containers in a reproductive state. That's when alarm bells began to ring. Why would they want to move around lethal bacteria if the reason for making it was to test new antibiotics on it in their own laboratory?'

Nick leaned forward. 'Tom mentioned something about sending some to the Yemen.'

'Yes,' said Gita. 'That was very recent and another thing that got me really worried. Just before I left for the club I had to go over to the outer admin office to pick up some mail. Accidentally I saw some paperwork relating to exportation that had just come in. It was another request to supply a batch of live experimental material, this time to a place in North Africa. The note was marked strictly confidential and said something about unconventional exportation procedures. I didn't have time to read any more as someone came into the office.'

'And that's not the only unconventional thing about this setup,' added Tom. 'We won't bother you with the details but a lot of the methods that the lab are using to make these bugs are not authorised by any science organisation that we know. They are bloody dangerous to say the least. That's how we heard about the lab in the first place. One of their technicians caught an infection. He was discovered in London with a raging fever. Luckily for the hospital they isolated him in time so it wasn't passed on. Unluckily for him their antibiotics didn't work. He died within a week.'

'What was he doing in London, and how did you know that he worked for the Javanese lab?' asked Nick.

'No idea why he was in London, but because of the rarity of the bug he was referred to the School of Tropical Medicine and they did some digging. Found a letter on him with an address I was given, or should I say noticed, during my research. That's how you found me at the lab that evening.'

The surly waiter turned up with steaming plates of ayam greng kalasan and gado gado. Nick grabbed a fried chicken wing.

'At last real food. Thank God it's not rice cakes.'

Tom helped Gita to rice and then spooned some of the gado gado into his bowl. 'Why rice cakes?'

'Another story,' mumbled Nick through his mouthful of chicken. 'Waiting for a jewel heist to be sorted.'

Tom realised that it was pointless asking any more questions so they sat there for a few moments without talking, chewing on their food to the accompaniment of the slow-turning fans overhead.

It was late afternoon and the low angled sunlight slanting in from the windows crept across the tables. The waiter cleared the empty plates and served up mugs of muddy coffee. Nick took a swig and grimaced.

'Should have taken your advice Gita and ordered the tea.' He could sense that Tom was still agitated but it wasn't his job to organise this project, he had only been sent to look after the guy. 'Okay Tom, what do you want to do next?'

'It's a problem. I've been asked to check out the lab and see if there's anything worth filming. I'm pretty sure there's something fishy going on but I've got no real proof and, if I had, I don't know how they would film it. Any suggestions?'

'Not my field Tom but, if I was you, I'd find out more about that export licence for the bugs. If it's crooked like you think it is you're halfway there.'

'Yeah but we've only got Gita's word for it. They could say she's lying.'

'There's only one way to find out,' said Nick, standing up and making a mimed scribbling gesture to the waiter. 'That's to go and take a look.'

Gita had taken some persuading but when Nick pointed out to her that it was a choice of that or being investigated by the Surabaya police she agreed to show them the office where she had seen the papers. It was possible but it wouldn't be easy. The main laboratory entrance was heavily guarded day and night with security cameras and alarms. The administration office was to the rear of the compound, guarded only by regular patrols. To enter the laboratory Gita had to not only use her key card but be accompanied by a security officer who would insert his card at the same time. Fortunately, she could access the administration building on her own as it only required one key card.

'Well Tom, looks like the lab is out of bounds, for the time being anyway. But if you're game and we look out for those dogs I'm sure we could take a peek at this suspect paperwork.'

Tom looked at his watch and nodded. 'If we leave now it should be dark by the time we get there. We could get in under the fence where I did before; that's if they haven't found it and filled the hole in by now.'

Nick paid the bill and added a few extra notes. 'Tell him it's not for a tip, it's for a takeout bag of raw beef,' said Nick to Gita. 'Ask him to bring it round to the car park.'

The road out of Surabaya was busy and it was already dark by the time they hit the outskirts. There was no moon and no street lights and without Gita it would have been impossible for them to have found the side road to the laboratory. Nick drove slowly, they were in no hurry and he didn't want to draw attention to themselves. They couldn't see any habitation but Gita said that amongst the rice fields there was the odd farmer living in a crude shelter, either palm-thatched huts or merely a piece of corrugated iron perched on a few poles. A four-wheel drive tearing along the poorly made-up road would cause gossip for miles. As a result it was past midnight when they saw the glimmer of the small industrial estate looming up before them. Nick switched the headlights off and crawled the final kilometre by the jeep's sidelights. On the outskirts of the complex was a rundown factory, a few rusty cars parked behind an old outhouse. Nick pulled the jeep in alongside one of them and switched off the engine. They sat there for a moment in silence in the cool interior of the vehicle.

Nick broke the atmosphere. 'Right, you all know what to do. I'll lift the wire. You and Gita get to the admin block as quickly and quietly as you can.' He lifted up the bag of raw meat from the car well. 'I'll deal with the dogs and join you when I can. You set?'

They nodded and opened the car doors to be hit by a wave of thick hot tropical air. Using only the light from their phone screens the three of them crept along the tree-lined pathway that led to the barbed wire perimeter. A hundred metres before the entrance of the compound they broke off the track and pushed their way through the wild grasslands. Apart from the odd scuffle and twitter from the night animals the air was soundless. After fifteen minutes Nick gauged that they were about parallel with Tom's last foray into the laboratory grounds. He pointed sideways and gestured for them to crouch down. They broke off from their current direction and crawled at ninety degrees towards the area where they thought the wire fence would be waiting. Nick's sense of orienteering could hardly have been better. As they cleared the final scrub and long grass they arrived within a few metres of the mown boundary that bordered the barbed wire enclosure. Tom pointed out the sign. *SUPAYA METU.*

'Keep out,' whispered Gita.

'Like a red rag to a bull,' muttered Nick.

Tom pointed along the fence boundary. 'Not far,' he said quietly.

The sky was black and there were no lit windows to pick out the laboratory within the compound but, once inside, Gita would be able to show them the way. They continued on all fours crawling alongside the periphery until they came to the tree root and depression where Tom had first broken in. Tom sighed with relief.

'It's not been disturbed,' he said softly. 'They've obviously not found it.'

'I'll need to make the hole a bit bigger for me,' said Nick. 'First, let's get you two through. Here, I'll hold the fence up, crawl through quickly.'

Tom and Gita slithered their small frames between the depression in the ground and the razor wire that was being lifted for them. They sat panting, covered in earth, on the other side. Nick started to dig at the soil with his large hands. 'You two go on, this won't take me long.' He held up the bag of meat. 'I'll deal with the dogs and catch up with you later.'

Gita pressed the button on her phone. Tom reached out suddenly and grabbed her wrist. 'Don't make a phone call now, someone might hear you.'

'I'm not making a call, I'm opening my compass App,' she snapped in a low but angry voice. 'I'm familiar with the grounds but if you hadn't noticed it's pitch black. I need to get a sense of direction.'

Tom snatched his hand back in surprise. This was quite uncharacteristic of the Gita he had known for the last twenty-four hours. Perhaps now she had committed herself and was on home ground she had become more confident.

'Sorry, stupid of me, lead the way.'

Gita studied the compass on her phone and pointed into the darkness. 'The admin block should be over there. I don't think we need to crawl now; if we tread quietly I think we should be all right. The security guards are on the opposite side next to the laboratory.'

Tom opened his hands in compliance. He followed this new bolder Gita into the night.

Nick took a note of their direction and continued digging. It took him longer than he had expected as, after a few tens of centimetres, he hit a rock. He crawled back into the bushes to find a piece of hard bamboo, sharpened it with his leatherman knife, and returned to the hole under the fence. He dug around the rock and it slowly gave up its grip when he prised the bamboo under it, using it as a lever. He glanced at the glowing figures on the dial of his watch. It had taken a lot longer than he had hoped. As long as those dogs were parading the perimeter and not smelling out his two companions in the middle. The hole wasn't as big as he would have liked but he was running out of time so he pushed his arms through and shoved as hard as he could. He got his head through easily but the fence clamped down on his broad shoulders.

'Fuck this,' he barked. 'Worse than a bloody army exercise.'

He pulled back again and attacked the bottom of the fence with the leatherman pliers. The wire was thick and they weren't really up to the job but with Nick's strength and tenacity some of the links finally gave way.

'Okay Coburn, you can't let those kids down, it better work this time,' he muttered slipping down onto the ground again. It was a tight fit, yet easier. The wire cut into his back and no doubt was spilling blood but at least half of his torso was through. If he wriggled his hips and pulled forward on his hands he should be okay. Just then a snarl came from the dark. Nick froze. He had left the meat on the other side of the fence. His body was filling the hole and his arms and hands were on the wrong side. He lay as still as he could but the dogs could smell him, or at least the bag of meat nearby. He heard them growling and snuffling closer.

Two hundred metres away Tom and Gita had found the administration hut. Gita used her phone light to find the card slot and slipped her key card into it. The door opened with a reassuring click. They crept inside. The only lights coming from the room were from softly humming computers and printers. Pinpricks of green and red throwing eerie shadows across the desks. Tom and Gita used the soft blue light from their phones to find their way to the filing cabinets at the back of the office. Their eyes were slowly becoming adjusted and it became easier to navigate their way around the room. Gita tried the drawer of the first cabinet she came to. It was locked. Tom groaned in exasperation but Gita signalled towards a desk drawer. He opened it and found a bunch of keys. She opened her hand and indicated that he should throw them to her. Not wanting to risk the noise, in case she dropped them, he walked around the desk and placed them carefully into her palm. He shone the phone light while she picked through them and inserted one of them into the lock. It didn't work. Patiently she tried another. On the third attempt the filing cabinet drawer slid open. Gita flicked through the files and triumphantly pulled one out. A large bang came from behind them and she immediately dropped it. Tom's heart nearly stopped. Gita swung around and took in a huge gulp of warm air.

'It's only the door,' she explained in a hushed voice. 'We forgot to close it behind us.'

Tom steadied himself against the wall and closed his eyes for a second. 'Shit, that's my fault I should have done that. I'll do it now while you pick up those papers.'

He walked back to the doorway and looked around outside before he shut it noiselessly. 'No one around anyway. Are those the documents?'

'Think so, here take a look.'

Tom took the assortment of official-looking documents from her and placed them on a desk. Some were written in Javanese and didn't make any sense to him but others emblazoned with formal looking stamps were written in English. He picked out a letter with a London address. It was a request for samples of incubating microbes. He had never heard of the species before. *Pseudomonas synthetica, klebsiella titanicus, eschericia fortida*. The forenames resembled gram-negative bacteria, bacteria that cause pneumonia and blood infections, and bacteria that were hard to kill.

'Is the export licence there?' whispered Gita from beside him. 'It's on a yellowy kind of paper.'

'It's difficult to see the colour of paper in this light, are you sure it wasn't written in Javanese?'

'No it's definitely in English. Most of the international documents are.'

Tom rifled through the file. Gita jabbed her finger at one of the pieces of paper. 'There, that's it. Export licence to northern Africa but the numbers that relate to the material, don't match.'

Tom peered more closely at the columns. Harmless-looking chemicals, routinely used in microbiology labs, were printed alongside four-digit reference numbers. 'What do you mean they don't match?'

'See this number here, alongside some sort of agar preparation. That's not what it refers to. I'm working on that specimen number in the lab. It's yet to be tested but we have to handle it through sealed cabinets. It could be highly contagious and lethal.'

'So you think they are shipping out this dangerous stuff under false names.'

'It looks like it. Look at the price per milligram; you could buy a tank full of chemicals for that.'

Tom carefully laid out the papers and started to take photographs with his camera phone.

'The flash is a bit bright,' said Gita. 'Why don't we just take them with us?'

Tom continued methodically. 'Can't be helped, if we steal them they'll notice and probably do some sort of cover-up. We need…' He stopped abruptly as he noticed something on one of the files.

'What's wrong,' asked Gita.

'Nothing, just a bizarre coincidence. This address here on one of the export forms. I've seen it before. It's in Nathalie's production notes.'

'Who's Nathalie?'

'My director. She's been in contact with these people here. It's the company in North Africa. They're asking for samples to be sent to their plant in Morocco.'

'She thinks they're helping terrorists too?'

'No, that's why it's really weird. I think she's just using them to get some background on drugs.'

'What would she say about this?'

'I've no idea. And that's another thing, I've never made a programme before. I'm supposed to be checking out stuff to film. Here we are creeping around in the dark worried about the phone flash drawing attention. How in the hell is she going to get a film crew in here?'

Gita pointed to his phone. 'Why don't you ask her?'

Tom stared at her. She had been so nervous in the company of her brother he had forgot how bright she was. 'Yes, stupid of me, she's seven hours behind, it will be late afternoon there.' He pressed the speed dial.

Nathalie's voice was as clear as if she was in the next room. 'Tom?'

'Hi Nathalie, hope I'm not disturbing you, just want a bit of advice.'

'No problem Tom, but haven't got long, I'm just about to board a plane for the States. Fire away.'

Tom thought it best to play down his situation. 'I've located the lab and I'm pretty sure they are up to no good. Found a lab researcher who agrees with me, and have some documents in front of me but can't remove them from the building.'

'Okay, just had my last call. Take stills and e-mail them to me.'

Tom flashed his thumbs across the face of the phone. 'Done.'

'Now use the video camera on your phone to take a bit of action. Put the papers on the desk and use someone's hand to turn them over and to point to anything you think is important. Take various sizes of shot. Make sure you've got a lot of light on it and that you keep the camera still. The lab assistant sounds good, we could interview her and get her to do some clandestine filming.'

Tom heard an airport announcement in the background. He was just about to tell Nathalie that it might be difficult to get Gita to do any filming when the door of the hut burst open. The porch light had been activated and outlined the silhouette of a man in a beret holding what looked like a small machine gun. Tom acted quickly and pointed the only weapon he had in his hand. The flash of his camera lit up the room.

Fourteen

The phone in Nathalie's hand went dead. The last boarding call had already been announced so she didn't try to reconnect; not unusual for a line to Indonesia to be broken off. She would get back to him from Los Angeles.

The plane was full, no seats to lie across. She did the maths. An eleven-hour flight and Los Angeles was seven hours behind. That meant she would get to her hotel just before midnight. Best to keep awake and try to sleep when she got there. The shoot was scheduled in the Infectious Diseases department of UCLA at 9.00 am sharp. She had got the call as she was returning to the office after her lunch with Geoff. Veronica had organised some confidential filming with Zormax concerning adding an Ebola vaccine to their portfolio. At the last minute her director had gone sick. An opportunity for both of them, she had said. She would pay Nathalie's flight if she stood in. As a bonus Nathalie could find out more about Zormax.

'It's a win-win,' Veronica had pleaded. 'I'm afraid I can't give you a fee because that's already been committed but the flight's booked and paid for. You did say you wanted to know more about that company.'

Nathalie had referred the idea to Geoff who in turn had referred it to Stefanie. Stefanie worked out that it would be possible for her to get a flight from Los Angeles to Surabaya and then on to Harare. If she accepted to film their legs with local Indonesian and African crew then it should be well within the budget. Nathalie was never keen on using local cameramen but this job was different; she needed to be as invisible as possible. Arriving with a cameraman, equipment and carnet would be like putting an advertisement in the paper. By late afternoon she had been at Heathrow and now here she was, on board, taking off in an Airbus A380.

As soon as the seatbelt signs were turned off Nathalie took a look at her phone. Tom's e-mail had not yet come through. She put it away and dug out the call-sheet and production notes that Medical Films had biked over. There had been a bit of a fuss about changing names on the ticket but Veronica had a contact in British Airways and it was somehow smoothed over. Nathalie still had a journalist's visa for the States which was the main thing. Bill Sharpe's name as director on the manifest was the only thing that would have told anyone that there had been a last-minute change. Although Medical Films didn't produce broadcast stuff they were still very professional. The call-sheet was better than most of Bagatelle's. Geoff's excuse would have been that investigative documentaries are shot on the hoof and it was pointless scheduling a day from minute to minute. Nathalie preferred a plan at least; one could always change it later. The production assistant who had written this had done her homework. The location, crew's names and phone numbers, as well as a do-able but tight schedule were all clearly laid out. Most production companies tended to think you could move from one location to another in minutes. Only the PAs who had actually been on a shoot realised that it took an hour or so to rig a proper lighting set-up. Anyone expecting more than five to ten minutes' finished footage in a ten-hour day was not really interested in making a quality film. No, the actual filming schedule looked alright. What was more daunting was the first item written on the list, *Meeting with Medicolegal Department to clear the script.* Nathalie had been to these sorts of pharmaceutical meetings before. 'Medical Legal department.' More like 'film prevention unit,' she thought. Every objection possible was made to what anyone could say. You would think the pharmaceutical company's lawyer was working for the other side. She hoped the trip would be worth it. She didn't really know what she was looking for. Geoff had said that if she had a sixth sense she should follow it. It was cheaper to get to Java and Zimbabwe via a free flight to Los Angeles more like it.

The plane touched down in LAX on time and Nathalie hailed a cab to the hotel written on her call-sheet, The Royal Palace just off Wilshire Boulevard. It was a simple three-storey hotel, within walking distance of the medical centre. Just perfect. Nathalie took a shower, set her alarm and slid between the crisp sheets. She turned to switch off the bedside light and her phone on the table reminded her of Tom's e-mail. She logged into the hotel's WiFi and tapped the envelope icon. A few items were in her inbox, most of them junk but she found Tom's attachments and opened them. There were about five documents in all, some in a foreign language, but a couple in English drew her attention. The print was difficult to read and phone screen too small to study them in detail so she reluctantly spun out of bed and reached for her laptop. When she expanded the documents, she thought she must be hallucinating from jetlag; there in the bottom right-hand corner of one certificate was a signature. Like many signatures completely indecipherable, but just above it a typed name – Biomedivac. Of course it could be possible that there was more than one company called Biomedivac in the world but surely not on a piece of paper next to an address in Morocco. Nathalie was not a great believer in coincidences and spent much of her sleep-disturbed night trying to work out why Professor Townes' outfit would be communicating with a suspect laboratory in eastern Java.

✳

It was only a twenty-minute walk from her hotel to the medical centre so Nathalie had an early breakfast and decided to take a stroll in the Los Angeles sunshine. As she made her way down Westwood Plaza through the university campus she recalled one of Geoff's old stories. He had been directing a shoot in the old UCLA; yes it was hard to believe but he did actually go out on shoots in those days. The old UCLA was apparently now closed but Geoff said it had some of the longest corridors in the world. According to one of the doctors he filmed there, long enough to use as a shooting gallery. Geoff had told her that the said doctor packed a loaded Magnum revolver in the top of his cowboy boots barely covered by his white lab coat. Nathalie never knew how much Geoff's filming stories were embellished but he swore this was true. 'The guy was really wacky, even smeared bacteria on door handles to get back at his colleagues,' he had told her. 'Anyone who crossed him would end up in the john for a week.' She hoped no one was smearing any bugs on the door handles of the new hospital because, as she'd learned in Africa, the Ebola virus was not to be played with.

The new UCLA Medical Centre was a classic modern building made up of a number of pale smooth blocks inscribed with, what Nathalie thought, a chequered tablecloth design. A number of small black page-like windows pierced this facade. She left the heat of the sunshine and walked into the air-conditioned reception.

'Nathalie Thompson, Medical Films,' she said offering an identity card to the person behind the desk. 'I believe a...' she glanced down at her call-sheet, 'Vince Page is meeting me here?'

A voice from over her shoulder brought her up sharply. 'That's me, Miss Thompson, welcome to Los Angeles.'

Nathalie turned around and had to crane her neck to look up at a very tall, dark-haired American.

He noticed her surprise. 'Sorry to startle you, I'm from Zormax. We'll just get you signed in here and I'll take you to meet the others.'

'The others' were an entourage of medical and legal personnel from the pharmaceutical company along with a key opinion leader from the Microbiology Department who had agreed to be interviewed. They were heavily engrossed in conversation when Nathalie turned up. She knew from her notes that the company wanted the endorsement from a non-company expert who could talk about Ebola, its devastating consequences and the possible mechanisms of a vaccine. This was all to be shot against the background of a modern laboratory, hence UCLA. This interview was to be followed by a more political and strategic statement from a senior company representative. Boring, but a 'piece of cake' in film terms. Two interviews with the interviewer's questions off-mic, one with a bit of lab background, the other in an office. Nathalie could do this sort of thing standing on her head. What she knew from experience was that the problem wasn't going to be the actual filming, it was going to be what these guys were allowed what, and what not, to say.

The Los Angeles film crew turned up on cue. Nathalie took them to one side, introduced herself to the cameraman, the sound recordist and the sparks, and told them it might be a little while before they could light the first location. First, no one had decided where that was yet and second, there was going to be a meeting to decide on the content. Why this hadn't been done before she had no idea but there you go. The crew sloped off to the coffee shop and Nathalie returned to the 'suits'.

She entered the middle of an argument about where they were going to hold the interview. The marketing manager wanted a high-tech exciting scientific background. The medical expert was explaining that the laboratories belonged to the hospital and he couldn't just let them in without permission. 'Besides,' he was saying, 'they contain some quite delicate experiments; we wouldn't want any cross contamination.'

Nathalie could see the marketing manager furiously whispering to his assistant asking why this had not all been cleared before. The solution was found by the doctor's secretary, who said that she knew of a small lab undergoing refurbishment, and she strode off to find someone to sign an authoritative bit of paper. It was pointless getting the crew to pre-rig without that bit of paper so Nathalie stayed to listen to the next piece of argument. This was a classic. Could the doctor say that the vaccine under speculation was 'safe'? According to the pharmaceutical lawyer, nothing was safe. Not even water. If even one patient turned up with a mild side effect they could sue, and suing meant millions of dollars. The marketing manager protested. The drug they were thinking of buying, and possibly developing, had a good safety record. They weren't comparing this product to a foodstuff. It was a highly effective drug where any reported side-effects were minimal compared to its benefits. Instead of ameliorating the situation this argument added fuel to the lawyer's fire.

'Ah, *effective*,' he said. 'If you use that word you have to qualify it with data.'

Nathalie had made these sorts of films before. They ended up with miles and miles of tiny illegible captions that were scrolled across the screen during the interview, each sentence qualifying or even contradicting what the opinion leader seemed to be suggesting. This key opinion leader was looking very confused. It appeared that rather than express his, quite knowledgeable, opinion he was being asked to parrot some sort of benign script. He was about to make a comment on this when his secretary returned to the conference room. The hospital had agreed that they could use the small laboratory and that a donation to the fund would be gratefully received. The marketing manager nodded in acquiescence and it was with relief that Nathalie asked to be excused and show her film crew where to set up.

The location was less than desirable. It was cramped, it had a row of windows facing the sun, and it looked more like a storeroom than a laboratory. She asked the sparks to ND the windows. This meant taking a roll of neutral density gel and taping them up to filter the sunlight. A bit like sunglasses for the window panes. She gently persuaded the soundman – she knew it wasn't really 'his job' – to see if he could rustle up some laboratory glassware that they could use as props. Nathalie then set to work with the cameraman rearranging the room. Perhaps they could sit the doctor behind some sort of bench containing agar plates. With a bit of backlight it would be quite atmospheric.

An hour later, the entourage turned up with a very nervous looking doctor in tow. Nathalie had pre-lit the room but wanted to see her interviewee in-situ before she made the final adjustments. He sat behind the desk on the chair that had been placed there for him, but protested when he saw some of the laboratory props.

'We don't use these in our antiviral experiments,' he started to explain.

'It's just for a bit of atmosphere Doctor, the audience this is aimed at won't know one end of the test tube from another,' intervened the marketing assistant. 'As long as you are happy with the notes that we've given you?'

Nathalie inwardly groaned. Notes. The last thing she wanted was the guy reading from a piece of paper. She decided it was time to take control.

'Just want you to be comfortable Sir, if you would just like to lean against the desk and look towards me, not at the camera; try to forget that. Just try to explain to me personally what you want to say.' She turned to the corporate employees. 'If you would sit at the back of the room and face away from the doctor, I think he'll find it more comfortable to speak. If at any time he says something that you think we will not be able to use, please would you wait until the end of the take and then address any comments to me. Are you okay with that?'

It was obvious that this young woman knew what she was doing so the lawyers and marketing men meekly huddled on their stools in the back of the room.

Nathalie took the list of questions she had been given and put them on her lap. 'Now Doctor, perhaps you would put your notes to one side and I'll ask you a question. My question will not be heard by the viewer, so it would be great if you could reflect the question in your answer. And one more thing, just before you answer, pause and look at me. I really am interested in knowing what you have to say and it would be difficult for us if you overlap my question. Okay, are we ready? Turnover and here we go.'

To everyone's surprise Nathalie's first few questions were nothing to do with the list that she had been given. They concerned the doctor's background, how he had been appointed to the university and what first got him interested in the subject of Ebola. During this time the key opinion leader visibly relaxed and started to learn the tricks of the trade. Not to glance at the camera, avoid the overlaps, and become an expert in reflecting the question in the answer. By the time she began to address the questions the company wanted her to ask, he was eating out of her hands. But then came the inevitable gremlins.

'Fridge!' interrupted the soundman.

Nathalie was cross. She had heard the machine switch on too, but she wanted to get to the end of the take before it was addressed.

'Sorry for the interruption Doctor, could someone please kindly turn that off, it's interfering with our sound.'

There was a delay of fifteen minutes or so whilst another discussion ensued about the legality of touching any of the equipment. In the end it was discovered that there was nothing in the fridge and a simple switch would solve the problem. Nathalie made a note on her pad to turn it on again before they left the room.

'Okay, now if you'll be patient with me, we will do those questions again but this time in a tight shot.' She turned to the cameraman. 'Really chunky, just crop the top of his head and down to his tie knot if that's okay.'

He nodded back and adjusted the lens. 'Framed. Ready when you are.'

Nathalie explained to the doctor that she needed this for editing reasons. 'They don't have to be exactly the same answers, just roughly what you said before. We'll use the best bits.'

It was lunchtime by the time they finished. The shots weren't too bad, the cameraman seemed to know what he was doing. Nicely framed, not too much space above the interviewee's head, and pleasant lighting. As for the content, she wasn't so sure. The corporate boys had been so restrictive on what he could and couldn't say that the poor doctor ended up by not saying much at all. Ebola was a terrible disease and people were working on vaccines, but the words 'safe' and 'effective' were avoided at all costs. She did get one interesting bit of science out of him when she went off-piste from the client's questions. Remembering her early discussion with Doctor Styne she asked her expert about lectins. He was surprised with her medical knowledge and enthusiastically launched into a detailed explanation of viral entry inhibitors which, against Nathalie's rules, one of the clients had put a stop to. Shame, she had thought, that would have made good scientific television.

The afternoon session was entirely different. The interviewee was one of the corporate bigwigs and was definitely in charge. The lawyer and marketing manager kowtowed to him as if he was royalty and made no comments on what he had or had not to say. The doctor offered them his office as a location and was liberated back to work in his laboratory. Unfortunately the office was on the corner of one wing opposite a building that was about to be demolished. In true filming encounter, the ball and chain man decided to swing into operation the second that Nathalie asked the first question. The 'suits' were so intimidated by their boss that they tried to ignore the situation. Nathalie shouted 'cut' and sent the sparks with a hundred dollar bill to see if the guy would stop for half an hour. It seemed to work. Silence. When the sparks returned Nathalie began her question again and as soon as she did the ball crashed into the building opposite.

'Sorry guys, we're going to have to move,' she said. 'If you'd like to take five, I'll see if we can get somewhere the other side of the building.' They all looked on in amazement as she calmly strode out of the room.

It was ten rather than five minutes later when she returned. 'Along the corridor, elevator to one floor up and there's a room in the opposite corner. Some kind research student says we can use it for an hour. If you would all come with me we will make it a wrap here and the crew will join us as soon as they can.'

The pharmaceutical group, including their hallowed leader, followed her like sheep as she led the way. The pristine corridor was full of white-coated scientists returning to their workstations. The first elevator car was full so they pushed the button and waited for a second. It arrived with a 'ding' and the doors slid open to reveal a large empty space. Nathalie gestured for them to enter, made her way in last and pressed the button for the next floor. She turned to watch the doors close. As they did so she thought she saw a familiar face in the crowded corridor. It was a fleeting glimpse but she was sure it was that of Rob Barnes.

Fifteen

'I'm Jan Roszak, CEO, Acquisitions and Mergers, Zormax.'

The CEO leaned comfortably in his chair looking at Nathalie who was sitting opposite. The lawyers and marketeers were positioned awkwardly standing at the back of the room avoiding eye contact. A click of the fingers and they would be practically genuflecting, thought Nathalie. She had no idea why these corporate suits were so frightened of their bosses. She had been asked to interview the guy but not to challenge any of his statements. If they wanted that, they had another thought coming.

'And would you tell me Jan,' she asked, purposely using his first name, 'why you are investing in Ebola vaccines and how you think this will benefit your current portfolio?'

The answer came out like a scripted politician's speech. It made sense but it was boring and definitely too long. She wasn't being paid for this gig, but she had taken it on in good faith; the least she could do would be to repay Veronica with a professional job.

'That's great Jan, but somehow I'm not convinced, and I'm not sure if your employees will be either.' She could hear a loud intake of breath from the back of the room. 'Also, I'm afraid it's too long and unless we can get it crisper I'm going to have to cut it down in the edit suite. Now if you can do it again, but this time more succinctly and from the heart then it will be your version rather than mine.'

She didn't turn around but could imagine the blood draining from the faces of the subordinates behind her. She'd interviewed these types before. They were used to sycophants saying 'yes' but they didn't get to be number one by chance. If you challenged them on their own level they would often come up with the goods. Her interviewee slowly pulled himself up in the chair.

'So, exactly how long would you like my answer to be Miss Thompson?'

Nathalie looked at her watch. 'One minute thirty would do it.'

Jan Roszak eyeballed her. 'When you are ready then,' he said calmly.

She directed the camera and asked him to begin 'in your own time.' The speech lasted exactly one minute and twenty-five seconds. It was to the point and contained a certain amount of emotion. It certainly felt like he meant it.

'And cut,' said Nathalie. 'If that's okay with sound, I think that's a wrap. Thank you Mr Roszak.'

Roszak swept out of the room, towing his entourage behind him like kite tails in the wind. The crew were left staring at each other. Nathalie broke the silence with sarcasm.

'And thank you Miss Thompson, nice to be working with you.'

The cameraman laughed. 'Well I thought it was a good job, would like to stay on and have a chat but I'm afraid I've got to be somewhere. Joe and Billy will make you a digital backup and store the gear.' He passed her his business card. 'Nice working with you. Any time you need crew in LA please look me up.'

After doing a few last-minute checks to make sure that everything would be okay he left with a wave. Joe made her the backup whilst Billy struck the lights and packed them onto his trolley. He told Joe that he would wait for him in the van. Nathalie hated this part of the shoot. When she had used old-fashioned celluloid, the camera assistant would pass her the cans of undeveloped film and she would ship them off to the laboratory. Today, in this digital world, the soundman would often spend hours downloading the material as a safety backup in case the original became corrupted. 'And this was meant to be progress,' she thought. Joe could sense her irritation.

'Not long now, just want to check this bit back and we're ready to go.'

Nathalie was about to tell him to take his time – she'd rather be safe than sorry – when a squawk came from his sound mixer.

'Is there a problem?' she asked.

'No, that's not on our recording, I'm afraid it's live. Your interviewee was so keen to get out of the room that he's left the tram wireless mic on his lapel.'

'Are you sure?'

Joe turned one of the knobs on his machine and handed her the headphones. 'Yeah, listen that's his voice isn't it?'

Nathalie could hear the distinctive voice of Jan Roszak talking to someone. The few words that she caught made her make a quick decision.

'You're right, and if your tram isn't here then he must have got it. I think you had better try and find him before he leaves the building. I'll stay here and look after the gear.'

Joe looked undecided. 'You sure?'

Nathalie was already feeling guilty but she knew that this was a great opportunity. 'Yeah absolutely, you had better hurry, I know those things are expensive and knowing the sort of guy he is I doubt if he'll return it.'

'Okay, I'll scour the corridors, you stay here. Don't touch anything. I'll be back as soon as I can.' Joe left the room.

Nathalie waited a few moments and then opened the door to check the corridor. Joe had already disappeared around the corner. She quietly shut the door and returned to the sound mixer on the table. The volume had already been turned up so she didn't have to touch it.

'Nothing illegal here Nathalie,' she said to herself. 'Just rest my head on the table next to the cans, and if I hear something who's to be the wiser.'

The voice of Jan Roszak came clearly out of the leather-padded earpiece. He was in conversation with someone but unfortunately for Nathalie that voice was off-mic and hardly audible. What had grabbed her attention were the words she had heard earlier, 'Moroccan plant.' This was the third time this North African location had been flagged up. She had to know why.

'... and you're absolutely sure you've left no paper trail between us and your requisition?' Roszak's tone of voice was far from the calm presence of his interview. 'We want it done but if anyone...'

Roszak was interrupted by a muffled interjection. Nathalie moved as close as she could to the earpiece but she still couldn't make out the words. She jumped as Roszak's voice cut in again.

'You've blown one chance, this is your last opportunity. If the Moroccan thing doesn't work we'll cut you out. Shit, now there's someone at the door, I told one of my goons to keep this private. Keep your face to the window, I'll get rid of them.'

There was a scraping noise as if someone had moved a chair across the floor and then an expletive before the tram went dead.

'Joe's found him,' thought Nathalie. 'Pity, it was just getting interesting.' She backed off from the table, took out a notepad and started writing. When Joe returned she didn't want to give him any clues that she might have been eavesdropping.

She didn't have to wait long. Joe burst in triumphantly waving the microphone.

'Got an ear-full, even though it was his own stupid fault for walking off with the thing.'

Nathalie looked up from her notes. 'Did he know that it was live?'

'Don't think so, I said I found it missing from my kit, he just tore it from his lapel and almost threw it at me.'

'No mention of his conversation being heard or recorded?'

Joe looked at her quizzically. 'No, don't think he realised the range of these things; anyway we only heard a couple of words, and I didn't say anything so...'

'Okay, just don't want any complaints to the production company; my first job for them.'

Joe nodded understandingly. 'I don't think you've got a problem there. He was just pissed off by being interrupted in his meeting. Gave his lackey on the door a real roasting. Anyway the recorder was packed away, there's no record of it so no one will know that the mic was live.'

That answered Nathalie's next question. She was hoping that she could hear more of the conversation. All she had was a few clips of the CEO talking to someone about Morocco. Could be completely innocent or could be very sinister. She suddenly remembered who she thought she had seen from the elevator earlier.

'Joe, where was it you said you found the guy?'

'I didn't, why?'

'I think I ought to go and apologise, say we should have taken the mic from him earlier.'

'We couldn't have, he just walked out, and besides I think he's forgotten about it by now.'

'I'd feel happier.'

'You're the director. Down the corridor, first left and about the fifth office along; could be room 502 or 503 I think. I'll pack up here and bring the media drives to the van.'

Nathalie gave him the thumbs up and left the room. The corridor was empty. The cold neon tubes created an eerie green hue on its walls. Nathalie felt conspicuous as she turned the corner and squinted through the narrow glass panels that were paired with each office door. The first two rooms were empty and the third had a solitary occupant bent over a computer terminal. She sidled up to the pane of the next room numbered 502 and was just about to peer in when a door was flung open from the adjacent office. Two men stormed out in heated discussion. Jan Roszak was telling the man with him that they shouldn't be seen together and to take different exits. The man with his back to her replied cursorily protesting that he had always been careful. She instantly recognised the voice of Rob Barnes and saw that he was about to turn towards her. If he recognised her she really would have some explaining to do. She turned on her heel and dived into the nearest office. It had been so quick that she didn't know if he had seen her or not. Anyway it was too late now. The woman at the computer terminal looked up in surprise.

'Excuse me, do you always burst in without knocking?'

'Sorry,' said Nathalie breathlessly. 'I've obviously got the wrong office, Doctor, er, Sykes told me to wait in room 502.'

'Room 502 is next door but it's not Doctor Sykes' office, whoever that is.'

Nathalie had no wish to return to the corridor for a while so she decided to play for time.

'I'm sure he said 502, this is B Wing isn't it?'

'B Wing?'

'Or maybe B Block. Sorry but I'm new here, on a visit from the UK.' Nathalie rummaged around in the pocket of her jeans. 'I wrote it down somewhere but I seem to have lost it.' She stressed her English accent, it had often worked for her in the past. 'You wouldn't be kind enough to have a plan of the campus, I'm sure I could remember if I saw a map.'

The woman wasn't taken in by this ruse at all, and was obviously busy and irritated by this unwelcome intruder. She started to reach for her telephone.

'No, I don't have a map and I don't think you should be wandering the corridors without any authorisation.'

Apart from confronting Rob Barnes the last thing Nathalie wanted was to be hauled out of this office by a campus security guard. Her hand was still in her pocket, apparently searching for the imaginary directions, and she scratched it on something sharp. Her plastic visitor's badge that she had been given at reception. She pulled it out triumphantly.

'Authorisation, yes, here it is, my visitor's pass.' She flashed it rapidly in front of the woman's eyes, hoping that it wouldn't be scrutinised too closely.

The woman released her hand from the telephone.

'Right.' Her tone still had a twinge of suspicion. 'Visitor's pass. I'm very busy Miss... what did you say your name was?'

Nathalie speedily searched for a name. She was certain that the woman had not had time to read it on her plastic card. 'Tanner, Elsie Tanner,' she blurted out.

'Well Miss Tanner, I suggest you go back to the reception and get your directions from there.'

Nathalie jumped at the opportunity. Surely Roszak and Barnes must have left the corridor by now. She spun around, opened the door and put her head around to get a glimpse of the corridor. It was empty.

'Thank you,' she said as a parting shot as she closed the door behind her and ran towards the stairwell. She took the stairs two at a time. There were five floors but she didn't want to bump into Rob Barnes at the elevators. Panting, she handed her badge in at reception on the ground floor and made her way to the parking lot. Joe and Billy were waiting for her.

'Did he accept your apology?'

'No, missed him. But you're probably right, let sleeping dogs...'

Joe looked mystified. Nathalie grinned. 'I'm sure you have that expression over here. Oh, and while we're on cultural differences, have either of you watched old reruns of *Coronation Street*?'

Joe and Billy looked at her as if she was mad.

'Never mind,' chuckled Nathalie. 'As long as the woman on the fifth floor is as puzzled as you are I'm okay.'

The last of the Californian sunshine leaked through the high-rise blocks of the university campus. Nathalie looked at her watch. It would be the early hours in London but around breakfast time in Surabaya. She would call Tom from the hotel. Medical Films had arranged all the paperwork and for a courier to pick up the media drives so all she had to do was to say goodbye to the crew and head off towards Wilshire Boulevard. The walkways were lined with students, folders underarm, returning to their residences. In the warmth of the evening, Nathalie envied them. Nostalgic perhaps, but it reminded her of those carefree university days without responsibility and accountability. Now she had decisions to make and a film to produce. Should she hang around and discover if she could find anything else about Rob Barnes or would it be wiser to make herself scarce and travel on to eastern Java to see if Tom had come up with anything to film there? Investigative documentaries were always a bit like this. A few scraps and leads but then suddenly you would get a coup. She made up her mind. If Rob Barnes spotted her on the campus there was no way that she would get a story. What that story was yet she didn't quite know. The conversation had been ambiguous and she had only heard half of it. Why would Zormax be interested in using Rob Barnes to access lethal synthetic microbes? For research perhaps. Or, the unthinkable. A means of laundering biochemical weapons for sale to a third party. No, following Tom's lead and the source of the microbes would be a better option. After all he had a laboratory worker who might be able to do some actual filming. If they could prove that the Javanese lab were manufacturing and selling these microbes to terrorists for nefarious purposes then she could tie in the Rob Barnes/Zormax connection later.

She realised that she had hardly had anything to eat since breakfast so dropped her bag off at the hotel and asked them to direct her to the nearest restaurant. The concierge recommended the Palomino, just along the Boulevard, a few metres from the hotel. He described it as 'rustic European' whatever that meant. She was so hungry that she didn't care if it was 'rustic anything', as long as they had a table. She needn't have worried, the restaurant was practically empty. She took a corner table so that she could phone Tom without drawing attention to herself and asked for a menu. Ironically the first thing on the list was a Moroccan humus and tzatziki starter, but she settled for the maple-marinated chicken salad. The descriptions of these dishes were as far from any European food she had tasted or she could imagine, rustic or not. One or two people had started to enter the restaurant. Nathalie decided to call Tom now, while she waited for her food and before it got too busy. She would ask him to find good locations where they could take clandestine shots of the laboratory exterior and arrange for a day when the lab assistant could be interviewed and they could do some undercover filming. He wouldn't have to worry about the kit and the crew, she would arrange that through Bagatelle when the office was open in a few hours' time. She took out her mobile and keyed in Tom's number. The phone rang and rang.

Sixteen

Tom opened his eyes and then closed them again. Shafts of bright light were coming through the shutters splintering into blinding rays. His body ached all over and he put his hands out to feel what he was lying on. Earth or concrete perhaps. The buzzing noise that had woken him was getting louder and more persistent. He opened his eyes again. This time more cautiously using his lids as shades. He turned away from the shutters to the inside of the room. It was stifling. He saw a shape draped across some sort of couch against the far wall. Now he remembered. They were in Gita's sister's house. He looked at his watch. 10.00 am. He'd only been asleep for three or four hours. The phone kept ringing. He rolled over and dug it out of his back pocket. It had made an indentation in his backside, reminding him that it would be the last time he would go to sleep on it.

'Hi, Tom here,' he managed to gasp, his voice rasping from the dryness in the air. 'Nathalie?'

'Thought there was something up, you took a long time to answer.'

'Sorry I was asleep.'

'Have I got the time difference wrong or something?'

'No, it's mid-morning but we've had a rough night.'

'We?'

'It's a long story.'

Nathalie took a sip from her cold beer and nodded to the waitress who was asking if she had finished her meal. 'Call's expensive but have got the time, fire away. You were going to tell me about those requisition papers you found.'

Tom's head was clearing. He now saw that there were four of them in the room. Gita's sister was on the couch, Gita on some sort

142

of mat on the floor and Nick propped up in a sitting position in the corner. He would feel worse than Tom when he woke.

'Give me a moment, I'll take this outside. Let the others sleep for a while.'

He limped to the door, still cramped from lying on the bare dusty floor. It was as hot outside as it was in. Sunlight danced in ribbons across the facing canal, but the palms were motionless in the still air. He looked down the row of shanty houses. The residents had either gone out for the day or had decided to keep in the shade, for the street was empty.

'Are you still there Nathalie?'

'Hearing you loud and clear Tom. Can't wait to hear about these papers. I think I've found another connection.'

'Oh yes, the papers. That's how we got into this mess.'

Nathalie knew better than to shout out a number of panicky questions so she just waited.

'Sorry I cut you off the other night. We had a bit of a problem.'

'No worries, I thought it was the reception.'

'No, not that sort of reception anyway. Gita, Nick and I had broken into the laboratory compound.'

'Gita?'

'Yes the lab assistant I told you about.'

'Go on.'

'Gita and I are quite small so Nick got us under the fence and told us he would follow on. It was dark but Gita knew the way so we found the admin hut and the papers that I sent you.'

Tom heard a noise from behind and turned to see Nick standing in the doorway.

'It's Nathalie.'

'Who's that Tom?' asked Nathalie.

'It's Nick, he's just woken up.'

'Can I talk to him?'

Tom handed the phone to Nick. 'She wants to talk to you.'

Nick winced as he reached out for the phone. He looked down at the bandages around his leg. Dark brown bloodstains were seeping through them.

'Hi boss. What's it like in sunny California?'

'Pretty dark at the moment Nick, it's late evening here. Tom is not exactly getting to the point. He said you're in a mess. I thought that was precisely what Geoff sent you out to avoid.'

'No damage done, I think. Could have been a lot worse.'

'Nick!'

'I just got held up. Have to lose weight. Got stuck under this bloody wire.' He rubbed his leg gingerly. 'Still got the scars to prove it. Anyway Tom and his girlfriend went on ahead and checked out the hut. Must have made a bit of noise because some runt of a guard crept up on them. Lucky for Tom I crept up on the guard. Lights out and thank you ma'am.'

'He isn't…?'

'No, he's fine, bit of a sore head but…'

Nathalie breathed a sigh of relief and then confronted her next concern. 'Did he recognise any of you?'

'We don't think so.'

'You don't *think* so.'

'I'll give it to him, Tom was pretty quick. Just as the guard opened the door he fired his phone flash at him. The guy was putting his hands to his eyes when I bopped him. Don't think he saw a thing, and we didn't wait to ask.'

'So why so long in reporting in.'

'Ah, that's down to me I'm afraid. We spent a while making it look like attempted burglary. You know, found the safe, jemmied it open, strew money around the place. By the time we'd done that it was getting light, and I wasn't very mobile to run for it, so we hunkered down in some bushes and waited all day until it got dark again. That's why we are all exhausted. Only got back four or five hours ago.'

Nathalie drained the last of her beer. The restaurant was getting busy and it was becoming more difficult to talk.

'Okay Nick, sounds like you did your best. Put me back to Tom.'

Tom took the phone from Nick's outstretched arm. 'Hi, did you get the picture?'

'Yes Tom, because of your quick thinking we've still got a chance to shoot this location.'

'Not so sure about that Nathalie. Don't believe he recognised us and they'll probably think it a bungled burglary...' Tom paused wondering how he was going to break the news. 'I'm afraid there's another problem.'

Nathalie closed her eyes. Geoff had abandoned the Afghanistan idea and that only left two key locations. The Indonesian laboratory and Zimbabwe. She couldn't afford to lose one of these now.

'Another problem? Which is?'

'It's Gita. She's been traumatised by the whole breaking-in thing. She's absolutely refusing to take a camera into the laboratory and even worse won't be interviewed.'

'Maybe after...'

'I've tried everything. Said we would protect her, film the interview in shadow, disguise her voice. It's no good. She is really scared. Said she's going to call in sick, make an excuse to resign.'

'You could stall her. Buy some time. See if she feels different after a day or two.'

Tom looked across at Nick who was now sitting in the dirt against the wall in front of the house. He'd already suggested this to Nick, but knew it was useless. Nick shrugged his shoulders.

'We've already bought all the time we can,' said Tom into the phone. 'Nick's policeman friend gave us forty-eight hours and that's nearly up. He said they can't turn a blind eye any longer. I think they're going to raid the laboratory this afternoon.'

'Shit,' said Nathalie. The couple in the booth opposite her turned to stare. She put up her hand in apology. 'Sorry, bad news.'

It really was bad news. She had already started to map out the programme. Undercover shots of a suspicious laboratory, paperwork showing nefarious dealings, an interview with a lab assistant explaining the dangerous nature of the microbes. Now this was all shot down in a single telephone call.

'Okay Tom. This is what we do. Go to the police station with Nick. See if you can negotiate with them to take a camera to the raid. I'm sure the police force there will have one for filming evidence. It'll be a crap camera, and Geoff will hate it, but beggars and all that. Say if we can have a copy of the footage we'll make their outfit look really good on broadcast TV.'

Tom thought for a moment, feeling slightly faint. Someone in the vicinity had started to prepare a meal. The scented smells of coconut and lemongrass stole across the veranda. He couldn't remember the last time he had eaten.

'Okay, that might just work. Nick's pretty persuasive. We'll give it a go. And if they agree, what do you want *us* to do?'

Nathalie snapped her reply. 'Go with them of course, we'll need someone to direct that police cameraman.'

✳

London's Soho district languished in the warm summer rain. Geoff pulled up his collar and ran the last few yards to the steps of Bagatelle's offices. It was early for him but Stefanie had arranged a teleconference with an international consortium concerning viewing rights. A pain in the arse but it had to be done. She greeted him with a double espresso and a warm croissant.

'Here, let me take that wet raincoat. You've time to dry off and drink this. The Italians have just called to delay the conference by half an hour.'

Geoff raised his eyebrows.

Stefanie predicted his thoughts. 'No problem though, I've rearranged with the others. They're okay about it. Give you time to look at your e-mails too. One from Nathalie a few minutes ago.'

Geoff ran a paper towel through his wet hair and took the croissant and coffee across to his desk. He switched on his computer and took a bite from the pastry as he waited for it to boot up. He hated early mornings, early for him anyway. He'd grown up with the old television production habits, start late finish late. A hangover from the days when TV broadcasts only started in the afternoon. Production meetings would tend to start late morning and then the studio directors would work late into the night. A lot different now of course. Thousands of channels, twenty-four hours a day. No such thing as standard hours. As and when needed had become the norm. Just like this bloody teleconference. Guys from all over Europe on different time zones. And now the delay. He could have had an extra half an hour in bed listening to Radio 4. The icons were now lit up on his screen and he had started to log into his e-mails when he was interrupted by the buzzer on his desk.

'Yes, don't tell me they've brought it forward again?'

Stefanie's placid voice came through the intercom. 'No Geoff, we have a visitor, wants to talk to Nathalie. I told him she's in the States but he said he was just passing and thought you might want to know some information he has.'

'Can't you take a message?'

'I suppose so but I think you would like to hear directly from him. It's Doctor Styne, you know the physician Nathalie was talking to about the Ebola virus. He has more news concerning that poor woman with memory loss.'

'I don't know why it's our problem, she just wandered in here off the street.'

'Yes, but Nathalie asked this man to report in any facts he could find out about her. She had Nathalie's card remember?' Stefanie's voice became a little more persistent. 'He's a busy man and has taken the time to come in, so I think the least we can do is to see him for a few minutes.'

Geoff knew when he was beaten. 'Oh all right, show him in,' he sighed. 'Just make sure I'm not late for that teleconference.'

Doctor Styne walked in cradling a cup of freshly brewed coffee. 'I understand Miss Thompson is away. I realise that you must be very busy but I thought I really must pass this information on.'

147

Geoff gestured to the seat the other side of his desk. 'Please sit down. No it's very kind of you to come in person.'

'Thank you Mr Sykes. I was passing a few blocks away and I thought...'

'I'm sure Nathalie will be very grateful. Now what would you like me to tell her?'

Doctor Styne sat down and placed his cup on the mat that Geoff pushed towards him. 'She was very keen to follow up on Esther Phillips.'

'Esther Phillips?'

'Yes, it's the name of the woman who stumbled into your office with memory loss. We've found her again. Although not exactly we – an associate of mine in the neurological unit.'

Geoff pulled a pad out of his desk drawer and plucked a lethally sharpened pencil from a Perspex pot. 'I'm not sure why Nathalie is so interested in this case but give me the details and I'll pass it on.'

As Styne took a sip of his coffee the aroma floated across Geoff's desk. The doctor sat back in his chair. 'At first, I must admit, I wasn't sure either but when I explain the situation that's just arisen, you may understand why she's been so keen to follow it up.'

The overhead sun had just begun to dip as the four unmarked police cars crawled slowly down the single-track road. Nick and Tom followed them in the 4x4, trying to keep their distance. Michael, Nick's policeman friend, had been adamant.

'I gave you forty-eight hours, more than I should have. Any more and it will be noticed by the top brass and I could lose my job. Besides, if it's as dangerous as we think it is we should stop it now.'

And stopping it now was what Michael was about to do. Twelve armed policemen in the lead with four guys, dressed in what looked like spacesuits, taking up the rear. The saving grace was that the unit had agreed to film the raid. Nick and Tom could come along as long as they kept out of the way. The guard at the gate looked puzzled to see the convoy.

'Passes?'

Michael held up his badge. 'This do?'

The guy in the beret with the gun over his shoulder glanced into the car to see the other heavily armed men. His only experience to date had been to wave his gun at kids and a few nosy passers-by. A threatening gesture to this lot wasn't going to work. He nervously reached for his walkie-talkie.

'Wait here, I'll call the boss.'

'You do that sonny, and while you're waiting lift that barrier or I'm afraid we will have to drive through it.'

The guard was at a loss of what to do. He looked at the barrier, then at his walkie-talkie. Michael made up his mind for him. The bull bars of his jeep crashed through the red-and-white striped obstruction.

'Tell your boss to meet us at the main entrance,' Michael shouted back, 'we've got a few questions for him.'

Nick trailed the cavalcade over the debris of the barricade and through the compound. As they pulled up at the entrance to the white painted concrete laboratory, Tom jumped out and ran towards the policeman with the camera.

'Did you get the smashing of the barrier?' he shouted.

The policeman looked at him sharply, 'I thought you were told to keep out of the way.' But it was obvious that he was enjoying this as much as Tom.

'Yeah I know, I'll just keep behind your shoulder. Two eyes better than one. If I see anything I'll just point. Okay?'

The police cameraman nodded. 'Okay, but if any shooting starts just drop on the floor and stay there. I don't want to be responsible.'

'Will do,' said Tom. 'Look over there, they're breaking into the door.'

Two officers were shattering the glass-panelled doors, swinging a heavy metal object with handles into the locked entrance. It gave way easily. Whoever had set up this institution hadn't really expected a brazen full frontal attack. The guys with the spacesuits poured in. Tom encouraged the cameraman to poke his lens through the open door to film what was going on. The laboratory workers froze. Tom couldn't see their expressions through their protective goggles but no doubt they were terrified. Calmly and methodically the white-suited policeman walked down each laboratory bench and began collecting the samples, placing them into airtight containers. Tom was startled by a loud retort from the other side of the compound. He and the photographer wheeled around to see a black Mercedes veering out of control.

'Some guy's trying to get away,' cried Nick from the seat of his 4x4. 'Jump in if you want to film the action.'

This wasn't exactly the brief that the cameraman had been given. Film the evidence, and any documents on site. Not an action-packed car chase. He hesitated, then with a glint in his eye jumped into the passenger seat next to Nick.

'Go, go, go,' he shouted. 'I think they've shot his tyres out.'

Tom nearly missed the ride as he swung into the lurching rear door of the moving vehicle. The Mercedes was now heading towards the perimeter on bare metal wheels, the rubber having been ripped off by police gunfire. The sharp spinning steel was now digging into the earth as the car left the tarmac and headed across the grass borders straight towards the exit gate. As the car came to a stop the door swung open and a suited dark-haired man leapt out and began to run. He didn't get very far. Michael had left two armed officers with the guard at the barricade. One put up his hand and told the man to stay where he was.

Tom could just about hear the conversation, which was cried out in English.

'Police, you are police? Help we are under attack from terrorists.'

'Not terrorists, this is a raid. Keep your hands where we can see them and come with us. We have some questions that need to be answered.'

Nick pulled up by the broken barricade. Tom and the cameraman jumped out to film the rest of the dialogue. The man in the suit was protesting loudly.

'Raid? What do you mean raid ? We are a legitimate biotech laboratory. Manufacturing microbial products for antibiotic research. What you are doing is dangerous, these microbes must be kept in sterile conditions. If they get out you will be responsible, I'll sue, tell the press, this is outrageous!'

Tom watched the cameraman film the rant. The guy sounded convincing. What if he had got it wrong? What if this laboratory really was a bona fide outfit? Not only would they have no film, he doubted that he would have a job. He was so wrapped up in his thoughts that Nick's hand on his shoulder made him jump.

'If you've got all that, I think we should head for the Records office. There's some stuff in there that should tell us whether this snake in the grass is lying or not.'

Seventeen

The London streets always appeared to resemble a toy town to Nathalie after the wide boulevards of Los Angeles. The cramped terraced Edwardian facades were like miniatures compared to the steel and glass towers of downtown LA. But they had their charm, and she was glad to be going back into her Fulham flat. And, for once, the sun was shining, filtering through the leaves of the trees lining Munster Road. She took a left turn and dragged her trolley bag across the broken pavements towards her small maisonette. She was exhausted. Geoff had called at the crack of dawn to give her the change of plan. She'd managed to get an eleven o'clock United flight from LA, but with a gruelling fifty-minute stop in Chicago. All in all, it had taken her more than thirteen hours. At least she would have time to regroup, wash and change her clothes before setting off to Zimbabwe rather than go the circuitous route via Surabaya. Geoff didn't sound at all pleased. 'Things are falling apart, get back here and sort it all out,' were his actual words. How she was going to do that she didn't know. From what he had told her the Surabaya thing was out of her control. She had less than an hour to unpack and shower before their arranged meeting. With a bit of luck he would have calmed down before then.

✻

She was greeted in Bagatelle's reception by Stefanie with raised eyebrows.

'Good morning Nathalie. I expect you're shattered but I'm afraid you're going to have to steel yourself for one last lap. Our esteemed leader is not in the best of humour.'

Nathalie smiled. 'Not for the first time Stefanie. Don't worry, I'll use the old whiteboard trick.'

Stefanie looked somewhat nonplussed.

'When he goes into a tirade, I just use the whiteboard to map out a programme plan,' Nathalie explained. 'He loves it. Works every time.'

'Rather you than me Nathalie, good luck.'

Geoff didn't offer her a coffee. A really bad start.

'I've had the commissioning editor on the phone again this morning. The channel would like an updated programme proposal and a broadcast schedule.'

'As you know, it's still in a state of flux. You know that, they know that. It's the name of the game.'

Geoff's eyes were dull and his voice flat. 'The name of the game is that they are pulling the funds if we don't turn up with your wild promises.'

Nathalie flinched in her chair. '*My* wild promises?'

'You're the one that put the proposal together.'

'Yes, under your instructions. You're the one who gave me the leads, said that it could be the investigative documentary of the year.'

'I hire you because you turn these so-called leads into great programmes. Not this time apparently according to the fracas in Surabaya.'

Nathalie stood up, put both her hands on Geoff's desk and stared him out. 'Oh it's a fracas is it? Me, trying to get your rookie assistant to direct a police camera shoot from the other side of the world. What else do you expect me to do?'

Geoff gestured for her to sit down. 'Okay, okay. Let's start again. I realise that you can't be in two places at once. But Bagatelle's reputation depends on high-end professional photography. Not wobbly scope and some ill-lit iPhone shots.'

Nathalie stayed standing. 'I didn't see any other option. Tom's inexperienced; Nick's great in a tight corner but no photographer. Our prime interviewee backs out and it's all about to kick-off. Yes, if I was on the spot maybe I could have got a professional crew and followed the raid. But I wasn't was I?' Nathalie pointed to the project file on the desk. 'And talking about raids, you said that you were expecting an e-mail from Tom with an update.'

Geoff flicked open the cover and handed her a long e-mail printout. 'Some good news and some bad news.'

'Are you going to tell me or do I have to sit and read all of this?'

'Read it later for the detail, but in essence the good news is that the police say they have footage covering the whole raid.'

'And the bad news?'

'They won't release the footage until they've reviewed it and see what's required for evidence. Don't want to compromise the legal proceedings.'

'But they'll let us have it when they've finished?'

'Yes, Nick's pretty sure about that, but there's another problem.'

Nathalie waited.

'The CEO of the lab who they've got in for questioning is still protesting his innocence. Says that the laboratory is synthesising microbes for selling to pharma companies who want bugs to test their new antibiotics.'

'And do they believe him?'

'No, but proving it is another matter. They have to get scientific experts to find out what sort of bugs they are making and see if the documents tying those bugs to any pharma companies are kosher.'

'That would make good TV, if they can make it stick.' Nathalie walked up to the whiteboard which made up part of Geoff's office wall. 'I still think we've got a great film here. The deadline may be a problem but you've sorted that before.' Nathalie grabbed a marker pen. 'Especially if you can persuade them that the story is worth waiting for.'

By lunchtime the board was a maze of interconnecting arrows and locations. Nathalie was right, Geoff came into his own when plotting a programme narrative. At the centre of the web was a circle around the words Zimbabwe and WEXA. On the periphery, the Javanese laboratory and its possible connection to Rob Barnes and Biomedivac. Both Zimbabwe and Java had a signpost towards Morocco. Zormax was highlighted with a question mark. The more they scribbled the more they realised that the storyline had yet to be drawn. Geoff pulled up two armchairs in front of the board. They sat back and stared at it for several minutes before he broke the silence.

'Your hunch about Rob Barnes and Zormax. Where does that take us?'

'A difficult one. He's definitely doing something covert with that company, and Tom found his name in the Indonesian lab. Could be industrial espionage. Sourcing microbes to test out antibiotics or antivirals for a rival company. If that's the angle, we could talk about the profits pharma companies make from selling drugs to countries who want a defence against bioterrorism. Or, worst case scenario, they're laundering microbial weapons for terrorists.'

'Sounds a bit extreme.'

'I know, but people like WEXA would be all too pleased to get their hands on these bugs.'

'Okay, so where does WEXA fit into our scenario?'

'They may be an incongruous group, but I think they're serious. They really would like to give the West a dose of African disease. Show us what it's like for dumping second-rate drugs into their pharmacies.'

'We have Biomedivac's vaccine for that?'

'Not if you read some of Rob Barnes' papers. Not as good as it's cracked up to be. Anyway, let's hope it won't need to be tested.'

'We'll need some footage to see how far they'll go though.'

'I've been thinking about that. Same old documentary dilemma. How far can we let them go before informing the authorities?'

Geoff got out of his chair and walked towards the board. He underlined the WEXA acronym. 'This is the core of our programme, without it not much else stands up. And, as I keep saying, without any proof we are wasting the authorities' time. We've got to go as far as we can. You've been doing this long enough to know when we've got to blow the whistle.'

There was a knock at the door and Stefanie walked in holding a plate of sandwiches. She looked at the whiteboard and grinned.

'Thought you might be hungry. Especially as Mr Sykes has dragged you halfway round the world without any sleep.'

Geoff turned around in his chair. 'I hope some of those are for me.'

Stefanie placed the plate on his desk. 'Oh, I expect she will share them with you, if you're nice to her of course.' She closed the door of his office softly behind her.

✳

Tom was lying on the bamboo bench under the veranda trying to keep in the shade. Across the vibrant green rice fields he could see the twin volcanoes in the distance topped with clouds. If he didn't know better it would have looked like smoke coming from their cones. The aromas of sesame oil and fish sauce drifted from the door behind him. Michael had insisted that they moved closer to Surabaya. Closer meant his uncle's house in a small village on the outskirts. Rafi from the Sun Hotel had been downcast.

'We can make you more comfortable here Mr Tom,' he had pleaded. 'It's very primitive there, only a few wooden huts and a well.'

Tom was looking at that well now. A woman in a brightly coloured sarong with a baby on her back was slowly drawing water into a bucket. A gentle breeze touching the surrounding palms accompanied the leisurely squeak squeak of the hand pump. If this was primitive, it couldn't be more idyllic. Michael's uncle, at least he said it was his uncle, he seemed to have thousands of them, was the ultimate host. Against many protests he had given up his bed to Tom and Nick, in place of the very bench Tom was reclining on now. Breakfast had been mango and papaya laced with lime and now he was preparing lunch. Somehow, through the grapevine, locals had

156

heard that Tom was fond of gado gado, which was true, but not for seven days in a row. But after what he'd been through in the last few days Tom wasn't going to mention that now.

Nick and Michael's uncle appeared in the doorway carrying plates of colourful food.

'Move over,' said Nick. 'Take one of these, you look like you need it; put some muscle on that skinny body.'

Tom took a plate from him. It looked vibrant; bright green cabbage, eggs and fried yellow tofu topped with what looked like a splash of tomato sauce.

'Thanks Nick and thanks Mr Chandrah.' He still couldn't get used to calling this wizened walnut-faced man Deddy as he had been asked to.

The old man gave a slight bow and returned to the interior of the hut. Nick sat down on the bench, his large thighs pushing Tom even further into the corner.

'I've been doing some phoning around. Bloody amazing isn't it, you can't get a good signal in Mile End, but out here in the jungle its five bars. Anyway, after your boss gave you that earful, filming with toy cameras and all that, I've managed to get you a professional crew. Not quite Hollywood standards but they do the local music videos here so can't be that bad.'

'Professional crew? But what's the point. All the action's over. And who's going to pay for it anyway?'

'Thought you were a film-maker. Of course the action isn't over. The police are doing a huge forensics job. Why do you think Michael invited us to be closer to Surabaya?'

'Yeah but that's all done at the police station. How are we ever going to get access to all of that?'

'Funny you should say that. I've just had a long chat with Michael too. He's agreed to bring out some photographs of the paperwork. And be interviewed, as long as you don't broadcast it before he sees it first.'

Tom looked at Nick with amazement. 'And the authorities will give us access to the police station?'

'Not exactly, this is between Michael and myself. The shoot has to be done here, don't think the authorities will know much about it.' Nick looked at the massive timepiece on his wrist. 'The crew should be here within the hour.'

Tom stared at his plate of gado gado, trying to get his head around all of this. 'O-kaay, so Michael and the crew are coming here.'

Nick had started to dig into his food, so his next words were spoken between a mouthful of bean shoots and peanut sauce. 'That's about it.'

'But Geoff will go ballistic. I'm not a film director. I was told to set it up and wait for Nathalie and, like I said, who's going to pay for all this?'

'Ah, Geoff will be fine. Once he's seen some proper footage from a real camera. And how difficult can it be? Just tell the guy where to point it.'

Tom let out a loud scream.

'Hey, it's not that bad, prices are diddly squat out here. This crew seem so keen that they might even do it for nothing.'

Tom didn't reply. He just sat there eyes wide, frantically waving his hands in front of his open mouth.

'Hey, you okay?'

Nick could just about make out the answer through Tom's swelling lips.

'Water, give me water. It's not ketchup, it's bloody chilli!'

The film crew turned up on time. There were four of them in a rusty shooting brake. One of them introduced himself to Tom.

'Hi, I'm Kevin, your cameraman,' he said in English with hardly a trace of an accent. 'This is Ahmad, Arief and Henry; sound, sparks and grip. Where would you like us to set up?'

Nick stepped off the veranda to shake Kevin's hand. 'I'm Nick, friend of Michael. I'm afraid you won't get much out of Tom at the moment, stupid bastard's swallowed a mouthful of neat chilli. Can hardly get his mouth open, his tongue has swollen so much. His arms are okay though so he will be able to point you to the right bits.'

Kevin didn't seem at all perturbed by this mute film director. 'That's all right, the others don't speak English anyway so I'll have to translate. Just let me know the sort of thing you want and I'm sure you'll be happy with the result. It's for the BBC isn't it?'

Nick knew this was the ace he had up his sleeve. Michael had told him that these guys would do practically anything to get on British television. That's why they were prepared to do this shoot for peanuts.

'Oh yes, and all the good documentary channels in the States,' he said, putting his arm around Kevin's shoulders. 'Make sure you give Tom your names, don't want to get the spelling wrong on the credits.'

Michael arrived as the crew were unpacking their gear. He was wearing a crisp white open-necked shirt and held a satchel of documents in his hands. Nick explained Tom's demise and Michael fell about laughing.

'Plusn sipp offer err,' mumbled Tom.

'I think he wants you to sit over there for your interview,' said Nick, pointing to a chair on the veranda and trying to keep a straight face at the same time.

Kevin leapt to their aid. 'Ah, interview; if you want it there we'll have to get some lighting up. I know it's outside but we'll have to balance that shade with this sunlight. It's pretty fierce so we'll need a few watts.'

Tom suddenly felt thankful for his condition. He'd never directed a film shoot before and this guy sounded like he knew what he was doing. Now he wouldn't sound like a fool. He could just sit there and point, and if they didn't understand him then he was sure that Kevin would sort it out. He put his thumbs up towards the crew and sat down to write a few questions that he thought would be useful to ask Michael.

The crew worked like clockwork. Lamp stands were erected, the tripod positioned on the veranda, and a microphone was placed on

159

a long metal arm. Then Arief started to shout something at Kevin from the other side of the hut.

'He wants to know where he can tap into the power for the lights,' he explained to Tom.

Tom shrugged.

'We don't have any power,' intervened Nick. 'Not that sort anyway, unless you can run your lights off butane gas.'

'Okay, no problem,' said Kevin, looking not in the least perturbed. 'We'll get a generator.'

The generator looked more like a rusty baked potato machine than an appliance that created electricity. Where it came from Tom couldn't say, but here it was wheeled out of the surrounding jungle.

'We need some flags,' said Kevin, and shouted orders at Henry, in what Tom could only guess was Malay. Why they needed flags God only knew.

He was answered twenty minutes later. The flags were flat pieces of plywood, painted black and mounted onto stands. Their purpose, to give some shade to the camera lens and some of the lights. A pain in his mouth was little price to pay for not sounding a complete idiot.

'Amazing isn't it,' said Nick drawing up alongside. 'Ask for this stuff in the West and there'd be requisition orders, stock checks and transport delays, yet here a couple of guys run off into the undergrowth and come back with a time machine and some handmade shades. Developing country? Who's developing what I'd like to know?'

Kevin declared that he was ready for the interview. Nick said he would read out Tom's questions. Kevin asked Michael not to look into the lens and pretend that he wasn't there.

'Just chat to Nick as if there are only the two of you. Try not to interrupt and overlap his question though, as it will be difficult to use that in the edit.'

Tom took a mental note of these instructions. Next time his mouth might be able to work.

The generator was fired up and the lights came on, but this time there came a shout from Ahmad.

'What's up?' asked Nick.

'I should think that's obvious,' replied Kevin. 'There's no way we can record sound with the noise from that generator. It sounds like a B-2 bomber.'

Another twenty minutes went by whilst fifty metres of cable were found and the generator, encased in huge sheets of Styrofoam, was placed as far from the veranda as they could put it. After all of this Tom started to wonder whether he really did want to be a budding film director, but when things had settled down the interview went really well. Michael was a natural. He described his suspicions about the laboratory near Sidoarjo and explained how an assistant working there, who didn't want to be named, began to confirm these suspicions. The microbes, which they had obtained from the raid, were very dubious and didn't appear to tie in with the export orders. These bugs, if released into the population, could be very dangerous.

At the end of the interview Kevin repositioned the lights and moved the camera to over Michael's shoulder.

'If you thumb through those documents, I'll take some big close-ups.' He looked up at Tom. 'You could use them as stand-alone shots or cut them into his interview so you could edit the soundtrack.'

Tom nodded vigorously, trying to work out how this would assist the editing. Thank goodness he had been given Kevin. This guy was a real saviour. Once more he made a mental note of the technique. The 'cutaways' as Kevin was calling them were not just giving the viewer more information, they would allow the editor to shorten bits of interview without the audience even knowing.

'Great,' said Kevin as he finished the last shot. 'We'll just check those back before we strike the lights. Do you want to do any GVs?'

Now that was one term that Tom had heard of. General Views. They were used to set scenes, as backgrounds to voice-overs, and just attractive pictures to give atmosphere. It sounded fun. He scribbled down some ideas on a piece of paper. Kevin raised his eyebrows, they were a bit ambitious. *Crowds of villagers walking through the marketplace. One villager stops Michael to ask him a question.*

But Kevin was not to be defeated. He asked Michael's uncle to wake the sleeping villagers from their siestas and to meet in the empty marketplace. The bemused gathering waited in a huddle. Kevin marked a line in the dirt and divided the crowd into two groups facing each other. He gently cajoled the elderly to stand at the front, and the young and the ones on bicycles and carts to wait at the rear. He positioned the camera to focus on the spot just above his eyeline.

'Place yourself about halfway back in one of the groups,' he asked Michael. 'Now, when I say "Tindakan" I want you all to walk or ride at normal pace towards each other. Got that?'

By the looks on their faces some did and some didn't, but when Kevin shouted the order, they all began to move. Kevin bent down to look through the eyepiece. He switched the camera on and to his delight watched a throng of villagers milling around in the marketplace. And on cue Michael walked into shot and was detained by a young man who held him there in deep conversation.

'And, cut!' exclaimed one jubilant cameraman.

Eighteen

Addis Ababa International Airport at six-thirty in the morning isn't the most congenial place to set up a small portable office. Especially if you have had hours on a plane with only fitful sleep. Nathalie had left Heathrow at nine o'clock in the evening with a head full of instructions and a pile of notes to go through. She had decided to try to sleep and put everything on hold until her four-hour stopover. She wouldn't arrive in Harare until around midday, and wouldn't be getting any respite then, so that was the plan anyway. The trouble with best laid plans is that they often go awry so here she was, exhausted, perched on a plastic waiting-room seat, trying to process all the information she had been given. She placed her hand luggage on the chair next to her. There was one good thing about six-thirty in the morning. The in-transit hall was practically empty. She undid the zip and pulled out her laptop and project file. While the laptop was firing up she glanced at the call-sheet. Stefanie had done a good job in a short time. The Holiday Inn in Harare had been booked and a meeting set up with the local film crew on the afternoon of her arrival. She only hoped that she could stay awake long enough to convey any sense to them. Her difficult meeting with Geoff had ended well. This was helped by the fact that a message arrived from Nick in Java proclaiming a triumph of photography and a promise of great action footage from the Indonesian police force. Nick was always the optimist and his e-mail sounded pretty good.

...high-quality professional footage of the local police force investigation and dramatic live-action of the laboratory raid. Credible evidence emerging concerning illegal and dangerous microbe manufacturing.

Geoff had made an instant reply asking Nick to stay on in Surabaya, to follow the progress of the investigation and, in Geoff's words:

Make sure you get your huge mitts on that footage!

And Nick would know that Geoff wasn't prone to exclamation marks.

In the same e-mail Tom was asked to take the next flight, or flights as it happened, to Harare to meet up with Nathalie. Nathalie looked at his schedule, it was worse than hers. Nearly twenty-four hours, with stopovers in Singapore and Johannesburg on the way. He was also checked into the Holiday Inn but she didn't expect to see him until the next morning. A *bing bong* from the departures board made her look up, but her onward flight was yet to appear. She looked at her watch, barely 7.00 am. It would be five in London, too early to make the call that she was anxious to make. As her meeting with Geoff had ended he suddenly remembered a message he had for her. A Doctor Styne had popped into the office to see Nathalie. The woman with transient global amnesia had now been found again. Her name was Esther Phillips. Apparently she was regaining some of her memory. She had been on some sort of drug trial that may have affected her recall. They were still trying to establish what the trial was about and where it took place. Esther was keen to thank Nathalie for her help in getting her to hospital. When Nathalie had exploded and demanded why Geoff hadn't told her this before, he looked genuinely surprised and wondered what all the fuss was about. And Nathalie had done just that on the first leg of her flight, wondered what it was all about. How on earth had that woman got hold of her business card? It had been too late to visit Esther before her trip but she was anxious to know the details and couldn't wait to talk to her.

Whiffs of breakfast were starting to trickle across the hall. The coffee shops and restaurants were opening up for business. Nathalie had turned down the offerings on the plane; first, she was trying to establish a normal sleep pattern and second, it looked inedible. Croissants and pastries were becoming international fare and there was little the airport could do to ruin those so she made her way to the nearest food outlet. She was the only customer and there was plenty of space to instal her laptop and lay out her papers. She nibbled at the croissant whilst tapping in her notes. The priority was to film the WEXA group under the guise of the immunisation film without drawing too much attention to themselves. The first obstacle would be to take in the confidence of the film crew. Lloyd had already checked them out and they seemed a pretty broad-minded bunch. A couple of them had got into trouble with the authorities some months back for so-called anti-establishment programming. It might not be a matter of worrying whether they would be politically against the exercise but more that they didn't want to get burned twice. She would have to tread carefully but in her past experience crews tended to leap at the opportunity to film hard-edged footage. Too many of them had spent hours in corporate offices or factory production lines churning out boring images and pointless interviews. She scheduled the WEXA part of the programme as 'filming local colour and interviews'. Any official studying her itinerary would be none the wiser. Two days had been allocated for the immunisation shoot in Shurugwi district. Although she would have liked to get the WEXA material in the can as soon as possible she had decided to schedule it for the second day. Her entourage would be all over them for the first day, fascinated by the ins and outs of a professional film shoot. By the second they would realise that it was a lot of standing around and setting up of lights and tripods. Most people let them get on with it by then. Lloyd had arranged for their WEXA contacts to be in Shurugwi and, for some of Bagatelle's dollars, had commandeered a couple of huts in the compound. It shouldn't be difficult for Nathalie to escape for a couple of hours to film scenes with some of the so-called villagers to get their opinion on the immunisation outreach programme, or so she was persuading herself anyway.

The coffee shop was filling up. A man balancing a hot mug of tea and a plate of pastries stared irritably at her. There were still a few other empty tables but it was evident that he wanted to sit at this one. She shuffled her papers into a pile and made room. He sat down without a word placing his steaming drink within centimetres of Nathalie's laptop. She was reluctant to pack all her stuff up and move to another place so she just nudged her laptop towards the edge of the table and tried to concentrate on her next task. There was a file of correspondence from Lloyd that Stefanie had printed out for her. A lot of it referred to his meetings with Temba Murauzi whilst she was in America. Unfortunately it seemed with each meeting Temba was getting colder and colder feet. She gleaned that he had visited the Biomedivac Moroccan plant earlier in the year. He had won a prize and it was some sort of exchange scheme with the university. It didn't seem as if Lloyd had got much more out of him on this topic. Initially when Lloyd had suggested Bagatelle Films could arrange a second visit as part of a scientific film he appeared interested. Now, it seemed that with each e-mail he was backing off, or at least becoming less enthusiastic. Lloyd had surmised that Temba was worried about the publicity the film would give him in his homeland. Lloyd also had a theory about this. When doing some background checks on the guy he had heard that Temba had frequented gay clubs. These were not only few and far between in Harare but also highly illegal. The homophobic laws in Zimbabwe had criminalised this activity for the last decade. Men could even get arrested for holding hands. If Lloyd's intuition was right then the last thing Temba would want was attention being drawn to himself to the wrong authorities. He thought that Nathalie would have a better chance of encouraging him to take part, explain the distribution of the programme and perhaps excite him more about the scientific content of the project. Nathalie thought about this for a while. Her knowledge of pharmacology wasn't that great, especially if she was going to persuade an expert. Her researcher, Tom, on the other hand had a degree in microbiology, she was sure they would speak the same language. And here came her dilemma. From the moment she met him she could tell Tom's sexual orientation. She felt slightly disturbed about her own internal debate. Would one gay guy relate more to another gay guy than anyone else? Or was that a weirdly prejudiced thing to think? Would she as a woman be better at persuading another woman than a man? She was brought up with a jolt by the man next to her nearly spilling his drink on her laptop as he rose to catch his plane.

'Excuse me,' she said sarcastically.

He walked away without even looking at her.

'And you have a nice day too,' she called after him.

She turned back to her notes. The interruption had cleared her head. Of course Tom was the right person to talk to him. It was nothing to do with their sexuality. Tom knew about bugs and that's what the film would be about, initially anyway. If it came up that Temba was worried about the publicity then Tom could tell him that it wouldn't be aired in Zimbabwe. She hadn't known Tom long but from their short meetings she found him a gentle, amenable sort of guy. If anyone could persuade Mr Murauzi to take part, it would be Tom. She logged on to the airport WiFi system and sent a note to Lloyd asking him to set up a meeting. Despite the long wait in this holding area she didn't want to become complacent and miss her next connection. She turned to her flight itinerary. The Ethiopian Airlines flight from Addis Ababa to Harare was due to take off at nine twenty-three, with the schedule claiming triumphantly 'seating with above average legroom'. Nathalie, who was below five foot four, was not impressed and began wondering what 'average legs' looked like. She checked her flight number against the boarding gate that was now showing on the departures board, packed up her stuff and trudged wearily out of the in-transit lounge.

✳

'Welcome back Miss Nathalie,' said Manny with a big smile, his large out-reached hands taking her bags.

It had been raining. One of those short sharp warm late summer downpours. The pavements were shiny with water, the sun steaming off the surface.

'Thank you Manny,' said Nathalie. 'I assume...my people have checked me in and prepaid again,' she continued, nearly spilling out the word Bagatelle in her tiredness.

'Of course Miss Nathalie, we've given you your same room and I've left a glass of cool juice to refresh you on your arrival. Would you also like me to send up some lunch?'

'No, thank you Manny the juice will be fine. I've got to rush out to a meeting, so after I've had a quick shower I would be grateful if you would ring for a taxi.'

'Certainly Miss Nathalie, I'll take this to your room and you just dial zero when you're ready. I'll have a taxi waiting before you can reach the lobby.'

Nathalie knew that in Harare this promise wouldn't exactly be watertight but she accepted his offer with a smile and let him lead her to the room.

Nathalie was right about the taxi. She called down as soon as she stepped out of the shower but she had to wait in the lobby for at least twenty minutes before it arrived. Although it was only a few minutes' ride to the production company near Alexandra Park she would still be late.

XXL Productions were one of the few places in Harare where you could hire crew and equipment. The problem was that they didn't have anyone capable of operating their best camera, a Canon C-300. Stefanie had suggested that they hire a lower spec camera and use one of their guys who knew how to use it but Geoff rightly said that anyone that could operate a C-300 would probably be relied on to get good pictures. Geoff was really mean with money but he strangely overcame this tic when it came to quality cinematography. The result was that they had pulled in a freelance cameraman from Victoria Falls and hired the C-300.

The taxi pulled up outside a modest looking building sporting an equally modest sign on its facade. The two Xs of XXL were composed of slashes of red but that was the last of the creative influence, otherwise it could have been the face of an accountant's office. Nathalie rang the bell. Noticing a small camera above the door she peered into it and stated her name. The door clicked open. Inside was a small square anti-room with yet another door. This had a wire-framed window inserted into it. She peered through to see an extensive lobby with a young African man sitting behind a large desk. She pushed at the door and it swung open. The young man rose to greet her.

'Ah Miss Thompson, we were expecting you earlier but no matter, Mike Jeffries has just arrived as well. I'll take you straight through.'

Mike Jeffries; Nathalie recalled the name from the call-sheet. One of the best cameramen in Zimbabwe according to the blurb. He'd driven eight hours to get here but because of the nature of the shoot had accepted a special rate. She was shown into a large meeting room with a central table surrounded by a number of upright chairs. A number of these chairs were occupied by what she assumed to be her film crew.

One of the men, a black Zimbabwean, stood up to greet her. 'Hi, I'm Canaan, I run XXL. Pleased to meet you Nathalie.'

She shook his hand and accepted the invitation to sit beside him. He introduced her to the other men in the room. Mike Jeffries, cameraman; Farai Hatendi, sound recordist; and Chris Anderson the spark. Nathalie tried not to show her concern that two of the crew were 'white Rhodesians'. She wondered what WEXA would think of that. After the formalities Canaan asked to excuse himself.

'I'm sure you guys have got a lot to talk about; Chris and Farai work for XXL so if you want any information about the company or the kit they will fill you in. Unless you particularly need me for anything I'll leave you to it.'

Nathalie waited until the door had closed behind her and sat back in her chair to address the three men.

'Hi, first of all thanks for coming to this meeting, especially you Mike; I know you've come a long way. As you know, the shoot is in two days' time, and I know it's normal to get your brief on the day but this shoot's a little bit different.'

She noticed that Chris and Farai leaned forward and put their elbows on the table at this point. These must be the two guys that had been warned for so-called subversive filming. She had checked their programme output. Mostly harmless documentaries for NGOs and charities. Nothing subversive that she could see. She hoped they wouldn't back out when they heard what she was about to say.

'Now I know my producer Geoff Sykes has spoken on the phone with Mike and given him a rough outline, but I want to make sure that you guys,' she looked directly at her potential sound recordist and sparks, 'are really on board with this.'

Farai spoke up. He had a soft lilting accent that Nathalie found quite mesmerising. 'Believe me Nathalie Thompson, if for the last five years you've been shooting films under strict censorship like we have, there is nothing more you would like to do than record something that, as you say, is "different". Chris and I have checked out your company on the internet and from what we can see you do some pretty far out stuff. You couldn't have hired a more willing crew.'

Nathalie felt a wave of relief followed by an immediate nagging concern.

'You haven't told anyone else that I'm from Bagatelle have you?'

Chris intervened. 'No, of course not. We assume that you got into the country under a pseudonym or some other pretext. If *we* are not allowed to film investigative documentaries then sure as hell our government isn't going to allow a foreigner to do it here.'

'Okay, right, but I really would like you to know what you're in for. At the end of the shoot I'll be going home. Now I'm pretty sure that we can do this without any sniff from the authorities but you live here; I need you to know the risks.'

The three men just sat in their chairs and waited.

Nathalie passed them their call-sheets. 'Here's the schedule. As you see it's under the guise of an NGO called Imunaid. Imunaid doesn't exist. As you've deduced we've created this company to gain access to film in the country. To make it work we've got to make this part of the shoot realistic. Film it as if we are really making a documentary on childhood immunisation. Also we could get some really good GVs for setting the scene in our real programme; African village life, ways in which disease could spread et cetera.'

Mike spoke up for the first time. 'And the title of this real programme?'

'There isn't one yet, but the project is going under the working title of "Bioterrorism".' She waited for the message to sink in.

Mike put his head on one side. 'Quite a change from filming bloody waterfalls,' he said quietly.

Nineteen

Tom was in a complete daze. A few months ago he would have given his eye teeth to jet around the world, now he wasn't so sure. His trip had taken nearly twenty-four hours. He had taken off and landed at three different airports in three different countries, not that he'd seen much of them. The four-hour stop in Singapore and the two-hour stop in Johannesburg were spent dragging his bag from one terminal to another and sitting in soulless airport lounges. Now he was in another, waiting for his bag to come off the carousel. He glanced at the row of international clocks on the wall. It was nearly 11.00 am Harare time. In an hour's time he was meant to be meeting Nathalie for lunch, and after that a rendezvous with this Temba guy to convince him to take part in their film. In this state he didn't think he could persuade a drowning man to take a lifebelt. He hadn't slept for nearly two days and was feeling really spaced out. Through the knot of bodies he spotted his case tumbling down the conveyor. He knew it was his, it had a large Day-Glo gaffer tape cross strapped across it. A tip given to him by Stefanie. He squeezed through the crowd, hoisted the case from the rubber rack and made his way towards the blinding sunlight streaming through the exit.

'Tom, over here.' Nathalie's voice.

He shaded his eyes and panned across the waiting crowd. No sign of her.

'Here, over here.'

His eyes, now becoming accustomed, spotted a dark-haired head bobbing up and down in the press. She pushed through the swarm of people and took his bag from him.

'Welcome to Zimbabwe,' she said. 'Follow me, I've got a cab waiting outside.'

Tom sat beside her in the taxi. His head still swimming. Glad to be out of the melée of the airport.

'You look absolutely blitzed,' said Nathalie. 'A good lunch and ten cups of espresso should put you right. I've booked just the place.'

The taxi sped north through the suburbs and towards the centre of Harare. Tom began to tell Nathalie about the laboratory raid in Surabaya but she told him to sit back and relax.

'Plenty of time for that over lunch, the ride is about half an hour so chill out and take in the city. We will both think more clearly with a bit of food inside us.'

The restaurant, claiming to be Italian, was just north of the botanical gardens; the location that Lloyd had chosen for Tom to meet Temba. It was unlike any Italian restaurant that Tom had ever visited. A vast thatch-like building was surrounded by a stream breached by the arc of a rather twee wooden bridge. Tables and parasols were scattered under the large trees. The arrangement looked rather inviting in the dappled light so they decided to eat alfresco. Nathalie ordered a margarita pizza for herself and a melanzani parmigiana with a double espresso for Tom.

She looked at her watch, 'Okay we've got a couple of hours before I have to go to the hospital to finalise the shoot tomorrow and you have to meet with Temba Murauzi. Why don't we kick off by you telling me about your Surabaya trip. I know Nick was pretty effusive but, how do I put it, Nick always looks on the bright side.'

Tom had prepared for this on his long-haul flights. He took out his notebook and methodically told Nathalie the story. His first trip to the laboratory and the dog attack, meeting Nick and eventually Gita. And finally, the laboratory raid and their filming in the village. He didn't mention about his mouth being full of chilli, only praising the cameraman for getting some really good pictures.

'Wow, I thought I had a baptism of fire on *my* first shoot,' exclaimed Nathalie. 'Seems tame after what you've been through. If Nick manages to get permission to air that police footage, with a bit of graphic manipulation it should look really good.'

Tom blushed with the praise.

'No really Tom, you've done well. Now we need to sew up this Zimbabwe part of the story.'

She told him about the arrangements with WEXA. Not guaranteed but Lloyd said it looked promising. Her meeting this afternoon was with the outreach team to finalise details about travel, accommodation and the next two days' filming. The film crew were well on board. Couldn't wait to get their teeth into clandestine documentary making. With a bit of luck they would have some telling footage in the can in two days' time. It was a pity that they had to go through the charade of an immunisation programme. The project on the ground looked really worthwhile and Nathalie felt quite guilty about taking them in.

'Will you need me on the shoot?' asked Tom expectantly.

'It depends. Let's see how your meeting with Murauzi goes. It's really important that we get this Moroccan thing, especially now you've found some sort of odd connection in Surabaya. If you need longer to get him on board then I would suggest you stay. Otherwise you could come on the shoot and help out. I could do with a good A.D.'

'A.D.?'

'Assistant director,' said Nathalie with a smile. 'I hear you've got some experience.'

The pitted and rusting sign at the entrance to the National Botanic Gardens had seen better days, as had the gardens. With a bit of tender loving care they could have been spectacular. Still, the wide open spaces and arboretums were welcome respite from the traffic in downtown Harare. Tom walked under the shade in the natural woodland. The roots of the trees were exposed as gnarled, knotted and twisted serpents but their canopies acted as biological verandas casting relieving shadows over the burned-out grass. He glanced at his tourist map. Through the Savannah, and past the odd asymmetric pyramid known as the Desert House, he would find the Auditorium. The blurb described it as a place for meetings and workshops but Lloyd had assured him that no formal events were taking place there today. After a ten-minute walk he saw it in the distance. A vast open-air structure under thatch. He hoped he would recognise Temba but Lloyd's description of a tall thin Zimbabwean with glasses was not very helpful. As he came closer he realised to his dismay that the shelter was already occupied. A photographer was lining up a wedding party for some album shots. The bride looked stunning, her bronze neck contrasting with the long white dress. The man with the camera was having difficulty in explaining the composition. One large guest was obscuring the mother of the bride and some good-natured banter was taking place.

'It's a popular location for wedding photographs.' A lightly accented voice came from behind his shoulder.

He turned to see Temba. It had to be him; tall, thin, wearing spectacles, an educated face.

'I hope I've got the right time,' said Tom. 'Lloyd said that there wasn't an event on this afternoon.'

'No you're fine, these wedding parties just turn up, they shouldn't be long.'

Tom put out his hand. 'Tom Finch, good to meet you.'

Tom felt a gentle hand press into his. 'Good to meet you too Tom.'

The two men strolled under the thatched canopy of the auditorium which shielded them from the direct sunlight. As Temba had suggested the party were now moving off to another location. He pointed to one of the large wooden pillars.

'Let's sit over there and we can talk.'

They walked over to a large piece of coconut matting, presumably left there by some convention or other. Temba squatted down cross-legged and invited Tom to do the same. Tom put down his bag, sat and leaned against the pillar.

'I don't know what Lloyd's told you but I don't think I want to do this,' opened Temba.

'I can understand that,' said Tom. 'I'd probably feel exactly the same but I've just been asked to come and have a chat with you. Could you help me out here?'

Temba made a slight shrug of his shoulders.

Tom reached into his bag and took out a notebook. 'I'm new to this game, even a bit of information would help.'

'Such as?'

'This Biomedivac company, how do you know them?'

'That's an easy one. I won this competition, pharmacologist of the year, huh. Anyway the prize was an exchange with a scientist from a top manufacturing plant in Africa. I would spend several weeks a year working on some of their stuff and one of their employees would lecture at the university about the real world. There were several companies involved in the project. I'd been to South Africa and Kenya so I chose Morocco. Sounded an interesting place.'

'And Biomedivac's plant's there?'

'Yeah, different companies in different countries, just happened to be them.'

'How long were you there?'

'Oh a couple of weeks I think. They really liked my work; I'd done a thesis on Ebolavirus glycoprotein in E. coli. Uh sorry glycoprotein is...'

'Yes I know what glycoprotein is, I did a microbiology degree.'

'Oh yes, Lloyd did tell me. Anyway they liked the stuff so much that they wanted me to go back to collaborate some more.'

'On Ebola?'

'That and other stuff. The idea is to link the R & D side with manufacturing.'

Tom scribbled a note in his book. 'What sort of other stuff?'

'Oh this and that, can't say too much, it's supposed to be confidential.'

From the askance expression on Temba's face Tom could see that he wasn't going to get much more on this topic. He repositioned himself to get more comfortable. 'So if you're going back there and we could get you in with the big cheese, I would have thought the filming would do your career some good.'

'It's not my career I'm worried about. You have no idea what it's like to be one of us in Zimbabwe.'

'One of us', thought Tom, what a strange expression. One that he hoped had gone out of currency a long time ago.

'I am right about that?' said Temba, looking at him out of the corner of one eye.

'I don't see what making the film has got to do with . . . with that,' said Tom making a face. 'I would have thought as a scientist, an African scientist, you could do some good by talking about antivirals, as a protection for populations as well as an antidote to bioterrorism. From what I've read your knowledge of adenoviral vectors and EBOV glycoproteins is up with the top researchers in the world. Surely this is your one chance to spread the word.'

'Wow, quite a speech Tom, and very complimentary, and it sounds like you've done your homework on some of my papers. But you live in the UK. Our laws are very different here. I have to be very careful. This publicity could turn on me.'

'I don't see how. I doubt if the programme will ever get aired here. And even if some government official got to see it, we are hardly going to publicise your private life. What's different in talking in a film than giving your lectures?'

'I suppose if you put it like that. It's just that I don't like drawing attention to myself. Have to live two sorts of lives you know.'

The shadow of the pillar was lengthening and running into the grassland beyond their shelter. Tom got up to stretch his legs. He stared into the distance. The high-rises of Harare leaked through the foliage. A grey backdrop to the plant life of the park. Of course he knew. He was one of the lucky ones, born in the right decade in a metropolitan city and now with a job in the media. Not one of his colleagues had turned a hair. How different it must be for Temba in Zimbabwe. Was he doing the right thing to persuade the guy to stick his neck out?

'So how does it work here?' Tom paced up and down under the auditorium roof. 'Do you have a community? Meeting places? I mean, I know it's illegal but things must happen.'

Temba got to his feet. 'Of course. There are places we can go. Sometimes it's convenient for the authorities to turn a blind eye. Often money changes hands. Other times, at a whim, they can raid the places and arrest people. It can get quite brutal. I've been fortunate, moved around, have a few friends that belong to what you might call the intellectual set. I can introduce you to some of them if you like.'

'Yeah, I would like that. I'm asking you to come into my world, why shouldn't I come into yours?'

'You free this evening?'

Tom remembered what Nathalie had said. 'Do what you can to get this guy on board.' 'Yeah sure. Where should we meet?'

'The last venue was just south of here near the golf club, but it moves about so I'll need to check.'

'Check?'

'Yeah, we use social media, safer that way.' Temba pulled out his mobile phone. 'Give me a minute to find the address.'

✳

The chief medical officer was looking with irritation at his watch. Joseph Karasa was meant to have arrived ten minutes ago. Nathalie used the hiatus in the proceedings to introduce her cameraman, Mike Jeffries, to Nurse Sue Jones. She had asked him to the meeting to assess what kit they might need for the locations. Now he was here she was really pleased that he had come from outside the district. No history there. Sue Jones seemed really impressed with the towering presence of Mike and they fell into conversation about landscapes and cinematography. Nathalie was glad to see they were getting along, she needed all the cooperation she could on this trip.

Joseph Karasa entered the room nonchalantly and ignored the daggers being thrown at him from the chief officer's eyes. He put his briefcase on the table and took the empty chair.

'I must apologise for being a little late,' he said softly. 'An emergency in A&E. I'm afraid the child died.'

There was an awkward silence around the table. Even the chief medical officer cast his eyes down for a while. Sue Jones broke the atmosphere.

'So sorry,' she said. 'I hope you have left someone with the family.'

'No family,' said Joseph.

'Oh,' Nurse Jones appeared uncomfortable for a moment before regaining composure.

'Work must go on I suppose. This programme for instance, will save the lives of many children.'

Nathalie felt the atmosphere in the room and intervened to support Nurse Jones.

'And that's why we're here. And again I must thank you for letting us intrude on your outreach programme. I must warn you that filming can be a little intrusive but I'm sure when you see the results you'll know that it's been worth it.'

'Intrusive?' The chief medical officer was back to his normal self.

Nathalie groaned inwardly, she should have known better. 'Oh there's no need to be concerned, we won't interfere with any of your procedures or anything. It's just that we sometimes need some time to set up lighting and position our cameras. Occasionally Mike and I will ask people to repeat a few things but this won't be when any serious care is going on.'

'Good, as long as they are allowed to get on with their jobs. I'm afraid I won't be coming on the, what do you call it, "shooting"? I'm going to leave you in the safe hands of Nurse Jones. Before you set up your things I would ask you to ask permission first.'

'Of course,' said Nathalie. 'Very good shooting depends on full cooperation and agreement between both parties. As you've heard Sue, Mike is very experienced and we'll do our best to keep you in the loop at all times.'

Nurse Jones smiled at Mike.

Nathalie was feeling good. She had breathed a sigh of relief when she'd heard the medical officer wasn't going to be nosing around.

Now it seemed as if Mike had Sue Jones eating out of his hand. Things were looking up.

'Now, I understand that Joseph, it's all right if I call you that isn't it?'

Joseph nodded.

'I understand that Joseph will be leading the team and procuring the present vaccines. Is that right?'

Joseph nodded again.

'Well what would be most helpful for us is for you to outline step by step the procedures you take. Where you go first, what the locations look like, what transport you use. The reason for this is that we need to plan our days so we can get the most footage out of the trip and to be able to tell the full story of the programme. Also Mike here needs to know what lights and power to bring. For instance, I believe some of the places don't have electricity and we may need a small generator.'

Nathalie had to lean forward to catch Joseph's hushed reply.

'We begin at the District Medical Centre. It's an L-shaped building with a veranda supported by metal poles. I believe the scene you will want to film there is how we take the vaccines from the fridge and place them in the cool box for the outreach jeep.' Nathalie was just about to ask him about the room but he anticipated her. 'The fridge is in a very small windowless room that's lit by fluorescents, but we have electric points if you want to add some more light.'

This was rare for Nathalie, someone appreciating what they really wanted.

'Go on,' she encouraged. 'How long does it take to drive the vaccines to the outposts?'

'About three hours, most of it on rough track. That's why we need a four-wheel drive. It's also useful to be a bit of a mechanic; it is known to break down.'

Nathalie's filming instincts jumped to the fore.

'That would make a good scene for us. Showing someone repairing the jeep. It would demonstrate how difficult it is to get this stuff to the kids.' Out of the corner of her eye she noticed the medical officer becoming aggravated. 'I mean we wouldn't hold you up much, we could fake the repair. If you are looking for donations this is just the thing we need. "Help buy a jeep for the programme", that sort of thing.'

Her natural enthusiasm carried the rest of the meeting. Mike said he had all the information he needed. Sue Jones and Joseph Karasa seemed happy and, best of all, the chief medical officer had given his blessing. The shoot was on and she had paved the way for her covert filming on the second day. As she packed her bag she couldn't resist sending a quick text to Tom.

Any progress?

Tom's reply came within seconds.

Working on it. Out this evening, don't wait up.

Enigmatic to say the least. She hoped that she hadn't put him in yet more danger.

Twenty

The club was not what Tom was expecting. From the exterior it appeared to be a coffee shop. Blinds down, a 'Closed' sign on the door. He texted Temba as instructed and waited outside. A few minutes later a young suited man opened the door and, checking the message on his mobile phone, let him in. It didn't look like a nightclub. Scattered tables and chairs were pushed back against the wall and along one side was a bar that was obviously used in the daytime to serve coffee and cakes. Someone had attempted to place a few discreet lamps on its surface and lined up a few bottles of spirits, but it still looked forlorn. There were about a dozen men in the room. Holding glasses, talking to each other as if they were at the opening of an art exhibition. He saw Temba in the corner of the room engrossed in conversation with whom he assumed to be, what they call, a 'white Rhodesian'. He thanked the man who had let him in and indicated that he would make his way to meet Temba.

'Hi,' greeted Temba. 'George, this is Tom. Tom, George.'

Tom shook George's hand.

'Hear you've come from the UK,' said George. 'Into the lion's den.'

'As bad as that,' joked Tom.

George shook his head. 'You've no idea. Anyway you're a brave guy to come to this place. Welcome, have a good time.'

Tom looked around. It didn't look like they were having much of a good time to him. More like an after-office drinks party.

George noted his expression. 'No worries Tom, it's early. Things start heating up later on. I'll leave you with Temba, he'll fill you in with the form.' With that he left them to join in another group.

Temba laughed. 'He's right Tom, we start off cool. Have a few people on the street checking things are okay, and later, well what you want. Music, more drinks, a few of us get together. They're all pretty safe, educated guys here so you needn't worry on that score.'

That was one thing Tom noticed as soon he had entered the room. They were all professional types. Solicitors or doctors perhaps. Temba was a pretty high up academic, no doubt these guys travelled in the same circles.

'You look awkward standing there Tom, let me get you a drink.'

They moved over to the makeshift bar and Tom asked for a vodka and tonic. The barman winked at him. 'Double, double?' he asked.

'Why not,' said Tom feeling he needed some Dutch courage to get through this evening.

After about an hour it felt like someone had flicked a switch in the club. It had become more crowded and someone had dimmed the lights. Music suddenly burst from some unseen speakers. Abba, really corny. But it worked. A few of the guys, lubricated by the cheap alcohol, started to dance. Others instinctively seemed to break off into pairs, falling into intimate conversations around the edge of the room. Tom sought out Temba. He was feeling a bit heady with all the vodka but, even though he'd rather be having a good time, he had a job to do.

'You're right, it's heating up,' said Tom, trying to stay steady on his feet. 'Have you thought more of the Moroccan trip? I'm sure you would find it really interesting.' He gestured around the room. 'I can't see there's any danger of anyone finding out about this stuff. In fact, the more you present yourself to the world as a serious scientist, the less suspicious your authorities might be.'

Temba took a sip of his whiskey. 'In what way?'

'Well, I imagine these guys think we are all pretty stereotypical. You know, flowered shirts, bushy moustaches. Eloquent academics in lab coats or formal suits hardly fit their bill. They'll be looking for guys who are hiding from the spotlight. Putting yourself out there talking soberly about pharmacology is bound to put them off the scent.'

Temba put his arm around Tom's shoulder, and put his face close to Tom's. For a minute Tom thought he was going to kiss him.

'Tom, you might be right,' said Temba, slurring his words. 'You're really a bright guy, you know that don't you. It's a pity you're not my type.'

'And what type's that Temba?'

'Oh you know, bushy moustache, flowery shirt,' Temba laughed. 'No, not really. But, I'll think about what you've said, sleep on it, tell you in the morning. Right?'

'Right,' said Tom.

'Now why don't you go and have a dance. I know George has being eyeing you up all evening.'

'I might just do that,' said Tom, heading towards George at the bar.

Nathalie woke early without the use of her alarm. She had left the hotel blinds open and the sun came streaming through. She leaned over to reach the hotel's internal telephone, punched in Tom's room number and waited. No reply. Still, he had left her a message yesterday afternoon; there was no need to worry yet. The shower in her room was either scalding hot or freezing cold. She chose the cold setting to wake herself up and pulled on an old pair of jeans and a T-shirt before ringing room service for breakfast. She resisted texting Tom. He was a grown up and, by his stories of Indonesia, more than capable. She would wait until after she had had something to eat. Manny brought her a plateful of scrambled eggs, toast and some pastries. She felt it wise to stoke up before travelling to the first location; who knows when or where she would get any lunch. The last morsel of toast had just entered her mouth when her mobile rang.

'Tom?' she mumbled through the crumbs. 'Where are you?'

Tom ignored her question. 'What time's the truck arriving?' asked Tom, referring to the crew's flatbed vehicle that had been arranged to pick them up from the hotel.

Nathalie, needlessly checked her watch. 'In about half an hour, are you coming?'

'If you want me to, I think I could just make it.'

'How did the Temba thing go?'

'Just got a text. He's on board.'

'A text? Isn't he with you?'

'No, he wanted some time to think it over. He's done that now and it's all go.'

'Think it over? So where have you been?'

'If I get in a cab now I'll just make it, wait for me won't you?'

The phone went dead.

Nathalie looked at the phone screen and shook her head, bemused.

'Okay Tom, I'll do that,' she said to herself and took a last swig of coffee.

The crew vehicle turned up five minutes early. Still no sign of Tom. Farai jumped out of the cab.

'Mike and Chris will ride in the back. Okay for you to sit alongside me in the front?'

'Fine,' said Nathalie looking up and down the street. 'Just waiting for my assistant if that's all right.'

'You're in charge, but I hope he is here soon. According to the schedule Mike gave me, the jeep is leaving the medical centre in a few hours' time. I've checked the map and we're cutting it quite fine.'

'We'll give him ten minutes,' said Nathalie, pulling out her phone and dialling Tom's number. She needn't have bothered. A taxi pulled up sharply behind the truck and Tom jumped out.

'Hope I haven't held you up,' he cried, grabbing his holdall from the taxi's backseat. 'Great driving,' he said to the driver thrusting some dollar bills into his hand.

'Just in time,' said Nathalie coolly, holding open the back door of the flatbed cab. 'Squeeze in.'

Traffic was light and the journey was fairly uneventful. It was difficult for Nathalie to question Tom about his meeting with Temba. She was in the front, Tom in the back and she didn't really want the crew to become involved. Besides, after a few miles Tom dozed off making conversation impossible. She spent the time talking to Farai in the driving seat next to her. He assured her that all the kit that she and Mike required was on the flatbed. Mizars, redheads and a 5K as well as a small generator. Mike had handled the Canon C-300 and was more than happy with it. They'd not worked together before but Mike had come with a reputation so he didn't see a problem there. Nathalie quite enjoyed this 'industry talk', and it took her mind off her anxiety about the WEXA filming.

The Zimbabwean plains were now stretching before them, the red earth protruding through the burned grass. It was a glorious day, the cloudless sky giving a magnificent backdrop to the scrubland. If the weather held they were going to get some great shots. The truck wheels droned over the tarmac spitting the odd chip of stone onto the grass verge. Cars were becoming fewer but they did pass the odd bicycle and donkey cart, both laden with brushwood. The frenetic metropolitan city of Harare had given way to rural Africa.

The District Medical Centre was just as Joseph Karasa had described it. An L-shaped building with a wide interlocked metal-strip roof. Staff in white and green uniforms were walking along the open veranda corridors. Farai drew up the truck at the entrance and Nathalie asked them to stay put whilst she announced their arrival. Joseph, dressed in a loose-fitting khaki uniform, was there to greet her.

'A slight change of plan I'm afraid. We have to deliver some of the vaccines to the local hospital before we drive into the bush.' He looked across at the flatbed truck. 'I see there are five of you, I'll have to ring the accommodation; I was told there would only be four.'

'That's no problem,' said Nathalie. 'I booked five rooms at the Midlands Hotel before we left.'

'Sorry, I thought you understood, because of the visit to the provincial hospital we'll not be staying in Gweru. The nurses and I will sleep in the jeep but I've booked your film crew in at a guesthouse in Shurugwi. We'll be starting off from there at sunrise tomorrow morning.'

Nathalie tried not to show her irritation. She'd been on enough film trips in developing countries to know how plans could change.

As long as they were at that village kraal tomorrow afternoon she would even sleep on the flatbed.

'Okay, Joseph, if the guesthouse can manage to squeeze one more in that would be great. Now, you mentioned yesterday that we could kick off by filming the outreach office; why don't you lead the way.'

Nathalie was not keen on the scene but the district medical officer had insisted. This was the hub of the administration. She would find district maps on the wall and their documentation on health statistics. Nathalie could not think of anything more boring than filming documents on health statistics but Geoff had said to keep them happy. He would even get one of the assistant editors to knock up a ten-minute video on the outreach programme so it could be sent to them later to stop them asking any awkward questions. But her reputation depended on getting an investigative documentary on television. Well-framed shots of the Zimbabwean countryside, hospitals and even perhaps children being given vaccines would be useful for her programme. A dusty old admin room didn't fit that bill. However, she was a professional so, if she was going to shoot it, it was going to look bloody good.

The sparks, Chris, was a quiet guy and got on with setting up the lamps without a fuss. Nathalie and Mike decided to use a panning shot that would be initiated by the movement of a desktop fan. The idea was to create the atmosphere of the stultifying heat in the office. Even though it was searingly bright outside the sunlight was on the wrong side of the building so Chris set up the 5K next to one of the windows. Tom watched on, taking on board all the activity with interest. He looked puzzled when Mike asked him to wet the window and stick some tracing paper to it.

'It'll defuse the light from the 5K, make it look like sunlight streaming across the desk,' Mike explained.

They rehearsed the shot. As the fan turned on its stand the camera followed it and then continued across the desk to find Joseph poring over some documents. On Nathalie's cue, Joseph rose from his position to move over to the map on the wall and stuck a pin in it.

'Great,' said Nathalie. 'We'll shoot that and then reposition to take a close-up of Joseph's hand sticking the pin in the map. In that way we can see the position of the actual village you are marking,' she explained to Joseph.

Mike may have spent most of his career filming Victoria Falls but somewhere along the line he must have gained experience with interiors. He was good; had an eye for composition, was skilful at lighting and, as a bonus, sensitive in handling the subjects he was filming. They checked the first take back on the playback to see if all the kit was working properly. Perfect. After that Nathalie didn't bother. As she said 'cut' she put up both thumbs and smiled.

Her cameraman started to move on for the next shot. 'Nice to have your confidence.'

'Used to shoot film, didn't see the results until it was developed days later. And you obviously know what you're doing.'

'Compliment accepted,' said Mike. 'How about we use the baby legs here and take a low angle shot across the desk. Hardly Ridley Scott but could make your guy's papers look a bit more interesting.'

They milked the office location for all its worth. If that didn't keep the medical officer happy nothing would. It was with relief that Nathalie heard that the outreach team were ready to load up the jeep. If she kept some of the faces out of this then the close-ups might be useful in her documentary. They moved the kit over to the vaccines' room. Again it was just as Joseph had described: pokey, lit by flickering fluorescents, with a background of dirty white walls.

'Can we kill the lights and use ours?' asked Mike.

Joseph nodded, 'If you think you can get them in here.'

'Only need a couple of small Mizars, no windows you see, no light to compete with.'

'What are Mizars?' Joseph, normally introverted and offhand, seemed to be becoming interested in the film-making process.

'Small Fresnel prism lights. Their lenses focus the light onto one particular area. Nathalie wants to make the room look intimate, need to see your hands on the packets of vaccines. Perhaps with a bit of vapour coming out of the fridge to show it's really cold.'

'Right, let's go then. As long as the fridge isn't left open too long, we've got a long way to drive and need to keep them as fresh as we can.'

Nathalie intervened. 'No problem Joseph. We'll rehearse the movement of you putting an empty packet into the cool box with the fridge lid closed before we go for the real take, happy with that?'

By now Joseph had got the hang of rehearsals, repeat shots and close-ups, so all went well in the vaccines' room and they were ahead of schedule to film the loading of the jeep. Shooting in the exterior made things move along even faster and, as Joseph was keen not to leave the vaccines in the cool box longer than necessary, they loaded up the crew truck and followed the outreach jeep onto the highway towards the provincial hospital.

After a few kilometres the jeep took a sudden side turning onto a smaller single-track metalled road. There was no warning and Farai was taken by surprise. He wrestled with the wheel and slew the flatbed to the left.

'Shit, Farai, I hope that stuff on the back's tied down,' shouted Mike, grabbing on to the seat in front of him.

Chris peered through the back window. 'It's still there, that webbing is really strong. Tom and I strapped it really tight, thought we'd get some potholes. Didn't make allowances for Farai's crap driving but it looks like it's passed that test as well.'

Farai had managed to get the truck back in control. 'Not my fault. Didn't bloody indicate, he knew we were following him.'

'Now then boys,' said Nathalie laughing. 'What is it with you men and driving prowess?'

The road became narrower and, as Chris had predicted, more potholed. The truck bounced from one ridge to another. Eventually the metalled road ran out altogether and they followed the jeep along a rutted earth track, stubble grass growing along the middle. They had had no rain here for a few days so clouds of red dust were thrown in the jeep's wake. Farai wound up the windows. The truck's air-con had seen better days but the stifling heat was better than being choked by lungfuls of dirt.

After about an hour there were some signs of life. The odd person here and there, carrying bundles, stepped aside to let the small convoy through. Next a few shanty buildings. Corrugated roofs, breeze block walls. And at last, through the dirt haze, a lopsided sign indicating they had entered a small provincial town. An arm extended from the window of the jeep in front of them. It pointed to another unmade side road. But this thoroughfare was wider. Small thatched shops lined either side, coloured plastic litter in the street. A party of schoolchildren, incongruously dressed in neat white shirts and pinafore dresses amongst the filth of the surroundings, streamed across the road. The outreach vehicle in front began to slow. Several metres to the front of it, a large wooden board on two poles. White with a large red cross. Underneath faded painted letters.

SHURUGWI REGIONAL HOSPITAL

Twenty-one

It was unlike any hospital Nathalie had seen before. A single-storey building with faded yellow stuccoed walls. The facade was bordered by a low wall holding up a thick concrete pillared veranda. In the centre half a dozen or so wide steps led to the entrance. The walls and steps were filled with seated people. Many clutching creased hospital cards, some wearing colourful headscarves, others grubby woollen beanie hats. Not one of them was in conversation, just staring blankly into the distance. They had evidently been waiting a long time. Nathalie followed Joseph into the building. They were confronted by an officer wearing a short-sleeved khaki shirt. The epaulets on his shoulders and sewn badges on his sleeves gave him a military appearance. He was partly concealed by piles and piles of manila folders. He continued stamping them loudly; ink pad to folder, ink pad to folder. Joseph coughed to interrupt him.

'We have your vaccines. They require refrigeration so if you don't mind I would be grateful if you would call the duty officer.'

The man looked up but persisted in stamping. The rhythm was mesmerising.

'Down the corridor, third door on the left,' he muttered laconically.

'Thank you,' said Joseph with emphasised politeness and gestured to Nathalie to follow him along the passageway.

The corridor was lined with chairs filled with yet more people clutching manila files. Some held infants in their arms, like the adults they were silent and staring. Posters on the walls warned of malaria, bilharzia, and typhoid. One contained a strip cartoon showing how to build a better Blair latrine. All in all, it was a pretty depressing place. But the worst was to come. Nathalie peered through the glass window at the first door she came to. The room looked more like a prison cell than a hospital ward. A number of iron beds, paint peeling, were aligned against the wall. The patients partially obscured underneath mosquito nets. A doctor in a white coat was pulling back one of the muslin curtains. He examined the little boy who was sitting cross-legged on a yellow knitted blanket, expressionless. Nathalie noticed that the doctor was wearing a mask and rubber gloves. What chance did the poor kid have in this environment? Joseph saw her concern and asked her to continue down the corridor.

'The care here is better than the surroundings, but I'm afraid the medical supplies are less than we would wish for. The West seem to think that they can dump their out-of-patent drugs on us and no one seems to be interested in developing a fail-proof malaria vaccine. If malaria was contagious then I'm sure the big pharma companies would pull one out of the hat pretty quickly.'

This was spoken softly but with an edge that Nathalie had not heard from Joseph before. This made her a little uneasy, for the way he said the word 'West' and the tone of his speech chimed with the sentiment that she had received from her WEXA friends. She would have to keep an eye on Nursing Officer Karasa.

The hospital duty officer was pleased to see them.

'Sorry to pull you out of your way but our stocks were becoming dangerously low.' He looked towards Nathalie. 'I've heard that you are filming the outreach team, and this may have upset your arrangements a little. Is there anything that we can do for you?'

'Well there is one thing,' replied Nathalie looking up at Joseph. 'That's if my friend here can spare the time. It would be great if we could get some shots of the hospital wards. They would be pretty emotive, especially as we are doing a prevention programme.'

Joseph shrugged. 'We won't be setting off until first light, so if you think it will really help. We've got to store the vaccines in the hospital fridge anyway so there's no problem there. Of course, it's up to the hospital.'

Nathalie's real motive was to get some good shots for her documentary. Wards full of infected people, a possible consequence of a bioterrorist attack. She gave the medical officer her soft open-eyed look. 'You bitch,' she thought to herself.

The Duty Officer fell for it. 'Of course, by all means. Let me know what you want and we will try to accommodate. Anything to help the immunisation programme, it's a valuable resource.'

Whilst Joseph unloaded the vaccines into the hospital's refrigeration unit, as a temporary store, the crew unpacked the flatbed. The sun was dropping and Mike said, in order to create the look Nathalie required – filtered light through the mesh surrounding the hospital beds with the silhouettes of the patients inside – he would need all the lighting they had. Nathalie tried to keep busy, helping to carry the lamp stands into the hospital. She was feeling really guilty; not only was she duping these poor people, she felt like a voyeur on other people's misfortunes at the same time. Still she had done it before. If you wanted to make great documentary films then you had to push for the pictures and live with your conscience.

'Small problem,' Chris's voice interrupted her musings.

'Which is?'

'Power, lack of it.'

'There are lights on in the hospital, there must be electricity somewhere.'

'Yeah, electricity but the wrong voltage. No way can we power up the lights you want.'

Tom overheard the conversation. 'What about the generator?'

'Too small,' said Chris. 'Only meant to power a redhead or two. Anyway, I don't think they would want that thing inside the hospital.'

Nathalie was in one of her stubborn moods. 'We've set most of the lamps now, I really would like to get that shot. Are you sure you can't get enough power?'

'Not unless someone turns the voltage up.'

'And that would fix it?'

'Yes but...'

Chris had no time to finish the sentence because Nathalie had started disappearing down the corridor.

Fifteen minutes later and Nathalie returned with a short Zimbabwean man wearing a boiler suit.

'Chris, this is Benson. He is responsible for the small power station in this town. From what I gather they keep the voltage low to spread it around a bit. Not enough for the community otherwise; too many brownouts.'

Chris just stood there open-mouthed.

'He doesn't know whether he can get all the power you want but he is prepared to go up to the station. It's on the hill about half a kilometre from here, and from what I can gather he'll wind the voltage up.'

'Shall I go with him?'

'No need, he says he'll give us all he's got.' Nathalie smiled. 'But there is one thing you can do, he's got a feeling that even with the adjustment there may not be enough. I want you to borrow a bicycle and cycle round the village asking everyone to switch off their lights and cooking appliances. Only for an hour of course.'

'You what?'

'Benson says that it's getting near suppertime; a big pull on the power at this time of day. He reckons people won't mind, especially if you tell them it's for the hospital. Take Farai with you, I understand he speaks Shona.'

Chris could tell that Nathalie was being serious and this was confirmed by the enthusiastic nodding of Benson alongside of her.

'I've been in this business a long time but there's always a first for everything,' he said and ran off to find a bicycle.

✳

One by one the lights came on. 'It's working,' said Mike with a big grin on his face. 'Bloody marvellous. A whole village goes without its supper and we get a great shot.'

'Don't,' said Nathalie. 'I feel bad enough already.' She took a quick look through the viewfinder. 'Still, you were right, those lights make all the difference. Now let's get this in the can and then everyone can get something to eat.'

It was dark by the time they had finished and Farai and Chris rushed around the village with torches shouting the all-clear.

'I wonder what would happen if you tried that in London,' joked Tom to Nathalie as he helped strap the kit back onto the crew truck.

'Be lucky to come back with just an earful. One for a good story in the edit suite though, that's if they believe you.'

Her remarks reminded Tom of his trip around Soho with Stefanie. 'Yeah, I'm looking forward to that bit, Geoff sent me on a tour of post-production houses. The animation studio looked amazing. Will we be using some of that stuff?'

'Depends. I only use graphics or animation if I can't tell the story through live-action although, in this case, I suppose we might need some footage to explain how bacteria and viruses work. When it gets to that stage I might ask you to help out with the brief. But before that we've got the tough bit to do. The crew are in on the act; tomorrow afternoon I'd like you to act as a decoy.'

Tom scratched his head, 'A decoy, in what way?'

'Apparently Nurse Jones is meeting us at the settlement where the immunisation is taking place. I want you to distract her and Joseph away from the huts where we are filming our WEXA contacts. Perhaps you could get them involved in some sort of conversation about infection and bugs or something. While we are off doing our 'boring' local colour shots, say you're the medical scriptwriter on our team and you need some help with it. I think she feels a bit undervalued so if you big her up I'm sure she would rather be talking to you than following us around in the mud.'

Tom secretly would have preferred to have been in on the interview with the so-called terrorists, but he knew he had to be a team player. 'I'll give it my best shot,' he said reluctantly.

'It's got to be better than that Tom,' said Nathalie seriously. 'If I don't get carte blanche with those guys we're really up the Swanee.'

Their guesthouse, the Miners Lodge, was hardly the Holiday Inn. It was a rundown wooden-slatted shack on the edge of the town. The Lodge had confirmed that they could accommodate five instead of four but there were still only two rooms and the fifth place was provided by a camp bed, hastily assembled, in one of them. The crew said that they would take the room for three. Farai and Chris drew lots for the camp bed. It was obvious that Mike wouldn't fit on it. Chris lost so the others offered to buy him a beer. Nathalie and Tom took the other room.

'At least it's got two single beds,' said Nathalie. 'One of the last shoots I was on I had to squeeze into one with the cameraman.'

'Lucky you,' quipped Mike.

'Didn't turn out that way,' replied Nathalie reflectively. She quickly changed the subject. 'Anyway that's the sleeping arrangements sorted out, let's hope we do better with the food.'

Tom reminded her that he was a vegetarian, and Farai recommended that it might be safer to avoid meat in a hostelry such as this so they all ordered sadza, balls of stiff maize that they could dip into a peanut sauce, with stewed vegetables. It didn't sound very appetising and indeed it wasn't but it washed down well with several bottles of local Bohlinger's lager.

They all had a pretty restless night and no one was in the mood for talking as they gathered their things together at five o'clock in the morning. Chris limped to the truck holding his back which had been bruised by the protruding bar of the camp bed. Nathalie had tossed and turned all night, her stomach grumbling with cramps from the sadza, and waking fitfully from darkest dreams. She tried to get her head around the day's plans.

'Tom,' she said hoarsely, sipping some water to moisten her dry mouth. 'Can you try and find "Mein host", pay the bill and get him to rustle up some packed lunches. I don't think there's any Michelin restaurants where we're going.'

'On it,' said Tom, taking the stairs two at a time.

'Youth,' sighed Nathalie at Mike who was rechecking the lenses in his case.

Mike managed a smile as he snapped the box shut. 'Come on old lady, I'll help you to the truck.'

They had just finished loading when Joseph pulled up in the jeep. He looked fresh as a daisy even though he had been sleeping in the vehicle all night.

'Follow me, I'll take it slow, the track is pretty rough into the bush. Your truck looks pretty robust and, if we are lucky, for the most part the road is dry so I think you should make it okay. If you run into trouble use your horn and flash your lights. There isn't a mobile signal where we are going. Well, that's it. I'll get going.'

Joseph wasn't joking about the road or 'track' as he had called it. The crew vehicle crawled and bounced along it, throwing them around in their seats. The sun was coming up, burning the sky. The burnt orange hue was bleeding into the horizon, creating a black sharp-edged frieze from the trees. The blue Toyota jeep in front of them heaved and yawed as it turned into yet another side alley in the maze of tracks that weaved into the bush. Now Nathalie understood why Joseph had mentioned that it was fortunate that the roads were dry. If there had been rain the now dusty channels, lined with red sandstone bluffs topped with bunches of grass, would have been rivers of mud. She closed her eyes and tried to let the bucking vehicle rock her to sleep.

They had been driving for two hours when the jeep in front of them dipped into a depression between a cluster of rocks. Farai pulled up the truck to wait and see what was going to happen. Nathalie woke with a start.

'Why are we stopping, are we here?'

Farai wound down the window and brushed some of the dust off the windscreen so that he could see more clearly. 'No, the jeep is navigating some sort of obstacle; just holding back for a bit.'

Nathalie jumped out of the truck and walked up to the hollow that the jeep had driven into. She noticed that the dirt track turned into a metalled road at this point. It was cracked and pitted but formed a sort of inverted bridge across a narrow wadi. To one side of the road there was water but, on the other, scattered boulders across a dry sandstone riverbed. Joseph was rocking the jeep slowly forwards and backwards to test the tarmac. It seemed to be holding.

Joseph shouted out of the window. 'Just making sure that this asphalt won't crumble into the river. It would be a hell of a job to get your truck out if it slipped in. I think it's all right but tell Farai to take a run at it, and he should get across okay.'

The Toyota slowly eased its way out of the gulley rupturing a few pieces of tarmac under its tyres.

'A run at it?' Farai didn't seem sure.

'That's what he said.'

'On your head then,' said Farai, slipping the clutch.

The truck wheels spun and it tilted headlong into the wadi. The flatbed with its load was far heavier than the jeep. The concrete and bitumen started to crunch under the weight. Farai hesitated.

'Keep going,' shouted Nathalie. 'We're slipping sideways.'

Farai put his foot down. The vehicle lurched forward, a rear wheel sliding off the road. Mike turned to look out of the back window.

'The kit's slipping, more gas Farai!'

Farai managed to get the truck into a lower gear, the front wheels spun and then gripped the subsiding road. With one last effort they climbed out of the basin and up onto the other side.

'Hope there's another way back,' said Tom, looking at the devastation behind them. 'No vehicle's going to cross that for a while.'

'We'll worry about that later,' said Nathalie, climbing out of the truck again. 'Meanwhile, we've got to repack that equipment, so why don't Mike and I use the opportunity to film our "jeep repair" scene.'

'Nearly replaced by the "crew-truck repair scene",' snorted Chris. 'I imagine you won't need any lights here so Tom and I will rejig the gear whilst you lot take your shots.'

Joseph wasn't keen on the delay but, when Nathalie explained that their adventure in the ditch had moved the equipment around on the back of their transport, he agreed to take part in the re-enactment. He pulled the jeep onto a nearby verge and propped up the bonnet with a stick. Mike asked him to lean over the engine with a spanner and pretend that he was fixing something. It didn't look convincing.

'Anyone smoke?' shouted Nathalie.

'I do,' shouted Chris, still wrestling with the generator on the back of the truck. 'Why, have you run out of cigarettes?'

'Not for me, but can you come over here and light one up for a moment?'

Chris had been long enough around this crazy girl not to ask questions. First, tell a whole village to stop cooking and now, have a smoke on the side of the road. He left Tom with the strapping and walked over to the jeep.

'Right, take your lit cigarette and crouch down behind that wheel.'

He did as he was asked.

'Head down more so we can't see you, that's it. Now blow as much smoke as you can into the engine. Better. Look okay to you Mike?'

Mike peered through the lens. 'Looks like a jeep with a blown gasket,' he said. 'Now if you can get Joseph to tinker a little I think we've cracked it.'

'Old commercials' trick,' explained Nathalie to Tom when they were on their way again. 'You remember those ads when someone lifts the lid on a steaming terrine of peas? Done the same way. A quick puff on a cigarette over some frozen peas, close the top quickly, and you've got ready-made steam. Believe me, you don't want to eat any of that food after it's been in a TV programme.'

The rest of the journey was uneventful. Plenty of ruts and potholes to navigate but no more riverbeds. At one point their narrow side-track crossed a large dirt highway. Locals were using the intersection for a makeshift market. Kids were selling papaya on a stall under a battered parasol, and some women were strolling up and down with enamel bowls laden with okra and sweet potato on their heads. This was a bit odd as there didn't seem to be any customers. The blare of a horn and a cloud of dust announced the answer. A cream and green 1950s single-decker bus drew up at the crossroads. It couldn't have been more crowded, people on the roof, hanging out of the windows, one even perched on the bonnet. A few people fell out and strolled towards the papaya stall. The women with vegetables walked up and down alongside the bus. Nathalie suddenly twigged the reason why they had the bowls on their heads. Arms thrust out of the bus windows and grabbed the sweet potatoes. Notes, or in some cases fruit, were stuck in the bowls in exchange. The scene was so colourful Nathalie couldn't resist getting a shot. After the wadi incident Mike had insisted on holding the camera on his lap. It didn't take long for them to jump out and film the scene. Joseph was getting impatient.

'One last shot,' pleaded Nathalie. 'That papaya stall is something else. Tom, give one of those kids a dollar and ask him to buy a papaya.'

The boy, about ten, took the dollar with suspicion but seeing the camera, meekly walked up to the stall and pretended to buy a piece of fruit from his friend.

'Thank you, you can keep the dollar,' called Nathalie.

The small boy ran up to her. 'Have you got HD video playback on that thing?' he asked eagerly.

Nathalie shook her head in disbelief; technology gets everywhere.

Twenty-two

By the time they had reached the broad river floodplain Nathalie felt like they had driven over most of the African interior. The three guys in the back had fallen asleep but she felt that she should stay awake to keep Farai company. It had been hard going and she could see that he was getting tired.

'Are we there yet?' she joked.

'You tell me,' yawned Farai without any hint of humour.

The jeep in front suddenly pulled up at the edge of the road.

'Perhaps this is it,' said Nathalie looking around.

But no, it was a false alarm. Joseph was pointing out of the window towards the shallow meandering river, brown sludge moving slowly across the landscape of endless grass and stubble.

She followed the directing finger to see three small boys shepherding cattle through the water.

'Sensed you might need a break,' said Joseph walking up to their truck. 'Before we have a bite to eat I thought you might be interested in this scene.'

Nathalie studied the diminutive cattle drivers. Two of them must have been only eleven or twelve and the other, well he looked about six.

'A bit young for that sort of job.'

'Common enough, rural area, not a school within miles. They grow up with it.'

'You didn't seem keen on me filming those other scenes. What's so special about this?'

'Bilharzia; we are carrying a vaccine for it. Imagined you would want to show what we're trying to prevent.'

Nathalie waited for the explanation.

Joseph gestured again towards the river. 'Typical breeding ground for the freshwater snails that harbour the larvae of schistosomes. These rivers are full of these nasty parasitic worms. They burrow into your skin and lay eggs in your gut. Kids like this can have them in their insides for years.'

Nathalie made a face. 'What's it do to them?'

'Diarrhoea, blood in the urine, dermatitis, you name it; in extreme cases, central nervous disease. Only second to malaria in this part of the world. So if you're looking for a scene of how these kids catch it, there it is in front of you.'

Nathalie looked shocked. She had got most of the local background shots she wanted for her documentary, but this information made her want to make Geoff's palliative immunisation video really worth it.

She called out to Tom, 'Tom, get those kids to go back over the river with their cattle, tell them we want to film them.'

The children didn't seem at all perturbed to guide their cows back across the waterway. Natural little actors.

Chris unloaded the camera tripod from the truck and set it up along one side of a small bridge. The midday sun was perfect and shards of light caught the movement of water as the cattle ploughed through the brown river. Mike raised his thumb as he took the shot. It was obviously looking pretty good.

'Tom?' asked Nathalie. 'Can you persuade them to do it again? I'd like to do some tight shots.'

'I thought there were snails in that river. Won't we be putting them at more risk of bilharzia?'

'Tom,' repeated Nathalie, with a stare.

Tom did as he was told. The small boys turned their cattle around and drove them back through the river as if they did this roundabout activity every day. This time Mike picked off close-ups of the kids' faces, feet and the legs of the cattle. Spliced into the wide shot in the edit they would make a vivid story.

'And cut,' said Nathalie, running up to the boys. 'Thank you so much, you were great, real stars.'

The three children looked up at her with beaming faces. Nathalie dug into her shoulder bag. She pulled out two packets of ballpoint pens and a wallet of cheap coloured felt tips.

'Here, prizes for being so brilliant.' She gave the pens to the two older boys and the felt tips to the youngest. 'Now you better get going, I hope we haven't made you late.'

The cattle were already meandering onto the other side of the bank and the boys didn't seem in a hurry to catch them up so Nathalie rejoined the crew and helped them repack the gear. Tom broke out the sandwiches and they sat down on the riverbank to have lunch.

'Hey, look at those kids,' laughed Farai.

Nathalie peered across the river. The two older boys were setting upon the little six-year-old and grabbing what she could only imagine were his coloured felt tips.

'Poor mite,' she said. 'Talk about law of the jungle.'

Farai was still laughing 'I wouldn't worry, I expect they'll get their due deserts when they get home. Imagine what their mother will say when she hears their story. I can see it all now. "Yeah yeah, some strange white people in the middle of the bush, now where did you really steal them from?"'

Nathalie looked crestfallen. 'You don't think really… I was only trying to…'

'I wouldn't give it another thought Nathalie. They had a great time and if you're still worrying about the snails in the river, they use that crossing every day. If they were going to catch bilharzia they'll have got it by now.'

They were interrupted by a roar from Mike. 'What in the hell is in these sandwiches?'

Nathalie stared down at the sandwich in her hand and peeled the two thin pieces of white bread apart. One single leaf of wilted lettuce. She saw Tom sloping off towards the truck.

'Tom! Next time you choose the bloody vegetarian option you can opt us out.'

The immunisation station was a riot of colour. Women in bandanna headdresses, children in bright clothes that looked like they had just been purchased from Mothercare. White bonnets, little floral frocks, multi-coloured shorts. The families were crouched patiently under the shade of an enormous Musasa tree. As the outreach jeep arrived they rose to their feet, clapped their hands and began to sing. An amazing unaccompanied song. In unison, harmonised and punctuated by warbling trills. It was electrifying. Shivers ran down Nathalie's spine.

'Mike and Farai, grab your gear and record everything that moves,' she shouted. As the two men rushed to their equipment Nathalie turned to Joseph.

'Why and what are they singing?' she asked.

'It's what they do. It's a health song. They are singing in Shona, "Be Zimbabwean, keep healthy, keep happy."'

'It's extraordinary,' said Nathalie. 'Here in the bush, miles from anywhere, a complete Zimbabwean choir.'

'We get it everywhere we go,' explained Joseph. 'A cultural thing, you know.'

Nathalie didn't know, it was a new experience for her. She crouched down under the tree behind her crew and took in the melody of the swaying crowd.

'Miss Thompson,' a voice came from behind her. 'Miss Thompson, welcome to Masbela. We were afraid that you might not make it.'

Nathalie turned to see Nurse Sue Jones in a starched white uniform. She held out her hand and Nathalie shook it warmly.

'Can't say the journey was without incident but with Joseph's good guidance we made it.' She turned to the singing masses. 'Isn't this wonderful.'

'I suppose for you it must be quite a sight, but we must press on. If you follow me I'll show you where we have set up our medical centre.'

The so-called medical centre was a trestle table covered with a tarpaulin cloth and a macabre butcher's hook-looking thing strung up from a large branch of the tree.

'Weighing scales,' explained Joseph seeing Nathalie's concerned face. 'The kids hold on to the hook and we take the measurement off the dial.'

He instantly demonstrated this by picking up a small child and held her so that she could reach the instrument. She grabbed on to the hook with both hands and dangled there whilst Joseph peered at the swinging needle and when it had stopped jotted down her weight.

'We weigh them all, check their health cards and then give them their jabs. Any children with particular problems will be looked over by Nurse Jones. I've explained to everyone what you're doing here so if you'd like to set up we'll begin.'

The clinic, if that's what you could call it, was very efficient. Queues of vibrantly dressed women, babes in arms, lined up before the table. Each child clung on to the hook and was weighed by Joseph before being immunised by Nurse Jones. Many of the children were bemused by this activity but others, not expecting the sharp needle in their arm, burst into tears. One little boy, with huge teardrops in his eyes suddenly caught the camera lens. It worked like a magic spell; the tears were arrested and his eyes widened with curiosity. Mike captured the whole scene in close-up.

'One for the final cut,' he mouthed quietly.

The queues of mothers and babies stretched for tens of metres and when Nathalie had obtained enough material she looked beyond them to the enclosure of conical thatched dwellings in the distance. There was no sign of Lloyd and she wondered if she would have to venture into the village on her own. If she was going to get these terrorists on film now was the time, when Nurse Sue Jones and Joseph were engrossed in weighing and immunising children.

She was startled by a gravelly voice.

'Are you Miss Nathalie?'

She spun around to see a diminutive ancient-looking man; wrinkled face, one solitary front tooth. Where he had come from she had no idea, he just seemed to appear from nowhere.

'Oh, I'm sorry, you startled me. Yes, that's me, why do you ask?'

'Been asked to give you a message.'

'Oh, who by?'

'He tells me you know his name. Newspaperman, you have to tell me his name before I give you the message.'

Nathalie looked around, this was really weird. Some kind of village elder in the middle of the bush with a mysterious message. Then she twigged; it had to be Lloyd. He wouldn't want the information landing in the wrong hands.

'It's Lloyd,' she said. 'He's asked you to give me a message?'

The man nodded and pointed towards the cluster of huts. 'My home is in the kraal. The men you have come to see are there.'

'Where's Lloyd?'

'He can't come,' the man gave a wide grin, his single tooth protruding bizarrely. 'He left me dollars and the message. You can have my house until morning.'

Nathalie shaded her eyes with her hand and peered towards the kraal. 'How do I know which hut is yours?' There was no reply so she turned to ask him again, but he had disappeared as silently as he had arrived.

Tom was helping Chris load some of the gear back onto the truck when he heard Nathalie shouting and waving her arms.

'No Tom, over here. We need that kit for our village stuff. Remember, some local colour shots and interviews with the residents about the immunisation programme.'

Tom realised that the announcement was meant for Nurse Jones and Joseph rather than him so he put his thumbs up and made his way towards Nathalie.

'We're on then?' he asked as he came alongside.

'Yes, I want you to ask the guys to bring the gear to the village. Those huts are windowless, just a small door and a hole in the roof for the fire smoke, so they will be pretty dark inside. The generator and a single redhead should do it.'

'Will do,' said Tom. 'You asked me to keep the outreach group out of the way but they look pretty busy, shall I come with you?'

'Sorry Tom, I know you're keen to watch but I can't risk someone nosing around. They're getting through these kids pretty quickly and when they're finished you need to keep them away from the location. Besides, the less of us in that hut the better. Don't want them getting stage fright. Just me, Mike and Farai; not even Chris. Once he has set up the generator I'll ask him to wait outside.'

Tom tried to hide his disappointment but it was obvious that he was unhappy. 'Fine, I'll tell Mike what you want and hang around the immunisation team until you've finished'

'Good, and Tom?'

'Yes.'

'It's important. Keep them away from those huts at any cost.'

'Of course, I get the message.'

Nathalie waited whilst Tom sloped off to give the crew their instructions. She watched him whisper into Mike's ear and then walk over to the immunisation table. He sat on the chair besides Nurse Jones and started to ask her questions as she was immunising the children. Whilst everyone was occupied Mike and the crew casually carried the equipment towards Nathalie.

'Okay,' she said quietly. 'The location is over there, in the kraal. I've no idea which hut it is but just act normal as if we are looking for local volunteers to talk about the vaccination scheme. I'm sure we'll soon find them.'

They strolled towards the village. Looking back Nathalie saw that Sue Jones and Joseph were so engrossed in their tasks that they didn't even notice them go. The kraal was a cluster of about a dozen mud-daubed shelters contained within a palisade of roughly hewn branches. There was a newly constructed Blair latrine on the fringe of the gathering of huts, a grey concrete circle with an opening like the old Parisian pissoirs. Elsewhere there were scatterings of spindly cacti and brown-tinged crops. The crew stood at the entrance and waited for Nathalie's instructions. The nearest hut was set upon an area of bare earth. A portly man, a yellow shirt hanging over his trousers, was leaning against a rusty makeshift table tinkering with something. He turned away as Nathalie approached. Beckoning the crew to follow her she moved further into the village. Outside the next hut she found a woman carrying a child on her back filling a hessian sack with grain. Nathalie walked up to her and took a guess.

'Could you tell me which one is the headman's hut?' she asked.

The woman stopped what she was doing and looked up at Nathalie, puzzled. She said something in a language that Nathalie didn't understand.

Farai who was close by offered to help. 'She doesn't speak English,' he explained. 'Shall I talk to her in Shona?'

Nathalie smiled at the woman, 'That would be great Farai. Could you ask her if we can visit the headman's home?'

Farai greeted the woman and became engaged in a soft melodic conversation. It seemed like a lot of words just to ask a simple question.

'And?' asked Nathalie impatiently.

'I'm trying to establish some sort of rapport; the woman is quite nervous, thinks you're some kind of official. I'm just reassuring her that we are helping the outreach team.'

'Oh, of course, sorry,' apologised Nathalie. 'Any luck?' she added tentatively.

'It's the large hut over there,' said Farai, the one with the brick around the bottom. 'She says we are expected.'

'Must be the right one then,' said Nathalie with relief. 'Thank her and bring all the stuff over. If you guys wait outside and set up the generator I'll go inside and check it out.'

Even with her small stature she had to bend down to enter the open doorway. Inside there was a shaft of light coming from the hole in the conical thatched roof. It lit up a wisp of smoke that was twisting its way towards the sky. The whole home was contained within one room. A small kitchen, a bed and an eating area. Two men were sitting on the floor cross-legged waiting, their faces obscured by headscarves. One of them was reading from a sheaf of papers. The other, who despite his disguise she recognised as being the 'middleman' she'd met earlier, was flicking through his mobile phone. Nathalie coughed and Middleman looked up.

'You have the camera?'

No formal niceties, thought Nathalie, recalling her last encounter and wondering where the other two men were. 'Outside, shall I invite them in?'

The man studying the papers, put them down. She had not met him before and he appeared different to the others. Smarter clothes, expensive watch, more alert, eyes studying her through the slit in the scarf. He spoke quietly. 'Them?'

'Yes, the cameraman and the sound recordist.' Nathalie looked around the hut. 'And we'll need to put a light up in here, but once that's done there'll only be the three of us.'

The man with the watch, whispered into the ear of his partner. Middleman spoke.

'Can you not do this on your own?'

'No,' said Nathalie. 'I don't know how to use a camera, or a sound recorder come to that, but you needn't worry, these are professional crew, used to this sort of stuff; they've sworn confidentiality.'

'Mr Rolex' as Nathalie was mentally tagging him, bent over and whispered to Middleman again.

After a moment's consultation Middleman spoke, 'Okay you can set up your equipment.'

Nathalie turned to the door to call in the crew but she was arrested by Middleman's next words.

'Before you ask them in, tell them what we do to traitors.'

Nathalie paused, nodded and walked out into the light. Of course she had told the crew about her and Lloyd's last encounter and they had shrugged it off. But Lloyd's absence made her wonder how anxious he was about the capability of these people. Still there was no turning back now. She asked Chris to fire up the generator and told Mike and Farai to set their gear up inside the hut. With only one lamp and a tripod it didn't take long. Nathalie had asked the crew to keep conversation to a minimum so when they were ready Mike just nodded towards the viewfinder to get approval for the shot. Nathalie peered down the lens. The scene was spectacular. Two hooded men set against the background of a primitive dwelling, their images lit by the glow of the burning wood fire. Mike had used the embers and the one lamp that he had to dramatic effect. It couldn't have been more atmospheric or menacing.

'Ready to go,' said Nathalie.

Twenty-three

'He's dead Geoff, you can have the footage.' Nick Coburn's voice was coming down the line as clear as if he was next door. But Geoff Sykes was hardly listening. He had the phone to one ear, was watching some rushes on a monitor in the corner of his office and signing some papers that Stefanie had thrust under his nose at the same time.

'Dead? Who's dead?'

'Are you taking this in Sykes? Or are you being your normal "I can do everything at once" self? If you are, switch that bloody television off, if that's the noise I can hear, and listen up. It's getting late here and I'd like to get to bed.'

Stefanie, hearing the Scotsman's voice coming down the phone, picked up the papers and switched off the monitor. As she left the office she turned to Geoff.

'You've dragged that poor man all over the Far East, the least you can do is to listen to what he has to say.'

She closed the door quietly before her employer had time to think of some witty response. Geoff Sykes put Nick on speakerphone and leaned back into his chair.

'Okay Coburn, I've had the third degree from Stefanie, I'm all ears.'

'Right, block off your calls, clear your desk of contracts and switch off any media. Things have happened here fast and I've got a lot to get through. Also, half of it I can't bloody understand. You should have left Tom here to do this stuff not me. Why is it that these scientists can't talk in words of one syllable?'

Geoff grabbed the moleskin notebook from his desk and took the sharpened pencil from behind his ear. 'I thought you wanted to get to bed. Stop blathering man and get on with it then. You said someone was dead.'

'Oh yes, the guy the police arrested at the laboratory. You know the CEO of the whole shebang. He's topped himself.'

'What?'

'Topped himself. At least, that's what they're saying. You can never tell in these places. Found in his cell hanging by his necktie. Bloody idiots. Shoelaces and neckties first thing you should take off them.'

'When did you hear this?'

'This afternoon. That would be probably early morning your time. Know what you're like so didn't ring until I had all the facts. Been most of the evening putting it all together. Like I say, would be a lot easier with Tom here. Maybe he could make more sense of this mumbo-jumbo.'

Geoff had known Nick long enough not to ask what was meant by 'mumbo-jumbo'. 'You said you had put it all together, why don't you start at the beginning?'

'Oh, right, I've written it down here. Wait a minute, I'll just take a sip of this and begin.'

'Water of course.'

'Yeah but it's got something in it. Right here we are. You're up to speed with the raid so I won't go into that. Anyway they interviewed Gita, the lab assistant, and analysed samples and documents from the laboratory to check out her story. The CEO guy was feigning outrage, saying that the lab was legit. The police asked him why he had to export such dangerous bugs if he was testing his own antibiotics. Simple he claimed, they were also synthesising microbes for selling to other pharma companies so that they could test *their* antibiotics. This of course will explain some of the export licences.'

'Sounds a good story,' said Geoff scribbling in his notebook. 'What were these bugs anyway?'

'Weird stuff with unpronounceable names. I'll e-mail them to you. Apparently they're some sort of man-made bugs, manufactured using methods that aren't officially approved. I read one of the reports but can't make head or tail of it. Something to do with gyroscopes I think. Anyway I'm sure Tom will decipher it for you.'

'What did Gita say about the bugs?'

'That's the interesting bit. Michael slipped me the transcript of her interviews.'

'Michael?'

'Keep up Geoff, my local police mate, the reason why we've got all this stuff in the first place.'

Geoff rose from his chair and walked to the window. It was nearly mid-afternoon and the streets were less crowded than usual. A lot of people on summer holiday he supposed.

'Yeah, sorry Nick, a lot of material passing through this office since the last time we talked. Doing seven films at the moment. One minute it's sleazy politics in Eastern Europe and the next some gang cartel in Buenos Aires. Mike, of course, the Indonesian police guy.'

'Yeah, anyway.' Nick's voice was becoming sarcastic. 'This Indonesian police guy gave me copies of the transcripts. Gita has sworn on oath that she was asked to manufacture these weird bugs with the precise ability to be easily transported and, wait a minute I've got it written down here, yes here it is, in-vitro I think they call it. That means outside of the human body.'

'I know what in-vitro means Nick, but didn't the owner say that they needed to export the stuff to other pharma companies?'

'Yeah, that's where his case became unravelled. First, they checked out the paperwork and the batch numbers on the invoices didn't correspond with the actual materials that were being sent. Gita's testimony reinforced this. She cited one particular case where the code of a nasty untested bug was interpreted as a harmless chemical with an exorbitant price. Then lo and behold none of the people at the addresses on the export forms admitted to have ordered the product.'

'They could be lying.'

'True, and the police are checking those out. One in particular might interest you.'

Geoff returned to his desk and pulled out the bioterrorist proposal file. He flicked open the pages. 'Go on.'

'It's a name that Tom said that Nathalie would be interested in. A company called Biomedivac in Morocco.'

'Yeah she mentioned it, what of it?'

'Their name and address was on an export form. The order, a particularly nasty bug. The company in Morocco have denied sending it, and the signature was indecipherable, but the police have since checked out the e-mail ISP-number; it can be traced back to the personal computer of someone called Robert Barnes.'

Geoff continued flicking through the file and scanning Nathalie's notes.

'Interesting. What are they doing about it?'

'Investigation ongoing, I would say, but as I said the guy at the centre of this is out of the picture. Police are saying that the evidence was getting so strong that he opted for suicide rather than spend a lifetime in jail. Problem is, they're under pressure out here. International investigations get very expensive. The lab has been closed down and the guy running it is dead so it's not a priority anymore.'

'And the police laboratory raid footage?'

'That's the good news. No trial so not needed. Michael has handed me a copy of the media files. Under strict instructions to not use it for a couple of weeks while the dust here settles.'

'That's not a problem, we won't be transmitting for a month anyway.'

'Oh and there's some bad news, for you anyway. I'm not allowed to transmit the files over the internet. Have to deliver it in person. Which means you'll have to dig into your pockets for my first class airfare.'

The internal light on Geoff's desk began to flash. Geoff put Nick on silent and pressed the intercom button. It was Stefanie informing him that his next meeting was waiting.

'Send them up Stefanie, I'll just get rid of Nick.'

He flicked the intercom off and the speakerphone on.

'Hi Nick got to go. Economy class and a pint of beer when you get here. Let me know your ETA,' said Geoff making the disconnection.

There was a gentle tap on his office door. Geoff frantically leafed through his diary to find out who he was meant to be seeing.

'Come in,' he shouted after a brief pause.

The door opened to reveal a slightly-built middle-aged man wearing a sports jacket. Geoff's eyes had at last found the name scribbled under today's time and date.

'Please sit down, uh Mr Townes. I hope you haven't been waiting long.'

The man walked over to the desk and shook Geoff's hand. 'Professor Townes actually, but you can call me James. Thanks for agreeing to see me.'

The penny was at last dropping. Professor Townes from Biomedivac. He had telephoned Stefanie to arrange a meeting to discuss Bagatelle's *Horizon* project on biotechnology and pharmaceuticals. Geoff had reluctantly agreed and Stefanie had made a date in the diary. He had planned to fob the man off with a few palliative remarks about the whims of commissioning editors but, after his telephone call with Nick, he was now forming another agenda altogether.

'No problem, this *Horizon* project could be very exciting and my film director Nathalie Thompson says that your company is leading-edge in this field. It's me who should be thanking you.'

'Well I hadn't heard from Nathalie for a while so I started to wonder what was happening. Called the BBC in fact to find out what was going on. They said they'd had a proposal from Bagatelle but for more information I should contact you. So here I am.'

'Quite understand. These things take time I'm afraid. We put in a proposal but then it's all got to be budgeted. Complicated schedules, broadcast bureaucracy. Even then we don't get the green light till the last minute, if at all. I'm afraid there's not much more I can tell you, especially as Nathalie's on another shoot at the moment.'

'She did say that she'd have liked to have another visit, see what and when we could accommodate any filming and talk about some of the scientific content.'

Geoff reached out to the stainless steel filing cabinet next to his desk and pulled out a drawer.

'She did mention it, but as I say she's abroad at the moment. Let me just look at the file.'

The *Horizon* file contained only one piece of paper so Geoff grabbed another behind it to make it look thicker. He flicked over a few pages pretending to look at the schedules.

'Ah yes, I see she's planning to contact you as soon as she returns next week. Sorry, we should have been in touch. Also, I believe she said she would like to have another chat with one of your colleagues, what's his name, here it is, Doctor Barnes I think.'

Geoff looked up as he said the name. There was discernible discomfort flickering across Professor Townes' face.

'She wants to see Rob? That might be difficult. He went to the States recently, on an independent research project. Problem is, no one's seen him since.'

✳

The Zimbabwean sun was dropping and the shaft of light drifting through the hole in the thatched roof was beginning to fade. The keen eyes of the two men facing Nathalie appeared sinister between the gashes of material that were wound around their heads.

'And turnover,' Nathalie spoke slowly and quietly. 'I know you can't identify yourselves but would you tell me what organisation you represent, and what it stands for.'

The wisp of smoke coiling from the fire in the centre of the room added to the ominous surroundings. The men looked at each other and then straight at Nathalie. The man with the expensive watch spoke first. His voice was measured and in an educated African accent.

'We represent an organisation called the Western Exploitation of Africa. For years our continent has been raped and raided for its people and wealth. First slaves then natural resources, and now commercial and political corruption. This is where life began. We have a continent of beauty and the raw materials to give health and happiness to all our population.'

The man paused and then in a sudden movement pulled out an assault rifle from behind his back. Nathalie froze and Mike jumped away from his camera for a second. But the man gently placed the rifle on his lap and continued to speak in a calm level voice.

'Violence. We didn't want to resort to this. But it seems that we have no choice. No one listens. That's why we want to be part of this film. The West have one last chance to listen to us. Otherwise we will unleash hell and give them a lesson they won't forget.'

There was silence in the hut only broken by the crackle of the burning embers. Nathalie took a deep breath. She addressed the man she had labelled Middleman.

'We're listening now. How is Africa being exploited? Aren't countries like China providing enormous investment?'

Middleman looked at his colleague and was given silent approval to speak.

'Last year trade between China and Africa was worth more than two hundred billion dollars. Twenty times more than it was fifteen years ago. Many Africans are saying that China is a better friend than the West. But China's extraction of billions of dollars' worth of African resources which are used to make manufactured goods are then sold back to Africans at marked up prices. This results in the value of African resources going to the West and East Asia rather than Africa causing further poverty on the continent.'

Nathalie waited but no more was forthcoming so she asked another question.

'But doesn't the West give you aid?'

The larger man, the one Nathalie was now mentally referring to as Rolex, sat upright.

'Aid!' he exploded. 'You call what they give us aid?'

Nathalie was taken aback by the change in his demeanour.

'I thought the figure in the last twelve years came to about five hundred billion dollars,' she challenged.

Rolex became calm once more.

'Loaned not given,' he said. 'In that time nearly six hundred billion was paid back, and there were still three hundred billion owing from previous loans. Such "aid" as you call it is just another way of bleeding the continent.'

Nathalie could feel the tension. She glanced up at Mike who was now glued to his lens and then at Farai who was sitting to one side pointing his muffler-covered microphone at their two interviewees. In other circumstances, the crew would be in charge telling the participants how to sit and when to talk. In this situation it seemed that the roles were reversed. These men were very much in control. One with a weapon on his lap, the other with a self-assured air.

'Let me give you an example,' said Middleman, idly poking the fire. 'When the World Bank and IMF began offering loans they forced us to privatise our economies. This allowed Western corporations free access to our raw materials and markets. It was a debt trap that Africa didn't realise until it was too late. Take Zambia. They pressurised them to privatise their copper industry. Zambia has the third largest copper reserves in the world, yet more than sixty per cent of Zambians live below the poverty line. Eighty per cent of the people live on less than two dollars a day. That's what we mean by exploitation.'

These protests were eloquent but Nathalie was desperate to get on to the topic of what these guys were going to do about their anger. She knew that she had to gain their trust to get that material. She mustn't rush it. She decided to go with another question.

'That sounds all very well but the West would say that Africa is its own worst enemy. Look at the corruption here.'

Rolex put up his hand to his colleague to indicate that he would field this question.

'It's true. Corruption gets most of the blame for why African countries have struggling economies, but tax evasion of the multinationals does more to cheat Africa of its wealth than its corrupt leaders. This money, wrongfully stolen from African countries, ends up in rich Western nations or is protected in their tax havens. Don't talk to us about corruption.'

Rolex was becoming heated again and Nathalie decided it was now time to strike.

'You say that the West isn't listening to you. Your arguments are very strong but I can't really see these organisations you're talking about changing their practices. What are you going to do about it?'

Outside the hut the sky had become blood red. The shadows from the trees were running against the burned earth. It would soon be completely dark. A few hundred metres away the immunisation outreach team were packing their remaining supplies into the cool box. The families had dissolved into the bush and Nurse Jones, Joseph and Tom were left on their own. Tom looked anxiously around for any signs of Nathalie. Surely she should be finished by now. He tried to distract Joseph by asking to help dismantle the weighing scales. This worked for a while but there was only so much equipment to pack up. All was nearly in the jeep when Tom remembered Nathalie's ruse.

'Nurse Jones?' Tom hoped that he wasn't betraying the anxiety in his voice. 'I wonder if you and Joseph could spare me a few minutes, because of my scientific background, I've been asked to write some of the script for your video.'

Nurse Jones was packing away the final sharps' bin into the back of the jeep. 'Of course Tom, but wouldn't it be better to do that back at the hospital, it's getting dark and we ought to be moving.'

'I'm afraid we've got to go back to London soon and may not get the chance. Besides if we sit in the front of the jeep we could have the light from the cab.'

'Right, I suppose if it doesn't take too long. Okay by you Joseph?'

Joseph heaved the collapsible table into the back of the jeep. 'Fine by me, but I'm sure you can give Tom all the information he needs. I'll go over to the kraal to see how the crew are getting on. I expect they are being held up by some village elder telling the stories of his ancestors. I'll help them get away without offending anyone.'

219

Tom started to panic. 'Oh I'm sure they'll be all right, in fact you might interrupt some important filming; won't you stay and…'

But Joseph was striding purposely across the grassland towards the village and didn't hear the rest of what Tom was trying to say.

Tom frantically searched for the phone in his pocket. He pulled it out but there was no signal. Nurse Jones was looking at him strangely.

'Is there a problem Tom? I thought you wanted to ask me some questions about the project.'

Tom was in a quandary. If he followed Joseph then Nurse Jones might follow too. He decided to stay. With a bit of luck Nathalie might talk her way out of this one.

'Yes, I mean no, no problem. Let's sit in the cab and I'll take some notes.'

By the time Tom had started to ask questions Joseph had reached the headman's hut. He saw the warm glow coming from the small entrance and bent down to enter.

'Ah Nathalie,' he said, 'I see you have met my friends.'

Twenty-four

There was a stunned silence in the hut. Nathalie looked first at Joseph Karasa and then at the two disguised men. Nobody else moved. After what seemed an age Rolex stood up. He slowly and deliberately placed his rifle against the mud wall, approached Joseph and held out his arms. Joseph responded and they hugged each other like brothers. After some seconds Rolex stood back and held his outstretched arms against Joseph's shoulders.

'You've arrived just in time,' he said. 'We were about to get to the interesting bit.' He looked over his shoulder at Nathalie. 'Aren't we Nathalie King, or should I call you Thompson.'

Nathalie's mind was racing. King was a name that Lloyd had seeded on her militant websites. She hadn't mentioned that name since but Rolex had obviously been doing some checking. And Joseph, what in the hell was he doing here. Hugging and kissing this activist like a long lost relative. Yet there was no imminent threat at the moment; the gun was in the corner, Farai was next to her and Mike was a pretty big guy. No need for immediate panic. She decided the best thing to do was to say nothing.

Joseph broke the hiatus. 'Yes, good cover don't you think. The model Imunaid worker.'

Rolex's eyes looked questioning.

Joseph smiled and nodded. 'Not a word about you to the outreach team. I also checked with the hotel. She was really beaten by the police, but they got nothing from her.' He nodded towards the crew. 'These guys seem legit too, professionals, not known for toeing the political line. If we want our message out there this is the best chance we've got.'

Nathalie's heart rate was returning to normal, but on the mention of the crew she thought about her sparks. He was meant to be outside minding the generator.

'Where's Chris?' she asked.

'Oh, outside doing his job. Don't worry, I didn't whack him or anything. I just approached from the other side of the hut.'

'And Tom and Nurse Jones?'

'Planning your little video in the jeep. They are fine, but we shouldn't leave them too long.'

Reassured that Tom and Chris were safe Nathalie decided to put her cards on the table.

'So you're a member of this group Joseph.'

'Are you shocked by that?'

'No, not shocked, a little surprised perhaps. Why didn't you tell me earlier?'

'I would have thought that was obvious. We can't be too careful. You could have been someone from Western intelligence trying to infiltrate our network. My friends here thought that we should take a look at you when you were off your guard. I'm pleased to say that you have passed with, what would you call it, flying colours? And, as I said, Tom won't keep Nurse Jones talking forever so I think that you should continue with your filming.'

Mike and Farai, who hadn't said a word during this confrontation, resumed their places behind the equipment. Nathalie asked her two interviewees to resume their places and stood with Joseph behind the camera. She was just about to tell the camera to turn over when her film sixth sense kicked in.

'Role...' she was about to say Rolex, and had to stop herself. 'The gentleman on the left had a gun on his lap during the last take. I think we should put it back there for continuity.'

Mike smiled and shook his head. What a nerve this slight young woman had. 'She's right. Joseph would you kindly pass your friend his gun.'

Joseph gingerly reach for the gun, holding it as if he hadn't touched such an instrument before, and passed it to Rolex who took it and replaced it casually on his lap.

'And so Miss Thompson, if I can call you that now, shall we resume where we left off. You were asking me what we would do if the West didn't listen to some of the grievances in our last remarks. Well if you turn on your camera we'll tell you.'

The tension in the hut was palpable. With Joseph Karasa now by her side, Nathalie directed the camera and asked her questions. What action would they take? What methods would they use? Would they give any warning? The answers from the two men were pretty comprehensive and quite worrying. They had no qualms about using explosives. Their plans were not to kill but to draw attention to the campaign. That's why they had agreed to be filmed. To show that they were serious and to publicise their cause and intent. Nathalie next asked them what they would do if these warnings were not heeded.

Middleman looked to his partner for approval before giving an answer. It sounded rehearsed but, despite that, it still put a chill in the air.

'We have a plan. One that may unfortunately endanger lives. And so it's an idea that we hope we will not have to put into action.'

Nathalie looked first at Joseph, who was standing impassively, and then back towards her interviewee.

'And what will trigger this?'

Rolex intervened. 'If we see no movement on any of our concerns. The cancellation of aid debt, the renationalisation of mining industries, the exposure of multinational tax evasion. Just one of these actions would stay our hand.'

Nathalie leaned forward and mimed silently to Mike that he should creep into a tight shot. 'From what?' she asked quietly.

She imagined the image as seen through the lens. The skein of smoke from the fire drifting across a face, ominous eyes peering through the scarf.

'They will find out.'

'But if I'm going to transmit this threat, no one is going to listen unless they know the consequences,' said Nathalie, a slight tinge of exasperation in her voice. 'That's if the threat isn't an idle one,' she added provocatively.

The response came like a firecracker

'This is no idle threat! We have already prepared the ground. This plan will involve more than explosives. We plan to give the West a dose of African disease. An ironic weapon considering that much of the disease here could be treated by the West if the pharmaceutical companies thought they could make profits from us.'

'A biological weapon, a terrifying prospect,' said Nathalie coldly. 'Also quite devastating. How do you propose to control it?'

'We are not monsters. Our aim is to frighten not kill thousands of people. Our blueprint is to spread the disease amongst a restricted population.' Rolex laughed sardonically. 'They may even find an antidote more quickly. One that we could use in Africa.'

Nathalie felt that she was now getting to the nub of her interview.

'An antidote to what?'

'Ebola of course, a virulent virus, causing slow and painful death. Also transmissible but eventually containable. The perfect weapon of fear.'

'So how do you propose to obtain the virus?'

'We have methods, trials have already taken place. I told you, this is no idle threat.'

'And how do you intend to spread it?'

Rolex suddenly got to his feet and placed his hand in front of the camera's lens.

'Enough, switch off your equipment, this interview is over. You have all that's necessary to persuade people to meet our demands. We have no intention of disclosing our methods. Even to you Miss Thompson.'

Nathalie glanced at Farai, to see if he had got the audio of that, and then turned calmly to Mike.

'You can switch the camera off now Mike, the gentleman is right, we have plenty of material to warn people of what could be done.'

At that moment Chris put his head through the door.

'Hey you guys, I think there's some movement from the jeep, looks like the nurse and Tom are making their way towards the village.'

'Shit,' snapped Nathalie. 'Joseph, can you intercept them, tell them that we're just wrapping here and we'll join them by the truck.'

Joseph nodded and made his way into the night. The crew hurriedly coiled the cables and packed the recording gear into the boxes. Nathalie stood to one side, debating with herself about her next move. It was a difficult one, this was a great opportunity to raise the issue of a meeting with Temba. The idea, to infiltrate this organisation even further and to gain further evidence of them obtaining Ebola and an antidote for its couriers. She was unsure of the legality of this entrapment. Also, although Temba had agreed to go to Morocco, he still had to be persuaded to take part in the sting. She turned to the two men who were now stamping out the fire.

'As you can see we've got to go. The interview, great stuff, I'm sure it will work. I'll be in touch through our normal contact. You know we are on your side, and to prove this, we may have something for you.'

'For the cause?'

'Of course, something to do with the safe handling of bio weapons. Have to check it out but let's say it looks promising.'

'You are full of surprises Miss Thompson, but you are right, that would be very useful to us. We will wait to hear.'

✴

The journey back to Harare would take them all night. The outreach jeep was returning to the district medical centre near Gweru but, now that the road behind was out and Farai had no idea where they were, Joseph agreed to drive the long way round and lead them to the main Gweru-Harare highway. The crew truck followed the jeep's red tail lights through the dusty tracks. Either side of them it was pitch black, not a rock or a blade of grass to be seen. Nathalie soon fell asleep as their vehicle lurched rhythmically from side to side.

She was woken by a splinter of light reflecting from the rear-view mirror. She blinked to clear the mist from her eyes.

'Harare?'

'I wish,' said a drowsy voice from the driver's seat.' Farai handed her a crumpled roadmap. 'Useless, none of the side tracks on it at all.

Even Joseph in front there has made a few wrong turnings. Now that the sun is coming up, should be a bit easier.'

Nathalie looked out of the window. They were still on dirt roads, the blue Toyota in front of them slowly navigating the ruts and potholes. Either side, the yellow grass was beginning to glow in the early dawn light. No trees, no houses, just miles and miles of flat featureless scrubland.

'You want me to drive?'

'No. Company rules, no insurance, as if that matters out here. You could wake Chris up though. He's a crap driver but it's better than me falling asleep at the wheel. I'll flash my lights to see if we can get creepy Joseph there to stop.'

'Creepy?'

'Yeah, springing that surprise on us in the hut, I nearly had a heart attack. Thought we were going to be abducted for a minute.'

Nathalie laughed. 'Must admit it surprised me too. Imagine what would have happened if he'd overheard us talking about the real purpose of the shoot.'

As it happened, Farai had no need to flash his lights. The jeep ahead slowed and pulled up at a major junction. A tarmac road stretched at right angles into the distance.

'At last,' sighed Farai. 'Must be the A5, the main Gweru-Harare road. They'll be turning south from here.'

Nathalie reached for the door handle. 'Let me out, I'll thank them and say our goodbyes. You wake up the guys in the back and swap places with Chris. I won't be long.'

Nathalie ran over to the jeep. Joseph wound down the window and she shook his hand.

'I want to thank you and Nurse Jones for the trip. I'm sure you'll be pleased with the results of the video. Flying back to London tomorrow so will keep in touch by e-mail.'

'No problem,' said Joseph. 'And thank you for the filming, I'm sure the publicity will work.' He handed her a scrap of paper. 'Here's my number. Any further help your organisation can give us, you can call that without having to go through the hospital bureaucracy.'

Nathalie folded the paper and put it in her jeans' back pocket. 'I'll keep it safe, thanks for going out of your way and leading us out of the bush.'

'It was either this or repairing that wadi road, and I didn't think Nurse Jones would be up to laying tarmac in the middle of the night.'

Nathalie looked over at the passenger seat but now she saw that Sue Jones was fast asleep. 'I suppose not but thanks all the same, we'd still be driving round in circles if we hadn't followed you. Also thank Nurse Jones and the chief medical officer for us. Despite our sideshow, I really hope that the immunisation video will help.'

'Me too,' said Joseph, putting the Toyota into gear and pulling out into the highway.

It was after nine in the morning by the time the film unit vehicle pulled up outside the Harare Holiday Inn. Nathalie and Tom said their goodbyes to the crew and took the media drives into the hotel.

'Breakfast for two in the coffee shop please Manny, we're both starving,' said Nathalie as she passed the reception desk.

The coffee shop was empty, and they chose a table by the window. Tom pulled up a chair opposite and folded his arms.

'So?'

'So why didn't you stop him coming to the village,' Nathalie fired back.

'Was it that bad? I thought by your attitude when we left that you'd either finished filming or managed to fudge it somehow.'

Nathalie fingered the menu, keeping Tom in suspense a little longer. 'Do you want waffles with your scrambled eggs?'

'Look I'm sorry Nathalie, it was either him or Nurse Jones. I didn't have an option. I've been waiting all night to know what happened. Are you going to tell me or not?'

'Tom, I've had a rough night, haven't eaten since your sumptuous lettuce sandwich, and am just getting over the shock of being confronted by a covert terrorist. If you don't mind I'll have some breakfast and then tell you the story. Until then, why don't you work out a plan and explain to me how you are going to get this Temba guy to collude with us in entrapping these activists.'

Tom hadn't seen Nathalie in this mood before. She was obviously really pissed off with him for not keeping Joseph at bay. Either that or she was suffering from lack of sleep.

They ate their breakfast in silence and Nathalie downed three cups of espresso before she spoke again. Then she told Tom of the events in the kraal headman's hut. She was still cross that Tom hadn't given her warning about Joseph's unannounced entry. She still had palpitations recalling the event. But fortunately the crew had kept cool heads and it had all worked out. They had got the footage she had come for and a possible lead for further contact.

'That's where you come in. We've not had time to talk about your liaison with Temba Murauzi. You've told me he's on board but not any details.'

'Liaison, I…'

'I don't mean that sort of liaison, I'm not interested in your private life. How much does he know about what we want to do in Morocco.'

'It wasn't like that anyway.' Nathalie's febrile demeanour was rubbing off on Tom. He too was suffering from lack of sleep. 'He's agreed to take up the position with Biomedivac in their laboratory. At the moment he thinks our filming is just for talking about antidotes for a possible Ebola bioterrorist attack.'

'We're in Harare for another afternoon. Do you think it's worth hooking up and mentioning that we're trying to snare a terrorist group? You could persuade him that he would be doing society a great favour if he would pretend to supply them with a protective antidote for their Ebola carriers.'

Tom stared out of the window. Traffic, the sun glinting from their paintwork, idled past in the street. Knots of people milled on the pavement; casual conversations, a far cry from the task that Nathalie was asking him to do.

'Too fast, too soon,' he said. 'We could frighten him off. He might even back out of the Moroccan trip. No, I think it best to tackle him when he's there. I've not known him long, need more time to get his confidence. Besides, outside of his own country I think he'd open up more.'

Nathalie thought for a while.

'You're right, stupid of me. Also stupid of me for playing you along back there. I was tired and grumpy. I'm sorry, there was no way you could have done anything else with Joseph and, besides, it worked out okay. You've done a good job with Temba, he's your contact and I trust you to play him in the right time in the right place.'

'Not sure, "play" is the right word. If this is a means of catching those guys red-handed, the little I do know of Temba, he might take part.'

'Yeah, corny phrasing. I'm still a bit caught up in all of this cloak and dagger stuff. You're right, we've got to keep level-headed on this one. I think this film could be really good but I mustn't lose sight of the fact that, although, as Lloyd would put it, this is a small-time amateur bunch, they could be really dangerous. My problem now is, if and when to tell the authorities. And which authorities? Zimbabwean or the UK? It's a bit out of my pay grade. I'll need to speak with Geoff.'

Manny entered the coffee shop with a 'top up'. Nathalie couldn't help wondering what he had said to the WEXA people who had questioned the hotel about Nathalie's behaviour and her trip to the police station.

'Sleeping dogs,' she said aloud.

Tom screwed up his face in bewilderment.

'Think we should get a nap,' she said. 'It's an early flight to Heathrow tomorrow.'

Twenty-five

Stefanie brought in a tray of sandwiches and placed them in the middle of the boardroom table. This was the first time that the full pre-production team had been present. Nick was in one corner rocking idly in his chair. Nathalie and Tom were seated on the other side of the table with a place between them that was soon filled by Stefanie. One empty chair at the end waited for Geoff.

'That bugger's always late,' moaned Nick, grabbing a sandwich from the tray.

'He's on his way,' explained Stefanie. 'Take it as a good sign. He's been viewing the rushes with Bob, if he didn't like them you can be sure he would have cut it short and be banging on this table right now.'

Nathalie leaned around Stefanie to address Tom. 'Bob's the editor on this project, lucky to have him; he's really good.'

The boardroom was windowless. Set up for video viewings. A large pull-down screen at one end and a projector setup high at the other. The lighting was warm and convivial but nothing like the natural sunlight that was streaming down on London's streets.

'Another idiot who spends all his days in a darkened room,' carped Nick. 'I don't know why Geoff wants me here, unless it's to apologise for cramming my legs into economy seats meant for...'

He was brought up by a glare from Stefanie. 'I know, I know, bloody political correctness; all I was going to say was, for people who aren't six foot three.' He reached for another sandwich. 'Well if the miser doesn't turn up soon I'll eat all his bloody sandwiches.'

'So which miser paid for these bloody sandwiches?' said Geoff striding through the door. 'Anyway, you can have them all. Bloody brilliant. The rushes that is.'

The atmosphere in the room changed. Tom breathed a sigh of relief, Nathalie a quiet smile and Stefanie rose to charge Geoff's plate with his favourite salt beef rolls.

'Thank you Stefanie, much appreciated; that's if Nick doesn't want them of course.'

Nick stopped rocking on his chair and placed his arms on the high-gloss table. 'Enough of the small talk. We gather you like the footage; do you mean our Java effort or Nathalie's African stuff?'

'Both. I think we've got the makings of a good film. Even the wobbly scope police video tells a great story, especially if Bob frames it using his magic box of tricks. And, Nathalie, I think you should be looking over your shoulder; Tom's footage of that Indonesian village is quite classy.'

Tom looked with discomfort at Nathalie. He was about to say something and then thought better of it.

'That sounds great Tom,' interjected Nathalie, in an attempt to cover his embarrassment. 'You should come down to the edit suite this afternoon, we could view it together.' She turned to Geoff. 'How's the audio on the WEXA interview?'

'As one would expect from a Thompson shoot. The whole scene is very atmospheric, eerily threatening. As I said I think we've got the makings of a good documentary. Nick's said that the Surabaya police don't want us to use their stuff for at least two weeks. But that's fine, I called the channel from the taxi on my way back. They're happy with a transmission date three weeks from today. Nathalie I'd like you to knock up some blurb for the *Radio Times* and the other rags. Always think seeing it in print gives a good incentive for finishing on time.'

'Is that wise Geoff?' asked Stefanie, noticing the look on Nathalie's face. 'From what I understand Nathalie's got quite a lot more to do. There's the Moroccan shoot to finalise and I believe she's not sure yet whether she can set up the sting we are depending on.'

'If I waited for every occasion a director wanted more time Bagatelle would be demoted to reality TV shows. Find a few mugs who want to be humiliated and shoot it live, shoot it quick. No, if we didn't stick our neck out we wouldn't have all these baubles,' he said waving his arm at the glass cabinet crammed with film awards. 'Not that I'm looking for glory; they're the means we get further commissions.'

Nathalie opened her file and handed out a typed agenda to everyone. 'Thanks for your concern Stefanie, but Geoff's right, I'd always like more time. Often a tight deadline gets the best out of a film. I can see the shape now but really do need these last pieces of jigsaw. I've outlined a to-do list. Now we know the timeline, we need to pull together to see if we can get through it.'

It was quite a long list. Tom wondered how Nathalie had managed to put this together in such a short time. To him the project seemed just a jumble of images and disconnected pieces of story. To Nathalie there was a strong narrative – an investigative film with a beginning, middle and end – with just a few holes to fill in. Realising the urgency of finishing the programme he puzzled at the first item on the agenda.

'Outreach immunisation video?'

'Yes, what of it Tom?'

'Is that important? I thought there was a tight timeline for the documentary, can't this wait?'

'Not really Tom. If we don't get them their video, they might start asking questions.' She handed Geoff half a dozen or so typed pages. 'I knocked out a short script on the plane, ought to be about six to eight minutes. Should keep them happy. With a bit of luck they'll not even see our finished article.'

Tom's admiration of Nathalie went up even further. Not only had she outlined a completion agenda but she had written a full blown script. 'How long will it take you to cut it together?' he asked.

Geoff was glancing at the pages. 'Needn't worry about that Tom, I've seen some of the footage. If I pass this to Bob he'll knock it up in no time. We are recording a voice-over tomorrow for one of our other projects, I'll ask the artist to add this on at the end. Should get it out to them by the end of the week. Okay with you Nathalie?'

'That would be good, get it out of the way. Tell them that sadly, due to lack of funds, Imunaid is closing down but they are welcome to use the video to look for donations.'

'I'll type up a letter,' said Stefanie, touching Nathalie on the shoulder. 'I know you feel a bit guilty about using them but knowing Bob's work, I'm sure the video will really do some good.'

'Hope so,' Nathalie straightened in her chair. 'Now on to item two. Morocco. I understand that Geoff's got Professor Townes' permission to film Biomedivac's plant. Where do we stand on that?'

'He's still keen as mustard, even though I've told him we've got a different programme strand,' replied Geoff. 'Given some dates. Problem is, film crew. Stefanie's done some digging but no one really suitable in Morocco.'

Nathalie turned to Stefanie.

Stefanie shook her head. 'Sorry, understood you wanted some really glossy high-tech shots of the lab. There are a few bits and pieces but no one we could really trust.'

'So what's the solution?' asked Nathalie.

'Granada. A really good group of people we've used before. I've booked tickets for you, Tom and John McCord. Sound and sparks will meet you at the airport with the kit and a vehicle. Taking the Tarifa ferry it's only about eight hours' drive to Casablanca. I've booked you into a hotel for the night, not swish but it's got parking. From there it's only three hours inland to the location. A bit isolated but Professor Townes says he can get you accommodation.'

'Sounds good,' said Nathalie. 'Especially if you can get John. I'm surprised he's free at such short notice.'

'Not sure he was but I know he likes to work with you. He says he owes you one for not turning up last time.'

Nathalie recalled the last time. She was making a documentary on the oceans. Hours before a shoot John had been run over; broken ribs and fractured leg, hardly in the position to operate a camera. Another cameraman had to be drafted in at the last moment.

Nick was pushing the crumbs around his plate. 'So, if I'm not going on this jolly jaunt why am I here?'

'That's next thing on the list Nick. While we are in Morocco Tom's trying to persuade Temba to take part in a sting. I've talked to Geoff about this and told him my concern about the legality of entrapment and the dangers of these WEXA guys actually carrying out their threats. He said you knew someone in the security services who we could contact if things got messy.'

Geoff interlocked the fingers of his hands and slowly started to turn one thumb around the other. 'I said *if* things get messy. There's no need to sound any alarms yet. All that we've got at present are some masked guys, shouting their mouths off, in a hut in the middle of the African bush. Nothing anyone can do if we shop them now. They're in Africa for a start and, even with Lloyd's help, it would be hell of a job to nail them. Now if this thing works, they take the bait and we get them on camera accepting what they think is an antidote for their bioweapon; *then* perhaps we could warn the authorities to keep an eye out for them.'

Stefanie began to look concerned. 'Don't you think we should let Nick warn these people? Imagine it if they really did spread Ebola around the country.'

'Pointless Stefanie,' said Nick. 'They'd just laugh at you. From what I can tell this is a small unknown amateur group, sabre rattling. And besides, what country? The so-called West is a pretty big catchment area.'

'I wouldn't have thought a few words in the right ear would hurt. I've been told that amateur terrorist groups can be the worst. Unpredictable, no set intelligence plans.'

'Exactly, unpredictable,' intervened Geoff. 'We don't want anyone causing a stir around our little group before we've got this film in the can. Nathalie, what sort of guys are these?'

'I had two meetings. At the first there was a guy who used quite sophisticated language, although his two compatriots were pretty basic I would say. On the filming day the more sophisticated guy brought another mate along. He seemed to be in charge. Educated voice, classier clothes, expensive watch. Smooth talker. Possibly from the professional classes. Certainly a lot less amateur than the first bunch I met. He could be dangerous.'

'Which is why we filmed him,' said Geoff with exasperation. 'Now if you have no real objections, we'll carry on until we sniff there's actually a real indication that they're going to spread some of this stuff. Then, and only then, we'll ask Nick to drop the word to the anti-terrorist squad. Okay?'

He didn't wait for an answer. 'Now, why don't you tell me how you're going to carry out this sting.'

Nathalie outlined her plan. She would negotiate with Townes to interview his protégé Temba Murauzi in the laboratories. This would make good TV she would tell Townes. Bright African guy explaining how anti-Ebola vaccines worked and how they could be used in a potential bioterrorist attack. She knew that Townes would be nervous about mentioning bioterrorism but she was sure he would come around when he realised that this could be a promotion for governments to stock up on his drug. During the two-day shoot Tom would find an opportunity to talk to Temba. He had struck up some sort of rapport so they had high hopes for a successful outcome. WEXA had already been primed to expect some further help. Temba would meet with them and explain; as a sympathiser, he could provide them with a new effective antidote for their couriers. He had been all over the papers as a star pharmacologist so it should appear quite convincing.

'So, you'll wire him with a microphone or, better still, hidden camera and get them admitting to their intent on tape,' concluded Geoff. 'Great stuff if you can pull it off. Confident Tom?'

'He's a sensitive sort of guy, the real incentive is to tell him that he could stop the deaths of hundreds of innocent people. I'd just need to take it slowly, drip-feed him with information over the two days. Not come out with, "Hey I want you to wear a wire and offer to help some terrorists" as an opener.'

Geoff grinned, 'It's a good job we've got you doing it rather than Nick then. Which reminds me, I'd like Nick to go with Nathalie to the meeting with Professor Townes tomorrow. We set it up to finalise the arrangements of the Moroccan shoot but Townes phoned this morning.' He noticed anxiety flashing across Nathalie's face. 'Oh don't worry, the shoot's still on. Remember I told you that thing about Rob Barnes. Yesterday the British police visited Biomedivac on behalf of their friends in eastern Java. Wanted to know why their letterhead is on a requisition e-mail. He seems quite worried, I told him that Nick would come over to help out.'

✳

Tom recognised the building as soon as they had turned the corner. The same anonymous looking terraced house with the dirty brick facade. Only the small plaque next to the doorway gave any indication that it had anything to do with the film industry.

'This is Reels,' Nathalie started to explain, as she pressed the intercom button. 'It's just one of the places that Geoff dry-hires from time to time.'

'Yes, it's the place Stefanie showed me when I started.'

'Oh, you've probably met Bob then. Geoff's chained him down to this grubby little edit suite for the last two months. Don't know why he puts up with it, plenty of other more swish places around.'

'Think Stefanie said it was something to do with money.'

'Geoff's always moaning about money. Channels wanting films by the yard rather than quality productions. Penny pinching budgets, not like the old days. He goes on and on. He makes enough, you should see his car. What he doesn't realise is that people like Bob are hard to find. He takes him for granted. One day, he'll up and leave.'

A fuzzy voice emitted from the intercom. 'Who'll up and leave?'

Nathalie realised that she had kept the button down and left the intercom open.

'Oh, is that you Bob? It's Nathalie.'

The buzzer sounded and a click indicated that the lock had been automatically opened. Nathalie pushed at the door and the two of them mounted the grimy concrete stairs to the edit suites. As they entered Tom frantically tried to remember what Bob had told him on the last visit. Digitising the rushes, sorting the bins, recording scratch voice-overs. The room reeked of the smell of oriental noodles, reminiscent of Java.

'Hi', said Bob. 'Sorry about the aroma, Chinese restaurant downstairs. Take a seat, I'll just finish off this last edit and show you what I've done to date.'

Nathalie sat in the wheeled metal armchair next to Bob and, as there was no other seat available, Tom perched behind them on the small sofa. Over Bob's shoulder he could see the three monitors flicker and recognised some of the pictures that Nick and he had taken in Indonesia.

'That's where we filmed Michael, isn't it?' Tom asked.

Bob's fingers moved over the keyboard, his eyes still staring at the screens. 'Michael?'

'Yes, the Javanese policeman.'

'Oh, is that what he's called. These are really good shots Tom, thought you were a novice.'

'Beginner's luck.'

'Either that or a bloody good cameraman,' said Bob still not turning to look at Tom. 'Didn't get any shot-list though.'

'That's my fault,' said Nathalie turning to Tom. 'Should have told you, but didn't realise that you were going to be directing anything. When shooting, we note down some time-code or time of day against the scenes we're taking. Helps Bob find things quickly.'

'Damn right,' said Bob. 'Had a hell of a job in sorting this lot out.'

'Sorry, I didn't realise.'

Nathalie spun round in the chair again. 'Not your fault Tom, it's difficult at the best of times if you haven't got a PA and you weren't supposed to know. We are glad just to have the shots.'

'Finished,' exclaimed Bob sitting back in his chair. 'I've just been playing about with some of these Indonesian rushes. Putting them in to some kind of story. Used the policeman's interview as most of the guide track and overlaid some of the other stuff taken later. The black holes are where I imagine you would want to put something like lab shots. Anyway see what you think.'

He pressed a key on the controls and the images came to life on the central monitor. Michael was seen walking amongst a crowd of villagers in a Javanese marketplace. As the camera cut into a close-up his voice came out from one of the speakers. He was explaining how the Surabaya police force had been given information about a clandestine laboratory in the countryside. After some description of the investigation the pictures jumped to a dramatic sequence of the police raid. These images were set into the frame of a mocked-up newspaper page containing shock headlines. Bob paused the film.

'A bit naff, I know, Geoff's idea.'

'No worries,' said Nathalie. 'He's concerned about the quality of the images but the content of the shots are good enough without the gimmicks. Carry on let's see the rest.'

Bob pressed the play button and they watched the remainder of his edit.

'Not bad,' said Nathalie when he had reached the end. 'We obviously need some state-of-the-art laboratory footage and perhaps some explanation of how these bugs work. Could use graphics for that. I like the use of the close-ups of the documents. We could do a dissolve from them to the plant in Morocco.'

Tom was amazed at how the pictures were beginning to tell a story. Suspicions of foul play, strange bacteria being manufactured in a laboratory, evidence of shipping the stuff to other countries, a dramatic police raid, and a car chase. There were a number of black spaces in the video but he could see that Nathalie was already planning the pictures that would be inserted.

'Looks amazing,' he said. 'Will you do your African story before or after?'

'Neither,' replied Nathalie. 'These aren't two different films. We'll inter-splice the African stuff with the Javanese footage, build up a narrative. Perhaps open with the general threat of terrorism today. Talk about the type of weapons used, and the frightening prospect of biological agents. Use the stories we've got so far and interweave them to show the threat and the possible countermeasures. This is a good start and I've got a better idea of what we need to get from the Moroccan plant. But no documentary's finished until the last gasp. Our coup will be if we can show that WEXA is a real threat. It could throw the whole programme on its head.'

She couldn't have spoken a truer word.

Twenty-six

London was waking up as the sun stole the last cloak of night. Nathalie squinted her eyes at the light trickling through the blinds of her Fulham flat. She turned over and pulled the duvet around her. The air was cooler signalling that the long hot summer was coming to an end. The phone on her bedside table began to vibrate. Surely she hadn't set the alarm this early. She tried to ignore it but realised that it was creeping along the wooden surface and about to plunge like a lemming onto the parquet floor. With one swift movement her hand shot out from the covers and grabbed the suicidal device. The screen announced that it was an incoming call.

'Nick, why in the hell are you ringing me at this time in the morning. Are you still on Java time or something?'

A Scottish drawl came down the phone. 'I wish. I've just been woken up too. Bloody Sykes. Says we are to pull our meeting with Townes forward. Forward means in the next half-hour.'

Nathalie checked the time on her phone. 'That's crazy, whoever wants to meet at six-thirty in the morning?'

'Townes does apparently. All in a panic. Just had the police round in a dawn raid. Went through his office like a pack of wolves. Something to do with the Surabaya lab. Geoff had told him that I'd been there and he wants to see us fast.'

Nathalie groaned. 'I don't know what he expects us to do. I can't even think straight this time in the morning.'

'Dress, get some coffee inside you, and I'll be round to pick you up in the next ten minutes.' The phone went dead.

Nick's car smelt like a transport café.

'Bacon roll?' He handed her a small greaseproof parcel.

Nathalie snapped on her seatbelt, unwrapped the paper and took a large bite. She closed her eyes as she chewed on the first succulent mouthful.

'Thought that would get you out of your bad mood,' said Nick pulling out from the curb. 'Nothing like a good healthy breakfast to start the day.'

Nathalie didn't take the bait. She was wondering how she was going to handle the meeting now this small hand-grenade had been thrown into the arena. Her original objective had been to smooth the way for the Moroccan shoot. Now this Rob Barnes' thing might really mess that up. She finished the roll, screwed up the paper and pushed it into Nick's ashtray.

'So what's Geoff told you?'

'Not a lot more than I said on the phone. This second visit from the police wasn't announced, unlike the first. They had a warrant. Nearly bashed his door down at four o'clock in the morning and marched him to the laboratory offices. Geoff said he's really scared, knew that I'd been in Surabaya and wondered if I could help. That's about it.'

'Did the police find anything?'

'Don't know, you will have to ask Townes.'

'Me? I thought it was you he wanted to talk to.'

'I'm just the monkey, I'll leave the agenda up to the organ grinder.'

Nathalie threw up her eyes; it was too early for her to think of a plan, she would just have to play it by ear.

'Okay then, I'll do most of the talking. We mustn't give Townes too much information, he might stop us filming his Moroccan plant. Oh, I think you've missed the turning; turn right here, we'll need to go round the block.'

This early in the morning it wasn't difficult to find a place to park. They could see the lights on in the laboratory building lobby so they walked up to the main entrance and pressed the bell. The door opened immediately. Townes must have seen them coming up the path. He looked dishevelled; mismatched jacket and trousers and a creased open neck shirt.

'Thank God you've come, I didn't know what to do. They've wrecked the offices. Luckily the warrant didn't extend to the lab but I think they're now trying to get access to that. It's a nightmare.'

Nathalie closed the door behind her.

'Calm down Professor Townes, we'll do what we can to help, but why don't you let us into your office and we can sit down and talk about it.'

'Of course. I'm sorry, my head is still spinning. Why four o'clock in the morning I don't know.'

Nick put out his hand, 'Nick Coburn, Professor, the guy who visited the lab in Java. Four o'clock in the morning; because that's the time when you're at your most vulnerable. If you have any information, they want to catch you off guard.'

'But that's the point, I don't have any information. I've no idea what Rob has got up to.'

Nathalie took James Townes gently by the elbow. 'Like I said Professor, let's go into your office and we can sit down and calmly talk it through.'

The office looked like a tornado had passed through it; papers were scattered around the room, filing cabinets left open and drawers upturned.

'Tidy bunch,' said Nick.

Townes sighed and shook his head. 'They said they would put it back but I'd had enough, just wanted them to go.' He gestured to the cluster of small armchairs nestling around a coffee table. 'Please sit, I'm afraid I can't offer you a drink, the staff won't be in until nine.'

Nick slumped into one of the chairs. 'No problem, we've had our breakfast. Did they find anything?'

Nathalie glared at him. 'Geoff said that you wanted Nick to come along as he's been to Surabaya recently. We'll help you all we can but I'm not sure if we know any more than you do. Why don't you start by telling us exactly what happened.'

Graven-faced, Townes sat down and told Nick and Nathalie about the first visitation from the police. They were just making enquiries. Some documentation involving the names of Rob Barnes and Biomedivac had come into their possession. They wanted to know what Professor Townes knew about it.

'I told them, nothing, never heard of the lab. Tried to contact Rob but couldn't get hold of him. Thought the police would leave me alone and go after Rob, but no, this morning...' James Townes gestured around the room.

Nathalie flicked her eyes at Nick indicating that she would take the floor. 'And did they take anything away?'

'No, not a thing.' Townes paused nervously.

Sensing there was more Nathalie interjected quietly. 'Not a thing, but...?'

Townes folded his arms and took a deep breath. 'I suppose I should tell you.'

Nathalie and Nick waited.

Townes leaned forward as if he didn't want anyone else to hear, even though there was no one else in the room. 'They wanted Rob's computer.'

Nathalie and Nick waited again in silence.

'I've done nothing illegal. That computer has proprietary confidential information. It's technically not Rob's. I told them that his personal computer might be in his flat.'

'So where is his company computer?' asked Nathalie softly.

Townes looked nervously around him, 'It's in the laboratory under some apparatus. I put it there after their first visit.'

'Perhaps we should have a look at that,' suggested Nick.

'I've tried, he's put a new cryptic password on it. Haven't had time to investigate further, and now this has happened, and I don't even know what it's about.'

Nathalie knew that she had to divulge something to Professor Townes. Geoff had already told him that Nick had been to Surabaya. She made a decision.

243

'Nick is with security,' she said hastily skipping what sort of security Nick was in. 'He was with the Indonesian police force when they raided the laboratory that contained some paperwork with Doctor Barnes' name on it. Now the consignment note could be quite legitimate, but the laboratory has been involved in some illegal practices so I expect the police want to clarify things.'

Townes spluttered. 'But I've never heard of any laboratory in eastern Java. Until this week I'd never even heard of a place called Surabaya.'

'There could be some very simple explanation,' said Nathalie, trying to calm the professor down. 'Rob could have just been requisitioning some equipment there because it was cheaper or something. Let's not jump to conclusions, but I'm sure we would know more if we could take a look at Rob's computer.'

Eventually James Townes agreed to fetch the computer. He placed it on the coffee table between them and typed in the Biomedivac company password. The laptop protested with a ding. No access.

Nick reached into his pocket, pulled out a notepad and pen and handed it to Townes.

'Do me a favour Professor. Write down Rob's date of birth, mother's maiden name, pet's name if he's got one, and the titles of any important papers he's written. There are other ways of getting into these things but I'd need to give it to a mate of mine, let's see if this works first.'

Townes scribbled away and Nick tapped in the words. After an hour they had exhausted the list.

'Okay your staff will be turning up soon, why don't you and Nathalie tidy up the office while I try one more trick,' said Nick staring at the piece of paper.

Nathalie was just putting the last drawer into place when Nick shouted 'bingo'. She and Townes rushed over to the laptop. The screen had changed and they could see icons of rows and rows of files.

'No idea what it means,' said Nick. 'But I stuck in this.' He handed Nathalie the piece of paper with the words *B amyloid* circled on it.

'It's a peptide,' said Nathalie thoughtfully. 'Something in a paper that was very important to him, but I thought you tried that before.'

'Yeah, but without the numbers.'

Townes began to stare at the files on the computer. 'Numbers?'

'I stuck numbers instead of the letters O and I,' said Nick. 'Common practice, luckily one followed by Rob.'

Townes sifted through the documents, most were familiar but one led to a file containing a series of unconventional correspondence.

'Lazy boy,' commented Nick. 'No passwords on the document, must have been in a hurry.'

'I didn't give permission for this,' said an outraged Professor Townes, pointing at an e-mail under the Biomedivac letterhead. 'Why would he order that?'

The order was for samples of bizarre pathogens. Ones that did not appear in any microbiological textbook. The price was high, but it appeared that it was being paid from a Biomedivac bank account, showing the delivery address, the company's lab in Morocco and the source, the laboratory in Surabaya.

Nathalie was careful with her words, 'It's possible that he wanted some bacteria to test on a new antibiotic idea that he was working on, or...'

'Or he was getting at me,' said Townes slowly and deliberately. 'He's always borne a grudge, an unwarranted one, but a grudge. If this gets out Biomedivac will be ruined.'

✳

On the way back to the office Nathalie explained to Nick about the problems that Rob Barnes had had with his original thesis. He genuinely believed that James Townes had taken his ideas and used them for the benefit of Biomedivac without giving him the credit. Whether this was true or not she didn't know but Townes' theory of a grudge seemed to fit the picture. When Nick had explained that it would be extremely difficult for the Surabaya police to lay any blame on the UK company, Townes seemed to be partially placated. They all agreed that it would be the best idea to leave the computer in the laboratory; if the UK police found it, then so be it. Townes could genuinely claim that he had nothing to do with the correspondence. However, more likely, the case would be dropped. The Indonesians had got their man and the rest was peripheral, not to say outrageously expensive to follow up. Rather than put the professor off the Moroccan filming, the events seemed to make him more enthusiastic. In fact he would accompany them on the shoot and check with the Moroccan lab first-hand whether they had any more information about the requisition of the illegal material.

'Spider's web,' said Nathalie.

Nick pulled the car up outside of Nathalie's flat and turned to her. 'What in the hell is that meant to mean.'

'It's all coming together,' she said opening the door. 'Your Indonesian thing, Roszak, Rob Barnes and Morocco. I knew it couldn't be coincidence.'

'Roszak, whoever he is, and Rob Barnes, are you losing it Nathalie?'

'Far from it Nick, spider's web, but I don't know who's in the middle, or why Rob Barnes happened to choose our lab in Indonesia.'

'Anyway, have to dash, I'll let you work on that one. Tell Geoff I'm around tomorrow if he wants me.'

'Will do,' she was about to say but Nick was already speeding down the road and weaving in and out of the mid-day London traffic.

The flat was cold and her bed unmade. Not very welcoming. Nathalie looked in the fridge for something to eat. A couple of natural yoghurts, three eggs and an old piece of ham which was curling up under the plastic wrapping. She looked at the sell-by date on the yoghurts, threw them away and made herself a ham omelette. She was just finishing the last morsel when her phone rang.

'Stefanie, you beat me to it, just got back to my flat. I'll be in later this afternoon to go through the shoot arrangements.'

Stefanie's cultured voice came from the other end. 'Good, it's still on then?'

'Absolutely, you can confirm the flights now if you wish.'

'I'll do that, but it's not the reason I'm calling. Do you recall that Esther Phillips woman who came into our office some time ago?'

'Of course, I've been meaning to try to get to see her. Geoff says she wants to thank me or something, but I've been so busy.'

'She's called in again. They have let her go home and she would like to meet with you. I've got her address; if you have the time perhaps you could drop in to see her on your way to the office. It's only a couple of Tube stops from here.'

✳

The apartment was in a large row of sombre-looking mansion flats. These buildings made Nathalie shudder, transient dwellings with common halls and stairways. There were about a dozen nameplates on the row of brass bell buttons. Nathalie made out the faded name of E Phillips and pressed one of them. The response was almost instant.

'Is that Miss Thompson?'

Nathalie looked around for a security camera but couldn't see one.

'Yes, Nathalie Thompson, is that you Esther?'

'Thank you for coming, your office said you would be round. Please come up, I'm on the first floor.'

That explained the reaction thought Nathalie. Stefanie had phoned on ahead. She pushed open the door and entered a cold black-and-white tiled entrance hall. In front of her an old wooden staircase spiralled up into the distance. She took the threadbare rust-coloured carpet and made her way to the first floor. Esther Phillips was there waiting for her.

'It's really good of you to come Miss Thompson, your office have said that you are very busy.'

'No problem Esther. Sorry I haven't been able to make it before, I've been travelling.'

Esther Phillips led her into her apartment. The furnishings had seen better days but they were neat and clean. The window on the far side looked out on to a courtyard and an open door to the right led into a small kitchen. In the centre of the room was a low oak table set with a teapot and two ornamental cups.

'Please sit down. I've been really embarrassed over these few weeks thinking about what I did that day. I really just wanted to thank you for your kindness and to apologise.' Esther pointed to the cups. 'Tea?'

Not exactly Nathalie's favourite beverage but she was too polite to say so. She sat down as invited. 'Thank you Esther that would be wonderful. So how are you now?'

Esther sat in the small armchair opposite and started to pour out the tea. 'I feel physically fine, it's just this terrible problem with memory. The doctors are marvellous, they've given me some medication and counselling and bit by bit some of it is returning. But not all I'm afraid.' Tears moistened her cheeks. 'A lot of my life is still completely missing.'

Nathalie took a cup and placed it on her lap. 'I'm really sorry Esther. What do you remember about the day we met?'

'Not a lot I'm afraid. I don't know if it's what the doctors have told me or my own memory. I just know that you were very kind, took me in and helped me to a hospital. That's why I wanted to meet you. I don't know what would have happened to me if you hadn't...'

Nathalie saw that Esther was about to burst into tears and so she decided to take a matter-of-fact tack. 'Anyone would have done the same Esther and, besides, I was with a doctor; it was he who got you to the hospital. I'm glad to see that you're okay.'

'I'm not sure about okay but as I said the doctors have been very good.'

Nathalie was beginning to feel uncomfortable. She'd done her duty, the woman had thanked her, perhaps she ought to go.

Esther Phillips stood up and took a cup and saucer over to the window. She stared out onto the courtyard. 'Miss Thompson?'

'Nathalie, please call me Nathalie.'

'Of course, yes Nathalie. Could you tell me one thing?'

'If I can.'

'I was told I had your business card, when did you give that to me?'

'I didn't, at least I'm pretty sure I didn't. I'm good at faces; if we had met before that day I'm sure I would have remembered.'

'So how did I get it? I knew that it was important, I'm sure someone told me that.'

'That's been puzzling me too Esther.'

Esther returned to the table, sat down and placed her cup on the surface. She looked sheepishly at Nathalie, 'I'm afraid I've got a little confession.'

Twenty-seven

The room went eerily quiet. Esther's cup clinked against the saucer and she fumbled with the hem of her cardigan. Nathalie waited a while and, when no further comment was forthcoming, leaned forward to touch Esther gently on the arm.

'What is it Esther? What's worrying you?'

Esther took a deep breath and shook her head. 'I'm really sorry Miss Thompson but one of the reasons I wanted you to come round was to find out more about my past. I really thought you must have known me. I had your card, I thought we may have worked together or even been friends. I hope you don't think badly of me inviting you around.'

Nathalie smiled at her. 'Not at all Esther. In fact I've a confession too, I'm as curious as to why you had my card as you are.'

Esther's hands were still shaking. She put the cup down to stop it rattling further. 'I've tried everything, even walking up and down to the outside of your office to see if I could remember anything. From time to time, especially after the medication, I get flashes of recall but it disappears as quickly as it comes.'

'What sort of recall?'

'The doctors have told me that I mentioned something about a place I stayed in once. Apparently the hospital wards reminded me of it. Also something to do with taking little pink pills. I thought maybe it was just recent memory because of my treatment, but they said the rooms and pills I described were totally different.'

'Can you remember anything about the place now?'

'Not really. As I said I can't remember if it's my recall or what the doctors have told me I said.'

Nathalie tried to normalise the situation by taking a sip from her cup. The acrid taste of the tea came as a shock to her and she remembered the smoky hut in Zimbabwe with Lloyd and the terrorists.

'Esther,' she said thoughtfully. 'You don't happen to have any cleaning fluid in your flat?'

Esther looked at her in surprise. 'Why, have you spilt something?'

'No, but I've just had an idea.'

'I'm not sure, the kitchen cabinet is where I keep things like that.'

'Do you mind if we take a look?'

'Of course not,' said Esther. 'The kitchen is straight through that door.'

The two of them made their way to the kitchen and Nathalie rummaged through the cupboard to find a small bottle of methylated spirits.

'I can't remember what I bought that for,' said Esther. 'But I can't remember much nowadays,' she added sadly.

Nathalie unscrewed the top and waved the cap under Esther's nose.

'Remind you of anything, a sense of place?'

Esther closed her eyes and thought for a while.

'The hospital you mean.'

'Yes but any hospital in particular?'

Esther took another sniff and closed her eyes again. Nathalie waited patiently and looked around the small kitchen. The usual paraphernalia. Hanging saucepans, kitchen cupboards and a small noticeboard attached to one wall. She walked up to it.

'Do you use this?' she asked holding up a thin folded booklet.

Esther opened her eyes and blinked getting accustomed to the light. 'What is it?'

'A monthly calendar, can I take a look?'

'By all means, I didn't realise that it was there.'

Nathalie flicked through the pages. The last few weeks were blank but further back were some entries in small spidery writing. Most were for items of shopping: *scouring pads, tomato soup, stock cubes.* Others were for appointments: *dentist, hairdresser,* and then the shock entry, *Clinic Dr B.* Nathalie folded over the page and took it to Esther.

251

'Did you write this?'

'I think it's my handwriting.'

'Does this mean anything to you?'

Esther stared at the words. *Clinic Dr B*. She closed her eyes and then shook her head.

'Sorry, it doesn't mean a thing.'

Nathalie looked at the date, May, several months ago. She was desperate to shake Esther Phillips to get more information out of her, but she knew it would be no good. Esther was a delicate frightened woman. One who had had her memory stolen from her. She had to be patient.

'Esther, it says here "clinic", I think that at some point you may have mentioned to the doctors that you were on a clinical trial. Is that right?'

Esther was becoming agitated, she walked up and down the kitchen. 'I don't know, I really don't know. I'm sorry, but I remember small things and then I forget them again, I don't know what I've said.'

'It's all right, I understand, but if you were on a trial there would have been paperwork. Where would you have kept that?'

Esther began to cry. 'I wish I knew, I can't pay the gas bill, I can't find my bank details, if it wasn't for the lady from Social Security...'

Nathalie ushered her back into the living room. 'I didn't mean to upset you Esther, I'm just trying to help. Can I look around your flat?'

'Please do, if you can find anything, anything that will help me get my life back.'

The flat was small and very tidy. Nathalie methodically went through the shelves and cupboards. Not a scrap of paper to be found.

'You're very neat Esther. I'm sure you would have put your paperwork in one place somewhere, but it's not in this room, do you have anywhere else?'

'My bedroom is through the other door over there,' said Esther pointing. 'You're welcome to take a look, I have nothing to hide,' she smiled forlornly. 'At least, I don't think I have.'

Nathalie went into the room. It was as well-ordered as the others: a small dressing table under the window; a few items of jewellery hanging on a ceramic hand. A standard size double bed filled most of the room. One small bedside table held some pots of pills. Nathalie began to walk around the bed to take a look when her feet touched an obstacle under the canopy. She leant down and found a thin brown leather suitcase. It was of the old-fashioned type with two locks either side of the handle. Nathalie flicked them open. Inside were a number of Manila folders. She studied them for a moment before taking them through to Esther in the living room.

'Esther, I think I've found your bank details,' she said opening one of the folders. 'And, if I'm not wrong, the reason why you were given my business card.'

✳

The silhouette of the Alhambra Palace cut into the ochre sky. The Moors had labelled it the crimson castle and it was not difficult to see why. Nathalie loved Granada. She had been here before on holiday but had missed the chance to visit Flamenco. They had one evening before driving off to Morocco; she wasn't going to miss it again. Tom and her cameramen John McCord had agreed to go with her. Walking along the valley between the two hills that dominated the city, they were seeking a nightclub under the ancient stone arches. It was easy to find; a dark-haired lissom woman dressed in a low-cut red polka dot gown leant against the corner of an alley. She was drawing erotically on a cigarette.

'Flamenco?' her husky voice exhaled the smoke as she made the invitation.

They nodded and she gestured towards a small doorway set in the rocks. Inside a young man took the money and showed them to a bench seat opposite a long table. They ordered a drink and looked around. It was very small. A low white-washed arched ceiling above their heads and a narrow room leading to a small wooden stage containing two rustic chairs. The room was lined with bench seats and tables like the one they were sitting at. When full it would only hold about thirty people.

'Who's for a cold beer?' perfect English with a slight Spanish accent, the waiter was clutching three large glasses of frothing gold liquid.

They all raised their hands, and gratefully took the drinks. It was hot in this part of Spain and even the thick stone walls around them provided little protection.

'Thanks guys, I appreciate you coming,' said Nathalie wiping the froth from her lips. 'We've got a long drive tomorrow but I really didn't want to miss this.'

'Cheers Nathalie,' said John McCord clinking her glass. 'Good to have some relaxation on these trips. Everyone thinks it's a glamorous life travelling with a film camera, they don't realise that most of the time we don't have time to take in the places we've landed in. Been to New York twenty times, most of it filming hospital interiors and offices. Never seen the Statue of Liberty.'

'Yeah but you get to see things through the back door,' said Tom. 'Stuff tourists can't get access to.'

John downed his drink in one and indicated to the waiter that he wanted another. 'True, but when you've done as much travelling for work as I have it's good to be a tourist from time to time.'

Within half an hour the club filled and the performers came to the stage. The show was everything they expected it to be. Raw, rhythmic and energetic. Despite the small platform the dancer flung herself into a hypnotic trance and the singer and guitarist filled the chamber with harmonic structures punctuated with sharp handclaps and a struck guitar. At the end of the evening the three left the club and walked into the warm evening air with the mesmerising sounds still filling their heads.

'I'm really glad we went to that,' said Tom. 'I never understood what all the fuss was about before. They were amazing.'

'Yeah, the real thing,' said John. 'Not the commercial crap you find in the tourist traps.'

'Thought you wanted to be a tourist,' laughed Nathalie. 'Come on you two, I'll buy you a nightcap in the hotel bar in exchange for a briefing, how does that sound?'

'Sounds like we've stopped being tourists,' said John. 'But, as I'm being paid for being here, why not.'

The hotel was set just below the old quarter of the town. It was modern with all the amenities and the staff had taken care to lock John's camera gear in a secure room. Nathalie knew that this was the only way John would have accepted the invitation to have a night out, otherwise he would have sat in his room the whole evening on top of the camera case. The bar was pleasant, warm lighting with low music. They sat in a corner and Nathalie handed out the call-sheets.

'We are being picked up early by the Spanish crew. Two of them, one sound, one sparks. We've got two trucks, they'll do the driving. Tom and I'll go with the sound guy, and John, you can ride shotgun with the sparks. We're catching the ferry at Tarifa and should be in Casablanca before nightfall. The next morning we have to cut across inland to the laboratory. Apparently the road is pretty rough so that's why we've got 4x4s. When we get there Tom will introduce us to Temba. We'll just proceed with filming according to the schedule leaving Tom to see if he can persuade Temba to take part in our sting in his own time. If he's successful we'll build in a private interview on camera. Any questions?'

John took his call-sheet and tapped on the table. 'No, just as we discussed. I had a chat with the sparks on the phone and he knows what he's doing so we should be okay on the technical front. Now, if you'll excuse me, I'm off to bed. See you at six.'

The two men rose and started to make their way to the elevators. Nathalie remained seated.

'Aren't you coming?' asked Tom.

'In a moment,' said Nathalie. 'Have to make a phone call to Stefanie. I've asked her to follow up something in London for me. Want to know how she got on.'

Sebastian and Axel turned up on time. They carefully loaded John's camera equipment into one of the trucks and were on the road within minutes. There was little traffic on the autopista and the olive groves sped past them at a hundred and twenty kilometres an hour. The idea was to get to Tarifa before eleven. From there it was only an hour's ferry ride to Tangier in North Africa. There was plenty of time to brief Sebastian, the sound recordist, and so Tom and Nathalie dozed in the back seat trying to catch up on some sleep. After a fuel stop and coffee they felt more alert and made conversation with their driver. Sebastian spoke perfect English, had worked for Bagatelle before and, from some of his stories, sounded pretty experienced. Nathalie felt in safe hands; there was nothing worse than getting to the edit suite with perfect pictures only to find out the sound was muffled.

'Any time you want to hear playback, just give me the nod,' he said. 'If I hear any background noise I'll tell you by lifting a finger. I know how directors get frustrated by a sound guy shouting out "cut" during a sensitive take.'

'Sounds like we are singing from the same call-sheet Sebastian,' said Nathalie. 'I wouldn't worry, you've come highly recommended. Stefanie thinks you are the real deal,' she chuckled. 'But that may be something more to do with your photograph.'

Tom saved Sebastian's embarrassment by intervening.

'Talking of Stefanie, did you get through to her last night?'

'That I did Tom, and very interesting it was too.'

'Are you going to tell me about it?'

'You've got your plateful with Temba so I was going to leave it till later but I might as well fill you in now, as you've asked.'

Tom looked at her with exasperation, 'Go on then, spill the beans, I knew that phone call was important.'

'I'm not sure if we've got the whole story yet but it's to do with Rob Barnes. Geoff kept telling me to leave it alone but I knew there was something not right with that guy.'

'I thought you'd sorted all that; why we found the Biomedivac paperwork in Surabaya.'

'Yes, but we still don't know how he found out about that particular laboratory, although I have a hunch on that.'

Nathalie turned around to look at the truck following them. 'Good they're keeping up, I hope when we get to that lab we'll find out a little more.'

'So that's all she said?'

'Who?'

'Stefanie, who else?'

'Sorry Tom, just remembering my second meeting with Rob Barnes. I left him with my bag for a moment, had all my papers in it. All your research on Surabaya.'

'You mean he could have taken a look.'

'Wouldn't put it past him, slippery character.'

'So is that what you talked to Stefanie about?'

'No, but it could be connected. Remember I told you about overhearing a conversation with Barnes and a guy called Roszak in Los Angeles?'

Tom nodded.

'Barnes is obviously up to something, trying to discredit Townes and Biomedivac. Could be jealousy, but I think it's more than that. Anyway I made a visit to that poor woman with memory loss, you know the one who had my business card.'

'How is she?'

'Not good Tom, I don't think she'll ever get her full memory back. She let me look around her apartment and I found some paperwork relating to clinical trials.'

'What, testing drugs on people with poor memory?'

'No, quite the opposite. The trial was testing a new Alzheimer's drug on healthy volunteers.'

Tom sat back in the seat of the truck and took in a deep breath. He was suddenly getting the idea.

'You're now going to tell me that the trial was Biomedivac's.'

'Precisely Tom, and the leader of the trial was Doctor Robert Barnes.'

Tom whistled. 'So that's where she got your card from, you told me you'd met Barnes earlier.'

'That's right, when I was starting research on this project. The thing we have to establish now is why he gave Esther my card. But I have a theory on that one too.'

They were approaching the Tarifa ferry. Nathalie was obviously not going to expound any further so Tom busied himself fishing out their documentation from his bag. The two trucks were waved into a short queue of cars and vans by a port official. They presented their passports and vehicle papers and after a short while were guided onto the roll-on roll-off ferry. They had been told the trip would only take an hour. An hour on a boat from Europe to Africa, it seemed strange, but the timetable was correct and it wasn't long before they were being shepherded into a large arrivals hall. The exit of this hall took longer than the passage of the ferry. One by one men in military type uniforms came up to them asking them to fill in paperwork. They did this repeatedly a number of times. Eventually a senior official, senior by his groomed grey beard and authoritative cap, walked up to Sebastian and asked him to go with him to the office. Sebastian kept very cool.

'Won't be a moment, have to technically import the vehicles,' he said to the others. 'Normal procedure. They're looking for a backhander,' he whispered to Nathalie.

Half an hour later the military bureaucrats opened the gates and the two film trucks drove into the outskirts of Tangiers. Once through the city Sebastian and Axel pulled over to fill up with diesel. John suggested that, as the journey to their hotel would take another four hours, they should take some lunch in the service station. All were in agreement so they bought sandwiches and soft drinks and sat around one of the restaurant's Formica tables.

'Not very Moroccan,' said Tom looking at the cloned service station decor.

'They've upgraded the roads and gas stations,' said Axel. 'We should be grateful, ten years ago it was difficult to find a fuel pump.'

'I was hoping for something more exotic; you know, decorative carpets, exotic pottery, hookah pipes.'

Nathalie laughed. 'Don't worry Tom. Next stop Casablanca.'

'Play it again Sam,' said Tom.

'He didn't say that!' they all shouted in unison.

Twenty-eight

Casablanca was one of those places that John McCord would call 'been but not seen'. The crew arrived in the dark and left before dawn. The GPS maps in the trucks didn't cover Africa and they navigated by the hand-drawn one given to Nathalie by Professor Townes. They took the A5 south towards El-Jadida, their headlights picking out the monotonous tarmac of the motorway. By the time they had reached their turnoff the natural light took over and they were able to see the unspectacular barren land on either side as they headed towards the Mid Atlas. The roads became narrower and the French road signs turned into Arabic. Passing cars became fewer and were gradually replaced with donkeys and carts. This was the Morocco that Tom was hoping for.

'I think we were meant to turn right back there,' he said peering at the map.

'Are you sure?' asked Nathalie. 'The professor told me that we couldn't miss it; the turning should be just after the vineyards.'

'Weird isn't it…' said Sebastian, swerving to avoid a large rock in the road. 'Who would have thought they would make wine here.'

'A hangover from French colonial days I think,' said Nathalie. 'Anyway, I'm sure we haven't passed them yet.'

Sebastian pulled the steering wheel over once more, this time to avoid an old lady on a pony. 'No hangover from last night, the hotel didn't sell alcohol.'

Tom was still wrestling with the map. 'A good job too; reading this map in a bucking truck is making me quite queasy. I'm sure we should have turned right back there, can't we ask someone?'

'Only if they can speak French,' said Sebastian. 'My Arabic's non-existent.'

Nathalie shouted and pointed in front of them. 'There, I told you so; look huge vineyards.'

Spread out before them were rows and rows of vines. They could almost be driving through central France apart from the fact that the vines were sprinkled with blue and orange plastic bags. Evidently, rubbish collection was not the priority here.

'Tragic isn't it.' said Nathalie. 'Idyllic rural life ruined by the import of non-disposable plastic.'

The little convoy made its way past the vineyards and through a small bustling town. Sebastian pulled up by a cluster of people and wound down the window. He asked directions to the laboratory, first in English and then in French, but the men just smiled at him. Nathalie took the map from Tom and held it out of the window. The men looked at it and kept smiling.

'Ask them if they know where the kasbah is,' said Tom. 'It's marked on the map, and is only ten kilometres from the lab.'

Sebastian shaded his eyes in a gesture to show that he was looking for something. 'Kasbah, kasbah?' he said.

It was evident that the men understood the word. They talked amongst each other and then pointed excitedly down a side alley. 'Kasbah, kasbah,' they repeated.

'Merci, merci,' said Sebastian, starting up the truck again and aiming for the turnoff. 'I hope there's only one bloody kasbah,' he muttered, winding up the window.

The road became rougher and then practically disappeared. Their only guidance for direction were the parallel ruts from past vehicles exposing the sand through the scrub. They were about to give up and turn back when Nathalie saw an extraordinary sandstone fortress in the distance.

'That's it,' she cried. 'We are nearly there, but why in the hell did they build a laboratory out here in the middle of the desert.'

The dilapidated but magnificent kasbah was perched in a meander of a wadi. As they approached they could see some greenery and buildings on the other side.

261

'That's why it's been so difficult,' said Sebastian. 'We should have come in from the other direction. Look over there, metalled roads leading to that modern compound.'

Fortunately, in one place the wadi was dry and the two 4x4s scrambled across it and onto the road on the other side. The compound entrance was barred by a series of gates and reception buildings. Nathalie showed her passport and the security guards waved them through. Professor Townes greeted them effusively.

'Ah, well done you've made it. I'm glad my map worked, without it you may have had some difficulty, it's a hard place to find.'

Nathalie didn't tell him how hard it was and just introduced the crew. They were shepherded through the pristine corridors to a small canteen where they were offered something to eat. It was a little early for lunch but Nathalie thought that it would be a good way to regroup and plan the rest of the day. She asked Professor Townes to join them to discuss the schedule.

She needn't have worried. He passed her a piece of paper with a step-by-step plan. First they would film the research laboratories – assistants had been primed to re-enact any procedures Nathalie wanted – and then they could record some interviews in the boardroom. The manufacturing plant and anything else she wanted to film could be scheduled for the second day. It sounded perfect but she noticed that Tom was becoming agitated.

'That's great Professor Townes. You mentioned in London that we could get an interview with Temba Murauzi, your exchange scientist. Tom here has met him before and I understand that he could talk us through how your vaccines could be used for antidotes. It would be good if we could do a scene in the lab with him. Obviously it needn't involve real viruses, but as long as we could mock it up in a realistic way.'

The professor appeared a lot more relaxed in these surroundings. He seemed to have forgotten the trauma of the London raid.

'Yes, I know we agreed that didn't we; on the condition that no proprietary information is disclosed of course.'

'Naturally,' said Nathalie. 'We'll be guided by you. Is Mr Murauzi in the building?'

'Doctor Murauzi. Yes he arrived yesterday. Doing some really important work for us. Several months ago he was adding his expertise to our experimental Alzheimer's drugs for trials. A real authority on chiral molecules you know. Busy man but I know he's agreed to give you an hour of his time. If you would like to take some of your general shots first then I'll send someone to fetch him.'

The laboratories were state-of-the-art. Glass-partitioned divided rooms, glinting apparatus and stainless steel surfaces. John and Axel worked hand in glove with the lighting and, from what Nathalie could see on monitors, the shots were extraordinary. They would make a great contrast and punctuation to the terrorists in the African bush. Her idea was to give a brief insight into how viruses worked and the methods used in combating them. This wasn't meant to be a science programme but she knew her audience; they wouldn't want academic detail but they would be insulted if she skirted around the issue. They had paused for a while for Sebastian to take some ambient sound when Nathalie noticed Tom waving to her from the other side of the partition. She tiptoed out of the room.

'What is it Tom?'

'Temba, I met him in the corridor, he's on for the antidote interview.'

Nathalie looked at him expectantly.

Tom shook his head. 'No, not yet, it's too soon. I'll broach the meeting with WEXA over a drink this evening. Apparently there's a social bar on the other side of the compound. I'll see if I can get him on his own. But change the subject, he's coming around the corner.'

Nathalie looked over her shoulder to see a smart young African man in a starched lab coat. As he approached she did a double-take; she was good at faces and she was sure that she had met this man before.

Tom introduced them. 'Hi again, this is Nathalie my director. Nathalie, Doctor Murauzi who I have been telling you about.'

Temba put out his hand, 'Temba please, good to meet you Nathalie.'

Nathalie was distracted in the briefing meeting. She kept trying to place the face, it was so annoying.

'Nathalie,' said Tom brusquely. 'Temba was asking you how his scene would fit into the programme. How much depth do you want to go into on antiviral mechanisms?'

'Sorry,' said Nathalie. 'Not too much detail, but it's got to be factual. A brief description of how viruses get into cells and how Biomedivac's vaccine hunts them down. Not too many long words, and definitely not a lecture; pretend you're trying to explain it to a favourite nephew or something.'

'And what about this thing on bioterrorism?' asked Temba. 'Tom tells me that's what the real programme is focusing on.'

'That's true,' said Nathalie. 'What we are trying to do with these scenes is show what the authorities could do in combating nefarious groups who might use these nasty weapons.'

Temba nodded thoughtfully. 'Okay, I'll do my best. I'll set up a slide with an Ebola virus and you can use our monitors to see what they look like. It's difficult to stop them breeding, and not all antivirals are effective, but I can give you the theory if you like.'

Nathalie thought that was rather a strange answer. Why not just explain how Biomedivac's vaccine worked, but she let it lie.

'Fantastic Temba. Like your idea of the microscope; how long will that take to set up?'

'Oh, ten to twenty minutes, just need to be sure that the virus is contained. Your guys will need to be given the protocols.'

'Absolutely,' said Nathalie. 'We don't want any accidents. I remember the time when a sparks started to eat a donut in the School of Tropical Medicine. The medic went ballistic, told him if he wanted to catch the last sample of smallpox in the country he was welcome. The poor guy spent the next ten minutes of the shoot washing his hands. Take as much time as you need, I'll follow on in a few minutes.'

Temba started to make his way down the corridor. Tom was about to follow but Nathalie pulled him back.

'What's the problem?' asked Tom. 'You're behaving a bit strangely, you kept staring at the poor guy.'

'Was it that obvious?' replied Nathalie. 'It was just something I couldn't get out of my head, anyway he didn't seem to notice. What I was going to ask you was to meet up with Townes while we're doing the interview. He said he'll go through the admin paperwork to see if he can find anything about that Rob Barnes' requisition. I'd like you to be there to check that he really is doing that.'

'You think he's got something to hide?'

'Not sure. Think he was genuinely surprised about Rob's e-mail but there's something else he's not telling us. Could be about the Alzheimer's trial. Keep your eyes open, let me know if you see anything unusual.'

'You're the boss.'

'Dead right I am and, next time, less of the cheek telling me I'm acting like a weirdo.' She turned on her heels and made her way to the lab.

✳

The sun was setting against the backdrop of the Moroccan desert when Nathalie at last called it a wrap. John McCord helped Axel store the lamps whilst Sebastian checked over the footage and backed up the video drives. Nathalie was pleased with the day's work. Temba turned out to be a real star; cool under the lights, he delivered his interview with succinctness and charm. Just the right tone she thought, full of information and without jargon. Nathalie had often heard the phrase 'they know their stuff but can't teach'. It was something she didn't agree with – if you really knew your stuff it shouldn't be difficult to tell other people about it.

'Great interview Temba. You're in the wrong business, you should be on TV.'

Temba lowered his eyes shyly and gave a slight shrug.

'If I wasn't in this business you wouldn't be filming me, but I can't pretend I didn't enjoy it.'

'I believe you're going to have a chat with Tom this evening, perhaps we can persuade you to do some more.'

'Someone taking my name in vain?' asked Tom walking around the corner.

Temba turned to him and smiled, 'No, Nathalie was just saying we are going to meet up, but I must change and take a shower first. See you in the bar at seven?'

'Great,' said Tom. 'See you then.' He flicked his eyes at Nathalie indicating he wanted to talk.

She took the hint.

'I'm afraid I won't be able to join you,' said Nathalie to Temba. 'Some prep to do for tomorrow's filming, and just before you go Tom, a quick word?'

Tom said goodbye to Temba and followed Nathalie into the nearest office. She put down her bag and sat on one of the desks.

'Well?'

Tom stood in front of her and took his phone out of his pocket.

'I think you might be interested in this. Met up with Townes as you suggested. We spent nearly an hour going through the laboratory paperwork. Not a sign of anything to do with the Surabaya lab. Not even any orders to do with procuring bugs of any sort.'

'So why are you waving that phone at me?'

'Townes was so keen to find something that he pulled out documents all over the place. One of which I'm sure he didn't mean me to see.' Tom handed Nathalie his phone. 'I took a quick photo.'

Nathalie looked at the image and spread her fingers across the screen so that she could read it. It was a report on a Biomedivac clinical trial in the UK. A lot of it was a maze of numbers and p-values, but the study topic was quite clear. '*Stage III trials to analyse the safety profile of altzamine in healthy volunteers*'. Altzamine was the name for Biomedivac's prototype drug for Alzheimer's disease.

Nathalie hastily scrolled down the list of subjects. It was no surprise to find E. Phillips amongst the twenty or so names.

'Are you sure he doesn't know you've got this?'

'Absolutely,' said Tom. 'He was engrossed the other side of the room, I was very careful.'

'You shouldn't have, but I'm glad you did,' said Nathalie. 'Did you have time to read it?'

'No it was in a folder marked confidential, just saw the title. Thought you would understand it better than me.'

Nathalie studied the screen in more detail, 'This is dynamite Tom. It appears that they withdrew the trial because there were what they call "anomalous results" in a small number of the participants.' She used a finger to scroll down a little further. 'Apparently all of them were taking capsules from a batch labelled #124. In fact, if my reading of the data is right, the group actually started losing memory. It seems as if they've tried to cover this up, or at least Townes has. Poor Esther Phillips is part of the collateral damage.'

'And Rob Barnes?'

'Exactly Tom. As the head of the clinical trial he would obviously have to have been involved. He couldn't come out with the results without Biomedivac's permission – confidentiality and all that.'

Tom took back his phone. 'So you think Barnes gave Esther your card in the hope that the publicity would get out.'

'That's about it, I'm a television journalist why wouldn't I follow it up? The world would hear the data and Biomedivac shares would plummet. Zormax could do a takeover and no doubt Roszak would give Barnes a place on the board. Unfortunately for Robert Barnes I didn't take the bait, meaning he had to try something else.'

'The Surabaya e-mail.'

'QED Tom. You had better text me that photo and wipe it from your phone.'

'What will you do with it?'

Nathalie slipped off the desk. 'Not sure yet, but I don't want you to be caught with it. We'll keep this to ourselves for the time being.

We have other fish to fry for the moment.' She looked at her watch. 'You had better go and get washed and changed; Temba Murauzi will be waiting for you in the bar and you need to be at your best if you are going to persuade him to take part in entrapping WEXA.'

There was hardly anyone in the bar. Looking around, Tom couldn't see Temba so he purchased two whiskeys and took a table in one dimly lit part of the room. He was feeling really nervous. He knew Nathalie was depending on him to do this deal. He had implied that he would be able to persuade this talented scientist to go undercover and expose the WEXA terrorists. Now it was crunch time he really was not so sure.

'Hi Tom, that drink for me?' Temba was dressed in a blue linen jacket and cream chinos. His smile lit up the room.

'Hope whiskey's okay,' said Tom standing. 'You're looking really good.'

Temba waved at him to sit down, 'Well, thank you, you don't look bad yourself.'

The two young men sipped their drinks and made small talk for a while. How was the club scene in Harare? What was George doing now? Was Temba dating at the moment? It became evident that Tom was stalling for time.

Temba stood up taking the empty whiskey glasses between his two fingers. 'Okay Tom, I'm going to recharge our glasses. While I'm doing that perhaps you could work out exactly how you're going to tell me why you've met me here tonight.'

The barman seemed to take an age and Tom was quite breathless by the time Temba returned.

'I'm going to need that,' he said, taking quite a large drink.

'I'll make it easy for you,' said Temba also taking a draft. 'I know this is something to do with your bioterror film, your director has hinted as much. What is it that you want me to do?'

Tom told him the story. The WEXA group. Their threat to spread disease amongst innocent people. The need for a Zimbabwean they could trust to infiltrate them and to get hard evidence on tape. He knew it was dangerous but it was for a very good cause. It could save a lot of lives.

✳

The next morning Nathalie called an early breakfast meeting, ostensibly to set out the day's filming, but really she was desperate to know the outcome of Tom's negotiations.

'So how did it go?'

Tom played with his bread roll. 'As you can imagine it was quite difficult. At first he said it was dangerous and why should he put his neck on the line.'

Nathalie was becoming irritated. 'Didn't you play the empathy card, tell him he could help stop these guys?'

'Yes I did all that, explained that all he had to do was to persuade them he was a sympathiser and could help out with anti-Ebola drugs to protect their carriers.'

'And did that work?'

'Not at first, but when I started relating the terrible symptoms that Ebola patients could get, it seemed to flick a switch.'

'So you think he'll do it?'

Tom grinned from ear to ear, 'Yep, hidden camera and all.'

'Amazing Tom, well done,' said Nathalie giving him a kiss on the cheek. 'Ebola symptoms you say.'

'That's right, just listed things like fever, red eyes, nausea, vomiting...'

Nathalie suddenly jumped up from the table nearly knocking the coffee cups over. 'That's it!'

'That's what?' said Tom steadying a cup.

'Where I've seen him before. I told you I never forget a face.'

Twenty-nine

The manufacturing plant was a modern low-rise building only a few tens of metres from the laboratories. The crew were fitted out with white overalls and headgear to prevent contamination. Axel remarked that they all looked like storm troopers out of a Star Wars movie.

'I don't suppose they had to wash their phaser guns down with disinfectant,' moaned John McCord, scrubbing his camera tripod.

'It's the only way they'll let us in,' said Nathalie. 'Unless you want to force your way through with light sabres.'

'Light sabres?' said Professor Townes, catching the last few words as he marched up to greet them.

'Oh nothing,' said Nathalie. 'Bad joke amongst film crew. Pretending we are in a good mood this time of the morning. And you Professor, how are you today?'

'Fine thank you Miss Thompson. I see my staff have kitted you out; sorry about the precautions but we can't be too careful here.'

'Quite understand Professor. Whilst the crew finish washing down their equipment, perhaps you could give Tom and me a quick tour so that we can plan what to shoot first.'

Townes led them through a number of air-locked doors to one of the production areas. Axel's reference to Star Wars couldn't have been more appropriate; robotics and space-suited technicians everywhere.

'This section is where we are preparing the prototype medications for our new Alzheimer's drug,' said Professor Townes waving towards a number of production benches. 'We take the active ingredients here and combine them with a neutral compound before inserting them into dissolvable capsules.'

'So this isn't the final production operation then?' asked Nathalie.

'No, this is a very small batch production. The active molecules are prepared in the laboratory across the road and transported here to make the trial medication. However the process is the same; once the trial data has been approved we can scale up very quickly.'

'And will that be soon?'

'Oh yes, very soon. Hoped to be up and running by now but, you know how things are. We had a small hiatus but that's all been smoothed out; by the end of the year I should think.'

Nathalie was tempted to say that she didn't think that Esther Phillips was a small hiatus but she bit her tongue.

'And the Ebola vaccine?'

'Ah, now that's a different process altogether. If you think this looks impressive, follow me, I'll show you the real thing.'

Professor Townes strode with purpose across the floor of the building and led them through another series of airtight cubicles to a vast gleaming hall, ten times the space of the prototype area that they had just left. He stood there for a moment and proudly turned his head from side to side.

'This, my dear guests,' he pronounced rather melodramatically, 'is what state-of-the-art pharmaceutical production looks like.'

So this is why the guy had let them come to Morocco. He was an egotist; this plant was his baby and, although it was tucked away in some African desert, it was the acme of all his achievements. The rows of glittering robotics stretched for hundreds of metres. Hardly a human in sight. Almost silently the machines moved as if being choreographed in some strange ballet. The liquids and powders were moved through coiled glass tubes to stainless steel vats and then into glass vials. Finally, mechanical hands placed these shimmering objects into soft containers that were boxed and branded *XEBO* with the Biomedivac label.

'Wow,' said Tom. 'That's a lot of vaccine.'

'At its peak, fifty million vials a year,' said Townes not taking his eyes off the machines. 'Enough to combat any future Ebola outbreak anywhere in the world.'

Nathalie ran her hand across one of the Biomedivac boxes. The last time she had seen one was in Harare. It was being used to treat a woman who the hospital claimed did not have Ebola. And the woman had a brother, a young lecturer who believed that the hospital was hiding something. And now she knew who that young man was; they had interviewed him yesterday. No wonder he responded when Tom had mentioned the symptoms of Ebola. Temba Murauzi was still angry.

The shoot went as smoothly as the day before. John, Sebastian and Axel swiftly rigged lights, took sound and photographed the space-age scenes to Nathalie's direction. By the end of the day they had filmed practically every process, from the prototype Alzheimer's drug production to the manufacturing and packaging of James Townes' 'pride and joy', the *XEBO* Ebola vaccine.

'I hope you got a close-up of our logo,' said Townes as he watched the crew store their equipment onto the trucks.

'Absolutely Professor,' said Nathalie. 'Thanks for the access. Now all that remains is for you to sign the permission forms for our transmission and, if you don't mind, I'll take the crew to the social bar for a drink, I think they deserve it.'

Townes signed the forms with a flourish and said, as he had a meeting in a nearby town, he would say his goodbyes at tomorrow's breakfast. It was with relief that Nathalie and Tom made their way to the bar without him.

'Smarmy bastard, isn't he,' remarked Tom as they picked out a table.

'I don't know about that,' said Nathalie. 'But he'll do almost anything to keep this place up and running. It's obviously his life's achievement.'

'Yeah, but he's so smug about it. Like some sort of Lord overseeing his manor.'

Nathalie took two ice-cold beers from the barman. 'With downtrodden serfs you mean,' she said, offering one to Tom.

'Serfs?'

'Like Rob Barnes. You can almost see his point. Gets stuffed by Townes, so wants his revenge.'

'What do think happened to him?'

'Lying low in the States I expect. Still hoping for the Biomedivac bubble to burst. With Roszak and Zormax behind him I wouldn't be surprised if he eventually succeeded.'

'How?'

'If the Alzheimer's trial scandal gets out, share prices will drop and they'll move in.'

Tom took a long gulp from his chilled lager and sighed, 'Are we going to be the ones to do that?'

'Yes, a dilemma isn't it. Stuff Townes and abet Barnes. Neither very savoury characters. And all we've got is one grainy photo.'

'We could take another look?'

Nathalie looked at him puzzled.

Tom held up a piece of plastic. 'I've got the key card to his office, he was in such a state that he left it behind. I meant to give it to him this morning, but...'

'Tom!'

Tom blushed. 'No, really I was but, you know what shoots are like, you get so...'

'And you don't think he knows you've got it?'

'Why should he, he would have asked for it wouldn't he?'

Nathalie sat back and downed her last mouthful of beer. She looked around the bar. 'So you left your wallet in his office.'

It was Tom's turn to look puzzled. 'Wallet? You want me to pay for the beers?'

'No Tom,' Nathalie had exasperation in her voice. 'If you've left your wallet in his room, after we've lined up some drinks for the crew, perhaps we should go and look for it.'

They crept along the corridor, looking furtively to either side.

'This is stupid,' said Nathalie. 'We look guilty, we should just walk normally, after all we're only looking for your wallet.'

273

Tom stood upright, looking even more conspicuous. 'Here it is second door on the right. Are you sure he's out of the compound?'

'You were there, he said he had a meeting. Anyway best knock to be absolutely sure.'

Tom knocked gently and put his ear to the door.

'Not a sound,' he whispered, carefully inserting the key card into the slot.

The office looked a complete mess. Drawers open, files strewn everywhere.

'Great,' said Tom. 'He's not had time to clear up from our search for Rob Barnes' documents. He won't notice if we've moved anything.'

Nathalie looked at him sharply.

Tom grinned. 'Whilst looking for my wallet,' he added.

'What was the file like?' asked Nathalie, fingering through a few folders.

'A4, red, word "confidential" stamped on the cover.'

'Oh great,' moaned Nathalie. 'That makes me feel a lot better.'

'You did ask. Why don't you start over by the window and I'll begin from this end.'

The search was more difficult than they had anticipated. There were dozens of red files with the word 'confidential' written on the cover. What made it worse was their contents. Even though Tom had a microbiology degree, these papers were about high-end commercial pharmaceuticals. Most of them contained rows and rows of data and coded indexes.

'This is hopeless,' said Nathalie. 'Can't you remember where you found it?'

'No, I was so concerned about not being seen that I just tucked it under a random pile of documents.'

'But the folder, surely it must have had some distinguishing mark on it or something.'

'No, it was pristine, exactly like this one,' Tom suddenly paused and stared at the piece of paper inside the file he was holding.

'What is it, have you found it?'

Tom didn't reply. He leaned over the paper and then sat down to study it even closer.

'Tom?'

Tom looked up. 'No, it's not the Alzheimer's trial, but if this is what I think it is, it's even more…'

Nathalie snatched the paper from him and poured over the document. 'Shit, I don't believe it, the bastards.'

She was brought up suddenly by a noise from behind them. The office door was slowly being opened. Tom and Nathalie rose to their feet and turned to confront the intruder.

'Hi, you two, someone said you were seen in this corridor,' John McCord, bearing a wide grin made the gesture of downing a glass of beer. 'Thanks for standing us the first round but we think it's our turn. Waiting for you in the bar.'

Tom started to mutter something about his wallet but Nathalie shoved him in the back. She grabbed the piece of paper from the file and pushed it into the back pocket of her jeans. 'Fantastic John, we're really parched, lead the way and we'll join you.'

John McCord left the room without taking a further glance. Nathalie and Tom followed, Nathalie softly closing the door behind her.

✳

The breakfast room in Biomedivac's Moroccan compound was similar to their staff canteen in London. More like a classy restaurant than corporate foodservice. Tom and the crew were already mopping up their scrambled eggs when Nathalie, bleary eyed, sat down beside them. They had had a late-night drinking session. John hadn't even mentioned or asked why they were in Townes' office. He probably didn't even realise the office was his. Nathalie thought it best to act normally, it was the last day of the shoot, they would only be travelling today and it was convention to celebrate. She had downed her several glasses of lager and stayed with them till late, even

275

though the document was burning a hole in her back pocket. When at last they had all turned in, she went to her room and plugged in her laptop. Line by line she went through the document, and line by line she checked it against the published data on the internet. She thought that she had a dilemma with disclosing the single trial data on the Alzheimer's drug. This was a thousand times worse. A confidential report on the final phase trials of *XEBO*. It was true that the early results were highly effective, not just with prevention but also with speeding recovery. However, later data was revealing that the drug was only effective against certain strains of Ebola. These strains were taken from the terrible outbreak in Guinea. The report in her hands outlined a clear warning. The drug seemed totally ineffective against some of the later strains that were now emerging. The researcher had recommended retesting and further collection of data. So far nothing incriminating there but the shock came with the next few lines, neatly handwritten in blue ink. In effect, the author of this script was asking for a review of the technician's credentials and suggesting that he should be fired for incompetence. The notes also instructed the various strains to be deleted from the documents and the generic name Zaire ebolavirus to be placed in their stead. Nathalie could of course check the handwriting against Professor Townes' but, even if it wasn't his, he must have known about it and, despite that, he was still producing fifty million vials a year of vaccine that might not work.

'You look terrible,' said Tom. 'I told you that you shouldn't have had that last beer.'

'It's not the beer Tom, it's that document you found. We, or rather I, have stolen it and I really don't know what to do.'

Tom leaned over to whisper in her ear. 'Have you photographed it?'

'Of course, why?'

'I've still got the key card. If you go over and say your goodbyes to Townes, keep him busy, I'll put back the paper and leave the card in his room. It'll give you time to think.'

Nathalie reached into her bag and handed Tom the document. 'You're a star Tom, I owe you one. Be careful.'

Tom secreted the paper in his jacket and left the restaurant. Nathalie put on a broad smile and walked up to James Townes.

'Professor, thank you so much for allowing us to film here, very impressive. I think you'll find the final programme very interesting.'

The enigmatic sentence was lost on Townes. 'Not at all, Miss Thompson, I thought you would find this high-tech institution to your liking. We really are pioneers you know.'

Nathalie looked at the man. He was obviously in his own world, and no person nor data would get in his way.

'It seems that way Professor. If you don't mind we would like to have a brief chat with your exchange scientist, Doctor Murauzi, thank him for his help.'

'Of course, please use the boardroom. I'm afraid I have to dash now, catch a plane to Paris, big convention there you know. Take all the time you need.'

Townes snapped his fingers at his secretary and started to walk to the exit.

Nathalie stood, grateful that he had not offered to shake her hand. 'Oh, Professor?'

Townes turned to see what she wanted.

'If you hear what happened to Rob Barnes, you will let me know won't you?'

Townes' face darkened. 'If I never see that man again I won't be sorry Miss Thompson. Goodbye to you, my staff will ensure you take the right road.'

Nathalie nodded and watched Townes disappear before she rejoined the crew.

'Okay you guys, as planned Seb and Axel will take John, Tom and me to the airport at Marrakech before they head back to the ferry. If you've finished your breakfast, why don't you load up and get some better directions. Tom and I will join you later; we just have some washing up to do.'

277

Temba was waiting for her in the boardroom. Tom arrived a few minutes later looking a bit sheepish but held his thumb up when Nathalie glanced at him.

Temba made the first opening. 'Professor Townes' secretary told me that you wanted a word.'

'Yes, we understand that you are travelling back to Harare tomorrow. Just wanted to make sure that you're okay with this covert filming thing,' said Nathalie sitting down beside him.

'I told Tom I would, I always keep my word.'

'Yes, I'm sure but…' Nathalie looked at Tom. 'I know that you and Tom have become friends, I just wanted to make certain that you understand the full consequences.'

Temba turned to look Nathalie straight in the eyes. 'This has nothing to do with Tom. From what I understand there is a group of terrorists who plan to spread Ebola to innocent victims. By my filming them admitting that they want a vaccine to protect their couriers, whilst making their attack, I can help you stop them.'

'That's about it Temba. All we have at the moment is some masked guys boasting about what they can do. If you can get their faces on camera, taking the antidote from you, we've got them.'

Temba rested his hands on the table. 'As I said, I always keep my word. Ebola is a terrible disease; I'll do anything I can do to prevent it.' He glanced towards Tom. 'No matter what the risk.'

'Okay.' Nathalie handed Temba a piece of paper. 'This is Lloyd's new phone number. A buy and burn mobile,' she explained. 'As soon as you get back give him a call and make a meeting. He'll brief you how to use a hidden camera and set up a rendezvous with some of the WEXA group.'

'And what do you want me to say?'

'You, as little as possible. Lloyd has convinced them you are a sympathiser and have a new anti-Ebola vaccine. The news coverage of your presence here gives that credence.'

'A new vaccine?'

'Yes, Lloyd has spread the word that you have access to an amazing new drug, one that is guaranteed to protect their couriers.'

'Where is this vaccine?'

'It doesn't exist. You have to take just any old vial; a placebo from the lab here will do. Don't worry, they won't have a chance to use it. All we need is for you to get them saying that they will.'

Temba thought for a moment. 'And you'll stop them in time? Their couriers won't have a chance to spread the disease?'

'Absolutely Temba. Get them on camera and we'll do the rest.'

They parted with warm handshakes. Temba went back to the lab and Tom and Nathalie made their way to their rooms to collect their bags.

'You think he'll be all right?' Nathalie asked Tom.

'You saw him on camera,' said Tom. 'He's a cool customer. He sounds fairly committed to me, and he's met Lloyd before.'

Nathalie felt the phone vibrate in her pocket. She pulled it out and looked at the screen. 'Talk of the devil. I just need to take this. Go on ahead, I'll meet you by the trucks.'

Nathalie slipped into her room and sat on the bed. She pressed the receive button and heard Lloyd's voice come down the phone.

'Nathalie?'

'Well no one else has got my phone,' said Nathalie.

'Can't be too careful,' said Lloyd.

'Sorry, stupid of me. What's up?'

'Met with two of the WEXA group last night.'

Nathalie's heart began to race. 'You're not going to tell me that the Temba meeting is off. We just spent the last two days persuading him to do the filming.'

'No, not that. It's still on, or I think it is. They are planning two attacks.'

'Two! What do you mean two?'

'They still want the vaccine for their second larger scale scheme. But they've become impatient, angry at some recent UK mining operation.'

'You are not being very clear Lloyd. What do you mean larger scheme?'

'Their big plan, a threat to shake the West out of complacency. But they're not sure if anyone will believe them so they're planning a smaller scale attack to show what they can do. I couldn't persuade them to wait for the vaccine, they've already sent someone to spread the virus.'

Thirty

Bagatelle's offices were unusually quiet. Geoff had taken a rare morning off to sort out some personal things and Stefanie was using the opportunity to sort out some files. The phone rang for the umpteenth time and she pressed the button on her remote headset to receive it.

'Bagatelle Films.'

'Stefanie, it's Nathalie.'

'Oh, wonderful to hear from you. How did things go?'

'Fine thanks. Tom, John and I are at Marrakech airport, taking the next flight back to Gatwick, but I need to speak to Geoff urgently.'

'I'm afraid he's at home. I've tried contacting him myself but his phone seems eternally busy. If you like, I'll keep trying until I get through and tell him to call you.'

'No good I'm afraid, we are about to board. Flight should take about three to four hours. If we are on time I'll get to the office around eight in the evening. Do you think he could come in and meet me there?'

'I'll ask. If not I'll tell him to ring you as soon as you land.'

'That's great Stefanie. We are on the EasyJet flight, perhaps you would track our arrival.' Nathalie disconnected the call.

Stefanie was about to return to her filing when she heard a loud cry. Geoff burst into the office, red faced, mobile in hand.

'I just don't believe this, we live in a Kafkaesque world. I have listened to so many options and so much music that I'm about to explode. Now listen, you...' Geoff threw the phone across the room. 'Hung up on again. Fucking artificial un-intelligence machines if you ask me. That's it, I'm not paying for my gas whatever they say. They can just come and collect the bloody money.'

Stefanie had heard these rants before. She picked up the phone and placed it carefully on his desk. 'How does a cup of coffee sound?'

'Black and strong,' replied Geoff sitting at his desk and putting his head in his hands. 'Give me a few moments to get this black dog off my back and I'll try to remember how to make normal conversation.'

Geoff's face had returned to its usual colour when Stefanie presented him with the double espresso.

'Thank you Stefanie, a lifesaver,' said Geoff, downing it in one.

'You've just missed her,' said Stefanie. 'Rang in from Marrakech, urgent apparently. She'd like to meet here in the office around eight o'clock this evening. That okay with you?'

Geoff scrolled through the diary on his telephone. 'Theatre date, but the critics say it's crap so if she says it's urgent.'

❊

Gatwick was jam-packed. Several flights had landed within minutes of each other and passengers were jostling to manoeuvre their place close to the luggage carousels. It was one of those rare times when the camera equipment came off first. John McCord heaved the boxes onto a trolley, said his goodbyes, and headed towards the carnet office. Nathalie and Tom waited for their personal bags. Finally Tom saw them; two small suitcases with huge orange gaffer tape crosses strapped around the sides.

'That's us,' he said. 'Are you sure you don't want me to come back to the office with you?'

'No point in two of us going. Go home, have a bite to eat and get some rest,' said Nathalie. 'You deserve it.'

Tom took the train but, as Nathalie had the rushes, she walked towards the taxi rank. There was a large queue so she stood in line. The line seemed to move slowly. She couldn't understand why at this busy hour there were so few cabs. She stood on tiptoe to see if she could see any coming around the corner. Her view was obscured by a number of people clambering aboard a shuttle bus. Then she saw a face that she knew. It was Joseph Karasa. What was he doing in London? A cold chill ran down her back. It couldn't be, could it? The last couple in front of her took their cab and another taxi drew up behind opening its doors for her. She ignored the cab, grabbed her bag and ran towards the bus. She stumbled as a man crossed her path. He picked up her bag and handed it to her. Without thanking him she grabbed it and continued running. The doors of the bus were closing. She just managed to get alongside when it drew out of the bay. Diesel fumes filled her lungs as the bus propelled itself into the departing traffic.

Surprisingly the M20 was relatively free of vehicles and it didn't take the taxi, which Nathalie eventually found, long to enter central London. As they approached Soho Square Nathalie could see the lights on in Geoff's office. She paid the driver, skipped up the steps and pressed in the code to enter. Geoff was at his desk reading through a script, he tilted his head to look over his glasses.

'Ah, the prodigal returns. How was the desert?'

Nathalie ignored the familiar prodigal line and sat in the chair opposite. 'Sorry to drag you in at this time, hope you haven't…'

'Haven't had to cancel anything? Nothing important. She's gone with her sister, says she prefers her company than my sleeping carcass anyway. So what's up, problems with the shoot?'

'Shoot went fine. Also stumbled on some interesting documents. But before I go into that, we have a problem.'

She had been rehearsing it in the cab. Geoff hated people who didn't get to the point. Despite her racing pulse she tried to deliver her speech calmly and deliberately.

'Lloyd has told me that WEXA has initiated a limited attack to prove that they can spread the virus. This afternoon I saw Joseph Karasa at Gatwick. I don't think the two are coincidental.'

She paused, her chest heaving. Geoff folded his hands together and tapped his thumbs.

'And do you have any evidence that he is carrying the virus?'

'No, but why else would Joseph Karasa be in London?'

Geoff unclasped his hands and reached for a side drawer in his desk. 'Many reasons; holiday, sightseeing, perhaps he has friends here.'

'Geoff, the last time I saw this guy he was in a smoky hut in a Zimbabwean village with a couple of masked guys with guns. Hardly the sightseeing type.'

Geoff pulled out a folder, placed it on his desk, and leafed through the neatly typed forms. He handed Nathalie one of the pieces of paper.

'Contact-sheet. Joseph Karasa works for the Harare hospital. Your contact there is a Nurse Sue Jones. Why don't you give her a call, ask her if she's received our immunisation video yet, and drop in the conversation if she knows where Joseph is.'

Nathalie closed her eyes. Blindingly obvious. Why hadn't she thought of that? She had thought they might phone the police, the anti-terrorist unit, anyone who might find this guy but Geoff was right, they would ask her for evidence. She started to reach for her phone. Geoff held up his hand.

'Before you do that, I think you should calm down and take a breather. You don't want Nurse Jones to detect any panic in your voice. Why don't you tell me about those interesting documents you came across?'

Nathalie took a deep breath and told him the story. How Tom had discovered that Townes had scrapped one of the trials for his new Alzheimer's drug. How the healthy volunteers taking batch #124 suffered memory loss and that one of these volunteers was Esther Phillips. She showed Geoff the photos on her phone and explained that this wasn't the only data that Townes had manipulated. It had been discovered that his Ebola vaccine was totally ineffective against some new strains of the virus. Despite this he was still selling millions of vials, and the data had been hidden from the drug authorities.

'The problem is,' said Nathalie, 'we got these illegally. I don't know what to do.'

Geoff studied the photographs of the documents. 'Well I do. Send me these, wipe them completely from your phone and leave it to me. And now that you are breathing more easily, take a drink from the water-cooler over there and go into the boardroom to make your call. It will be better without me hovering over you.'

Joseph Karasa stepped out of Victoria station and made his way along Vauxhall Bridge Road. This was his first time in London and the sights and sounds were strange to him. The streets were wet with a recent downpour, but the smells from the pavement were unlike any he had experienced before. A leaden metallic taste rather than the brackish soil of the African bush. A mass of people tumbled towards him, weaving in and out, and he held on tightly to his small travel bag. It had been easy getting the visa. Members of the hospital team had done this trip many times before. The Child-Aid agency liked to see representatives of the recipients of their aid. It gave the charity kudos and the tangible reward of a speech from someone who had seen what their life-changing gifts could do, encouraged more donations. Joseph had volunteered to be this year's delegate and had been given the all-expenses-paid trip as a reward for his dedication to the immunisation programme. He stopped to look at his London street map, so suddenly that someone lurched into him and the bag fell off his shoulder. He dropped the map and picked up the bag, scrabbled to open the straps and frantically dug in between his clothes to find the container. To his relief it was intact, cushioned between the soft lens-cloth in a glasses case.

Nathalie had been unable to get through to Sue Jones and Geoff had sent her home. She had spent most of the night awake anticipating a response to her message even though she knew this was stupid, Harare was only a couple of hours ahead of London. Finally the blue light flashed on her phone. She grabbed it from the side table and tried to focus her tired eyes on the screen. 7.00 am and a message. Sue Jones? No, Lloyd. It was asking her to call him on a new number. She dialled and it didn't take him long to pick up.

'It's on today.'

Nathalie's head was full of Joseph Karasa. 'They're doing the attack today?'

'No, the covert filming. Temba is flying in this morning and I'm picking him up at the airport. Haven't got much time to teach him how to use the camera, they say they want to meet him this afternoon.'

'Do you know anything about Joseph Karasa?'

'Who?'

'The immunisation guy, is he the one that is doing the initial attack?'

'Karasa, immunisation guy. Ah yes you did mention him. No idea. They've not told me who or when they're doing that. Are you still okay with this filming thing? If you've told the authorities about a possible attack and WEXA hear about it it'll really scupper that.'

Nathalie hadn't thought about the consequences for her programme. She was so wrapped up in the idea of stopping anyone spreading the Ebola virus. 'No, I mean yes, go ahead with the filming. We haven't told anyone about the potential attack yet, not enough evidence. Have a lead though, will follow that through first. Any change of plan and I'll call you.'

'Are you sure? It's our necks on the line you know.'

Nathalie did know, she still couldn't get the vision of the machete cutting into that oil drum out of her head. 'Any news and I'll call, promise. This number?'

'Yes, I'll keep the phone for two days. If I don't hear anything and all goes well I'll send the video through to Bagatelle's encrypted drop-box this evening.'

Lloyd ended the call. Nathalie was about to dial Sue Jones' number when her phone rang. A Zimbabwean number.

'Nathalie Thompson?'

Nathalie recognised the voice. 'Yes. Sue Jones?'

✳

The Child-Aid agency was only a few hundred metres from Joseph's bed and breakfast. The accommodation was poor by London standards but for Joseph it had been pure luxury. He had spent the previous evening with a takeaway in his room watching television and this morning had consumed several bowls of cornflakes taken from the Tupperware container. He had pressed his jacket by putting it under the mattress and by doing it up disguised the wrinkles from his only shirt. He watched himself in the mirror as he neatened his tie. He had been waiting for this a long time.

The agency was not what Joseph was expecting. Instead of a pristine steel and glass premises it was in the middle of a rundown terrace in a Pimlico side street. He checked the number of the address on his sheet of paper. Yes it was number 27 but did he have the right road? Then he noticed the small sign in the doorway. *Pimlico Child Aid, First floor.* He pressed the bell and waited. After a few moments the door opened to reveal an elderly man in shirtsleeves and braces. He looked Joseph up and down and thoughtfully put his head on one side.

'You'll be here for the charity lot then,' he said in an accent that Joseph could just about understand.

Joseph showed him his sheet of paper. 'Nurse Karasa, I believe this is the premises of Child-Aid.'

'That's what the sign says.' The man stood there passively.

'I have an appointment.'

'Don't they all,' said the man. 'Just wish they wouldn't use me as their doorman.'

'Doorman?'

'Oh, forget it laddie, take the stairs, it's the first cream door on the right.'

The man disappeared into the dark interior without another word. Joseph looked at the threadbare carpet on the narrow wooden staircase in front of him. He straightened his tie, took a deep breath and made the steep upward climb. This was meant to be the easy part.

The door was opened by a thin young woman wearing spectacles. She greeted him like a long lost relative.

'Joseph, welcome to our agency, such a long way to come, we are so privileged.'

She shook his hand vigorously. 'Come, come in, my colleagues are eager to meet you, cup of tea?'

Joseph didn't know what to say. He had expected a lecture hall and a few rows of suited representatives. Instead he was shown into a small damp Victorian parlour boasting a few odd chairs and a small group of volunteers. Most were dressed as if they had bought their clothes from charity shops. This was going to be difficult. These people were really caring. His plan was to read the short institutional speech from the typed sheet he had been given from the hospital, make his excuses and then disappear. His next appointment, the real reason for his visit, was on no formal agenda but they were not to know that. He looked at his watch. He still had time. He accepted the offer of a cup of tea and sat with it on his lap facing the expectant expressions. He left the prepared speech neglected in his pocket.

'Perhaps they don't realise it but the children of Africa are indebted to your care,' he began.

❋

As soon as she had got the information from Sue Jones, Nathalie had rung Geoff. Now she, Geoff and Nick Coburn were sitting in his office.

'So that's the story Nick,' said Geoff. 'Here's the address. Could be completely innocent, the guy might really be on a charity jolly, or on the other hand...'

'He could be spreading the Ebola virus,' completed Nathalie.

'But we don't want you sparking off an international incident,' said Geoff. 'And we don't want any premature disclosure buggering up our film.'

'Geoff,' exploded Nathalie. 'If it means stopping people catching Ebola, who cares about the film.'

'I'm just asking Nick to be sensitive, not always his strong point. Of course, if he's carrying any of that nasty stuff, we'll stop him. But we don't want his mates to know, anyway not before we get them on film.'

Nick was looking at the address. 'He's right Nathalie, and it's not just for his bloody movie, I'm sure the security services would prefer to have the whole gang rather than one of their sacrificial lambs.'

'Sacrificial lambs?'

'You don't think they've left any trail connecting him to them do you? No, if he gets caught they'll wash their hands of him. That's why you need to get their faces on camera.' Nick got to his feet. 'Anyway, I'd better go and check out this Child-Aid outfit. Although it's not exactly the place I'd visit to start an Ebola epidemic.'

Thirty-one

The visit to the charity had taken longer than Joseph had planned and the guilt-generating applause was still ringing in his ears as he hurried towards the Tube station. He felt conspicuous but in the busy London streets no one seemed concerned about the dark Zimbabwean man paying for his ticket and tracing out his journey on the underground map with his finger. The train was crowded even in the middle of the afternoon. All the seats were occupied and so he stood clutching his bag against his chest like a baby, anxious not to bump into the sides of the careering carriage. His destination was near the end of a line. He hadn't realised how long London's underground system was. It took nearly an hour. Fortunately with each stop the crowd in the carriage thinned, eventually providing spaces in the seating. He sat, still holding his cargo close.

He was the only one left in the carriage when his stop arrived, the signs slowing down through the grimy windows. The turnstiles were open, no one to take his ticket, and so he strolled into the late afternoon sunlight squinting his eyes to take in the scenery. This was not like the London he had left. A few derelict buildings were scattered among some not so green fields. More like a Zimbabwean township than a metropolitan capital. His map was easy to follow and hardly necessary. The lane was signposted and he could see the warehouses in the distance, just like the photographs. If there was a guard he must have been patrolling the other side of the compound, for the gatehouse stood empty. Joseph pulled his collar around his neck, it was getting cold, and walked slowly towards an outer building. The door was unlocked, he was told it would be. Inside the row of lockers. He opened the nearest and pulled out the grey overalls. One size fits all. The white fitted mob-cap and mask completed the uniform. Now 'one of the guys' he made his way towards the main warehouse. He was ignored by a forklift truck operator and given a passing nod by an identically clothed man who was struggling with a large wooden pallet. The building was as large as an aircraft hangar. The interior was lit by strings of cold fluorescent lights. Slotted aluminium shelves held row upon row of brown cardboard boxes reaching far into the distance. Joseph pulled out his sketch of the warehouse. Aisle 6, row 29. He patted the front of his overalls, just to make sure that it was still there. Stupid really, he had checked the canister several times before transferring it from his bag and putting it into his inside pocket. The aisles were clearly marked, the rows less so. He counted them off, twenty-six, twenty-seven, twenty-eight, and studied the labels on the next shelf. They corresponded. How and who had gleaned this information he had no idea but they had done their job well. He reached up for one of the boxes and almost dropped it in fright.

'Oi you!'

Joseph turned around, almost too quickly.

A man in a cheap suit thrust a clipboard into his hands.

'You're on time. Makes a change from the regular. Keep this up and you'll have his job.'

Joseph stared at him over his mask, breathing heavily.

'Don't worry lad, I don't bite, that is if you count these boxes properly.' The man looked at his watch. 'You've got half an hour, then if you've finished you can knock off okay?'

Joseph nodded, stared at the clipboard and then at the man.

'Right, get on with it then.'

Joseph turned and pretended to count the boxes with his fingers. He heard the footsteps of the man walk away through the corridor of box-laden shelves. When the footsteps had faded he turned to check the aisle. Not a soul in sight. He turned back to the boxes only this time not to count them but to carefully prise one open. His heart was beating so loudly that he thought it might be echoing around the warehouse. When he had volunteered for this task he had been angry. Hundreds of

African mine workers killed in an accident that was waiting to happen. The British company had put profit over safety. A not uncommon practice. Peaceful protest had done nothing, it was time they had to listen. This would be a warning. Next time it would be worse, a lot worse. He looked over his shoulder before slipping the plastic bottles out of their containers and his hand trembled as he took out the hypodermic from its case. The meeting with Child-Aid had really shaken him. These weren't anonymous Western suits, donating for their consciences. They were kind men and women with a genuine care for children's health. He slowly plunged the needle into the vial. How many innocent children would this action affect? He had been reassured that this would be targeted at adults, but what if they passed it on? The UK wasn't like Africa, they had the best antibiotics, isolation units. It would be bad but they eventually would contain it. If their threats succeeded more would benefit in the long term, and he had come this far. The clear liquid trickled into the hypodermic. He was careful not to spill any onto his skin. The plastic bottles had a seam. The best place he had been told. The faces of the charity group still haunted him. But then he remembered the fate of the miners. He had seen pictures of the crushed and mangled bodies. It had been avoidable but they did not, would not listen. He made a decision. He had seen first-hand the symptoms of Ebola. It was a terrible way to die. They would listen now.

His lodgings had been booked for two nights. Tomorrow was meant to be a day off, a day sightseeing, taking in the culture of a country he was about to attack. He carefully lifted one of the bottles and inserted the needle into the seam. There was no way he could stay here. He would go straight to the airport, change his ticket and take the last flight to Harare. He would inform Sue Jones and the hospital that he had to return early to attend to a sick relative. No one would be the wiser. He gently pushed down the plunger. Not too deep, he had many bottles to do. He had come this far…

It was dark by the time Nick returned to Bagatelle's offices. There appeared to be no one about, but a glow under the door of the boardroom gave the indication that there was a presence. He went in. The whole team were sitting around the boardroom table, the large monitor on the wall lit up with a single drop-box icon. Temba's video from Harare was due at any moment.

'The fucking bastard's disappeared,' Nick used the expletives, foregoing any greeting formalities. 'Chased him all round London, first to the charity and then to his digs. No sign of him.'

He had phoned Geoff as soon as he had reached the Child-Aid offices. Admittedly he had taken a few minutes pretending that he represented a corporation wanting to donate to their charity. After that it didn't take long to establish that they had just been visited by a young Zimbabwean who had provided evidence of the benefits that their contributions had made. Without trying to make it too obvious that he was searching for him, Nick then had to devour several cups of tea before ascertaining that the young man had left and they had no idea where.

The room at the bed and breakfast address that Sue Jones had provided was empty. The accommodation had been booked for two nights but the young African man had taken what little luggage he had with him. He was probably exploring the city. If the gentleman would like to leave his number then when he returned they would ask him to call. Other than the lack of luggage there was nothing suspicious. Karasa had attended his scheduled meeting and had checked into his digs. Nothing he could call out the security forces for. On Geoff's approval Nick had called one of his many contacts and for fifty quid had posted him outside the B&B.

'Just called him again to see if he's awake,' said Nick. 'Got an earful about how cold it was but still no sign of him. Sorry guys.'

Geoff pointed to a seat. 'Did your best. We still don't know if he has anything to do with this Ebola threat. Doesn't sound like he had time to do much to me. Perhaps the charity thing was the real deal.'

'No,' said Nathalie. 'Everything is too coincidental. The guy's never been to London before. Why today when we've been told that there's a threatened attack? Don't you think it fishy that there is no luggage in his room and he's not turned up?'

'The country's strange to him,' said Geoff gesturing to Stefanie to check the video link. 'Probably doesn't trust anyone with his stuff. First trip to London? Living it up in the nightclubs most likely.'

'Joseph is not that kind of guy. Serious, a bit intense. I'm sure there must be a reason why he's not returned to his digs.'

'Well, when it comes to you, let us know,' said Geoff, pointing at the screen. 'But after this. Looks like Lloyd is transmitting the video to our drop-box.'

He was right, the icon on the screen was flashing to show that someone was sending through a file. Stefanie walked up to the computer and hovered her hand over the keyboard.

'Are you all ready?' she asked.

'As ready as we'll ever be,' said Nathalie anxiously.

There was no attached message to the video. It started with a wobbly shot of Lloyd counting to ten and asking Temba to angle his baseball cap a little lower.

'Just checking out the equipment,' explained Geoff unnecessarily.

The video then went to black and cut in again to a tracking shot along a hotel corridor. A door opened and the person wearing the camera was greeted by two black Zimbabweans. Some time was spent manoeuvring whilst the three men gathered around a low coffee table.

'Those the guys?' asked Geoff.

'Difficult to say,' said Nathalie. 'They had masks on. They look about the same build. Hush though, let's listen to their voices.'

The sound quality was very poor but they could just about make out what was being said. The two men began by boasting about their current operation. Their operative had arrived in the target area. If he had been successful all that they had to do was to wait for the first victims to be declared and then for the Ebola to spread.

Nathalie was hoping that Temba would ask who the operative was, but he was silent, the camera just dipping up and down slightly. He must have been smiling for the larger man smiled back and thanked his comrade for offering to help the cause.

The camera again slowly nodded up and down, Temba was really playing this cool.

'I told him to let them do the talking,' explained Nathalie. 'Even with what they've said so far we've got them, and we've also got the video so Temba must be okay.'

'Unless it's a live feed,' said Tom, who had been quiet until now.

'If it's live, I hope someone's bloody recording it,' said Geoff.

'All being laid down to the hard drive,' said Stefanie quietly, pointing to the computer.

Geoff sighed, 'Technology again; all in the ether, in my...'

'In your day, you wouldn't have got a micro-camera into a baseball cap visor,' interrupted Nick. 'Why don't you all shut up so we can hear what's being said.'

They hadn't missed anything. After taking a drink, Temba put down the cup of tea he had been offered. For the first time, they heard him speak. His voice was clear and without any sign of nervousness.

'I understand you are looking for an anti-Ebola virus drug to protect your agents. Aren't they using one already?'

As he spoke the camera moved from one man to the other. Nathalie noticed a large watch on the wrist of one of them. It was the man who she had nicknamed Rolex who fended the answer.

'They have been yes, something called *XEBO*. Unfortunately it's not reliable. In fact we have just heard that the person who obtained the virus for us has died. If our demands are not met we need something more effective for our large-scale attack. Our contact, Muzi, tells us that you have such a drug.'

There was a pregnant pause in the room. The two men in the chairs opposite sat back casually and sipped their tea. Nathalie couldn't stand the tension.

'Tell them you have one,' she shouted at the screen. 'Get them to say they will use it for their large-scale Ebola attack.'

But Temba said nothing of the sort. After what seemed an age he asked another question.

'You say that one of your agents has died? Is that the person you have sent to launch your initial attack?'

Rolex, put down his teacup. 'Fortunately, to the best of our knowledge, no. He knows the consequences and has decided to take the risk. We trust he will return safely from his trip. No, Salina died this morning in a Harare hospital. She caught the disease several months ago when obtaining the virus for our cause. She was a brave warrior and…'

The rest of his sentence was lost as the camera lurched violently to one side and the picture cut to black as it hit the floor.

'Christ,' called out Tom. 'They've shot him!'

Nick put his hand on Tom's arm, 'Don't think so Tom, we would have heard the report on camera. I think something that they said made him faint.'

The screen was still black and the room full of white noise. Geoff got to his feet. 'Nathalie take my office, ring Lloyd on that number he gave you. Find out what's going on. Nick, we've got our footage, time to give your security mates a call. Say we're pretty sure a Zimbabwean guy is planting the Ebola virus in the country. The Karasa thing could be a coincidence but, like Nathalie, now I don't think so. They could start by looking at his hotel and the charity. If they need any evidence tell them that they can have a squint at this footage. Stefanie, make sure we've got a backup of those files.'

Nathalie left the room and dialled Lloyd's number. He picked up immediately.

'Did you get it?'

'Yes, what happened at the end?'

'Not quite sure. I recorded it a few doors down from their hotel room. Had to be close enough to pick up the signal. About five minutes after we lost transmission Temba stumbled into my room.

Looked like he'd seen a ghost. Garbled something about telling them he'd swooned with jetlag and told me that he had to check on a woman at the hospital.'

Nathalie was relieved and disturbed at the same time. 'So he's all right? Did they know he was filming them? Did they accept the placebo drug?'

'He's not injured, if that's what you mean and I don't think they knew what we were doing, otherwise I'm sure they would be in here by now. Placebo drug? I've no idea, he said that he had arranged to meet them again to give them a drug that would really work.'

Nathalie was very confused, this wasn't the plan at all. 'Where, when? What does he mean by that?'

'No idea, the guy looked really crazy. That's all he said, tore off the camera and ran out of the room.'

Nathalie returned to the boardroom and told Geoff and Tom what Lloyd had said. She could see that Tom had been shaken and now looked visibly relieved.

'Looks like he got away with it,' said Geoff, studying Nathalie's face. 'I've seen that look before Miss Thompson, come on out with it.'

'I can't be sure,' said Nathalie thoughtfully. 'Somehow swooning over jetlag is one thing and collapsing on the floor is another. I think I know why Temba fainted.'

Geoff waited patiently.

'It was at the mention of the woman who died in the hospital. It was as soon as he heard her name: Salina.'

'You think he knew her?' Geoff asked.

'More than that, the first time I set my eyes on Temba Murauzi was in Central Harare Hospital. I think that Salina was his sister.'

'So the guy didn't know she was working for WEXA.'

'Why should he. I think he was angry because the hospital were denying that she had Ebola. They said she had a non-specific infectious disease but he knew they were lying. He's a pharmacologist, he would know what her *XEBO* treatment was for.'

'And she caught Ebola whilst getting it for these terrorists?'

297

'Evidently, it's not the easiest thing to contract but if she had some exchange of fluids somewhere...'

'What is it Nathalie, you've got that look again?'

'Fluid exchange. He just can't smear the virus on door knobs and seats, it would probably die within minutes. They need a way of getting the virus into people's body fluids. If we can think of ways in which they could do that, we may have a chance to stop them.'

Thirty-two

The watery light was indicating an early autumn. It had been four days since Nick had alerted the authorities but no action seemed to have been taken. They were given hundreds of videos with threatened terrorist attacks and this was just one of them. They had asked Bagatelle to contact Harare to see if Mr Karasa had returned there. Nathalie duly contacted Sue Jones with yet more excuses to talk about the immunisation video and on gentle probing heard that Joseph had arrived in the country, albeit a day early, to visit a sick relative. Nathalie was walking past Geoff's office hearing a conversation between him and Nick complaining that the whole thing had been a hoax when Tom rushed up the stairs.

'Did you hear the radio?' He was breathless.

'Calm down,' said Nathalie. 'What radio Tom?'

'The *Today* programme, on the news this morning.'

'No Tom, busy working trying to salvage my programme. Broadcasters going cold on it, not enough meat apparently.'

'Well, there might be some; meat I mean.'

Nathalie pointed to the boardroom. 'Well we better go in there, don't want Geoff and Nick adding more fuel to the thing.'

Tom followed her into the boardroom and perched himself on the corner of the long table.

'The news, not conclusive but it's possible, that WEXA's boast of an initial attack could be true.'

Nathalie turned pale. 'How come?'

'There's been a spate of hospital admissions in Guildford. They're saying it's early flu. Difficult to treat. Telling vulnerable people to get their jabs.'

'And you think…'

'It's Ebola, possibly. Something in the report didn't sound right. Shall I chase it up?'

'Absolutely Tom,' said Nathalie. 'And I'm coming with you.'

Superficially Guildford Hospital looked like any other on a busy Thursday yet Nathalie could sense a raised presence in the air. More police cars than usual, a quiet hurrying around the intensive care unit. She tried the usual trick of posing as a patient's sister but it didn't work. She was grilled for her identity and the name of the patient. The concern of the receptionist made her more suspicious so she and Tom made their exit and concealed themselves by the bushes outside the ambulance dock. Two hours later they were just about to change their plans when an ambulance pulled up. Screens were hurriedly pulled across the road but not before Nathalie spotted the trolley being wheeled from the back doors.

'Shit,' she said quietly.

'What's up?' asked Tom who hadn't seen the action.

'I'm afraid our Mr Karasa, or, if not he, someone else has succeeded. I've never seen flu victims delivered in an airtight tent by guys dressed up in containment gear before. I think you're right Tom, it's Ebola.

Nathalie and Tom returned to the office to find a reception committee. The blinds in Geoff's office were pulled down. Tom was asked to wait outside and Nathalie was shepherded in by Stefanie who then left and closed the door behind her. Stern faces turned to her. Geoff was swinging uncomfortably in his chair faced by two smartly dressed men and Nick.

'Nathalie, please sit down,' said Geoff in an uncharacteristic tone. 'These gentlemen are from, what they loosely call, the security services. I think we owe you an apology.'

'The Ebola outbreak in Guildford,' said Nathalie, still standing.

'Told you she was a smart journalist,' snapped Geoff.

The more thickset man leaned forward. 'And where did you hear that Miss Thompson?'

'Not heard it, seen it,' replied Nathalie. 'Just returned from the hospital actually, security and spacesuits everywhere.'

The services' men hid their surprise and outlined their position. The country was on high alert. Cases of suspected Ebola had been reported in Guildford and Staines. At first these were genuinely thought to be flu but one experienced doctor had alerted the epidemiological service. Efforts were made to find out if the suspected patients had flown in from possible source countries but at the moment this was drawing a blank. The security services were alerted earlier this morning. They had contacted Harare to talk to the police there but they had received nothing but obfuscation and denial. Bagatelle was their obvious next port of call. Nathalie could hardly believe her ears when Geoff started negotiating with the security officers. He was offering full cooperation and access to all their files and knowledge about the Ebola threat but hinted in return that he wanted privileged access to any filming opportunities.

The officers had obviously faced such cynicism before. 'Naturally in this case of national emergency the less people in the loop the better,' said the man in the pinstriped suit. 'In time you may have access to material but for the moment we are issuing a DSMA notice.'

'DSMA notice?' asked Nathalie.

'Defence and security media advisory notice,' explained Geoff. 'Means they want us to keep this stuff close to our chests for a while.'

He looked at the two officers. 'As long as we eventually get sole use for the stuff we're getting that's fine by me. At last we're going to get a great programme.'

Nathalie felt red with rage. Here they were discussing what might or might not have been a preventable terrible disease, and all Geoff was worried about was his programme. She was about to explode with expletives but thought better of it. Even now they had no concrete evidence that Joseph Karasa had anything to do with the affair. A thought came to her.

'CCTV.'

Geoff looked puzzled.

'CCTV,' she repeated. Can't we trace Joseph's movements from the Child-Aid centre?'

One of the security officers rose from his chair and made ready to leave. 'Already checked Miss. No cameras in that side street I'm afraid. We know the time he left but no other camera in the area picked him up.'

✳

DSMA notice or not, the wind of the Ebola outbreak caught fire. Over the next few days case after case was reported in the Home Counties. Isolation units were set up and guidance printed on every general practitioner's door. Speculation was rife. Many were convinced that a nurse travelling from Sierra Leone, although not presenting symptoms herself, had spread the disease. Fake news on Facebook and Twitter contrived every possible conspiracy theory, from imported food contamination to Martian invasion. Along with the major television networks Geoff had his cameras everywhere, but even he was distressed and sickened by the terrible symptoms.

'We reported Karasa as soon as we received Temba's video,' he said sadly to Nathalie. 'I know you blame me but we still don't know if he had anything to do with it. As for WEXA, you heard what the security guy said, they get threats like that every day.'

'We could have, should have, done more Geoff. The warnings were there.'

'We don't make the news Nathalie, we document it. Without your research the authorities wouldn't have the stuff they have.'

'That's no consolation. Nineteen cases and rising and two already dead. And this is meant to be a shot across the bow. If they really do a large-scale attack what on earth is that going to be like?'

'Well let's hope that's not going to happen. We haven't seen their threat posted yet, and if the terrorists' guys can persuade the

Zimbabweans to find your Mr Rolex I'm sure they will put him out of business.'

'I've told them about Temba's plan to meet up with them again, but he and Lloyd have gone off the radar. It's so difficult. The Zimbabwean government are just ignoring us. Some say they are even gloating over the crisis here.'

'Giving us a dose of African disease. That's what they said wasn't it,' said Geoff. 'Well looks like they've bloody done it.'

✳

One week after Joseph had returned to Harare there were nearly thirty cases of Ebola, and those were only the confirmed ones. Three people, all vulnerable or elderly, had died and the death toll was expected to rise. The health service was trying desperately to contain the situation. Special portable isolation units had been set up and some schools had been shut. Epidemiologists were working frantically on trying to trace the source and patterns of the disease outbreak. Media security had been tight and the public had no idea of the authenticity of the WEXA threat. GCHQ had quickly discovered their internet posting. This was downgraded and interwoven with other more likely threats. To the general web browser it was just one of many unlikely scams trying to take opportunistic publicity. The headline news from the broadsheets and public broadcasting still laid the blame at the door of the nurse who travelled from Sierra Leone. It was very convincing.

'Clever bastards,' said Nick staring at the web page. 'Shove the real threat in amongst other nutters' publicity and confuse Joe public.'

'Can I see that?' asked Tom.

Nathalie sighed and walked to the other side of the room whilst Nick turned the screen towards Tom.

'Looks pretty professional,' said Tom. 'Facts and figures of exploitation and their demands for a fairer Africa. And look here Nathalie, a reference to your promise of a video. "In the forthcoming days we will broadcast our case on British television". Sounds like they believed you.'

Nathalie pressed her head against the window. 'I don't want reminding Tom. I sat in a tent drinking tea with those bastards. Promised Lloyd and Temba, wherever they are, that we would prevent any attack. Look where that's led us. Those poor people, and we're still no closer to knowing the source or how they did it.'

Geoff burst into the room catching the end of her sentence. 'Ah now that's where you're wrong. Put a researcher onto the case. Given special permission to follow the epidemiologists' reports. There seems to be a pattern for the outbreaks.' He threw a map onto the table. 'Take a look at this.'

The four of them huddled around the map. Geoff pointed to circles of shaded colour around a number of towns in the south-east of England.

'Here, here and here. Tight spots where patients have been diagnosed. Not in Scotland, Wales or the North of England. Just around these towns.'

'Water supply?' suggested Nick.

'Doesn't fit,' said Geoff. 'There's some more localised source. I'll let you mull it over, if you get any ideas pass it on to the researcher.'

He started to leave the room but turned back to watch them still pouring over the map. 'Oh yes, and by the way, really odd one this, nearly all of the victims seem to have been short-sighted.'

Later that day Nathalie returned to her flat in Fulham. She lay on her bed exhausted anticipating another sleepless night. She played with the phone in her hand turning it over and over in her palms. She dialled Lloyd for the umpteenth time. The phone was dead. He did say he would discard it after a few days but, although she knew it was useless, she kept trying in case he reactivated it. The British authorities had discarded Joseph Karasa's involvement in the outbreak. The Harare Hospital and the charity had confirmed that the visit was official, and the Zimbabwean authorities pointed out that he had returned openly to the country. Unless the UK had any concrete evidence they were wasting the Zimbabwean police force's time. Nathalie knew from her own experiences that even if they did have evidence the Harare police would have been uncooperative. At the mention of WEXA, the Zimbabwean authorities just laughed. There was no such organisation in the country. Britain was just stirring up trouble by pointing the finger of their disease outbreak at Zimbabwe. The next time Zimbabwe had a reported epidemic perhaps they would point the finger the other way. It was a mess, but a mess that Geoff was revelling in. Each day they had more footage for their programme. As soon as the source was discovered and the DSMA notice was lifted they would finish the programme, perhaps even turn it into a series. Nathalie reluctantly turned to her script. Each day it was looking blacker. More and more people contracting the disease from an unknown attacker. When she had started her programme on bioterror it seemed a distant threat. Now that threat was real the whole thing seemed less attractive.

The phone rang.

'Lloyd?'

'No, it's Tom, isn't my name on your screen?'

'Sorry Tom, didn't check, wishful thinking.'

'Well that's what I've been doing. I remembered you telling Geoff that Ebola was not that easy to catch. They needed to get it into people's bodily fluids.'

'Yes that's right.'

'I've been trying to think how they could do that.'

'Yes Tom, get to the point.'

'I think Geoff's researcher has given us the answer.'

Nathalie's voice became more irritable. 'Tom!'

But Tom was not to be hurried in his moment of glory.

'They were short-sighted. Needed some help with their vision.'

The penny dropped. Nathalie shouted out the answer. 'Lenses, contact lenses. The maniacs have put it into contact lens solution.'

'Only an idea.'

'No, it's a brilliant idea. Explains the localised outbreaks. The spread isn't through contact contagion, the authorities have been amazing at isolating people. Clarifies why new cases are just popping up out of thin air. Someone buys some solution, sticks it in their eyes. Oh God, we've got to stop them. I'm cutting you off Tom, have to ring Nick, he'll get some of his security mates onto it.' She pressed the off button and then the speed dial.

Thirty-three

The meeting had been scheduled for two in the afternoon. Geoff had been isolated with some security service officers and a high-ranking government official in a backstreet office in Whitehall all morning. He even had his phone switched off, a first for Geoff. Now, halfway through the afternoon, he was ensconced in his office with Bagatelle's lawyer. He had even refused coffee, another first for Geoff. Poor Stefanie almost had her head bitten off as she poked it around his door. Nathalie, Tom and Nick though were flooded with the stuff as cup after cup was brought into the boardroom.

'You're very kind, but we can't take any more,' said Nathalie handing her the empties. 'How much longer do you think he will be?' She looked unnecessarily at her watch, the large clock on the wall clearly stating four o'clock.

'Your guess is as good as mine Nathalie, you know what he's like once he's got his teeth into something. Dotting I's crossing T's.'

Nick stood up to stretch his legs. 'If you've got anything stronger than coffee I'll take it. Don't understand all this hush-hush stuff we all know what's happened.'

What had happened in fact, was that Tom's theory was right. Patient's houses were searched for contact lens solution and tested for the virus. Within hours batch numbers were collated and the source traced to a warehouse on the outskirts of north London. The conditions and security there were pretty shoddy but fortunately the stock control less so. Twenty-four hours later and every single contaminated bottle had been destroyed. The spontaneous outbreaks stopped immediately. The proven cases of Ebola had been restricted to under fifty, it had been estimated that if the source hadn't been found the numbers would have reached the hundreds. Worse still,

307

if the primary cases had spread some people were talking in the thousands. The paper press had somehow circumnavigated the schedule notice, got wind of the lens solution source, and were hinting at bioterrorism. Geoff had protested to the authorities and had been called to this morning's top-level meeting. Just before two he had stormed into the office and demanded that the company's lawyer meet with him immediately. They had been in his room ever since.

It was five o'clock when Stefanie returned to the boardroom.

'He is ready for you now,' she said with a sigh.

Nick took a coin from his pocket, tossed it, and slapped it on to the back of his wrist. 'Good news or bad news?'

'No comment,' said Stefanie. 'But it won't be long before you'll find out.'

One by one they trooped into Geoff's office. He was sitting at his desk, angle-poise on, despite the time of day, hunched over a file scribbling frantically.

Nick walked over and rapped on the desk. 'Now when you said two o'clock, we didn't realise you meant New York time.'

Geoff looked up at Nick and then at the wall clocks. 'Ah yes, sorry. Needed to know the legal position.' He rose from his chair and slapped Nick on the back. 'Which I do now.'

He gestured to the four easy chairs circled around a coffee table in the corner of his room. 'Please sit, we've got a lot to get through.'

The sun was now at a low angle casting strips of light from the blinds across the room. Nathalie sat, squinted and then rose to adjust the slats to deflect the glare from her eyes. On her way back she looked over Geoff's shoulder at the document in his hand reading *Top-Secret and Highly Confidential.*

'So, we're going to be all sworn to secrecy,' she said.

Geoff smiled. 'Well, not exactly, in fact quite the opposite. We've got the green light to broadcast whatever we want, or nearly whatever we want anyway.'

Tom's mouth dropped open.

'And a lot of it, young Tom, is down to you,' added Geoff.

'Okay Mr Secret Service,' said Nathalie sitting and pulling out her laptop. 'Tell us the story.'

Geoff sat back, enjoying the moment, looking at the expectant faces. Eventually he put his hands behind his head and began.

'Secret Service pleased with Tom's hint for the source and realise that the bioterror attack cat is out of the bag so they want us to put out our programme pronto. They know that they may come under some criticism for not acting on our first tipoff but think the best thing is damage control by putting the whole thing out in the open. Also it will show our WEXA friends that we're onto them and any second attempt is likely to be well and truly snuffed out.'

Nathalie could hardly believe what she was hearing.

'Who will have editorial control?'

'We will, no interference from them whatsoever. The sting of course is that we are legally responsible for everything we say. Hence our lawyer.'

'And we can use all our footage; the WEXA interview in the hut, Temba's covert video?'

'Every single yard of it.'

Nathalie was tapping at her laptop. 'What about the Joseph Karasa story?'

Geoff removed his hands from behind his head and placed them on the coffee table. 'Ah, that's one thing that we may have to leave out. The police interviewed the warehouse staff. Rum lot by all accounts, no health and safety, crap security. I think they are going to shut the place down, especially after all the bad publicity. Anyway, spoke to the manager there. Apparently he saw a black guy by the lens solution stock. Thought he was a temporary, even gave him a job to count the packaging.'

'Then if it's in our time-frame, we've got him,' said Nathalie. 'It must have been Joseph Karasa'.

'Oh yes,' said Geoff. 'I can see that going down well. They all look the same syndrome. Don't be stupid Nathalie. The guy was wearing a mask, he had dark skin, like thousands of people in this country. He might be from WEXA, or he might not. No one saw the guy tampering with the bottles and there is not one shred of proof that Joseph Karasa went near the place. Anyway he's safely tucked up in Harare and we don't need him. The African story is fine without him. And we've got the great stuff from Indonesia to intercut with it. The message is that bioterror threats from any source are worth taking seriously.'

Nathalie stopped typing. Geoff was right, even if Joseph was part of the Ebola plan, there was no way they would get him into an English court. But Geoff's last statements reminded her of something that she had put to the back of her mind.

'Indonesia. I've been so wrapped up in the Ebola attack that I forgot to ask you what we're doing with this Townes, Biomedivac thing.'

'Ah, you may have forgotten Miss Thompson but I have not,' said Geoff tapping his nose, 'I have a cunning plan, leave it to me.'

✳

The cutting room was what Nathalie's mum would have called 'like Piccadilly Circus'. Tom had just proudly brought in the final sequences of the Ebola animation, Bob was subtitling the Temba covert footage and Nathalie continued to hammer away at the voice-over script on her laptop. It had only been three days since what they were now calling their 'summit meeting' in Geoff's office and Nathalie was trying to get the most up-to-date information into her film. Shots of the Home Counties' hospitals were now accompanied by a more optimistic note. No more cases, the ones infected being handled by expert teams. Geoff had sent a stringer to the warehouse. The shots were a sorry sight. Boarded-up gates, police tape around the perimeter. The message here was that the threat was still alive, the public needed to be calm but vigilant. They had filmed an interview with a government spokesperson. The authorities were doing everything that they could. The anti-terrorist unit was still making overtures to the Zimbabwean police force but, as the attack was not on their soil, they were currently disinterested and uncooperative.

Geoff burst into the edit suite. A rare visit.

'How is it shaping up?'

Bob finished typing his last caption and turned around from the editing consul. 'Think you've got a winner Geoff, BAFTA material. Moves along like an express train. Once I've got Tom's animation and some scratch music tracks in, could show you a rough-cut.'

Nathalie looked up from her script. 'Hang on, director's prerogative to see the first viewing. Don't want you washing my dirty linen in public.'

Geoff raised his hand. 'All right, all right, I'll wait for the call. Just popped in to show you today's papers.' He handed Nathalie a copy of the *Evening Standard*.

She took it from him and Geoff laughed as he saw her jaw drop. The headline said it all.

Oxford professor caught in cover-up scandal.

Nathalie read the first paragraph aloud. 'Professor James Townes has resigned from his brainchild Biomedivac after the disclosure of documents showed that condemning safety and efficacy data had been suppressed. The company is now in liquidation and it is rumoured that the US giant Zormax is planning a takeover of the assets. Professor Townes is currently under investigation by the police.'

'Whoa,' exclaimed Tom. 'So Rob Barnes got his revenge after all.'

Geoff took back the paper. 'Not without a price though Tom. I got Nathalie's friend from Medical Films to do some digging. Apparently Doctor Barnes was lined up for a senior management position at Zormax. But as soon as it became public that he was part of the Alzheimer's trial with batch #124, and had tried to discredit Biomedivac by requisitioning some suspect microbes, they dropped him like the proverbial plague.'

'Where is he now?' asked Nathalie.

'On the run in the States I think. I expect he rues the day he looked into your bag to find Tom's Java lab research.'

'If that's what he did,' said Nathalie. 'I was only in the loo for a few minutes.'

'Well, however he got the information, it's backfired,' said Geoff, about to leave the cutting room.

Nathalie snapped her laptop shut and grabbed the paper from under his arm. 'Talking about getting information, how did this lot get hold of those documents without us being named as the source?'

Geoff smiled and waved his mobile phone at her. 'Twitter, Nathalie Thompson. You are obviously not on it, otherwise you would have seen that the anonymous photos of those documents have gone viral.'

Thirty-four

Temba Murauzi strolled down the foot-worn earthen path hemmed by the long grasses that were touched with evening dew. He took in the peat laden African air and listened as he heard the growl of Lloyd's jeep disappearing into the distance. It had been his last meeting with Lloyd; last because Lloyd had taken a prestigious position with a South African television news network. He was starting tomorrow and had asked Temba not to disclose his whereabouts.

'No problem,' Temba had said. 'As long as it's reciprocal. Good of you to set up this final rendezvous.'

The location of the rendezvous was ironic. A small group of abandoned circular thatched huts where Lloyd had first been threatened. Now it was Temba's turn but this time the roles would be reversed and the action far more subtle than the crashing down of a machete. The dilapidated mud buildings were several hundred metres away and Temba had time to think about the events over the last six months. He had seen the documents from Geoff's anonymous Twitter account. They were broadcast everywhere. Each time, a reminder of that terrible day when he first arrived as an up-and-coming pharmacologist in Morocco. He hadn't been looking for the Ebola vaccine data, it had been misfiled and given to him by mistake. The anger surged through him as he saw the deception. At that time his sister was still struggling with the disease, a disease being treated with an ineffective drug. It was easy to take his revenge. He had been asked to help with their new Alzheimer's drug. He was an expert in chiral molecules. The same compound could have a left-handed and right-handed version, almost indistinguishable but mirror images. But the properties of these chemicals could be quite different. He used to tell his students about the difference between oranges and lemons. Same molecules, different tastes. All that he had to do was to switch molecules in a single batch. Batch #124. In earlier trials the left-handed molecule had been abandoned, a side-effect of terrible migraines. Batch #124 was allocated to a small trial for side-effects. A simple switch from the approved right-handed molecule would screw the results. He hadn't known about the memory loss. He would never forgive himself for the consequences to patients such as Esther Phillips.

The hut could be picked out by the thin wisp of brown smoke threading its way through the blood red sky. It was a beautiful evening, cigar-shaped clouds lit up by the falling sun. Temba thought of his sister, brainwashed by the men he was about to meet. Now she was dead. The rage started to flow through his body, but this would be no good to him. He stood for a moment waiting for his heartbeat to still. He crouched under the low opening of the shelter and made his entrance.

'Welcome brother,' Joseph Karasa stood to shake his hand. The other two men were wrapped in blankets huddled around the fire. They remained seated but nodded their heads and smiled.

The large man with the Rolex put out his hand, not to shake but to receive. 'You have the new antidote?'

Temba reached into his shoulder bag and pulled out several packets of pills. 'Of course, capsule form, easier to administer.'

The smaller man spoke. 'It seems that the West have ignored our demands. They were fortunate enough to restrict our little hors d'oeuvre, but they were frightened for a while. Next time it will be real terror. Unfortunately the attack is so bold that it is also at risk to us. Your antiviral, it's effective?'

'Very,' said Temba. 'May need a few days to work, so I would suggest you take some now. Three a day until the day of the attack.' He handed out the pink capsules.

'No time like the present,' said Joseph swallowing some and passing the rest to his colleagues.

Temba watched as they each took the maximum dose.

314

'I am sure they will work for you comrades,' he said. 'Now I must go, I don't want people searching for me.'

'We understand,' said Joseph. 'We will stay here until nightfall, you should have time to reach the nearest village by then.'

Temba looked carefully into the eyes of each man, before turning and leaving through the primitive doorway. Instead of returning the way he had come he took the opposite direction, away from the village and into the bush. As he strolled clear of the path and through the grasses he reached into his pocket and pulled out the last pack of capsules. He placed half a dozen into his mouth and swallowed hard, then, still walking, turned over the box to look at the label. Batch #124.

'Drugs to forget.'

Also by Martin Granger

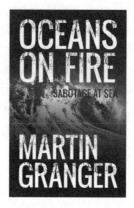

When Nathalie Thompson's cameraman doesn't show at the airport alarm bells start to ring. But, with a TV commission on the table and a job to do, she sets off across the world to make a documentary on ocean energy and its positive effects on climate change.

As the camera rolls Nathalie's worst nightmares slowly unfold; accidents happen, drilling rigs sink and marine structures are mysteriously damaged. At the same time a US senator, involved in a controversial new law concerning ownership of the seas, is caught in a sordid sex scandal.

With rumours of bribery and corruption at every turn there's more to her film footage than shale fracking and ocean engineering. In her quest to uncover the truth, Nathalie is in for a nasty surprise as she finds herself embroiled in a dangerous world of conspiracy, mayhem and sabotage.

OCEANS ON FIRE

One

The ice-biting wind hurled itself into the ship's anemometer. The needle on the bridge flickered, forty-two knots and rising. A man in glistening yellow oilskins leant over the rail and stared at the black waters heaving towards the horizon. The waves must be reaching nearly eight metres. It was a strange sensation, here he was somewhere in the Southern Ocean in a maelstrom and yet he could balance a coffee cup in the palm of his hand without spilling a drop. He stretched out an arm to prove the point. The deck he was standing on was as sound as rock. It was a scene that he must have described a hundred times to the various dignitaries or students who had visited the vessel. What was the line he opened with? *Even in the roughest seas this ship can drill through six miles of water and three miles of rock.*

It was a great line but, unless he had seen it with his own eyes, he doubted whether he would have believed it. The *IOD Revolution* was held steady by means of a computer-controlled positioning system. Sam Armstrong's speciality was ocean floor sediment and the Earth's climate; and he just had to know how this thing worked. The ship's engineer was only too pleased to have the opportunity to tell him.

'We put a beacon on the sea floor right next to the drilling point. There are a number of hydrophones attached to the ship's hull that pick up the signals. Our computers work out the arrival times and send messages to the ship's twelve bow thrusters to keep us in position.'

Sounded simple, yet, when you were standing stock still on what you knew was a ship floating on thrashing Antarctic waters, it still felt crazy. He drank the last of his coffee and was tempted to throw the plastic cup into the waves. It was one of those 'standing on the top of a cliff' moments – an imperative for him to jump off. Sam was a dyed-in-the-wool environmentalist, a geologist dedicated to removing the threat of climate change. He opened the flap of his oilskin's pocket and dropped the cup into it.

A shout came from the deck above him. He looked up and tried to lip-read the words over the noise of the wind. The first officer was waving at him like a traffic cop on speed.

'Trouble?' he shouted back. It was useless; his question was just wrapped into the air and taken away with the spray. He pointed to his ear and shook his head violently. Then he pointed upwards and mouthed the word 'up'. Why he mouthed it and didn't shout it he couldn't work out. It was just one of those things you did. Maybe if someone couldn't hear, it was done to bring some sort of equality into the conversation. He made his way gingerly across the drenched deck to the nearest stairway. The ribs on the iron steps had been painted so many times they were almost smooth and he had to hang onto the handrail to stop himself from slipping.

The first officer grabbed his hand to help him up the final rung.

'You're needed on the bridge. The chief engineer wants to start drilling and the captain needs your advice.'

This wasn't the first time Sam had been called in to act as a referee. The 'International Ocean Drilling Project' was over time and over budget. They had set out six weeks ago to drill ten kilometres of core samples from the southern ocean floor. This would tell them about the state of the Earth's climate in the Antarctic region over the last ten million years. Their various government sponsors were impatient for the results but the seas had been high and, even with computerised positioning, it had been difficult to drill. To date, they had only brought up half of the target cores. This had led to tension on the bridge. The captain and the chief engineer were standing like chess players on either side of the chart table.

'Come in, Sam,' invited the captain without taking his eyes off the chief engineer. 'Otto here thinks we're in an ideal position to drill.'

Otto began to protest. 'I didn't say ideal, I said...'

The captain raised his hand. 'Otto has informed me that the sea conditions are well within the tolerance of the drilling rig, and that we should start drilling the next core. I've pointed out to Otto that I'm responsible for the safety of the crew on this ship and, no matter what the international committee says, I'm not going to risk the lives of these men for a few feet of clay.' The captain arrested Otto's next interruption with a military stare. Otto closed his mouth without saying a word.

'Even...,' The captain turned to face Sam, '... even if that clay gives them an argument to keep their jobs at the next election.'

Sam was aware of the undertones of this statement. For days now, discussions around the captain's table had centred on the ethics of their task. Some governments were leaning heavily on the scientists to come up with data to show that their economic policy of burning fossil fuels would have little effect on the climate; others wanted figures to prove a case of impending doom.

'Captain, I'm a scientist and, as a scientist, I want to know the truth. Otto, on the other hand, is an engineer and if he says that it's safe to drill, I believe him.'

Otto looked at the captain and shrugged as if to say, 'I told you so'.

The captain turned to the bridge's instrument panel and studied the mass of flickering needles and blinking lights. Cold hard rain started to hammer against the windscreen. The pause was just becoming uncomfortable when the captain turned to speak.

'Okay, you two, let's get this straight. I will position the ship for drilling and your team will play it by the book. All procedures to be followed with no shortcuts. I want to be informed about any sign of trouble immediately. Then the decision will be down to me. If I say abandon the bore and cut the drill string, you cut it. Is that understood?'

Otto was about to say that there wasn't going to be any trouble when Sam took him by the arm and started to guide him out of the bridge.

'Absolutely, Captain,' he said. 'We will give you the drilling co-ordinates and procedures in writing within the hour.'

Sam half ushered, half pushed Otto down the stairs to B-deck. From the colour of Otto's neck he could see that he was fuming. This was confirmed when they reached the operation's cabin.

'What the fuck do you mean?' exploded Otto. 'Give you the procedures in writing. He knows what the bloody procedures are, and if he doesn't, he should do by now. What a waste of fucking time. As if we haven't got enough to do in this bloody storm.'

'Calm down, Otto, we've got our way. He says you can drill, just get on with it. I'll ask one of the university trainees to fill in the forms. I'm supposed to be teaching them something, anyway.'

'I hope they learn fast because I'm not waiting any longer. This sea's getting rougher by the minute. We've already dropped the guide cone onto the sea floor. If we don't get that drill string in soon we really will be in the shit.'

The pieces of drill were made up of rigid steel pipes nearly half a metre in diameter. When they were all screwed together to make a six-mile-long drill string, it behaved just like that, a piece of string. It wasn't easy to get such a long drill to bite into hard rock so Otto and his team had come up with a way of making it stick. Ten minutes later Sam was explaining this to his university trainee in his cabin.

'Okay, so they've lowered this huge aluminium cone onto the seabed. Technically, we should have logged this operation into the project book, so you can do that now and make up some sort of figure in the time column. Now the next thing we do is to use sonar to find its exact position and keep adding on bits of pipe until the drill bit wobbles around in the inside of the cone.'

The trainee seemed genuinely interested. 'How do we know when it gets there?'

'We can see it; there's a camera on the end of the drill. We can even take a photo to show the captain it's there.' Sam's right eyelid flickered. 'Keep him in the loop, if you know what I mean.'

'And then?'

'And then we fill the cone up with concrete so the drill tip stops wobbling and bites when we switch it on.'

'Amazing! How far down will we drill this time?'

'Three miles; enough core sediment to show the changes in climate over the last ten to twenty million years. But before we go too deep we have to bring up a sample from a few hundred metres. It's a pain but it's procedure. And with the mood the captain's in right now we can't afford to skip it, however stupid it seems.'

'What do you mean "stupid", Sir?'

'Well, it's never happened; a gas bubble, that is.'

Sam could see that he was losing his trainee. The poor boy had been thrown in at the deep end. Three years at university studying oceanography and then, as some sort of government PR exercise, a two-month postgraduate jaunt on the *IOD Revolution*, the most sophisticated deep-sea laboratory drilling ship in the world. No one had really thought through what to do with these students. Once on board, there was no way they could get off before the end of the trip. Two of the three had spent the last few days throwing up below decks. The survivor was an enthusiastic lad, although not the sort of experienced assistant Sam would have chosen.

'You've seen some of the clay cores that we've brought up in the lab, haven't you…' Sam said this rather as a statement than a question. 'They are soft cylinders of striped sediment encased in plastic tubes, yes? Well, when the first core hits the deck someone rushes up with a syringe and sticks it into the clay. They pull the plunger out and literally run back to the lab to see if it contains any gas. If it does, we get the hell out of there as fast as we can.' Sam folded his arms and waited for the inevitable question. It didn't come so he asked it himself.

'Why? The theory is that if there is gas in a core, there could be a gas chamber in the sediment under the ocean. And if our drill punctures that chamber it could release the gas into the ocean as a massive bubble. A bubble you don't want to be sitting on top of.'

The student sat there trying to think of something to say. Sam made an upward waving motion with his fingers. When his hands had reached eye level he clapped them together.

'Bloop,' he said and then laughed at the look of surprise on his trainee's face.

'You needn't worry, I've checked the surveys; we are nowhere near any gas fields. Tonight, you're going to do the syringe sample and take the negative results to the captain because...?'

'Because it's procedure, Sir.'

Sam handed over the paperwork to his student and began to struggle back into his wet oilskins. 'Absolutely, young man; you should go far.'

On deck Sam could hear the familiar rumble of metal pipes as an underscore to the high-pitched, gusting winds. Otto had given the order to prepare the drill. It was an odd system, partially automated but with the final joints being made manually by two riggers on either side of the drilling rig. The fifty metre-long drill pipes had to be brought up horizontally from the hold and then turned through ninety degrees to hang in the cage-like derrick. Two 'fucking idiots', as Otto liked to call them, then positioned one pipe on top of another so that they could be screwed together. Drilling on a stable oil platform is dangerous; drilling on a ship in high seas borders on the insane. Sam found Otto on the viewing platform.

'Jumping the gun a bit, aren't you? I said I'd give the captain the co-ordinates in writing.'

'Well, give them to him then. By the time he reads them the bit should be near the seabed; that is if the bloody sea hasn't snapped it off by then.'

The noise from the drill rig and wind was now so loud that Sam had to cup his hands like a megaphone and scream out his words. 'I thought you said the conditions were okay for drilling.'

He couldn't hear Otto's reply and it was obvious that Otto wasn't going to make the effort to repeat it, so he pulled his oilskin hood over his hard hat and headed for the instrument room.

The front of the ship was a haven compared to the metal mayhem of the drilling quarters. Three floors of pristine laboratories packed with screens, computers and scanners. Bespectacled, white-coated technicians shuffled between rock samples and the space-age technology. Normally, Sam would have stopped to ask for some of the latest paleoclimate results but this evening he headed straight for the positioning computer terminal.

'I need a printout of the entry cone location for the captain.'

The technician turned to look at him. 'I could just phone it up to the bridge, if you want.'

'Not today. We have to do it by the book. I'll send one of the students down to collect it. Oh, and while you're at it, could you show him how to analyse the test core gas sample; I expect the captain will want that in writing too.'

The technician gave him a knowing look. 'Sure thing, Sam. You look whacked, why don't you take a rest? It will be a while before we cut the first core. Promise I'll wake you when it comes up.'

※

The hammering on the cabin door was getting louder. Surely the drilling hadn't started yet; he had only just closed his eyes. Sam turned over in the bunk and pulled his arm from the blanket so that he could look at his wristwatch. The muffled noises outside had now reached fever pitch.

'Dr Armstrong, open the door, open the door!'

Sam leapt from the bunk and threw the catch. His trainee was standing there, his face as white as the paper he was clutching. Sam, still drowsy with sleep, tried to take in the scene.

'What the hell do you think you're doing?'

'It's the sample core; it's got gas in it.' The piece of paper was thrust into Sam's hands. 'Sixty per cent hydrocarbons; it could be a gas field.' Sam looked down at the paper.

'Calm down, Jeremy, there are no gas fields around here.' He nodded to the charts on the table. 'The surveys are pretty clear about that. Who took the measurements?'

'I did, Sir. The "chem ops" person showed me how to do it.'

Sam reached for his shoes and belt and began to put them on. 'Has he checked these results?'

'No, Sir, I came down here as soon as I saw the figures. You said it could be dangerous and that we would have to get out quickly.'

Sam smiled. 'I said we would have to get the hell out of here. I also said no one's ever heard of a ship being sunk by a gas bubble. Look, it's the first time you've done this test and…well, never mind that. Let's go up to the lab and we'll stick another syringe into that clay.'

Sam was still smiling as he led the trainee across a wave-swept A-deck when it happened. The ship bucked like a rodeo bull. Sam was thrown into the air like an athlete off a trampoline. The breath was crushed out of him as his body smashed back onto the metal surface. The skin on his face started to rip as he slid down the seawater-soaked incline. His arms and legs flailed to take a grip but the deck was now nearly vertical. The guard rail hurtled towards him – the only thing between him and the ocean – when he was pulled up sharply with a jolt and a sharp pain stabbing through his thigh socket. A thick coil of metal chain had wrapped around his ankle. For a moment his body dangled in the air, crashing from side to side into the air vents. A screaming, howling noise and then icy darkness. The foam and black freezing water entered his lungs. Sam tried to kick free but the huge iron links of the chain around his leg were pulling him down. He tugged frantically at them but it was pointless; they were impossibly tangled. Below him was six miles of water. He would either die of cold or the pressure would crush him like an imploding drink's can. He thought about inhaling a deep draft of seawater when his bruised hand caught on something. In his belt was a large serrated work knife. He pulled it from its sheath, screwed his eyes shut and placed the blade just below his knee bone. To his surprise he didn't feel a thing as it made the first deep cut into his flesh.